INVISIBLE
PLANETS

An Anthology of Contemporary Chinese Science Fiction

Translated and edited by KEN LIU

HEAD
of ZEUS

First published in the United States of America in 2016 by Tor Books, a registered trademark of Macmillan Publishing Group, LLC

First published in the United Kingdom in 2016 by Head of Zeus Ltd
This paperback edition first published in 2017 by Head of Zeus Ltd

1 3 5 7 9 8 6 4 2

ISBN (PB) 9781786692788
ISBN (E) 9781784978648

Printed and bound by CPI Group (UK) Ltd, Croydon, CR0 4YY

Head of Zeus Ltd
First Floor East
5–8 Hardwick Street
London EC1R 4RG

WWW.HEADOFZEUS.COM

COPYRIGHT ACKNOWLEDGMENTS

All text reprinted by permission of the authors

"The Year of the Rat" by Chen Qiufan. First Chinese publication: *Science Fiction World,* May 2009; first English publication: *The Magazine of Fantasy & Science Fiction,* July /August 2013, translated by Ken Liu. English text © 2013 by Chen Qiufan and Ken Liu.

"The Fish of Lijiang" by Chen Qiufan. First Chinese publication: *Science Fiction World,* May 2006; first English publication: *Clarkesworld,* August 2011, translated by Ken Liu. English text © 2011 by Chen Qiufan and Ken Liu.

"The Flower of Shazui" by Chen Qiufan. First Chinese publication: *ZUI Ink-Minority Report,* 2012; first English publication: *Interzone,* November-December 2012, translated by Ken Liu. English text © 2012 by Chen Qiufan and Ken Liu.

"A Hundred Ghosts Parade Tonight" by Xia Jia. First Chinese publication: *Science Fiction World,* August 2010; first English publication: *Clarkesworld,* February 2012, translated by Ken Liu. English text © 2012 by Xia Jia and Ken Liu.

"Tongtong's Summer" by Xia Jia. First Chinese publication: *ZUI Novel,* March 2014; first English publication: *Upgraded,* ed. Neil Clarke, 2014 (Wyrm Publishing), translated by Ken Liu. English text © 2014 by Xia Jia and Ken Liu.

"Night Journey of the Dragon-Horse" by Xia Jia. First English publication in this volume, translated by Ken Liu. English text © 2016 by Xia Jia and Ken Liu.

"The City of Silence" by Ma Boyong. First Chinese publication: *Science Fiction World,* May 2005; first English publication: *World SF Blog,* November 2011, translated by Ken Liu. English text © 2011 by Ma Boyong and Ken Liu.

"Invisible Planets" by Hao Jingfang. First Chinese publication: *New Science Fiction,* February–April 2010; first English publication: *Lightspeed,* December 2013, translated by Ken Liu. English text © 2013 by Hao Jingfang and Ken Liu.

To my authors, who entrusted me with their dreams

CONTENTS

ESSAYS

INVISIBLE
PLANETS

INTRODUCTION: CHINA DREAMS

by Ken Liu

This anthology collects a selection of short speculative fiction from China that I've translated over the years into one volume. Some have won awards in the United States, some have been selected for inclusion in various "Year's Best" anthologies, some have been well reviewed by critics and readers, and some are simply my personal favorites.

China has a vibrant, diverse science fiction culture, but few stories are translated into English, making it hard for non-Chinese readers to appreciate them. I hope this anthology can serve as an introduction for the Anglophone reader.

The phrase "China Dreams" is a play on President Xi Jingping's[1] promotion of the "Chinese Dream" as a slogan for China's develop-

---

[1] All Chinese names in this anthology are given with surname first, in accordance with Chinese custom.

ment. Science fiction is the literature of dreams, and texts concerning dreams always say something about the dreamer, the dream interpreter, and the audience.

Whenever the topic of Chinese science fiction comes up, Anglophone readers ask, "How is Chinese science fiction different from science fiction written in English?"

I usually disappoint them by replying that the question is ill-defined . . . and there isn't a neat sound bite for an answer. Any broad literary classification tied to a culture—especially a culture as in flux and contested as contemporary China's—encompasses all the complexities and contradictions in that culture. Attempts to provide neat answers will only result in broad generalizations that are of little value, or stereotypes that reaffirm existing prejudices.

To start with, I don't believe that "science fiction written in English" is a useful category for comparison (the fiction written in Singapore, the United Kingdom, and the United States are all quite different, and there are further divisions within and across such geographical boundaries), and so I wouldn't even know what baseline I'm supposed to be distinguishing "Chinese science fiction" *from*.

Moreover, imagine asking a hundred different American authors and critics to characterize "American science fiction"—you'd hear a hundred different answers. The same is true of Chinese authors and critics and Chinese science fiction.

Even within the limited selection of this anthology, you'll encounter the "science fiction realism" of Chen Qiufan, the "porridge SF" of Xia Jia, the overt, wry political metaphors of Ma Boyong, the surreal imagery and metaphor-driven logic of Tang Fei, the dense, rich language-pictures painted by Cheng Jingbo, the fabulism and sociological speculation of Hao Jingfang, and the grand, hard-science-fictional imagination of Liu Cixin. This should give a hint of the broad range of the science fiction written in China. Faced with such variety, I think it is far more useful and interesting to study the authors as individuals and to treat their works on their own terms rather than to try to impose a preconceived set of expectations on them because they happen to be Chinese.

This is all a rather long-winded way of saying that I think anyone who confidently asserts a definitive characterization of "Chinese science fiction" is either a) an outsider who doesn't know what they're talking about or b) someone who *does* know something, but is deliberately ignoring the contested nature of the subject and presenting their opinion as fact.

So I will state right up front that I do not consider myself an expert on Chinese science fiction. I know enough to know that I don't know much. I know enough to know that I need to study more—a lot more. And I know enough to know that there are no simple answers.[2]

China is going through a massive social, cultural, and technological transformation involving more than a billion people of different ethnicities, cultures, classes, and ideological sympathies, and it is impossible for anyone—even people who are living through these upheavals—to claim to know the entire picture. If one's knowledge of China is limited to Western media reports or the experience of being a tourist or expat, claiming to "understand" China is akin to a man who has caught a glimpse of a fuzzy spot through a drinking straw claiming to know what a leopard is. The fiction produced in China reflects the complexity of the environment.

Given the realities of China's politics and its uneasy relationship with the West, it is natural for Western readers encountering Chinese science fiction to see it through the lens of Western dreams and hopes and fairy tales about Chinese politics. "Subversion" in the pro-West sense may become an interpretive crutch. It is tempting, for example, to view Ma Boyong's "The City of Silence" as a straightforward

2   There is, in fact, a fairly vibrant body of academic scholarship about Chinese science fiction, with insightful and interesting commentary by scholars such as Mingwei Song, Nathaniel Isaacson, and others. Panels on Chinese science fiction are quite common at academic conferences on comparative literature and Asian studies. However, my impression is that many (most?) genre readers, writers, and critics in established science fiction fandom are not familiar with this body of work. The scholarly essays generally avoid the pitfalls I warn about and are nuanced and careful in their analysis. Readers seeking an informed opinion are urged to look up these works.

attack on China's censorship apparatus, or to read Chen Qiufan's "The Year of the Rat" only as criticism of China's education system and labor market, or even to reduce Xia Jia's "A Hundred Ghosts Parade Tonight" to a veiled metaphor for China's eminent domain policies in the service of state-driven development.

I would urge the reader to resist such temptation. Imagining that the political concerns of Chinese writers are the same as what the Western reader would like them to be is at best arrogant and at worst dangerous. Chinese writers are saying something about the globe, about all of humanity, not just China, and trying to understand their works through this perspective is, I think, the far more rewarding approach.

It is true that there is a long tradition in China of voicing dissent and criticism through the use of literary metaphor; however, this is but one of the purposes for which writers write and for which readers read. Like writers everywhere, today's Chinese writers are concerned with humanism; with globalization; with technological advancement; with tradition and modernity; with disparities in wealth and privilege; with development and environmental preservation; with history, rights, freedom, and justice; with family and love; with the beauty of expressing sentiment through words; with language play; with the grandeur of science; with the thrill of discovery; with the ultimate meaning of life. We do the works a disservice when we neglect these things and focus on geopolitics alone.

Despite the diversity of approaches and subjects and styles, the authors and stories collected in this anthology represent but a thin slice of the contemporary Chinese science fiction landscape. Though I've tried to balance the selection to reflect a range of viewpoints, I'm aware of the narrowness of my scope. Most of the authors collected here (with the exception of Liu Cixin) belong to the younger generation of "rising stars" rather than the generation of established, prominent figures such as Liu Cixin, Han Song, or Wang Jinkang. Most of them are graduates of China's most elite colleges and work in highly regarded professions. Moreover, I've focused on award-winning authors and stories rather than popular fiction published on the web, and I've prioritized works which I think are more accessible in translation than works requiring a deeper understanding of Chinese culture and history. These biases and omissions are necessary, but not ideal; the reader should thus be cautious about any conclusions they may draw from the stories here being "representative." My fondest hope is that each story here at least adds a layer to the reader's understanding and awareness of a literary tradition different from the one they might be used to.

To round out the collection and provide a more comprehensive overview of Chinese science fiction, I've included three essays at the end of the book by Chinese authors and scholars. Liu Cixin's essay, "The Worst of All Possible Universes and the Best of All Possible Earths," gives a historical overview of the genre in China and situates his own rise to prominence as the premier Chinese science fiction author within that context. Chen Qiufan's "The Torn Generation" gives the view of a younger generation of authors trying to come to terms with the tumultuous transformations around them. Finally, the essay by Xia Jia, who holds the first Ph.D. degree issued for a specialization in the study of Chinese science fiction, "What Makes Chinese Science Fiction Chinese?", offers a starting point for academic analysis of this body of work.

Noted translator William Weaver compared translation to a performing art. I like that metaphor. When doing a translation, I'm engaging in a cultural and linguistic performance, an attempt to re-create an artifact in a new medium. It is a humbling and thrilling experience.

I feel incredibly privileged to have had the chance to work with the authors in this anthology. In many instances, what began as professional collaboration has turned into personal friendship. From them I've learned much not just about translation, but also about writing fiction and living life across the boundaries of cultures and languages. I'm grateful that they entrusted their work to me.

I hope you enjoy the result.

CHEN QIUFAN

A fiction writer, screenwriter, and columnist—with a side gig as a product marketing manager for Baidu, the Chinese web giant—Chen Qiufan (a.k.a. Stanley Chan) has published fiction in venues such as *Science Fiction World, Esquire, Chutzpah!,* and *ZUI Found.* Liu Cixin, China's most prominent science fiction author, praised Chen's debut novel, *The Waste Tide* (2013), as "the pinnacle of near-future SF writing." Chen has garnered numerous literary awards, including Taiwan's Dragon Fantasy Award and China's Galaxy (Yinhe) and Nebula (Xingyun) Awards. In English translation, he has been featured in markets such as *Clarkesworld, Lightspeed, Interzone,* and *The Magazine of Fantasy & Science Fiction.* "The Fish of Lijiang" won a Science Fiction and Fantasy Translation Award in 2012, and "The Year of the Rat" was selected by Laird Barron for *The Year's Best Weird Fiction: Volume One.*

The three stories collected here, "The Year of the Rat," "The Fish of Lijiang," and "The Flower of Shazui," showcase Chen's unique aesthetic of melding a global, post-cyberpunk sensibility with China's traditions and complex historical legacy. By turns cynical, hopeful, playful, and didactic, Chen captures the zeitgeist of contemporary China, a culture going through a shocking transition and transformation. For more on how Chinese science fiction reflects this aspect of the Chinese experience, see Chen's essay, "The Torn Generation," at the end of this book.

A native of Shantou, Guangdong Province, and a graduate of Peking University, one of the China's most elite colleges, Chen speaks the Shantou topolect as well as Cantonese, Mandarin, and English (the spelling of his English name ["Chan"] reflects the Cantonese pronunciation). A language virtuoso, he has written speculative fiction stories in Classical Chinese—a feat akin to a contemporary English writer composing a story in the language of Chaucer—as well as Cantonese and Modern Standard Chinese. The linguistic divisions and diversity of his native land provide both backdrop and metaphor for his novel *The Waste Tide,* which I'm translating into English. "The Flower of Shazui" is set in the same universe as *The Waste Tide* and offers a glimpse into that world.

THE YEAR OF THE RAT

It's getting dark again. We've been in this hellhole for two days, but we haven't even seen a single rat's hair.

My socks feel like greasy dishrags, so irritating that I want to punch someone. My stomach is cramping up from hunger, but I force my feet to keep moving. Wet leaves slap me in the face like open hands. It hurts.

I want to return the biology textbook in my backpack to Pea and tell him, *This stupid book has eight hundred seventy-two pages.* I also want to give him back his pair of glasses, even though it's not heavy, not heavy at all.

Pea is dead.

The Drill Instructor said that the insurance company would pay his parents something. He didn't say how much.

Pea's parents would want something to remember him by. So I had taken the glasses out of his pocket and that goddamned book out of his waterproof backpack. Maybe this way his parents would remember how their son was a good student, unlike the rest of us.

Pea's real name is Meng Xian. But we all called him "Pea" because one, he was short and skinny like a pea sprout, and two, he was always joking that the friar who experimented with peas, Gregor "Meng-De-Er" Mendel, was his ancestor.

Here's what they said happened: When the platoon was marching across the top of the dam of the abandoned reservoir, Pea noticed a rare plant growing out of the cracks in the muddy concrete at the edge of the dam. He broke formation to collect it.

Maybe it was his bad eyesight, or maybe that heavy book threw him off balance. Anyway, the last thing everyone saw was Pea, looking really like a green pea, rolling, bouncing down the curved slope of the side of the dam for a hundred meters and more, until finally his body abruptly stopped, impaled on a sharp branch sticking out of the water.

The Drill Instructor directed us to retrieve the body and wrap it in a body bag. His lips moved for a bit, then stopped. I knew what he wanted to say—we'd all heard him say it often enough—but he restrained himself. Actually, I kind of wanted to hear him say it.

You college kids are idiots. You don't even know how to stay alive.
He's right.

Someone taps me on the shoulder. It's Black Cannon. He smiles at me apologetically. "Time to eat."

I'm surprised at how friendly Black Cannon is toward me. Maybe it's because when Pea died, Black Cannon was walking right by him. And now he feels sorry that he didn't grab Pea in time.

I sit next to the bonfire to dry my socks. The rice tastes like crap mixed with the smell from wet socks baking by the fire.

Goddamn it. I'm actually crying.

The first time I spoke to Pea was at the end of last year, at the university's mobilization meeting. A bright red banner hung across the front of the auditorium: "It's honorable to love the country and support the army; it's glorious to protect the people and kill rats." An endless stream of school administrators took turns at the podium to give speeches.

I sat next to Pea by coincidence. I was an undergraduate majoring in Chinese literature; he was a graduate student in the biology department. We had nothing in common except neither of us could find jobs after graduation. Our files had to stay with the school while we hung around for another year, or maybe even longer.

In my case, I had deliberately failed my Classical Chinese exam so I could stay in school. I hated the thought of looking for a job, renting an apartment, getting to work at nine A.M. just so I could look forward to five P.M., dealing with office politics, etc., etc. School was much more agreeable: I got to download music and movies for free; the cafeteria was cheap (ten yuan guaranteed a full stomach); I slept until afternoon every day and then played some basketball. There were also pretty girls all around—of course, I could only look, not touch.

To be honest, given the job market right now and my lack of employable skills, staying in school was not really my "choice." But I wasn't going to admit that to my parents.

As for Pea, because of the trade war with the Western Alliance, he couldn't get a visa. A biology student who couldn't leave the country had no job prospects domestically, especially since he was clearly the sort who was better at reading books than hustling.

I had no interest in joining the Rodent-Control Force. As they continued the propaganda onstage, I muttered under my breath, "Why not send the army?"

But Pea turned to me and started to lecture. "Don't you know that the situation on the border is very tense right now? The army's role is to protect the country against hostile foreign nations, not to fight rats."

Who talks like that? I decided to troll him a bit. "Why not send the local peasants, then?"

"Don't you know that grain supplies are tight right now? The work of the peasantry is to grow food, not to fight rats."

"Why not use rat poison? It's cheap and fast."

"These are not common rats, but Neorats™. Common poisons are useless."

"Then make genetic weapons, the kind that will kill all the rats after a few generations."

"Don't you know that genetic weapons are incredibly expensive? Their mission is to act as a strategic deterrent against hostile foreign nations, not to fight rats."

I sighed. This guy was like one of those telephone voice menus, with only a few phrases that he used all the time. Trolling him wasn't any fun.

"So you think the job of college graduates is to fight rats?" I said, smiling at him.

Pea seemed to choke, and his face turned red. For a while, he couldn't say anything in response. Then he turned to clichés like "the country's fate rests on every man's shoulders." But finally he did give a good reason: "Members of the Rodent-Control Force are given food and shelter, with guaranteed jobs to be assigned after discharge."

The platoon has returned to the town to be resupplied.

In order to discourage desertion, all the students in the Rodent-Control Force are assigned to units operating far from their homes. We can't even understand one another's dialects, so everyone has to curl his tongue to speak Modern Standard Mandarin.

I mail Pea's book and glasses to his parents. I try to write a heartfelt letter to them, but the words refuse to come. In the end, I write only, "I'm sorry for your loss."

But the postcard I write to Xiaoxia is filled with dense, tiny characters. I think about her long, long legs. This is probably my twenty-third letter to her already.

I find a store to recharge my phone and text my parents at home. When we're operating in the field, most of the time we get no signal.

The shop owner takes my one yuan and grins at me. The people of this town have probably never seen so many college graduates (though right now we're covered in dirt and not looking too sharp). A few old men and old women smile at us and give us thumbs-ups— but maybe only because they think we're pumping extra money into the town's economy. As I think about Pea, I want to give them my middle finger.

After the Drill Instructor takes care of Pea's funeral arrangements, he takes us to a cheap restaurant. "We're still about twenty-four percent away from accomplishing our quota," he says.

No one answers him. Everyone is busy shoveling rice into his mouth as quickly as possible.

"Work hard, and let's try to win the Golden Cat Award, okay?"

Still no one answers him. We all know that the award is linked to the bonus paid to the Drill Instructor.

The Drill Instructor slams the table and gets up. "You want to be a bunch of lazy bums all your life, is that it?"

I grab my rice bowl, thinking that he's going to flip the table.

But he doesn't. After a moment, he sits down and continues to eat.

Someone whispers, "Do you think our detector is broken?"

Now everyone starts talking. Most are in agreement with the sentiment. Someone offers a rumor that some platoon managed to use their detector to find deposits of rare earth metals and gas fields. They stopped hunting for rats and got into the mining business, solving the unemployment problem of the platoon in one stroke.

"That's ridiculous," the Drill Instructor says. "The detector follows the tracer elements in the blood of the rats. How can it find gas fields?" He pauses for a moment, then adds, "If we follow the flow of the water, I'm sure we'll find them."

The first time I saw the Drill Instructor, I knew I wanted to hit him.

As we lined up for the first day of boot camp, he paced before us, his face dour, and asked, "Who can tell me why you're here?"

After a while, Pea hesitantly raised his hand.

"Yes?"

"To protect the motherland," Pea said. Everyone burst out in laughter. Only I knew that he was serious.

The Drill Instructor didn't change his expression. "You think you're funny? I'm going to award you ten push-ups." Everyone laughed louder.

But that stopped soon enough. "For the rest of you, one hundred push-ups!"

As we gasped and tried to complete the task, the Drill Instructor slowly paced among us, correcting our postures with his baton.

"You're here because you're all failures! You lived in the new dorms the taxpayers built, ate the rice the peasants grew, enjoyed every privilege the country could give you. Your parents spent their coffin money on your tuition. But in the end, you couldn't even find a job, couldn't even keep yourselves alive. You're only good for catching rats! Actually, you're even lower than rats. Rats can be exported for some foreign currency, but you? Why don't you look in the mirror at your ugly mugs? What are your real skills? Let me see: chatting up girls, playing computer games, cheating on tests. Keep on pushing! You don't get to eat unless you finish."

I gritted my teeth as I did each push-up. I thought, *If someone would just get a revolt started, I'm sure all of us together can whip him.*

Everyone else thought the exact same thing, so nothing happened.

Later, when we were eating, I kept on hearing the sound of chopsticks knocking against bowls because our hands and arms were all trembling. One recruit, so sunburned that his skin was like dark leather, couldn't hold his chopsticks steady and dropped a piece of meat on the ground.

The Drill Instructor saw. "Pick it up and eat it."

But the recruit was stubborn. He stared at the Drill Instructor and didn't move.

"Where do you think your food comes from? Let me explain something to you: the budget for your food is squeezed out of the defense budget. So every grain of rice and every piece of meat you eat comes from a real soldier going hungry."

The recruit muttered, "Who cares?"

Pa-la! The Drill Instructor flipped over the table in front of me. Soup, vegetables, rice covered all of us.

"Then none of you gets to eat." The Drill Instructor walked away.

From then on that recruit became known as Black Cannon.

The next day, they sent in the "good cop," the district's main administrator. He began with a political lesson. Starting with a quote from *The Book of Songs* (tenth century BC) ("rat, oh, rat, don't eat my millet"), he surveyed the three-thousand-year history of the dangers posed to the common people by rat infestations. Then, drawing on contemporary international macro-politico-economic developments, he analyzed the unique threat posed by the current infestation and the necessity of complete eradication. Finally, he offered us a vision of the hope and faith placed in us by the people: "It's honorable to love the country and support the army; it's glorious to protect the people and kill rats."

We ate well that day. After alluding to the incident from the day before, the administrator criticized the Drill Instructor. He noted that we college graduates were "the best of the best, the future leaders of our country," and that instruction must be "fair, civil, friendly" and emphasize "technique," not merely rely on "simplistic violence."

To close, the administrator wanted to take some photos with all of us. We lined up in a single rank, goose-stepping. The administrator held up a rope that the tips of all our feet had to touch, to show how orderly we could march.

We follow the flow of the water. The Drill Instructor is right. We see signs of droppings and paw prints.

It's getting colder now. We're lucky that we're operating in the south. I can't even imagine making camp up north, where it's below freezing. The official news is relentlessly upbeat: the Rodent-Control Force units in several districts have already been honorably discharged and have been assigned good jobs with a few state-owned enterprises. But among the lucky names in the newsletter I don't recognize anyone I know. No one else in the platoon does, either.

The Drill Instructor holds up his right fist. *Stop.* Then he spreads out his five fingers. We spread out and reconnoiter.

"Prepare for battle."

Suddenly I'm struck by how ridiculous this is. If this kind of slaughter—like a cat playing with mice—can be called a "battle," then someone like me who has no ambition, who lives more cowardly than a lapdog, can be a "hero."

A gray-green shadow stumbles among the bushes. Neorats are

genetically modified to walk upright, so they are slower than regular rats. We joke among ourselves that it's a good thing they didn't use Jerry—of *Tom and Jerry*—as the model.

But this Neorat is on all fours. The belly is swollen, which further limits its movement. Is the rat preg—ah, no. I see the dangling penis.

Now it's turning into a farce. A bunch of men with steel weapons stalk a potbellied rat. In complete silence, we slowly inch across the field. Suddenly the rat leaps forward and rolls down a hill and disappears.

We swear in unison and rush after it.

At the bottom of the hill is a hole in the ground. In the hole are thirty, forty rats with swollen bellies. Most are dead. The one that just jumped in is still breathing heavily, chest heaving.

"A plague?" the Drill Instructor asks. No one answers. I think of Pea. If he were here, he would know.

Chi. A spear pierces the belly of the dying rat. It's from Black Cannon. He grins as he pulls the spear back, slicing the belly open like a ripe watermelon.

Everyone gasps. Inside this male rat's belly are more than a dozen rat fetuses: pink, curled up like a dish of shrimp cocktail around the intestines. A few men are having dry heaves. Black Cannon, still grinning, lifts his spear again.

"Stop," the Drill Instructor says. Black Cannon backs off, laughing and twirling his spear.

The Neorats were engineered to limit their reproductive capacity: for every one female rat born, there would be nine male rats. The idea had been to control the population size to keep up their market value.

But now it looks like the measures are failing. The males before us died because their abdominal cavity could not support the fetuses. But how could they be pregnant in the first place? Clearly their genes are trying to bypass their engineered boundaries.

I remember another possible explanation, something Xiaoxia told me long ago.

※

Even though I'd had Li Xiaoxia's phone number in my handset for four years, I never called her. Every time I took it out, I lost the courage to push the CALL button.

That day, I was packing for boot camp when I suddenly heard Xiaoxia's faint voice as though coming from far away. I thought I was hallucinating until I saw that I had butt-dialed her. I grabbed the phone in a panic.

"Hey," she said.

"Uh . . ."

"I hear you're about to go kill some rats."

"Yeah. I can't find a job . . ."

"Why don't I take you out to dinner? I feel bad that we've been classmates for four years and I hardly know you. It'll be your farewell meal."

Rumor had it that luxury cars were always parked below her dorm, waiting to pick her up. Rumor had it that she went through men like a girl trying on dresses.

That night, as we sat across from each other eating bowls of fried rice with beef, her face devoid of makeup, I finally understood. She really had a way of capturing a man's soul.

We wandered around the campus. As we passed the stray cats, the classrooms, the empty benches, suddenly I missed the school, and it was because of memories I wished I had made with her.

"My dad raised rats, and now you're going to kill rats," she said. "In the Year of the Rat you're going to fight rats. Now that's funny."

"Are you going to work with your father after graduation?" I asked.

She was dismissive of the suggestion. In her eyes, the business of raising rats was not all that different from working on a contract manufacturing assembly line or in a shirt factory. We still didn't control the key technologies. The embryos all had to be imported. After the farm workers raised them, they went through a stringent quality-control process, and those that passed were exported, implanted with a set of programmed behaviors overseas, and then sold to the wealthy as luxury pets.

All that our country, the world's factory, had to offer was a lot of cheap labor in the least technology-intensive phase of the operation.

"I heard the escaped rats had their genes messed with," Li Xiaoxia said.

She went on to explain that just like how some contract manufacturers had tried to produce *shanzhai* iPhones by reverse engineering and messing with the software, so some rat farm owners were trying to reverse engineer and mess with the genes in their rats. Their goal was to raise the ratio of females and the survival rate of babies. Otherwise their profit margin was too low.

"They say that this time the rats didn't escape," she continued, "but were released by the farm owners. It was their way of putting pressure on certain branches of the government to gain more handouts for their industry."

I didn't know what to say. I felt so ignorant.

"But that's just one set of rumors," she said. "Others say that the mass escape was engineered by the Western Alliance as a way to put pressure on our country in the trade negotiations. The truth is ever elusive."

I looked at the young woman before me: beautiful and smart. She was way out of my league.

"Send me a postcard," she said. Her light laugh broke me out of my reverie.

"Eh?"

"To let me know you're safe. Don't underestimate the rats. I've seen them . . ."

She never finished her sentence.

※

From time to time, I feel many bright eyes are hidden in the dark, observing us, analyzing us, day or night. I think I'm going a little crazy.

By the bank of the river, we discover eighteen nests—low, cylindrical structures about two meters in diameter. Several physics majors squat around one, discussing the mechanical structure of interweaving sticks. On top is a thick layer of leaves, as though the makers wanted to take advantage of the waxy surfaces of the leaves to keep water out.

"I've seen primitive tribal villages like this on the Discovery Channel," one of the men says. We all look at him oddly.

"It doesn't make sense," I say. I squat down, considering the trails of tiny paw prints that connect the nests to one another and the river, like an inscrutable picture. *Do the rats have agriculture? Do they need settlements? Why did they abandon them?*

Black Cannon laughs coldly. "You need to stop thinking they're people."

He's right. The rats are not people. They're not even real rats. They're just carefully designed products—actually, products that failed quality assurance.

I notice something strange about the paw prints. Most seem smaller than usual and only lead away from the nests. But in front of each nest there is one set that is bigger in stride length and deeper, with a long drag mark down the middle. The bigger trails only go *into* the nests but don't come out.

"These are"—I try to keep my voice from shaking—"birthing rooms."

"Sir!" A man stumbles over. "You have to see this."

We follow him to a tree. Underneath there's a tower made from carefully stacked rocks. There's a sense of proportion and aesthetics in the pattern of their shapes and colors. From the tree, eighteen dead male rats hang, their bellies open like unzipped sacks.

A light layer of white sand is spread evenly around the tree. Countless tiny prints can be seen in the sand, surrounding the tree in ever-widening rings. I imagine the ceremonial procession and the mystical rituals. It must have been as wondrous as the scene in Tiananmen Square, when the flag is raised on National Day.

"Oh, come on! This is the twenty-first century. Man has been to the moon! Why are we using these pieces of scrap metal?" Pea, his head now shaven so that he looked even more like a pea, stood up and protested.

"That's right," I echoed. "Isn't the government always talking about modernizing defense? We should have some high-tech toys." Others in the barracks joined in.

"AT-TEN-*TION*!"

Complete silence.

"High-tech toys?" the Drill Instructor asked. "For the likes of you? You college kids don't even know how to hold a pair of chopsticks straight. If I give you a gun, the first thing you'll do is shoot your own nuts off! Now pack up. We're mustering in five minutes for a twenty-kilometer march."

We were issued the following kit: a collapsible short spear (the head could be disassembled into a dagger), an army knife with a serrated blade, a utility belt, a compass, waterproof matches, rations, and a canteen. The Drill Instructor had no faith we could handle anything more advanced.

As if to prove his point, at the end of the practice march, three of us were injured. One fell and sat on the blade of his knife and became the first to be discharged from our platoon. I don't think he did it on purpose—that would have required too much dexterity.

As we neared the end of training period, I saw anxiety in most eyes. Pea couldn't sleep, tossing and turning every night and making the bed squeak. By then I had gotten used to life without TV, without the Internet, without 7-Eleven, but each time I thought about the idea of impaling a warm, flesh-and-blood body with a carbon fiber spear, my stomach churned.

There were exceptions, of course.

Whenever one of us passed the training room, we could see Black Cannon's sweaty figure practicing with his spear. He assigned himself extra drills, and constantly sharpened his knife with a grindstone. Someone who knew him from before told us that he was a quiet kid in school, the sort that got bullied by others. Now he seemed like a bloodthirsty butcher.

Six weeks later, we had our first battle, which lasted a total of six minutes and fourteen seconds.

The Drill Instructor had us surround a small copse. Then he gave the order to charge. Black Cannon went in first. Pea and I looked at each other, hesitated, and brought up the rear. By the time the two of us got to the scene, only a pool of blood and some broken limbs were left. They told me that Black Cannon alone was responsible for eight kills. He chose to keep one of the corpses.

At the meeting afterward, the Drill Instructor commended Black Cannon and criticized "a small number of lazy individuals."

Black Cannon skinned his trophy. But he didn't properly cure it, so the skin soon began to rot and smell and became full of maggots. Finally his bunkmate burned it one day when he was out.

Morale is low.

It's not clear what's worse—that the rats have figured out how to bypass the artificial limits on their breeding capacity, or that they have demonstrated signs of intelligence: construction of structures, hierarchical society, even religious worship.

My paranoia is getting worse. The woods are full of eyes, and the grass is full of whispers.

It's night. I give up on trying to sleep and crawl out of the tent.

The early winter stars are so clear that I think I can see all the way to the end of the universe. The sound of a lone insect pierces the silence. My heart clenches with a nameless sorrow.

Sha! I turn around at the sound. A rat is standing erect on its hind legs about five meters away, like another soldier missing home.

I duck down for the knife in my boot sheath. The rat crouches down, too. Our eyes remain locked. The second my hand touches the knife, the rat turns and disappears into the woods. I grab the knife and follow.

Normally I should be able to catch it in about thirty seconds. But tonight, I just can't seem to close the distance between us. From time to time, it even turns around to see if I'm keeping up. This infuriates me.

The air is full of a sweet, rotting smell. I take a break in a small clearing. I feel dizzy. The trees around me sway and twist, glistening oddly in the starlight.

Pea walks out of the woods. He's wearing his glasses, which ought to be thousands of kilometers away in his parents' possession. His body is whole, without that hole in the chest from that tree branch.

I turn around and see my parents. My dad is wearing his old suit, and my mom is in her plain dress. They're smiling. They look younger, their hair still black.

Tears roll down my face. I don't need logic. I don't need sense.

The Drill Instructor finds me before I die of hypothermia. He tells me that I have enough tears and mucus on my face to fill a canteen.

Pea finally said something meaningful. "Living is so . . ."

He didn't finish his sentence. Tiring? Good? Stupid? You could fill it in however you wanted. That was why I said it was meaningful. Compared to his old way of talking, this new style was forceful, to the point, and left plenty of room for imagination. I admit it—all those literary criticism classes did teach me something.

For me, living was so . . . unbelievable. Half a year ago, I never imagined that I would get to bathe only once a week, that I'd be sleeping with lice in the mud, that I'd fight other men my age for a few stale *wowotou* biscuits, that I'd tremble with excitement at the sight of blood.

Human beings are far more adaptable than we imagine.

If I hadn't joined the Rodent-Control Force, where would I be now? Probably wasting my time on the Internet all day, or maybe staying at home with my parents so we could sit around and drive one another nuts, or maybe carousing with a gang of social misfits and wreaking havoc.

But today, when the Drill Instructor gave the order, I was out there, waving my spear like a real hunter, chasing rats with their furs of all different colors. The rats were stumbling on their hind legs, designed more for cuteness than function, and screamed in their desperation. I heard that rats certified for export were given further surgical modifications so they could vocalize better. I imagined those rats screaming, in English, "No!" or "Don't!" and then looking down as the spear impaled their bellies.

Eventually the platoon developed an unwritten code. After a battle, every man handed the Drill Instructor the tails of the rats he had killed so a tally could be made. The records were supposed to influence what jobs we'd be recommended for after discharge.

They knew just how to motivate us; this was just like final exams and posting scores.

Black Cannon got the most commendations. His kill figure was probably already in the four digits, far ahead of anyone else. My own record was below average, barely passing, not unlike in college. Pea was at the very bottom. If I didn't help him out now and then by handing him a few tails, he would have zero kills.

The Drill Instructor pulled me aside. "Listen, you're Pea's friend. Straighten him out."

I found Pea behind a pile of leaves. I made a lot of noise to give him a chance to put away the pictures of his parents and to wipe away the tears and mucus on his face.

"Homesick?"

He nodded, hiding his swollen eyes from me.

I pulled out a photograph from my inner pocket. "I think about home, too."

He put on his glasses and examined the picture. "Your parents are so young."

"This was taken years ago." I looked at my father's suit and my mother's dress, still new looking. "I guess I'm not much of a son. All these years, all I've done is make them worry. I never even helped them take a new picture." My nose felt itchy.

"You know about macaque monkeys?" Pea asked. It was impossible to follow Pea's thoughts. His mind was like a wire mesh, and ideas traveled across it by jumping. "Scientists discovered mirror neurons in their brains, too. So like humans, they can understand how other monkeys feel and think. They have a mirror in their minds for empathy. You understand?"

I didn't.

"Empathy. You can always say something that gets me right where I need it. So I think you must have an excess of mirror neurons."

I punched him lightly. "You calling me a monkey?"

He didn't laugh. "I want to go home."

"Don't be stupid. The Drill Instructor would never give permission. And it will look terrible in your file. How will you ever find a job?"

"I just can't do it." Pea stared at me, speaking slowly. "I think the rats didn't do anything wrong. They're just like us, doing the best they can in this world. But our role is to chase them, and their role is to be chased. If we swapped roles, it would make no difference."

I couldn't think of anything to say, so I just put my hand on his shoulder.

On the way back to camp, I bumped into Black Cannon. He smirked at me. "Playing therapist for that sissy?"

I gave him the finger.

"Be careful that you don't drown along with him," he called out.

I tried to use my mirror neurons to understand what Black Cannon was thinking and feeling. I failed.

The Drill Instructor stares at the map and the detector, looking thoughtful.

According to the detector, a large pack of rats is moving toward the edge of our district. At the rate we're marching, we should be able to catch them in twelve hours. If we can kill them all, we will have completed our quota. Yes, we'll be honorably discharged. We'll have jobs. We'll go home for New Year's.

But there's a problem. Regulations say that Rodent-Control Force units may not cross district borders for kills. The idea is to prevent units from overly aggressive competition, stealing kills from one another.

The Drill Instructor turns to Black Cannon. "You think we can contain the battle so that the whole operation is within our district?"

Black Cannon nods. "I guarantee it. If we end up crossing district lines, the rest of you can have all my tails."

We laugh.

"Fine. Let's get ready to leave at eighteen hundred hours."

I find a landline public phone at a convenience store. First I call my mom. When she hears that I might be coming home soon, she's so happy she can't speak. I hang up after a few more sentences because I'm afraid she'll cry. Then I dial another number before I can stop myself.

Li Xiaoxia.

She has no idea who I am. Undaunted, I recount our entire history until she remembers.

She's now working at a foreign company's Chinese branch: nine to five, plenty of money. Next year she might go overseas to take some classes at company expense. She seems distracted.

"Have you gotten my postcards?"

"Yeah, sure." She hesitates. "Well, the first few. Then I moved."

"I'm about to be discharged," I say.

"Ah, good. Good. Stay in touch."

I refuse to give up. "Do you remember how when we parted, you told me to be careful of the rats? You said you had seen them. What did you see?"

A long and awkward silence. I hold my breath until I'm about to faint. "I don't remember," she says. "Nothing important."

I regret the money I wasted on that call.

Numbly I stare at the scrolling ticker on the bottom of the static-filled TV screen in the convenience store: "The rodent-control effort is progressing well." "The Western Alliance has agreed to a new round of trade talks concerning the escalating tension with our country." "Employment opportunities for new college graduates are trending up."

Well, even though the rats have now bypassed the limits on their reproductive rates, our quota hasn't been adjusted in response. It makes no sense, but I don't care. It looks like we'll have jobs, and the export numbers will go up again. It doesn't seem like what we're doing here matters.

It's just like what Xiaoxia said: "They say that . . ." "Others say that . . ." It's just rumors and guesses. Who knows what really happens behind closed doors?

No single factor means anything. Everything has to be contextualized. There are too many hidden relationships, too many disguised opportunities for profit, too many competing concerns. This is the most complicated chess game in the world, the Great Game.

But all I can see is my broken heart.

For the last few days, Pea had been going to the bathroom unusually frequently.

I followed him in secret. I saw him taking out a small metal can with holes punched in the lid. He carefully opened it a crack, threw some crackers inside, and murmured quietly into the can.

I jumped out and held out my hand.

"It was really cute," he said "Look at the eyes!" He tried to appeal to my mirror neurons.

"This is against regulations!"

"Just let me keep it for a few days," he begged. "I'll let it go." His eyes looked like the baby rat's, so bright.

Someone as nervous and careless as Pea was no good at keeping secrets. When the Drill Instructor and Black Cannon stood in front of me, I knew the game was up.

"You are sheltering prisoners of war!" Black Cannon said. I wanted to laugh, and Pea was already laughing.

"Stop," the Drill Instructor said. We stood at attention. "If you can give me a reasonable explanation, I'll deal with you reasonably."

I figured that I had nothing to lose, so I came up with an "explanation" on the fly. Black Cannon was so furious when he heard it I thought his nose was going to become permanently twisted.

Pea and I worked together the whole afternoon to dig a hole about two meters deep into the side of a hill. We lined it with a greased tarp. Pea didn't like my plan, but I told him it was the only way we could escape punishment.

"It's really smart," Pea said. "It can even imitate my gestures." He gave a demonstration. Indeed, the little rat was a regular mimic. I tried to get it to imitate me, but it refused.

"Great," I said. "Its IQ is approaching yours."

"I try to see it as just a well-engineered product," Pea said. "A bundle of modified DNA. But emotionally I can't accept that."

We hid downwind from the hole. Pea held a string in his hand. The other end of the string was tied to the leg of the baby rat at the bottom of the hole. I had to keep on reminding Pea to pull the rope once in a while to make the rat cry out piteously. His hands shook. He hated doing it, but I made him. Our futures were at stake here.

My whole idea was founded on guesses. Who knew how these artificial creatures felt about the bonds of kinship? Did adult rats have any child-rearing instincts? How did their new reproductive arrangement—one female mating with multiple males, each of whom then became "pregnant"—affect things?

One male rat appeared. It sniffed the air near the hole as if trying to identify the smell. Then it fell in. I could hear the sound of its claws scratching against the greased tarp. I laughed. Now we had two rats as bait.

The adult male was much louder than the baby rat. If it really had a high IQ, then it should be issuing warnings to its companions.

I was wrong. A second male rat appeared. It came to the side of the trap, seemed to have a conversation with the rats in there, then fell in.

Then came the third, fourth, fifth . . . After the seventeenth rat fell in, I worried that the hole wasn't deep enough.

I gave the signal. In a second, men with spears surrounded the trap.

The rats were building a pyramid. The bottom layer consisted of seven rats leaning against the side of the trap. Five rats stood on their shoulders in the next layer. Then three. Two more rats were carrying the baby rat and climbing up.

"Wait!" Pea yelled. Carefully he pulled the string and slowly separated the baby rat from the adult rats carrying it. The minute the baby rat dangled free of the adults, the adult rats screamed—and I heard sorrow in their voices. The pyramid fell apart as the spears plunged down, splattered blood beading against the plastic and rolling down slowly.

In order to rescue a child who was not directly related to them, the rats were willing to sacrifice themselves. Yet we exploited this to get them.

I shivered.

Pea pulled the baby rat back to him. Just as the baby was about to complete this nightmarish journey, a boot came out of nowhere and flattened it against the earth.

Black Cannon.

Pea jumped at him, fists swinging.

Black Cannon was caught off guard, and blood flowed down the corner of his mouth. Then he laughed, grabbed Pea, and lifted his skinny body over his head. He walked next to the trap, filled with blood and gore, and got ready to toss Pea in.

"I think the sissy wants to join his dirty friends."

"Put him down!" The Drill Instructor appeared and ended the madness.

Because I came up with the plan, I received my first commendation. Three times during his speech, the Drill Instructor mentioned "college education," but not once sarcastically. Even Black Cannon was impressed with me. He told me when no one was around that all the tails from this battle should be given to me. I accepted, and then gave the tails to Pea.

Of course I knew that nothing would make up for what I took away from Pea.

※

Farm fields, trees, hills, ponds, roads . . . we pass like shadows in the night.

During a break, Black Cannon suggests to the Drill Instructor that we divide the platoon in half. He will choose the best fighters and dash ahead while the rest follow slowly. He looks around and then adds, meaningfully, "Otherwise, we might not be able to complete the mission."

"No," I say. The Drill Instructor and Black Cannon look at me. "The strength of an army comes from all its members working together. We advance together, we retreat together. None of us is extraneous, and none of us is more important than any others."

I pause, locking my gaze with the furious Black Cannon. "Otherwise, we'll be no better than the rats."

"Good." The Drill Instructor puts out his cigarette. "We stay together. Let's go."

Black Cannon walks by me. He lowers his voice so that only I can hear. "I should have let you roll down the dam with the sissy."

I freeze.

As Black Cannon walks away, he turns and smirks at me. I've seen that curling of the lips before: when he warned me not to drown along with Pea, when he stomped on the baby rat and lifted Pea over his head, when he sliced open the bellies of the male rats.

Black Cannon was next to Pea that afternoon. They said that Pea left the path because he saw a rare plant. But without his glasses, Pea was practically blind.

I should never have believed their lies.

As I stare at Black Cannon's back, memory surfaces after memory. This is the most difficult journey I've ever been on.

"Prepare for battle," the Drill Instructor says, taking me out of my waking dream. We've been marching for ten hours.

In my mind, the only battle that matters in the world is between Black Cannon and me.

It's dawn again. The battlefield is a dense forest in a valley. The cliffs on both sides are steep and bare. The Drill Instructor's plan is simple: one squad will move ahead and cut off the rat pack's path through the valley. The other squads will follow and kill every rat they see. Game over.

I sneak through the trees to join Black Cannon's squad. I don't have a plan, except that I don't want him out of my sight. The forest is dense, and visibility is poor. A faint blue miasma permeates the air. Black Cannon sets the pace for a fast march, and we weave between the trees, among the fog, like ghosts.

He stops abruptly. We follow his finger and see several rats pacing a few meters away. He gestures for us to spread out and surround them. But by the time we get close, the rats have all disappeared. We turn around, and the rats are still just a few meters away.

This happens a few more times. All of us are frightened.

The miasma grows thicker, filled with a strange odor. My forehead is sweaty, and the sweat stings my eyes. I grip my spear tightly, trying to keep up with the squad. But my legs are rubbery. My paranoia is back. *Things* are watching me in the grass. Whispers in the air.

I'm alone now. All around me is the thick fog. I spin around. Every direction seems full of danger. Desperation fills my head.

Suddenly I hear a long, loud scream in one direction. I rush over but see nothing. I feel something large dash behind me. Another loud, long scream. Then I hear the sound of metal striking against metal, the sound of flesh being ripped apart, heavy breathing.

Then silence, absolute silence.

It's behind me. I can feel its hot gaze.

I spin around, and it leaps at me through the fog. A Neorat as large as a human, its claws dripping with blood, is on me in a second. My spear pushes its arms against its chest, and we wrestle each other to the ground. Its jaws, full of sharp teeth, snap shut right next to my ear, the stench from its mouth making it impossible for me to breathe. I want to kick it off me with my legs, but it has me completely pinned against the ground.

I watch, helplessly, as its bloody claws inch toward my chest. I growl with fury, but it sounds like a desperate, loud scream.

The cold claw rips through my uniform. I can feel it against my chest. Then a brief, searing moment of pain as it rips through my skin and muscles. The claw continues down, millimeter by millimeter, toward my heart.

I look up into its face. It's laughing. The mouth forms a cruel grin, one I'm very familiar with.

Bang. The rat shudders. The claws stop. It turns its head around, confused, trying to find the source of the noise. I gather every ounce of strength in my body and shove its claws away, then smash my spear against its skull.

A muffled thud. It falls against the ground.

I look up past him, and see a bigger, taller rat walking toward me. It's holding a gun in its hands.

I close my eyes.

"You can all have a real drink tonight," the Drill Instructor said. He revealed a few cases of beer next to the campfire.

"What's the occasion?" Pea asked happily. He grabbed a chicken foot out of the big bowl and gnawed on it.

"I think it's somebody's birthday today."

Pea was still for a second. Then he smiled and kept on gnawing his chicken foot. In the firelight I thought I saw tears in his eyes.

The Drill Instructor was in a good mood. "Hey, Pea," he said, handing Pea another beer, "you're a Sagittarius. So you ought to be good at shooting. But why is your aim at rats so awful? You must be doing a lot of other kinds of shooting, am I right?"

We laughed until our stomachs cramped up. This was a side of the Drill Instructor we never knew.

The birthday boy ate his birthday noodles and made his wish. "What did you wish for?" the Drill Instructor asked.

"For all of us to be discharged as quickly as possible so that we can go home, get good jobs, and spend time with our parents."

Everyone went quiet, thinking that the Drill Instructor was going to get mad. But he clapped, laughed, and said, "Good. Your parents didn't waste their money on you."

Now everyone started talking at once. Some said they wanted to make a lot of money and buy a big house. Some said they wanted to sleep with a pretty girl from every continent. One said he wanted to be the president. "If you're going to be the president," another said, "then I'll have to be the Commander-in-Chief of the Milky Way."

I saw that the Drill Instructor's expression was a bit odd. "What do you wish for, sir?"

We all got quiet.

The Drill Instructor poked at the fire with a stick.

"My home village is poor. All of us born there are stupid, not much good at schooling, not like you. As a young man, I didn't want to work the fields or go to the cities and be a laborer. It seemed so futile. Then someone said, 'Go join the army. At least you'll be protecting the country. If you do well, maybe you'll become a hero, and then you can return home and bring honor to your ancestors.' I'd always liked war movies and thought it exciting to wear a uniform. So I signed up.

"Poor kids like me knew nothing except how to work hard. Every day, I trained the longest and practiced the most. If there was a dangerous task, I volunteered. If something dirty needed to be done, I did it. What did I do all that for? I just wanted an opportunity to be a hero on the battlefield. It was my only chance to do something with my life, you know? Even if I died, it would be worth it."

The Drill Instructor paused, sighed. He kept on poking at the fire with his branch. The silence lasted for a long time.

Then he looked up and grinned. "Why are you all quiet? I shouldn't have ruined the mood." He threw away his branch. "Sorry. I'll sing a song to apologize. It's an old song. When I first heard it, you weren't even born yet."

He was not a good singer, but he sang with his whole heart. The corners of his eyes were wet.

"... *Today all I have is my shell. Remember our glory days, when we embraced freedom in the storm? All life we believed we could change the future, but who ever accomplished it . . . ?*"

As he sang, the flickering shadows from the fire made him seem even taller, like a bigger-than-life hero. Our applause echoed loudly in the empty wilderness.

"Let me tell you something," Pea said. He leaned over, sipping from a bottle. "Living is so . . . like a dream."

The loud noise of the engine wakes me.

I open my eyes and see the Drill Instructor, his lips moving. But I can't hear a word over the noise.

I try to get up, but a sharp pain in my chest makes me lie down again. Over my head is a curved metallic ceiling. Then the whole world starts to vibrate and shake, and a sense of weight pushes me against the floor. I'm in a helicopter.

"Don't move," the Drill Instructor shouts, leaning close to my ear. "We're taking you to the hospital."

My memory is a mess of random scenes from that nightmarish battle. Then I remember the last thing I saw. "That gun . . . was that you?"

"Tranquilizer."

I think I'm beginning to understand. "So what happened to Black Cannon?"

The Drill Instructor is silent for a while. "The injury to his head is pretty severe. He'll probably be a vegetable the rest of his life."

I remember that night when I couldn't sleep. I remember Pea, my parents, and . . .

"What did you see?" I ask the Drill Instructor anxiously. "What did you see on the battlefield?"

"I don't know," he says. Then he looks at me. "It's probably best if you don't know, either."

I think about this. If the rats are now capable of chemically manipulating our perceptions, generating illusions to cause us to kill one another, then the war is going to last a long, long time. I remember the screams and the sounds of flesh being torn apart by spears.

"Look!" The Drill Instructor supports me so that I can see through the helicopter cockpit window.

Rats, millions of rats are walking out of fields, forests, hills, villages. Yes, walking. They stand erect and stroll at a steady pace, as though members of the world's largest tour group. The scattered trickles of rats gather into streams, rivers, flowing seas. Their varicolored furs form grand patterns. There's a sense of proportion and aesthetics.

The ocean of rats undulates over the withered, sere winter landscape and the identical, boring human buildings, like a new life force in the universe, gently flowing.

"We lost," I say.

"No, we won," the Drill Instructor says. "You'll see soon."

We land on a military hospital. Bouquets and a wheelchair welcome me, the hero. A pretty nurse pushes me inside. They triage me quickly and then give me a bath. It takes a long time before the water flows clear. Then it's time to feed me. I eat so quickly that I throw it all up again. The nurse gently pats my back, her gaze full of empathy.

The cafeteria TV is tuned to the news. "Our country has reached preliminary agreement with the Western Alliance concerning the trade dispute. All parties have described it as a win-win . . ."

On TV, they're showing the mass migration of rats I saw earlier from the helicopter.

"After thirteen months of continuous, heroic struggle by the entire nation, we have finally achieved complete success in eradicating the rodent threat!"

The camera shifts to a scene by the ocean. A gigantic multicolored carpet is moving slowly from the land into the ocean. As it touches the ocean, it breaks into millions of particles, dissolving in the water.

As the camera zooms in, the Neorats appear like soldiers in a killing frenzy. Crazed, each attacks everything and anything around itself. There're no more sides, no more organization, no more hint of strategy or tactics. Every Neorat is fighting only for itself, tearing apart the bodies of its own kind, cruelly biting, chewing others' heads. It's as if some genetic switch has been flipped by an invisible hand, and their confident climb toward civilization has been turned in a moment into the rawest, most primitive instinct. They collide against one another, strike one another, so that the whole carpet of bodies squirms, tumbles into a river of blood that runs into the sea.

"See, I told you," the Drill Instructor says.

But the victory has nothing to do with us. This had been planned from the start. Whoever had engineered the escape of the Neorats had also buried the instructions for getting rid of them when their purpose had been accomplished.

Li Xiaoxia was right. Pea was right. The Drill Instructor was also right. We are just like the rats, all of us only pawns, stones, worthless counters in the Great Game. All we can see is just the few grids of the board before us. All we can do is just follow the gridlines in accordance with the rules of the game: Cannon on eighth file to fifth file; Horse on second file to third file. As for the meaning behind these moves, and when the great hand that hangs over us will plunge down to pluck one of us off, nobody knows.

But when the two players in the game, the two sides, have concluded their business, all sacrifices become justified—whether it's the Neorats or us. I think again of Black Cannon in the woods, and shudder.

"Don't mention what you saw," the Drill Instructor says. I know he means the religion of the rats, Black Cannon's grin, Pea's death. These things aren't part of the official story. They're meant to be forgotten.

I ask the nurse, "Will the migrating rats pass this city?"

"In about half an hour. You should be able to see them from the park in front of the hospital."

I ask her to take me there. I want to say good-bye to my foes, who never existed.

THE FISH OF LIJIANG

Two fists are before my eyes, bright sunlight reflecting from the backs of the hands.

"Left or right?"

I see myself reaching out with a child's finger, hesitating, and pointing to the one on the left. The fist flips, opens. Empty.

The fists disappear and reappear.

"One more chance. Left or right?"

I point to the one on the right.

"You're sure? Want to change your mind?"

My finger hesitates in the air, waving left, then right, like a swimming fish.

"Final answer? Three . . . two . . . one."

My finger stops on the left.

The fist flips, opens. Other than the bright sunlight, the hand is empty.

A dream?

I open my eyes. The sun is bright white and hurts my eyes. I've been dozing in this Naxi-style[1] courtyard for who knows how long.

---

1 The Naxi are an ethnic group living in parts of southwestern China. Lijiang, Yunnan Province, is a center of Naxi culture.

I haven't felt this comfortable in such a long time. *The sky is so fucking blue.* I stretch until my bones crack.

After ten years, everything here has changed. The only thing that remains the same is the color of the sky.

Lijiang,[2] I'm back. This time, I'm a sick man.

※

Twenty-four hours ago, I had a multiplicity of identities: an office drone with a strict routine, the master of a gray Ford, the prospective owner of a moldy apartment tucked into a hidden fold of the city, a debt-ridden parasite, etc.

Now I'm just a patient, a patient in need of rehabilitation.

It's the fault of that damned mandatory physical exam. On the last page of the report were the words, "PNFD II (Psychogenic Neural-Functional Disorder II)." Translated into words normal people can understand, they say that I'm messed up and I must take two weeks off to rehabilitate.

My face flushed, I asked my boss whether I could be exempted. I *felt* the stares of everyone in the office burning into the back of my neck. *Schadenfreude.* They were delighted that the "boss's pet" was shown to be human after all, weak in the head, collapsing under the stress.

I shuddered. That's office politics for you.

The boss spoke slowly, methodically. "You think I want this? I have to pay for your mandatory vacation! People working at other companies can't get rehab even if they need it. But the new labor law requires it of us. Our company is a proper globalized business; we have to set an example. . . . Anyway, if you get worse, your disease will turn into neurosyphilis and infect the rest of us. Better that you leave now, yes?"

Ashamed, I left the boss's office and cleaned out my desk. I ignored

2   The Lijiang region is famous for the pristine beauty of Jade Dragon Snow Mountain and the Old Town of Lijiang, an ancient city of orderly waterways and bridges and a UNESCO World Heritage Site.

the stares. *Keep on looking, you neurosyphilitic assholes. I'll be back in two weeks, and we'll see who gets to be assistant manager at the end of the year.*

On the airplane, I listened to the snores around me, unable to fall asleep. I'd been dealing with insomnia for more than a month. Actually, I'd been dealing with a lot of things: upset stomach, forgetfulness, headaches, fatigue, depression, loss of libido . . . maybe it really was time for me to rest for a while.

I flipped through the in-flight magazine. The pictures of the tourist sights around Lijiang were so beautiful they almost seemed fake.

Ten years ago, I had nothing and no cares. Ten years ago, Lijiang was a paradise for those who liked to exile themselves from civilization. (Or to put it less pretentiously, that was where young people who fancied themselves "artists" slept with one another.) Ten years ago, I carried everything I owned on my back (still had some muscles then). A map of the ancient city in my pocket, I wandered through it from morning till midnight, chatted with every woman who was alone, fell asleep to the accompaniment of song and alcohol.

Now I'm back. I have a car, a house—everything a man should have, including erectile dysfunction and insomnia. If happiness and time are the two axes of a graph, then I'm afraid the curve of my life has already passed the apex and is on its inexorable way down to the bottom.

※

I stay still, thinking of nothing. Sunlight falls from the tops of the high walls into the yard, which smells of Chinese mahogany. I don't know how much time has passed. My watch, mobile, and any other gadget capable of displaying time have been taken away by the staff of the rehabilitation center.

The ancient city has no computers and no TV. But some of the inhabitants have decided to rent out the space on their foreheads and chests. Tiny LCDs are embedded into their skin, showing all kinds of ads twenty-four hours a day. Like I said, this is no longer the Lijiang I knew.

Strangely, my desire to get better as soon as possible so that I can get back to the office is fading in the sunlight, like the fading smell of the Chinese mahogany.

My stomach growls, once. I decide to go find something to eat. My stomach seems the only way I have left to tell time—oh, also my bladder and the shifting lights in the sky.

The slate-lined street has few pedestrians—this part of the city is reserved for the use of the rehabilitating patients. There *are* many stray dogs, however: fat, thin, all kinds.

On the flight here I heard a joke. Serious economic criminals, in addition to the death penalty and life imprisonment, can now be sentenced to a third kind of punishment: becoming experimental subjects for consciousness transfer operations in Lijiang so that they can be turned into dogs. Normally, because these experiments often fail, no one volunteers. But the idea of living in Lijiang is so attractive—even as a dog—that many have jumped at the opportunity.

Seeing how these dogs are so obsequious before pretty girls and so nervous before city inspectors, I almost think the joke is reportage.

I finish a bowl of soy chicken, find a café, and sit with a cup of black coffee. I flip through a few books I've always been meaning to read (and will never finish) and think about "the meaning of life."

Is this how you get better? Without any physical therapy, medication, special diet, yoga, yin-yang dynamics, or any other kind of professional care? Is this the meaning of the slogan plastered all over the rehabilitation center: "Healthy Minds, Happy Bodies"?

I have to admit it: I have a great appetite; I'm sleeping well; I'm relaxed; I feel better even than I did ten years ago.

Even my nose, which has been stuffed up for several weeks, can now pick out the fragrance of sachets in a coffee shop. *Wait. Sachets?*

I lift my head. A girl in a dark green dress is sitting across from me, holding a drink that smells delicious and looking at me with a big smile on her face. This is like the hook for some French film, I think, or maybe a dream, either sweet or terrifying.

※

"So you're in marketing?"

The woman and I are walking together in the light of the setting sun. The stone-paved street is bathed in a golden glow. Lovely smells waft from the snack bars.

"Sure. You can also say I'm in sales. How about you? Office lady? Civil service? Police? Teacher?" Then I add a bit of flattery. "Actress?"

"Ha! Keep on guessing." She seems to enjoy my attempt at humor. "I'm a special-care nurse. Surprised?"

"So even nurses can get sick and need rehab."

After dinner, we go to a bar. She's disappointed by the decline in the level of service in Lijiang. "What happened to all the fun people who used to run this place?"

From one of the waiters we find out that the place is now owned by Lijiang Industries (stock code #203845), backed by several wealthy conglomerates. The local owners the woman knew sold because they either could no longer afford to keep the place running or could not afford a new license. Everything is so much more expensive now. But the stock of Lijiang Industries is doing very well.

The ancient city at night is filled with the spirit of consumerism, but we can't find anywhere we want to go. She has no interest in hearing Naxi folk music played by a robot orchestra: "Sounds like a braying donkey with its balls cut off." I don't want to see a folk dance demonstration by a bonfire: "Like a human barbecue." In the end we decide to lie down on our bellies by the side of the street, watching the little fish swimming in the waterway.

In the waterways of Lijiang live schools of red fish. Whether it's dawn, dusk, or midnight, you can see them hovering in the water, facing the same direction, lined up like soldiers on a parade ground, ready for inspection. But if you look closer, you'll see that they aren't really still. In fact, they're struggling against the current in order to maintain their position. Once in a while, one or two fish become tired and are pushed out of the formation by the current. But soon, tails fluttering, they fight their way back into place.

It's been ten years since I last saw them. *They*, at least, haven't changed.

"Swim, swim, swim. Before you know it, life is over." I repeat the same words I said ten years ago. "Just like us," she says.

"This is the hidden meaning of life," I say. "At least we still can choose how to live." I sound so pretentious I want to gag.

"But the reality is that I didn't choose you, and you didn't choose me."

My heart skips a beat. I look at her. I really haven't thought about inviting her to come back to my hotel; I still don't feel the return of my libido. This is a misunderstanding.

She begins to laugh.

"I was quoting a song. You don't know it? Well, I'm pretty beat. Why don't we meet up again tomorrow? You're fun."

"But how do I find you . . ." I suddenly realize that I don't have my mobile.

"I'm staying here." She hands me the card from a hotel. "If you're too lazy to walk there, just get a dog."

"A dog?"

"You really don't know? Any stray dog would do. Take a piece of paper, write down the time and place you want to meet at, and stick it in the dog's collar. Then swipe the hotel card through the collar."

"You're not kidding?"

"You need to read your Lijiang guidebook."

※

I don't know how long I slept.

I think it's the afternoon of the second day, but the position of the sun tells me it's morning. Except I have no way of ascertaining that it's not the morning of the third day, the fourth day, or a morning that comes after a dream that lasts a lifetime.

Maybe that's the trick to full rehab: just don't dream about business reports and my boss's fat face.

I look for a dog. But the dogs here have sharp noses. They can smell the failure on me and run away. I'm forced to buy a packet of yak jerky. I feed a dog—a real son of a bitch—until it's stuffed. Finally I get it to carry my message.

In case she forgets who I am, I sign the note, "Last Night's Fish."

I wander the streets. I enjoy the sun and the idleness. No one here has any sense of time anyway, so she can come whenever she wants to.

I see an old man sitting in a corner with a falcon. The falcon and the man are both full of energy. I go up to them with my camera.

"No pictures!" the old man shouts.

"Five yuan! One dollar!" the falcon shouts in a mixture of Sichuan-accented Mandarin and English.

Fuck! They're both robots. The city has nothing authentic anymore. I turn around angrily.

"Do you want to know why the sky in Lijiang is so blue? Do you want to hear the legend of the Jade Dragon Snow Mountain?" Seeing that I'm about to go away, the old man changes his pitch and even his accent. Now he sounds like a man from urbane Suzhou. "I know everything there is to know about Lijiang. One yuan only for each piece of information."

Why not? I just want to kill some time. Might as well hear his lies. I take out a coin and stick it into the falcon's beak. *Clink!* A panel opens in the falcon's chest, revealing a pink-glowing keypad.

"To hear why the sky of Lijiang is so blue, press one. To hear the Legend of Jade Dragon Snow Mountain, press two. . . ."

Enough. I press "1."

"Modern Lijiang relies on condensation control and scatter index standardization. The technology is able to maintain sunny days with probability above ninety-five-point-four-two-six percent. Through microadjustments to the atmospheric particle content, it is able to maintain the hue of the sky between Pantone2975c and 3035c. The system is designed by . . ."

Damn it. I feel sad. Even the sky, so beautiful it's like the pristine sky present at Creation, is fake.

"Looking for UFOs?" the woman asks as she puts her hands on my shoulders from behind.

"Can you tell me if anything here is real?" I mutter.

"Sure. There's you. There's me. We're real."

"Real sick," I correct her.

※

"Tell me about yourself. I love getting to know someone."

We're now back in the bar. Through the window we can see the fish in the waterway below, swimming, swimming, going nowhere.

"Let's play a game," she says. "We take turns guessing facts about the other person. If the guess is right, the other person drinks. If the guess is wrong, the guesser drinks."

"Sure. We'll see who gets drunk first."

"I'll go first. You work for a big company, right?"

"Ha. My boss's favorite saying is, 'We're a proper, global, modern, big' "—I lower my voice—" "factory.' "

She giggles.

I can't remember if I told her anything about my company in the past. But I take a drink anyway.

"Your patients," I ask, "are all important people, right?" She drinks.

"You're an important man at your company," she says. I drink.

"I'll ask something more interesting," I say. "You've had patients who made passes at you, haven't you?"

She blushes and drains her glass.

"You must have many girlfriends," she says. I hesitate for a second, and drink. *"Had" is a form of "have,"* I tell myself.

"You are not married," I say.

She smiles, not answering.

I shrug, taking a drink.

Only after I'm done does she lift her glass and drink.

"Not fair! You tricked me," I say. But I'm happy.

"It's your own fault for being impatient."

"Fine, then I'm going to guess that you have insomnia, anxiety, arrhythmia, irregular periods . . ." I know I've been drinking too fast. I know I'm going to regret this, but I can't stop talking.

She glares at me and drinks. Then she adds, "Whatever symptoms you have, I don't. Whatever symptoms I have, you don't."

"We're both here, aren't we?"

She shakes her head. "You think nothing has meaning."

"That was before I met you," I say in what I think is a seductive tone. Now I'm just shameless.

She ignores me. "You're often anxious because you hate the feeling of the seconds slipping away from you. The world is changing every day. And every day you're getting older. But there are still so many things you haven't done. You want to hold on to the sand. But the harder you squeeze, the quicker the sand slips from the cracks between your fingers, until nothing is left . . ."

Coming from anyone else, the words would just be pop psychology, pseudo intellectualism, cheap spirituality. But somehow, coming from her, they sound like the truth. Every word strikes against my heart, making me wince.

I drink by myself in silence. Her smile begins to multiply: two, three, four of her . . . I want to ask her something, but my tongue is no longer obeying.

She looks embarrassed. She whispers to me, "You're drunk. I'll take you back."

So I've failed again.

※

It takes a long time for me to remember where I am.

During the time I'm thinking, the sun shifts through six window squares. It marches across three more window squares before I've washed away the smell of alcohol on my body and the vomit in the bathroom.

I guess Miss Nurse hasn't taken good care of *this* patient. I have a splitting headache.

I don't want to send a dog after her. Indeed, I'm a bit scared to meet her. Maybe she's a telepath? It makes sense to have a telepath as a special-care nurse, right? Especially if the patient can no longer speak.

The biggest fear is for someone else to understand what you really fear.

A shar-pei enters my room and barks at me. I take out the slip of paper tucked into its collar.

She wants me to go with her to listen to robots playing Naxi folk music, which she'd described to me as a donkey braying with its balls cut off. She signed her note, "I'm No Telepath."

Screw you! You bourgeois bitch! I kick the shar-pei. It whimpers.

In the end, curiosity overcomes fear. I wash, get dressed, go to the concert hall. She's dressed all in yellow. I nod at her.

But she ignores my attempt to remain distant. She walks right up to me, takes my hand in hers, and drags me inside.

"Stop pretending," she whispers in my ear. I have to struggle to keep from her how aroused I am.

They begin to play. It does sound like a donkey braying. It's an insult to real Naxi music, the sort I heard ten years ago.

The robots swing back and forth, pretending to play all sorts of Naxi instruments, and recorded music streams from speakers embedded into the seats. The robots are clearly made in China: stiff, ridiculous movements; limited repertoire of gestures; monotonous expressions. Only robot Xuan Ke[3] is made with any kind of care for detail. Once in a while he even acts as though he's completely absorbed by his performance. I worry that he'll swing so hard his head falls off.

"I thought you didn't like donkey-braying," I whisper into her ear. The fragrance of sachets surrounds me.

"This is one part of our rehabilitation."

"Yeah, right."

I try to kiss her. But she dodges out of the way, and my lips meet her fingers.

"Back in your office, on your desk, there's a tiny gray alarm clock. It's shaped like a mushroom, and it often runs fast."

Her tone is calm, but I'm stupefied. That clock was a gift from the

3 The name of a famous Naxi music scholar.

company when I won Employee of the Month. How does she know about it?

I lost the drinking game—maybe that was an accident. But this . . .

I continue to stare at her profile. The donkey-braying music washes over me like a tidal wave. I seem to have also become a robot musician. I strain to play my foolish song of seduction, but she sees through me with no effort. I have nothing in my chest but a mechanical heart made of iron.

※

We end up in bed together.

She acts as though this is nothing special. But not me. A man is such a strange animal: fear and desire are expressed by the same organ. For the former, he loses control of the organ and it lets out urine; for the latter, he loses control of the organ and it fills with blood.

Is this part of our rehab, too? I can imagine myself mocking her. But I don't, because I fear how she'll answer.

"Who are you really?" I can't help myself.

Her voice is muffled, indistinct. "I'm a nurse. My patient is time."

In the end she does tell me her story.

She works for a place called "Time Care Unit." Only the most important men of the business world get to go there.

The old men are like mummies, their bodies plugged full of tubes and wires. Twenty-four hours a day they must be watched and cared for. Every day, all kinds of people come to visit. They dress in sterile biosuits and stand around the beds, communing with the old men, reporting and receiving instructions in silence.

The old men never move. Each of their breaths takes hours. Once in a while, one of them moans like a baby, and someone makes a record of it. Looking at all the biological signs, they should all be considered dead. The numbers shown on their machines never change. But they remain in that place for years, decades.

She tells me that they are receiving "time sense dilation therapy." She calls them "the living dead."

The therapy began some twenty years ago. Back then, scientists discovered that by controlling the biological clock of an organism, it was possible to reduce the production of free radicals and slow down aging. But the decay of the mind and its eventual death could not be reversed or halted.

Someone made another discovery: the aging of the mind was intimately connected with the sense of the passage of time. By manipulating certain receptors in the pineal gland, it was possible to slow down one's sense of time, to dilate it. The body of a person receiving time sense dilation therapy remains in the normal stream of time, but his mind experiences time a hundred, a thousand times slower than the rest of us.

"But what does this have to do with you?" I ask.

"You know that women who live together synchronize their biological rhythms, like menstrual cycles?"

I nod.

"It's the same thing with us nurses who care for these living dead, day in, day out. Once a year, I have to come to Lijiang to rehabilitate, to remove the effects time dilation has on my body."

I feel dizzy. Time sense dilation is used on those old men because of the need to maintain stock prices or to delay power struggles among successors. But what if the dilation is applied to a normal person? I try to imagine experiencing a hundred years within a second. But my imagination is not up to the task. To extend time to near infinity is to slow it down until it's almost still. Then isn't the mind under such dilation immortal? What's the need for a body made of flesh?

"Remember what I told you? I didn't choose you, and you didn't choose me," she says, smiling almost apologetically.

I begin to feel anxiety again, as though my fingers are wrapped around a handful of sand, leaking grains.

"You're the other half of me, cloven by Zeus's thunderbolt."

The words sound to me like a curse.

She's leaving.

She tells me that her rehabilitation period is up.

We sit in the dark. In front of us is the imposing mass of Jade Dragon Snow Mountain, its snowy peaks reflecting the silver moonlight. Neither of us speaks.

The donkey-braying music loops again and again in my head.

"Remember that alarm clock on your desk?" she asks.

Although time sense dilation therapy is very expensive, the opposite procedure—time sense compression—is not. The procedure is cheap enough to be commercialized. Several large conglomerates have invested in it, and taking advantage of certain loopholes in China's labor laws (and the complicity of the government), they've been conducting secret trials on Chinese employees of international companies.

That alarm clock is a prototype time sense compressor.

"So we are all lab mice," I remember mocking myself at her revelation. Even my boss is a mouse—he also has one of those clocks on his desk.

"It doesn't matter if you know the truth," she says. "The theoretical basis for time sense compression does not exist."

"Does not exist?"

"Theoretical physics says it's impossible, so they had to base it on the philosophy of Henri Bergson. It's all about intuition."

"What are you talking about?"

"I don't know." She laughs. "Maybe it's all nonsense."

"You're telling me that my disease, this PNFD II or whatever it's called, is the result of time sense compression?"

She doesn't say anything.

But it makes sense. Time passes quicker in my mind than it does in the real world. Every day I'm exhausted. I'm always working overtime. I accomplish so much more in twenty-four hours than others. No wonder the company thinks I'm a model employee.

Clouds drift over and hide the moon, eliminating the reflected light on the snowy peaks. Everything grows darker like after they lower the lights in a theatre.

A bright red laser beam lands on the snowy cliffs—5,600 meters above the sea—now acting as a giant screen. The laser creates shifting patterns, telling an animated tale, the creation of the world. A myth has been bowdlerized to mass entertainment. I'm not in the mood to appreciate it. The dancing lights only make my heart beat irregularly.

Time sense compression is wonderful for improving productivity and GDP. But there are many side effects. The mismatch between subjective time and physical time causes metabolic problems that accumulate into severe symptoms.

The conglomerates that invested in the technology created the rehabilitation centers in China and lobbied to change the labor laws to institutionalize the idea of "rehabilitation"—and so hide the truth.

They discovered that those suffering from the side effects of time sense dilation and those suffering from the side effects of time sense compression can help one another, be one another's cure.

"I'm the yang to your yin, is that it?" So her interest in me is limited to my value as a medical device. My middle-aged male ego is hurt.

"Sure, if you insist on thinking about it that way." Her tone, at least, is compassionate.

"What about the donkey-braying music?"

"It's a way to harmonize our biorhythms."

I wait for her to stroke my ego by telling me that compared to her previous rehabilitation biorhythm partners, I'm better looking, more interesting, more special, etc. But she says nothing of the kind.

"What about the dogs?" I'm running out of things to say before she leaves.

"They started out as regular dogs. But because they're exposed to so many patients with out-of-sync senses of time, the structures in their brains have changed."

"I have only one last wish." I stare at her bright eyes, like a pair of fireflies, in the darkness. "Come and look at the fish in the waterways with me. Maybe they're the only creatures in this world who live real lives."

The fireflies brighten. She touches my face lightly. "Actually . . ."

I silence her lips with my fingers. I shake my head. I've succeeded. There's no need for her to tell me what she's going to tell me, the three heaviest words in the world.

But she gently moves my hand away, and says three words, three different words.

"Don't be stupid."

※

I'm alone by the waterway, staring at the fish.

She's gone, leaving behind no way to contact her. Sand pricks my palms. No matter how hard I squeeze, it slips away.

Fish, oh, fish, you're the only ones left to keep me company.

Suddenly I feel an intense jealousy of these fish. Their lives are so simple, so pure. There's only one direction—against the current. They do not have to hesitate, overwhelmed by an endless array of choices. But if I really lived a life like that, maybe I'd still complain. A man is never content with what he has.

Suddenly I want to spit at myself for my self-love, self-pity, self-obsession, self-self. But in the end I do nothing.

I look at one single fish: it's pushed away from its school by the current. Once, twice, thrice. It falls behind, waves its tail madly, and returns to its position.

Fuck. It's tough.

But wait.

Why is it always this one fish? Why are its trajectory and movement always exactly the same?

I wait, unblinking.

Two minutes later, that same little fish again drifts away from the school, again waves its tail madly, again returns to its position.

I lift the stone in my hand.

The stone falls through the holographic fish and sinks to the bottom of the waterway.

I have nothing left in my hand, not even a single grain of sand.

※

My rehabilitation over, I'm on my return flight with my not-so-healthy mind and not-so-happy body. The airplane hasn't taken off yet, but the cabin is already filled with snores.

I guess some people at least have been fully rehabilitated.

Suddenly the idea of returning to that concrete jungle to struggle against my fellow time-compressors disgusts me.

The plane takes off. Cities, roads, mountains, rivers—everything recedes into a small chessboard composed of parti-colored squares. In every square, time flows faster or slower. The people below throng like a nest of ants controlled by an invisible hand, divide into a few groups, are stuffed into the different squares: time flies past the laborer, the poor, the "third world"; time crawls for the rich, the idle, the "developed world"; time stays still for those in charge, the idols, the gods . . .

Without warning, two fat hands belonging to a child appear before me, balled into fists side by side, holding the entire world.

"Left or right?"

I look to the left and then to the right. I'm frightened. I have no way to pick.

Mocking laughter.

I lunge and grab both fists and force the fingers open. Both are empty, both are lies.

"Sir, sir!"

The pretty flight attendant wakes me. Now I finally remember the origin of that dream. It was my cousin who tormented me as a child. His favorite game was to force me to guess in which hand he had hidden the candy he took away from me. He loved to tease me because I was always hesitant, always had trouble deciding.

"Sir, would you like soda, coffee, tea, or something else?"

". . . you."

She blushes.

I smile at her. "I just want coffee, black."

This is the only truly free choice I have left.

THE FLOWER OF SHAZUI

Summers in Shenzhen Bay last ten months. Mangrove swamps surround the bay like congealed blood. Year after year, they shrink and rot like the rust-colored night that hides many crimes.

To the east of the mangroves, north of Huanggang Port between Shenzhen and Hong Kong, is Shazui Village, where I'm staying for now.

I've hidden here for half a year. The subtropical sun is brutal, but I've grown even paler. The five urban villages, Shazui, Shatou, Shawei, Shangsha, and Xiasha—or literally, "Sand Mouth," "Sand Head," "Sand Tail," "Upper Sand," "Lower Sand"—form a large, dense concrete jungle at the heart of Futian District. The names of the villages often give one the illusion of living in the mouth of some giant, mythical monster named "Sand" which, while separated from the head, remains alive.

Big Sister Shen tells me this used to be a sleepy fishing village. But with the economic reforms and the opening up of China, urbanization brought construction everywhere. To get more compensation when the government exercised its eminent domain powers, villagers raced to build tall towers on their land so as to maximize the square footage of the residential space. But before they could cash in, real estate prices had risen to the point where even the government could no longer afford to pay compensation. These hastily erected buildings remain like historical ruins, witnesses to history.

"The villagers built a story every three days," she says. "Now that's what you call the Speed of the Special Economic Zone."

I imagine these buildings growing as fast as cancer cells, finally settling into the form they have today. Inside the apartments, it's always dark because there's so little space between the buildings that tenants in buildings next to each other can shake hands through the windows. The alleyways are narrow like capillaries and follow no discernible pattern. The stench of rot and decay permeates everything, sinks into everyone's pores. Because the rent is cheap, every kind of migrant can be found here, struggling to fulfill their Shenzhen dream: the high-tech, high-salaried, high-resolution, high-life, high-Shenzhen.

But I prefer this lower-end version. It makes me feel safer.

Big Sister Shen is a good person. She's originally from the Northeast. Years ago, she bought this building from a native family that was moving overseas. Now she lives the life of a happy landlady. With the rent rising daily, her net worth must be in the tens of millions, but she still lives here. She took me in despite the fact that I had no identity papers, and gave me a small booth to practice my trade. She even prepared a fake file for me in case the police ever show up. She never asks me about my past. I'm grateful, and I try to do a few favors to repay her.

From my booth at the door of the Chinese medicine shop, I sell a combination of body films and cracked versions of augmented-reality software. Body films are applied to the skin, where they display words or pictures in response to the body's electrical signals. In America, they use the technology as a diagnostic tool, monitoring patients' physiological signs. But here it has become part of the street culture of status display. Laborers, gangsters, and prostitutes all like to apply the films to prominent or hidden parts of the body so that, in response to changing muscle tension or skin temperature, the films can show various pictures to signal the wearer's personality, daring, and sex appeal.

I still remember the first time I spoke with Snow Lotus.

Snow Lotus is from humid, subtropical Hunan, but she decided to name herself after an alpine flower. Even at night, her pale skin glows like porcelain. Some say that she's Shazui Village's most famous "house phoenix"—a prostitute who works out of her home. I often see her walking and holding hands with different men, but her expression is always composed, with no hint that anything sordid is going on. Indeed, she exudes an allure that makes it impossible to look away.

Shazui Village is home to thousands of prostitutes at all price levels. They provide the middle- and lower-class men of both Shenzhen and Hong Kong with all varieties of plentiful, cheap sexual services. Their bodies are like a paradise where the tired, dirty, and fragile male souls can take temporary refuge. Or maybe they are like a shot of placebo so that the men, after a moment of joy, their spirit restored, can return to the battlefield that is real life.

Snow Lotus is not like any of the others. She's Big Sister Shen's good friend and comes often to shop at the Chinese medicine store. Every time she passes my booth, her perfume makes my heart skip a few beats. I always try to restrain myself from following her with my eyes, but I never succeed.

That day, Snow Lotus tapped my shoulder lightly from behind. "Can you help me fix my body film? It won't light up," she said.

"I can take a look." I had trouble hiding my rising panic.

"Follow me," she whispered.

The dim stairs were as narrow as intestines. Her apartment was nothing like what I had imagined. The color scheme was light yellow, decorated with many homey, warm details. There was even a balcony that allowed one to see the open sky. In Shazui, this was a real luxury.

She led me into her bedroom, and, keeping her back to me, she slid her jeans down to her knees, revealing a pair of blindingly white thighs and lacy black panties.

My hands and feet felt cold. I swallowed with difficulty, trying to moisten my dry throat.

Snow Lotus's elegant finger pointed to her panties. I was still not ready. My heart was full of fear.

"It won't light up," she said. She hadn't taken off her panties. She was just pointing to the octagon-shaped film depicting a *bagua* that had been applied right above her tailbone.

I tried to disguise my disappointment. Carefully, I examined the film with my diagnostic tools, doing my best not to pay attention to her smooth, silky skin. I tweaked the thermal response curve of the capacitance detector. "It should be okay now. Try it." I let out a long-held breath.

Suddenly Snow Lotus began to laugh. The almost-invisible hairs on the smooth skin below her waist stood up like a miniature patch of reeds.

"How am I supposed to try it out?" She turned around to look at me, her tone teasing.

I believe that no straight man in the world can resist that look. But in that moment, I felt insulted. She was treating me as just another customer, a consumer who exchanged money for the right to make use of her body. Or perhaps she thought that this was how she'd pay for my services? I didn't know where my childish anger came from, but without saying another word, I took out a heating pad and held it against her waist. After thirty seconds, the yin-yang symbol in middle of the *bagua* lit up with the character for "east," glowing with a blue light.

"East?" I asked, not understanding.

"That's my man's name." Snow Lotus's expression was back to being calm and composed. She pulled up her jeans, turned around, and saw the question on my face. "You think a prostitute should have no man to call hers?

"He likes to take me from behind. I put the film here to let all my customers know they can mount me if they're willing to spend the money, but there are some things they cannot buy." She lit a cigarette. "Oh, how much do I owe you?"

I felt a sudden, inexplicable sense of relief.

※

The man named East is Snow Lotus's husband, and also her pimp. His business involves traveling between Shenzhen and Hong Kong, smuggling digital goods. Others tell me that he's addicted to gambling. Most of Snow Lotus's earnings are lost by him at the gaming table. Sometimes he even forces her to service some older Hong Kong customers with . . . special desires. But even so, she still wears his name on her waist, declaring that she belongs to him.

This is such a cliché that it reminds me of many old Hong Kong gangster movies. But that's just daily life in Shazui.

Snow Lotus is unhappy. That's why she often comes to Big Sister Shen for help.

Like many in Shazui, Big Sister Shen also has multiple jobs. One of them is shaman.

Big Sister Shen claims to be a Manchu. Some of her ancestors were also shamans, she says, and so she has inherited some of their magical powers, enabling her to speak to spirits and to predict the future.

One time, when she was a little drunk and in a talkative mood, she described the great, empty deserts of the far north, where one's breath turned to ice, and where her ancestors had once performed magical ceremonies while dressed in ferocious masks, dancing, twirling in the blizzard, drumming and singing, praying for spirits to take over their bodies. Even though that was a hot day, with the temperature hovering near forty degrees Celsius, everyone in the room had shivered as she told her story.

Big Sister Shen never allows me to enter the room where she performs her magic. She says that because I don't want anything, my heart isn't pure, and so I will harm the atmosphere for the spirits.

An endless stream of customers comes to seek her services. They all say that she has real power—one look, and she can tell everything about you. I've seen the people who leave her room after the magic sessions: their faces are filled with a dreamy look of satisfaction.

I've seen that expression many times: young women carrying their LV Speedy bags, wealthy urbanites on the hunt for beautiful women at the V Bar of the Venetian, politicians who appear on TV every night for the six-thirty Shenzhen news—all of them wear that same expression on their faces, a very Shenzhen expression.

They are like the johns who come to Shazui every day. They go to the Chinese medicine store for some extra-strength aphrodisiac and then reappear with a confident smile. But I know that the aphrodisiac contains nothing but fiber, and it has no effect except causing them to shit regular.

In this city, everyone needs some placebo.

※

Snow Lotus comes to Big Sister Shen again and again. Each time she leaves as if enlightened, but soon after, she returns, her face full of unhappiness. I can imagine the kind of troubles that someone like her must endure, but I can't help wanting to know more. I have many technical ways to satisfy my curiosity, but they all require that I set foot first in Big Sister Shen's room. I know the only way is to become a disciple.

"I need the aid of spirits," I tell Big Sister Shen. I'm not lying.

"Come in." Big Sister Shen has seen countless men. She can spot a liar from a mile away.

The room isn't big, and it's dimly lit. On the wall I can see paintings of shamanistic spirits, the chaotic brushstrokes probably the result of a drug-addled brain. Big Sister Shen sits in front of a square altar covered by a red flannel cloth. On top of the altar are a mask, a cowhide drum, a drum whip, a bronze mirror, a bronze bell, and other ritual implements. An electronic prayer machine begins to recite sutras. She puts on the mask, and through the hideous eyeholes, I can see an ancient and alien light in her eyes.

"The Great Spirit is listening," she says. Her voice is low and rasping, full of an indisputable sense of dignity.

I can't resist her power. There's a story locked away in the darkest corner of my memory, but it has never ceased to torment me. Sin is like wine. The more it is hidden from sunlight, the more it ferments, growing more potent.

Suddenly I startle awake. My subconscious has been playing

a trick on me. It's not curiosity about Snow Lotus that caused me to step into this room, but the inner desire to be free of repression, to seek relief.

"I'm from outside the Fence. I was an engineer." I try to control my breathing, to steady my voice.

I'm from outside the Fence. I was an engineer.

Back in 1983, before I was born, a barbed-wire fence 84.6 kilometers long and 2.8 meters high was built to divide Shenzhen into two parts. Inside the Fence is the 327.5 square kilometers of the Special Economic Zone; outside is a wilderness of 1,600 square kilometers. They say that the purpose of the Fence was to provide some relief for the border checkpoint between Hong Kong and Shenzhen. Before 1997, when Hong Kong was ruled by Great Britain, there used to be many waves of illegal border crossings.

The Berlin Wall never truly fell.

The Fence and its nine checkpoints separated not only people and traffic, but also different systems of law, welfare, tax benefits, infrastructure, and identity. The area outside the Fence became Shenzhen's "mistress." Because of its proximity to the Special Economic Zone and its vast tracts of undeveloped land, it attracted many labor-intensive, though low-value-added, industries. But every time "outside the Fence" was mentioned, a Shenzhener's first thought was of the deserts in Hollywood westerns: a poor, backward place where the roads were always under construction, where running red lights had no consequences, where crime was rampant and the police powerless.

Yet history always surprises us with similarities. Shenzhen also had its own version of the taming of the West.

In 2014, the government's decision to finally tear down the Fence received unprecedented opposition. Shenzheners living inside the Fence believed that they would be overwhelmed by migrants from the other side and suffer increased crime. But those living outside the Fence opposed it even more. They felt that they had been abandoned by those inside the Fence back when the Special Economic Zone grew, and now that development had run into a wall due to the scarcity of developable space, they were being exploited for their only resource: land. If unopposed, increased rent and prices would drive the low-income population out of their homes. Young people even dressed up in Native American garb and tied themselves to the Fence to prevent it from being torn down.

The factory where I worked was one of the electronics manufacturers affected by the change. Every year we relied on orders from Europe, America, and Japan for augmented reality gear components to earn foreign currency. At the same time, our margins were being squeezed by the declining value of the dollar against the yuan. If commercial rent and wages also rose, then there would be nothing left for profit. The owner announced at an all-hands meeting that everyone should be prepared for layoffs.

I was a mold engineer. I wanted to do something to make as much money as I could before I was let go. Everyone thought that way.

Our clients gave us prototypes for unreleased products so we could design the molds ahead of actual production. Following strict NDAs and security procedures, RFID chips embedded in the prototypes sent out signals at 433 MHz and communicated with dedicated receivers through a proprietary over-the-air protocol. If at any time a prototype left a designated area, an automatic alarm would sound. If the prototype weren't returned to the designated area within three hundred seconds, the machine would activate a self-destructive mechanism. Of course, if that were to occur, the factory would lose all international credibility and be blacklisted by clients and get no more business.

Throughout the Pearl River Delta, experienced and crafty buyers solicited secret prototypes at high prices. Getting their hands on such prototypes and reverse engineering them would bring these *shanzhai* electronics manufacturers tens of millions in profits. These days, getting rich unethically was easier than running an honest business.

I had lined up everything: a willing buyer, a price, a way to deliver the goods, and an escape route. But I still needed one more thing, a helper, someone to divert the attention of the crowd and lure away the security guards. I couldn't think of anyone better for the job than Chen Gan, who was also from my hometown.

I understood Chen Gan. He was a shy young man. His wife had just given birth to their second daughter, and he was worried about how he would be able to afford his first daughter's elementary school tuition. As a migrant, he could not have his household registration in Shenzhen and had to pay an extra fee for his daughter to go to the regular school. Without that money, he would have to send his daughter to a different school, a low-quality place set up for the children of migrant workers. He would often look at a picture of his little girl and say that he didn't want her to repeat the path he had walked.

I made a deposit into his bank account: not too much, just enough to cover the extra fee for the school.

For the Chinese, what reason could be more compelling than "for my child"?

At the agreed-upon time, I heard the sound of loudspeakers outside my building. I knew that Chen Gan was already playing his role. In the middle of the yard, he had covered himself in gasoline and held a lighter in his hand. He declared that if the owner didn't pay him enough severance, then he would light himself on fire. As security guards rushed anxiously into the yard with fire extinguishers, no one paid attention as I took the emergency stairs up to the roof, clutching the stolen prototype.

I was one of only five individuals in the factory authorized to touch the prototype. Taking advantage of opportunities afforded by my duties, I had tested the RFID trigger mechanism several times. The logs appeared to only record the latitude and longitude of the device, but not the altitude. This hole allowed me to devise an effective method of delivery to the buyer.

On the roof, the wind blew strong and cold, like the moment before the first drops of rain. Almost all the workers in the factory had congregated in the yard to watch how the self-immolation drama would end. If the owner gave in to Chen Gan's demands, tomorrow hundreds more would be waiting for him, doused in gasoline.

But I'd known the owner for three years. He was the sort who would encourage Chen Gan to go ahead and use the lighter, and then he would light a cigarette from the smoldering pile of ash.

A dragonfly-like remote-controlled helicopter approached from afar, humming, and landed on the roof. Following directions, I tied the prototype to the bottom of the helicopter. Unsteadily, it began to rise. I anxiously watched this fragile machine, on which the lives of two men, and perhaps of even more, depended.

The maximum communication distance between the RFID chip and the receiver was about sixty feet. The roof was already close to that limit.

The helicopter hung in the air as if waiting for more direction. I didn't know how the buyers intended to deal with the self-destructive mechanism or if they were going to crack the communication protocol and substitute in a false signal to fool the device. That was all beyond what I could control.

For a moment, I thought the helicopter might never leave. But it did eventually depart the roof, and then disappeared into the gray sky.

Calmly, I rode the elevator down and squeezed myself into the gaping crowd. I made sure that Chen Gan saw me. He nodded almost imperceptibly, gave me his trademark shy smile, and dropped the lighter.

The security guards were on him immediately and wrestled him to the ground.

It was time to leave, I thought.

I got on the intercity bus to Dongguan. But before the bus had even started its engine, my phone began to vibrate insistently. Given what I knew about the owner, I never would have had much time. But I hadn't expected to be caught so quickly.

Maybe it was the closed-circuit cameras, or maybe Chen Gan sold me out. But I didn't care anymore. I just wanted him to be all right, to live long enough to see his daughter go to school.

I threw away my phone, got off the bus, and got on the bus going the opposite direction, inside the Fence, into Shenzhen. Instinctively, I knew that was the safer direction.

This was how I came to be in Shazui Village.

For the last half year, I've tried every which way to find out news about Chen Gan, but have heard nothing. I thought I was sufficiently indifferent, indifferent to the point that I could abandon my useless conscience. But often I would awaken in the middle of the night, breathless. In my dreams, Chen Gan, smiling his shy smile, would burn and turn into a pile of ashes. Sometimes I would even dream of his two daughters, crying, burning with him, also turning into ash.

I knew that I could no longer hide from myself.

"Please tell me if he's all right." My face is covered in tears even though I don't remember crying.

The wooden shaman mask glowers at me with its round eyeholes, orange light reflecting off the surface. The face is that of an angry goddess. Through the eyeholes I can see a strange glint in her eyes: sparkling blue flashes, very high in frequency.

Suddenly I understand. The mask is nothing more than a fucking well-made disguise for a pair of augmented reality glasses.

All this time, I've thought that Big Sister Shen is just a fraud pretending to be a medium and making her money by telling her clients what they want to hear. But she actually has real power. Guessing conservatively, her information privilege level must be set to at least level IIA or above, giving her the power to access an individual's private file based on facial recognition.

But even so, without professional-grade analysis filter software, how can she glean any useful information out of that torrent within such a short time? It would be like finding a needle lost in the sea. I can only credit her shaman genes, like Dustin Hoffman in *Rain Man* being able to tell how many matches are in a box with a single glance.

The lights behind the eyeholes flash faster. My heart accelerates.

"He's doing well."

Hope rekindles in my heart.

"At least there, he no longer needs to worry about money." Big Sister Shen points toward the sky. Then she adds, "I'm sorry for your loss."

I suck in a deep breath. Even though I was expecting it, now that the fear has settled into reality, I still feel a deep helplessness. The whole world seems to have lost focus, and nothing can be relied on.

I know that in this world, there's only one thing I can do to try to atone, even if it will provide only illusory comfort for my conscience.

"I want a working bank account number for Chen Gan's family."

Money was once my placebo. Now I no longer need it.

It's dark by the time I leave Big Sister Shen's room. I look around at Shazui, where lights are just being turned on behind windows. People are bustling every which way, filling the air with hope. But my heart is like a dead pool of water. I open my hand. Emptiness.

My subconscious has played another trick on me. I did indeed install the bug below the rim of the altar. I thought I was there for Chen Gan, but in the end I couldn't forget about Snow Lotus.

I smile, a Shenzhen-style smile.

Snow Lotus doesn't look well.

Her face is pale. She's wearing large shades that cover her eyes and half her face. Without speaking to anyone, she goes straight to Big Sister Shen's room.

I put on my headset and turn on the receiver. After a static-filled moment, I hear the sound of the electronic prayer machine.

"He hit me again." Snow Lotus's voice is tearful. "He said that I haven't been turning enough tricks. He needs more money."

"This is your own choice." Big Sister Shen's voice is calm, as if she's used to hearing this.

"I should go with that Hong Kong businessman."

"But you don't want to leave him."

THE FLOWER OF SHAZUI | 83

"I've been with him for ten years! Ten years! I was once a girl who didn't know anything, and now . . . I'm nothing but a cheap whore!"

"You want another ten years just like these?"

"Big Sister . . . I'm pregnant."

Big Sister Shen is quiet for a moment. "Is it his?"

"Yes."

"Then tell him. You're bearing his child. You cannot be a whore anymore."

"He'll tell me to abort it. This is not the first time. Big Sister, I'm getting old. I want to keep this child."

"Then keep it."

"He'll kill me. He will."

"He won't," I say.

Hearing your own voice from the air as well as the headset is a very odd sensation. I'm standing at the door to the room, watching a surprised Snow Lotus turning to look at me. Her face is as smooth as porcelain, except for her swollen, bruised right eye. My fists are squeezed so tight that the nails puncture my skin.

Here's my plan. Even though it's against my original aim, I have to admit that it's the most likely to succeed.

Her husband is addicted to gambling. He's also like every other gambler under the sun: superstitious. We need to allow him to make a connection between his child and good luck. *For my child.* My heart feels a tinge of bitterness.

Every morning, Snow Lotus will mumble a string of meaningless numbers as if talking in her sleep.

Her obsessive husband habitually seeks inspiration for his bets from anything, whether it's the colors of the Teletubbies or the phone number on advertising brochures. Then he'll discover that she's mumbling the winning lottery numbers from the day before.

Snow Lotus will tell him that she had a strange dream: she dreamed that a beautiful rainbow-colored cloud floated out of the east and drifted into her belly.

After seven days of this, we'll come to the best part of the show.

My professional skills will finally come into use. I'll arm Snow Lotus with wireless earbuds and augmented reality contact lenses. But the key will be a special black unitard. At first glance, it looks like regular long underwear, but specially designed fibers will deform and harden when electrically charged, resulting in precisely defined areas of tension and force, strong enough to stop a bullet.

With the addition of an array of electrodes and a communication chip, I can turn the unitard into a remote-controlled puppet suit, allowing me to pose the wearer in any position.

"Why do you want to help me?" Snow Lotus asks. She still thinks that men are only interested in her body.

"For karma." I laugh. Big Sister Shen often says this to her customers. With the remote control, I direct the unitard-wearing Snow Lotus into various sexy poses.

"Without any clothes, I can pose even better."

I lower my head, pretending not to hear. I continue to fiddle with the controls. Suddenly, like a warm cloud descending from the sky, two soft, pale arms are wrapped around my chest. Her voice is against my back, fills my chest, my heart, my lungs, flows up my spine into my eardrums. The voice seems to come from the bottom of my heart, and also seems to come from very far away.

"Thank you," she says.

I want to say something, but in the end I say nothing.

Big Sister Shen and I are seeing what Snow Lotus is seeing.

After the dim stairs, we come to the familiar pale yellow apartment. The man named East is sitting in front of the TV, watching horse races in Hong Kong, cursing all the while. Snow Lotus walks into the kitchen, preparing to make dinner.

The picture suddenly becomes still. Then a man's two arms are wrapped around her breasts, like the way she had held me.

"Don't," she says.

The man does not answer. The picture suddenly shakes, and now her face is close to the faucet, her head lowered into the sink. The faucet is on, and the water rises, covering the vegetables and the fruits before draining into the overflow hole with tiny bubbles. Now the picture begins to shake rhythmically. Then come the heavy breathing, sighing, and the occasional moaning.

I can turn off the video and audio feed, but I don't. I observe all this almost grimly, experiencing a mixture of anger, jealousy, and disgust churning slowly in the pit of my stomach until they merge into a single feeling. I struggle to imagine what Snow Lotus is feeling, especially since she is not making a sound, not a single sound, while all this is happening under the gaze of two outsiders.

Finally she finds some relief. She closes her eyes.

In the semidarkness, blurry patches of light penetrate her eyelids and tremble lightly. A hand is on my shoulder. It's Big Sister Shen. She sees and knows all.

We wait until midnight. I can hear even, rhythmic snores coming from next to Snow Lotus. I lift her left hand, indicating that I'm ready. She clears her throat in response.

Now begins the fake séance.

I manipulate the puppet suit and lift her legs high up; then I make her torso rigid and drop her legs, using them as a lever to lift her upper body off the bed. I let her body drop, bouncing her legs even higher. Switching thus between potential and kinetic energy, the rigid body of Snow Lotus soon behaves like a coin striking hard ground, quickly bouncing and making a frightening ruckus against the bed.

"What the fuck is the matter with you? It's the middle of the night!" The man named East, rudely roused from slumber, feels for the bedside lamp and turns it on. Then, with another great noise, East is bounced off the bed onto the floor.

"Fuck! Fuck! Fuck!" His curses are full of fear and shock.

As she continues to bounce, Snow Lotus's body seems to no longer be restrained by gravity. She is like a puppet pulled up by invisible strings. Up, down, up again, she springs from the mattress. For a moment, she seems to be floating in air. The yellow ceiling comes closer, and then recedes, like some kind of breathing membrane. The edges of our vision show signs of barrel distortion as the membrane relaxes.

"That's enough." Big Sister Shen puts a stop to my madness. Our goal isn't to scare this man away.

I have to admit that controlling Snow Lotus's body is addictive, as though it compensates for something subconsciously.

The amplitude of the bounces lessens. Snow Lotus's body is once again quietly lying in bed. I relax the fibers in the puppet suit. Now she is spread out like a floppy corpse.

Just like we planned, she begins to cry. Babbling incoherently, she describes her nightmare and the strange news.

"It . . . it says that if we take care of it, it will repay us, like with those lottery numbers . . ."

"Who is *it*?"

"Your child."

The man gets up from the floor. His face is wooden, as though he has been overwhelmed with too much information. He holds in his hands a fruit knife that he grabbed from somewhere. Approaching Snow Lotus, he caresses her belly, and then lifts his head to gaze into her face. Under the warm glow of the lamp, this seems like a happy scene from a soap opera. Next will come the promise to welcome new life, followed by the deep kiss of love.

The glimmer in his beautiful eyes suddenly turns cold, dark, like a pool of black water.

"The doctor told me that my sperm is no good." Slowly he rubs the flat of the knife across her belly. "Now tell me whose bastard this is. Then get rid of it."

"It's yours." Snow Lotus's breathing is now very rapid. Her voice trembles on the verge of tears.

"You think you're the Blessed Virgin Mary? You fucking whore!" He slaps her hard. The picture tilts. The dressing mirror shows two silhouettes. The composition is perfect in the dim light.

"It's yours," she repeats, her voice weak.

The knife is now right in front of her face, the thin, sharp edge glowing with a cold light. I can no longer sit and watch. I lift Snow Lotus's hands, grab the man's wrist and the knife handle, and turn the knife around. He's unprepared for her speed and strength and doesn't know how to react.

Snow Lotus's entire body leans forward, pushing the tip of the knife toward her husband's chest.

"Stop!" Big Sister Shen yells. But I'm not doing anything. It's Snow Lotus. I don't even have a chance to restrain her.

The knife, with all of Snow Lotus's weight behind it, sinks into the man's skin, through muscle and ribs, through his heart. Crimson liquid oozes out of the wound and spreads like wildflowers. He looks up, gazing past Snow Lotus as though he sees an existence even darker, further away, until the last light of life disappears from his eyes.

The picture stays still for a while. Stunned by the sudden turn of events, we don't know what to do. Snow Lotus suddenly begins to run. Everything in front of us is shaking violently. She runs toward the balcony, toward that patch of open night sky.

This time I don't miss. Before she leaps into nothingness, I restrain her. Snow Lotus stops like a frozen flower and falls heavily against the floor. Angrily she screams, struggles, and finally howls in desperation.

Death is the best placebo.

In this instance, I agree with this view.

Sirens shatter the dawn in Shazui Village. Accompanied by the police, Big Sister Shen and I walk through the crowd and duck into the police car. Snow Lotus is sitting in the back of another car, handcuffed. From the side, her porcelain cheeks are lit alternately by flashes of blue and red. She does not lift her head.

Eyes lowered, the roar of the engine in her ears, her silhouette trembles, blurs, and then disappears into the distance.

I recall the first time I spoke with Snow Lotus, and I begin down the long road of regret.

XIA JIA

As an undergraduate, Xia Jia majored in Atmospheric Sciences at Peking University. She then entered the Film Studies program at the Communication University of China, where she completed her Master's thesis, "A Study on Female Figures in Science Fiction Films." Recently, she obtained a Ph.D. in Comparative Literature and World Literature at Peking University, with *Fear and Hope in the Age of Globalization: Contemporary Chinese Science Fiction and Its Cultural Politics (1991–2012)* as the title of her dissertation. She now teaches at Xi'an Jiaotong University.

She has been publishing fiction since college in a variety of venues including *Science Fiction World* and *Jiuzhou Fantasy*. Several of her stories have won the Galaxy (Yinhe) Award and Nebula (Xingyun) Award, China's most prestigious science fiction honors. In English translation, she has been published in *Clarkesworld* and *Upgraded*, both edited by Neil Clarke. "A Hundred Ghosts Parade Tonight" won an honorable mention in the Science Fiction and Fantasy Translation Awards in 2013 and was selected by editor Rich Horton for his "Year's Best" anthology.

Xia Jia describes her own style as "porridge SF," in contrast to the perennial (and, in my opinion, pointless) debate over the distinction of "hard SF" from "soft SF." (These terms have slightly different meanings in the Chinese SF community than the Anglophone SF community. Generally, "hard SF" in Chinese refers to the inclusion of more technical material.) Her stories in this anthology, "A Hundred Ghosts Parade Tonight," "Tongtong's Summer," and "Night Journey of the Dragon-Horse," showcase the range of her style. Reviewer Lois Tilton described "A Hundred Ghosts" as "literary science fiction . . . where exceptional prose mingles the tropes of SF and fantasy and inform us that such distinctions are not so important."[1] "Night Journey of the Dragon-Horse" is a brand-new story that has never been published in English.

Besides writing fiction, Xia Jia is also a brilliant translator from English into Chinese. Her translations, like her own writing, are lucid, elegant, and graceful. Her translation of my novella, "The Man Who Ended History," is in many ways an improvement on the original.

In 2014, Xia Jia became the first Ph.D. in China with a specialization in science fiction. Her academic work on Chinese science fiction has been called groundbreaking, and she has presented her results in China as well as abroad. The critical essay she provided at the end of this book tries to tackle the question of what makes Chinese science fiction Chinese. (Most of her academic work is published under the name "Wang Yao," as "Xia Jia" is a pen name used mainly for fiction.)

Xia Jia is also a filmmaker, actress, painter, and singer.

---

1   http://www.locusmag.com/Reviews/2012/02/lois-tilton-reviews-short-fiction
-early-february-2/

A HUNDRED GHOSTS
PARADE TONIGHT

AWAKENING OF INSECTS, THE THIRD SOLAR TERM:

Ghost Street is long but narrow, like an indigo ribbon. You can cross it in eleven steps, but to walk it from end to end takes a full hour.

At the western end is Lanruo Temple, now fallen into ruin. Inside the temple is a large garden full of fruit trees and vegetable patches as well as a bamboo grove and a lotus pond. The pond has fish, shrimp, dojo loaches, and yellow snails. So supplied, I have food to eat all year.

It's evening, and I'm sitting at the door to the main hall, reading a copy of *Huainanzi,* the Han Dynasty essay collection, when along comes Yan Chixia, the great hero, vanquisher of demons and destroyer of evil spirits. He's carrying a basket by the crook of his elbow, the legs of his pants rolled all the way up, revealing calves caked with black mud. I can't help but laugh at the sight.

My teacher, the Monk, hears me and walks out of the dark corner of the main hall, gears grinding, and hits me on the head with his ferule.

I hold my head in pain, staring at the Monk in anger. But his iron face is expressionless, just like the statues of the buddhas in the main hall. I throw down the book and run outside while the Monk pursues me, his joints clanging and creaking the whole time. They are so rusted that he moves as slowly as a snail.

I stop in front of Yan, and I see his basket contains several new bamboo shoots, freshly dug from the ground.

"I want to eat meat," I say, tilting my face up to look at him. "Can you hunt some buntings with your slingshot for me?"

"Buntings are best eaten in the fall when they're fat," says Yan. "Now is the time for them to breed chicks. If you shoot them, there won't be buntings to eat next year."

"Just one, pleeeeease?" I grab onto his sleeve and act cute. But he shakes his head resolutely, handing me the basket. He takes off his conical sedge hat and wipes the sweat off his face.

I laugh again as I look at him. His face is as smooth as an egg, with just a few wisps of curled black hair, like weeds that have been missed by the gardener. Legend has it that his hair and beard used to be very thick, but I'm always pulling a few strands out now and then as a game. After so many years, these are all the hairs he has left.

"You must have died of hunger in a previous life," Yan says, cradling the back of my head in his large palm. "The whole garden is full of food for you. No one is here to fight you for it."

I make a face at him and take the basket of food.

The rain has barely stopped; insects cry out from the wet earth. A few months from now, green grasshoppers will be jumping everywhere. You can catch them, string them along a stick, and roast them over the fire, dripping sweet-smelling fat into the flames.

As I picture this, my empty stomach growls as though already filled with chittering insects. I begin to run.

The golden light of the evening sun splatters over the slate slabs of the empty street, stretching my shadow into a long, long band.

I run back home, where Xiao Qian is combing her hair in the darkness. There are no mirrors in the house, so she always takes off her head and puts it on her knees to comb. Her hair looks like an ink-colored scroll, so long that the strands spread out to cover the whole room.

I sit quietly to the side until she's done combing her hair, puts it up in a moon-shaped bun, and secures it with a pin made of dark wood inlaid with red coral beads. Then she lifts her head, reattaches it to her neck, and asks me if it's sitting straight. I don't understand why Xiao Qian cares so much. Even if she just tied her head to her waist with a sash, everyone would still think she's beautiful.

But I look seriously and nod. "Beautiful," I say.

Actually, I can't really see very well. Unlike the ghosts, I cannot see in the dark.

Xiao Qian is happy with my affirmation. She takes my basket and goes into the kitchen to cook. As I sit and work the bellows next to her, I tell her about my day. Just as I get to the part where the Monk hit me on the head with the ferule, Xiao Qian reaches out and lightly caresses my head where I was hit. Her hand is cold and pale, like a piece of jade.

"You need to study hard and respect your teacher," Xiao Qian says. "Eventually you'll leave here and make your way in the real world. You have to have some knowledge and real skills."

Her voice is very soft, like cotton candy, and so the swelling on my head stops hurting.

Xiao Qian tells me that Yan Chixia found me on the steps of the temple when I was a baby. I cried and cried because I was so hungry. Yan Chixia was at his wit's end when he finally stuffed a handful of creeping rockfoil into my mouth. I sucked on the juice from the grass and stopped crying.

No one knows who my real parents are.

Even back then, Ghost Street had been doing poorly. No tourists had come by for a while. That hasn't changed. Xiao Qian tells me that it's probably because people invented some other attraction, newer, fresher, and so they forgot about the old attractions. She's seen similar things happen many times.

Before she became a ghost, Xiao Qian tells me, she lived a very full life. She had been married twice, gave birth to seven children, and raised them all.

And then her children got sick, one after another. In order to raise the money to pay the doctors, Xiao Qian sold herself off in pieces: teeth, eyes, breasts, heart, liver, lungs, bone marrow, and finally her soul. Her soul was sold to Ghost Street, where it was sealed inside a female ghost's body. Her children died anyway.

Now she has white skin and dark hair. The skin is light sensitive. If she's in direct sunlight, she'll burn.

After he found me, Yan Chixia had walked up and down all Ghost Street before he decided to give me to Xiao Qian to raise.

I've seen a picture of Xiao Qian back when she was alive. It was hidden in a corner of a drawer in her dresser. The woman in the picture had thick eyebrows, huge eyes, a wrinkled face—far uglier than the way Xiao Qian looks now. Still, I often see her cry as she looks at that picture. Her tears are a pale pink. When they fall against her white dress, they soak into the fabric and spread like blooming peach flowers.

Every ghost is full of stories from when they were alive. Their bodies have been cremated and the ashes mixed into the earth, but their stories still live on. During the day, when all Ghost Street is asleep, the stories become dreams and circle under the shadows of the eaves like swallows without nests. During those hours, only I'm around, walking in the street, and only I can see them and hear their buzzing song.

I'm the only living person on Ghost Street.

Xiao Qian says that I don't belong here. When I grow up, I'll leave.

The smell of good food fills the room. The insects in my stomach chitter even louder.

I eat dinner by myself: preserved pork with stir-fried bamboo shoots, shrimp paste–flavored egg soup, and rice balls with chives, still hot in my hands. Xiao Qian sits and watches me. Ghosts don't eat. None of the inhabitants of Ghost Street, not even Yan Chixia or the Monk, ever eat.

I bury my face in the bowl, eating as fast as I can. I wonder, after I leave, will I ever eat such delicious food again?

MAJOR HEAT, THE TWELFTH SOLAR TERM:

After night falls, the world comes alive.

I go alone to the well in the back to get water. I turn the wheel and it squeaks, but the sound is different from usual. I look down into the well and see a long-haired ghost in a white dress sitting in the bucket.

I pull her up and out. Her wet hair covers her face, leaving only one eye to stare at me out of a gap. "Ning, tonight is the Carnival. Aren't you going?"

"I need to get water for Xiao Qian's bath," I answer. "After the bath we'll go."

She strokes my face lightly. "You are a foolish child."

She has no legs, so she has to leave by crawling on her hands. I hear the sound of crawling, creeping all around me. Green will-o'-the-wisps flit around like anxious fireflies. The air is filled with the fragrance of rotting flowers.

I go back to the dark bedroom and pour the water into the wooden bathtub. Xiao Qian undresses. I see a crimson bar code along her naked back like a tiny snake. Bright white lights pulse under her skin.

"Why don't you take a bath with me?" she asks.

I shake my head, but I'm not sure why. Xiao Qian sighs. "Come." So I don't refuse again.

We sit in the bathtub together. The cedar smells nice. Xiao Qian rubs my back with her cold, cold hands, humming lightly. Her voice is very beautiful. Legend has it that any man who heard her sing fell in love with her.

When I grow up, will I fall in love with Xiao Qian? I think and look at my small hands, the skin now wrinkled from the bath like wet wrapping paper.

After the bath, Xiao Qian combs my hair and dresses me in a new shirt she made for me. Then she sticks a bunch of copper coins, green and dull, into my pocket.

"Go have fun," she says. "Remember not to eat too much!"

※

Outside, the street is lit with countless lanterns, so bright I can no longer see the stars that fill the summer sky.

Demons, ghosts, all kinds of spirits come out of their ruined houses, out of cracks in walls, rotting closets, dry wells. Hand in hand, shoulder to shoulder, they parade up and down Ghost Street until the narrow street is filled.

I squeeze myself into the middle of the crowd, looking all around. The stores and kiosks along both sides of the street send forth all kinds of delicious smells, tickling my nose like butterflies. The vending ghosts see me and call for me, the only living person, to try their wares.

"Ning! Come here! Fresh sweet osmanthus cakes, still hot!"

"Sugar-roasted chestnuts! Sweet smelling and sweeter tasting!"

"Fried dough, the best fried dough!"

"Long pig dumplings! Two long pig dumplings for one coin!"

"Ning, come eat a candy man. Fun to play and fun to eat!"

Of course the "long pig dumplings" are really just pork dumplings. The vendor says that just to attract the tourists and give them a thrill.

But I look around, and there are no tourists.

I eat everything I can get my hands on. Finally I'm so full that I have to sit down by the side of the road to rest a bit. On the opposite side of the street is a temporary stage lit by a huge bright white paper lantern. Onstage, ghosts are performing: sword-swallowing, fire-breathing, turning a beautiful girl into a skeleton. I'm bored by these tricks. The really good show is still to come.

A yellow-skinned old ghost pushes a cart of masks in front of me.

"Ning, why don't you pick a mask? I have everything: Ox-Head, Horse-Face, Black-Faced and White-Faced Wuchang, Asura, Yaksha, Rakshasa, Pixiu, and even Lei Gong, the Duke of Thunder."

I spend a long time browsing, and finally settle on a Rakshasa mask with red hair and green eyes. The yellow-skinned old ghost thanks me as he takes my coin, dipping his head down until his back is bent like a bow.

I put the mask on and continue strutting down the street. Suddenly loud Carnival music fills the air, and all the ghosts stop and then shuffle to the sides of the street.

I turn around and see the parade coming down the middle of the street. In front are twenty one-foot-tall green toads in two columns striking gongs, thumping drums, strumming *huqin,* and blowing bamboo *sheng.* After them come twenty centipede spirits in black clothes, each holding varicolored lanterns and dancing complicated steps. Behind them are twenty snake spirits in yellow dresses, throwing confetti into the air. And there are more behind them, but I can't see that far.

Between the marching columns are two Cyclopes in white robes, each as tall as a three-story house. They carry a palanquin on their shoulders, and from within Xiao Qian's song rolls out, each note as bright as a star in the sky, falling one by one onto my head.

Fireworks of all colors rise up: bright crimson, pale green, smoky purple, shimmering gold. I look up and feel as though I'm becoming lighter myself, floating into the sky.

As the parade passes from west to east, all the ghosts along the sides of the street join, singing and dancing. They're heading for the old osmanthus tree at the eastern end of Ghost Street, whose trunk is so broad that three men stretching their arms out can barely surround it. A murder of crows lives there, each one capable of human speech. We call the tree Old Ghost Tree, and it is said to be in charge of all of Ghost Street. Whoever pleases it prospers; whoever goes against its wishes fails.

But I know that the parade will never get to the Old Ghost Tree.

When the parade is about halfway down the street, the earth begins to shake and the slate slabs crack open. From the yawning gaps, huge white bones crawl out, each as thick as the columns holding up Lanruo Temple. The bones slowly gather together and assemble into a giant skeleton, glinting like white porcelain in the moonlight. Now black mud springs forth from its feet and crawls up the skeleton, turning into flesh. Finally, a colossal Dark Yaksha stands before us, its single horn so large that it seems to pierce the night sky.

The two Cyclopes don't even reach its calves.

The Dark Yaksha turns its huge head from side to side. This is a standard part of every Carnival. It is supposed to abduct a tourist. On nights when there are no tourists, it must go back under the earth, disappointed, to wait for the next opportunity.

Slowly it turns its gaze on me, focusing on my presence. I pull off my mask and stare back. Its gaze feels hot, the eyes as red as burning coal.

Xiao Qian leans out from the palanquin, and her cry pierces the suddenly quiet night air: "Ning, run! Run!"

The wind lifts the corner of her dress, like a dark purple petal unfolding. Her face is like jade, with orange lights flowing underneath.

I turn and run as fast as I can. Behind me, I hear the heavy footsteps of the Dark Yaksha. With every quaking, pounding step, shingles fall from houses on both sides like overripe fruits. I am now running like the wind, my bare feet striking the slate slabs lightly: *pat, pat, pat.* My heart pounds against my chest: *thump, thump, thump.* Along the entire frenzied Ghost Street, mine is the only living heart.

But both the ghosts and I know that I'm not in any real danger. A ghost can never hurt a real person. That's one of the rules of the game.

I run toward the west, toward Lanruo Temple. If I can get to Yan Chixia before the Yaksha catches me, I'll be safe. This is also part of the performance. Every Carnival, Yan puts on his battle gear and waits on the steps of the main hall.

As I approach, I cry out, "Help! Save me! Oh, Hero Yan, save me!"

In the distance, I hear his long ululating cry and see his figure leaping over the wall of the temple to land in the middle of the street. He holds in his left hand a Daoist charm: a red character written against a yellow background. He reaches behind his back with his right hand and pulls out his sword, the Demon Slayer.

He stands tall and shouts into the night sky, "Brazen Demon! How dare you harm innocent people? I, Yan Chixia, will carry out justice today!"

But tonight, he forgot to wear his sedge hat. His egg-shaped face is exposed to the thousands of lanterns along Ghost Street, with just a few wisps of hair curled like question marks on a blank page. The silly sight is such a contrast against his serious mien that I start to laugh even as I'm running. And that makes me choke, and I can't catch my breath, so I fall against the cold slate surface of the street.

This moment is my best memory of the summer.

COLD DEW, THE SEVENTEENTH SOLAR TERM:

A thin layer of clouds hides the moon. I'm crouching by the side of the lotus pond in Lanruo Temple. All I can see are the shadows cast by the lotus leaves, rising and falling slowly with the wind.

The night is as cold as the water. Insects hidden in the grass won't stop singing.

The eggplants and string beans in the garden are ripe. They smell so good that I have a hard time resisting temptation. All I can think about is stealing some under the cover of night. Maybe Yan Chixia was right: in a previous life, I must have died of hunger.

So I wait and wait. But I don't hear Yan Chixia's snores. Instead, I hear light footsteps cross the grassy path to stop in front of Yan Chixia's cabin. The door opens, the steps go in. A moment later, the voices of a man and a woman drift out of the dark room: Yan Chixia and Xiao Qian.

Qian: "Why did you ask me to come?"

Yan: "You know what it's about."

Qian: "I can't leave with you."

Yan: "Why not?"

Qian: "A few more years. Ning is still so young."

"Ning, Ning!" Yan's voice grows louder. "I think you've been a ghost for too long."

Qian sounds pitiful. "I raised Ning for so many years. How can I just get up and leave him?"

"You're always telling me that Ning is still too young, always telling me to wait. Do you remember how many years it has been?"

"I can't."

"You sew a new set of clothes for him every year. How can you forget?" Yan chuckles, a cold sound. "I remember very clearly. The fruits and vegetables in this garden ripen like clockwork, once a year. I've seen them do it fifteen times. Fifteen! But has Ning's appearance changed any since the year he turned seven? You still think he's alive, he's real?"

Xiao Qian remains silent for a moment. Then I hear her crying.

Yan sighs. "Don't lie to yourself anymore. He's just like us, nothing more than a toy. Why are you so sad? He's not worth it."

Xiao Qian just keeps on crying.

Yan sighs again. "I should never have picked him up and brought him back."

Xiao Qian whispers through the tears, "Where can we go if we leave Ghost Street?"

Yan has no answer.

The sound of Xiao Qian's crying makes my heart feel constricted. Silently I sneak away and leave the old temple through a hole in the wall.

The thin layer of clouds chooses this moment to part. Icy moonlight scatters itself against the slate slabs of the street, congealing into drops of glittering dew. My bare feet against the ground feel so cold that my whole body shivers.

A few stores are still open along Ghost Street. The vendors greet me enthusiastically, asking me to sample their green bean biscuits and sweet osmanthus cake. But I don't want to. What's the point? I'm just like them, maybe even less than them.

Every ghost used to be alive. Their fake mechanical bodies host real souls. But I'm fake throughout, inside and outside. From the day I was born, made, I was fake. Every ghost has stories of when they were alive, but I don't. Every ghost had a father, a mother, a family, memories of their love, but I don't have any of that.

Xiao Qian once told me that Ghost Street's decline came about because people, real people, found more exciting, newer toys. Maybe I am one of those toys—made with newer, better technology until I could pass for the real thing. I can cry, laugh, eat, piss and shit, fall, feel pain, ooze blood, hear my own heartbeat, grow up from a simulacrum of a baby—except that my growth stops when I'm seven. I'll never be a grown-up.

Ghost Street was built to entertain the tourists, and all the ghosts were their toys. But I'm just a toy for Xiao Qian.

Pretending that the fake is real only makes the real seem fake.

I walk slowly toward the eastern end of the street until I stop under the Old Ghost Tree. The sweet fragrance of osmanthus fills the foggy night air, cool and calming. Suddenly I want to climb into the tree. That way, no one will find me.

The Old Ghost Tree leans down with its branches to help.

I sit hidden among the dense branches and feel calmer. The crows perch around me, their glass eyes showing hints of a dark red glow. One of them speaks. "Ning, this is a beautiful night. Why aren't you at Lanruo Temple, stealing vegetables?"

The crow is asking a question to which it already knows the answer. The Old Ghost Tree knows everything that happens on Ghost Street. The crows are its eyes and ears.

"How can I know for sure," I ask, "that I'm a real person?"

"You can chop off your head," the crow answers. "A real person will die with his head cut off, but a ghost will not."

"But what if I cut off my head and die? I'll be no more."

The crow laughs, the sound grating and unpleasant to listen to. Two more crows fly down, holding in their beaks antique bronze mirrors. Using the little moonlight that leaks through the leaves, I finally see myself in the mirrors: small face, dark hair, thin neck. I lift the hair off the back of my neck, and in the double reflections of the mirrors, I see a crimson bar code against the skin, like a tiny snake.

I remember Xiao Qian's cool hands against my spine on that hot summer night. I think and think until tears fall from my eyes.

WINTER SOLSTICE, THE TWENTY-SECOND SOLAR TERM:

This winter has been both dry and cold, but I often hear the sound of thunder in the distance. Xiao Qian says it's the Thunder Calamity, which happens only once every thousand years.

The Thunder Calamity punishes demons and ghosts and lost spirits. Those who can escape it can live for another thousand years. Those who can't will be burned away until no trace is left of them.

I know perfectly well that there's no such thing as a "Thunder Calamity" in this world. Xiao Qian has been a ghost for so long that she's now gone a little crazy. She holds on to me with her cold hands, her face as pale as a sheet of paper. She says that to hide from the Calamity, a ghost must find a real person with a good heart to stay beside her. That way, just as one wouldn't throw a shoe at a mouse sitting beside an expensive vase, the Duke of Thunder will not strike the ghost.

Because of her fear, my plan to leave has been put on hold. In secret I've already prepared my luggage: a few stolen potatoes, a few old shirts. My body isn't growing any more anyway, so these clothes will last me a long time. I didn't take any of the old copper coins from Xiao Qian, though. Perhaps the outside world does not use them.

I really want to leave Ghost Street. I don't care where I go; I just want to see the world. Anywhere but here.

I want to know how real people live.

But still I linger.

On Winter Solstice it snows. The snowflakes are tiny, like white sawdust. They melt as soon as they hit the ground. Only a very thin layer has accumulated by noon.

I walk alone along the street, bored. In past years I would go to

Lanruo Temple to find Yan Chixia. We would knock an opening in the ice covering the lotus pond and lower our jury-rigged fishing pole. Winter catfish are very fat and taste fantastic when roasted with garlic.

But I haven't seen Yan Chixia in a long time. I wonder if his beard and hair have grown out a bit.

Thunder rumbles in the sky, closer, then farther away, leaving only a buzzing sensation in my ears. I walk all the way to the Old Ghost Tree, climb up into its branches, and sit still. Snowflakes fall all around me, but not on me. I feel calm and warm. I curl up and tuck my head under my arms, falling asleep like a bird.

In my dream, I see Ghost Street turning into a long, thin snake. The Old Ghost Tree is the head, Lanruo Temple the tail, the slate slabs the scales. On each scale is drawn the face of a little ghost, very delicate and beautiful.

But the snake continues to writhe as though in great pain. I watch carefully and see that a mass of termites and spiders is biting its tail, making a sound like silkworms feeding on mulberry leaves. With sharp mandibles and claws, they tear off the scales on the snake one by one, revealing the flesh underneath. The snake struggles silently, but disappears inch by inch into the maws of the insects. When its body is almost completely eaten, it finally makes a sharp cry and turns its lonesome head toward me.

I see that its face is Xiao Qian's.

I wake up. The cold wind rustles the leaves of the Old Ghost Tree. It's too quiet around me. All the crows have disappeared to who knows where, except one that is very old and ugly. It's crouching in front of me, its beak dangling like the tip of a long mustache.

I shake it awake, anxious. It stares at me with two broken-glass eyes, croaking to me in its mechanical, flat voice, "Ning, why are you still here?"

"Where should I be?"

"Anywhere is good," it says. "Ghost Street is finished. We're all finished."

I stick my head out of the leaves of the Old Ghost Tree. Under the slate gray sky, I see the murder of crows circling over Lanruo Temple in the distance, cawing incessantly. I've never seen anything like this.

I jump down from the tree. As I run along the narrow street, I pass dark doors and windows. The cawing of the crows has awakened many of the ghosts, but they don't dare to go outside where there's light. All they can do is peek out from cracks in doors, like a bunch of crickets hiding under houses in winter.

The old walls of Lanruo Temple, long in need of repairs, have been pushed down. Many giant mechanical spiders made of steel are crawling all over the main hall, breaking off the dark red glass shingles and sculpted wooden molding piece by piece and throwing the pieces into the snow on the ground. They have flat bodies, blue-glowing eyes, and sharp mandibles, as ugly as you can imagine. From deep within their bodies comes a rumbling noise like thunder.

The crows swoop around them, picking up bits of broken shingles and bricks on the ground and dropping them on the spiders. But they are too weak, and the spiders ignore them. The broken shingle pieces strike against the steel shells, making faint, hollow echoes.

The vegetable garden has been destroyed. All that remains are some mud and pale white roots. I see one of the Monk's rusted arms sticking out of a pile of broken bricks.

I run through the garden calling for Yan Chixia. He hears me and slowly walks out of his cabin. He's still wearing his battle gear: sedge hat on his head, the sword Demon Slayer in his hand. I want to shout for him to fight the spiders, but somehow I can't spit the words out. The words taste like bitter, astringent paste stuck in my throat.

Yan Chixia stares at me with his sad eyes. He comes over to hold my hands. His hands are as cold as Xiao Qian's.

We stand together and watch as the great and beautiful main hall is torn apart bit by bit, collapses, turns into a pile of rubble: shingles, bricks, wood, mud. Nothing is whole.

They've destroyed all of Lanruo Temple: the walls, the main hall, the garden, the lotus pond, the bamboo grove, and Yan Chixia's cabin. The only thing left is a muddy ruin.

Now they're moving on to the rest of Ghost Street. They pry up the slate slabs, flatten the broken houses along the sides of the street. The ghosts hiding in the houses are chased into the middle of the street. As they run, they scream and scream while their skin slowly burns in the faint sunlight. There are no visible flames. But you can see the skin turning black in patches, and the smell of burning plastic is everywhere.

I fall into the snow. The smell of burning ghost skin makes me vomit. But there's nothing in my stomach to throw up. Instead, I cry during the breaks in the dry heaves.

So this is what the Thunder Calamity looks like.

The ghosts, their faces burned away, continue to cry and run and struggle in the snow. Their footprints crisscross in the snow like a child's handwriting. I suddenly think of Xiao Qian, and so I start to run again.

Xian Qian is still sitting in the dark bedroom. She combs her hair as she sings. Her melody floats in the gaps between the roaring, rumbling thunder of the spiders, so quiet, so transparent, like a dreamscape under the moon.

From her body come the fragrances of myriad flowers and herbs, layer after layer, like gossamer. Her hair floats up into the air like a flame, fluttering without cease. I stand and listen to her sing, my face full of tears, until the whole house begins to shake.

From on top of the roof, I hear the sound of steel clanging, blunt objects striking against one another, heavy footsteps, and then Yan Chixia's shouting.

Suddenly the roof caves in, bringing with it a rain of shingles and letting in a bright patch of gray sky full of fluttering snowflakes. I push Xiao Qian into a dark corner, out of the way of the light.

I run outside the house. Yan Chixia is standing on the roof, holding his sword in front of him. The cold wind stretches his robe taut like a gray flag.

He jumps onto the back of a spider and stabs at its eyes with his sword. The spider struggles hard and throws Yan off its back. Then the spider grabs Yan with two sharp claws and pulls him into its sharp, metallic, grinding mandibles. It chews and chews, like a man chewing kimchee, until pieces of Yan Chixia's body are spilling out of its mandibles onto the shingles of the roof. Finally Yan's head falls off the roof and rolls to a stop next to my feet, like a hard-boiled egg.

I pick up his head. He stares at me with his dead eyes. There are no tears in them, only anger and regret. Then, with the last of his strength, Yan closes his eyes, as though he cannot bear to watch any more.

The spider continues to chew and grind up the rest of Yan Chixia's body. Then it leaps down from the roof and, rumbling, crawls toward me. Its eyes glow with a deep blue light.

Xiao Qian jumps from behind me and grabs me by the waist, pulling me back. I pry her hands off me and push her back into the dark room. Then I pick up Yan Chixia's sword and rush toward the spider.

The cold blue light of a steel claw flashes before my eyes. Then my head strikes the ground with a muffled *thump*. Blood spills everywhere.

The world is now tilted: tilted sky, tilted street, tilted snow falling diagonally. With every bit of my strength, I turn my eyes to follow the spider. I see that it's chewing on my body. A stream of dark red fluid drips out of its beak, bubbling, warm, the droplets slowly spreading in the snow.

As the spider chews, it slows down gradually. Then it stops moving. The blue light in its eyes dims and then goes out.

As though they have received some signal, all the other spiders also stop one by one. The rumbling thunder stops, plunging the world into silence.

The wind stops, too. Snow begins to stick to the spiders' steel bodies.

I want to laugh, but I can't. My head is now separated from my body, so there's no way to get air into the lungs and then out to my vocal cords. So I crack my lips open until the smile is frozen on my face.

The spiders believed that I was alive, a real person. They chewed my body and tasted flesh and saw blood. But they aren't allowed to harm real people. If they do, they must destroy themselves. That's also part of the rules. Ghosts, spiders, it doesn't matter. Everyone has to follow the rules.

I never imagined that the spiders would be so stupid. They're even easier to fool than ghosts.

The scene in my eyes grows indistinct, as though a veil is falling from the sky, covering my head. I remember the words of the crows. So it's true. When your head is cut off, you really die.

I grew up on this street; I ran along this street. Now I'm finally going to die on this street, just like a real person.

A pair of pale, cold hands reaches over, stroking my face.

The wind blows and covers my face with a few pale pink peach petals. But I know they're not peach petals. They're Xiao Qian's tears, mixed with snow.

TONGTONG'S SUMMER

Mom said to Tongtong, "In a couple of days, Grandpa is moving in with us."

After Grandma died, Grandpa lived by himself. Mom told Tongtong that because Grandpa had been working for the revolution all his life, he just couldn't be idle. Even though he was in his eighties, he still insisted on going to the clinic every day to see patients. A few days earlier, because it was raining, he had slipped on the way back from the clinic and hurt his leg.

Luckily he had been rushed to the hospital, where they put a plaster cast on him. With a few more days of rest and recovery, he'd be ready to be discharged.

Emphasizing her words, Mom said, "Tongtong, your grandfather is old, and he's not always in a good mood. You're old enough to be considerate. Try not to add to his unhappiness, all right?"

Tongtong nodded, thinking, *But haven't I always been considerate?*

Grandpa's wheelchair was like a miniature electric car, with a tiny joystick by the armrest. Grandpa just had to give it a light push, and the wheelchair would glide smoothly in that direction. Tongtong thought it tremendous fun.

Ever since she could remember, Tongtong had been a bit afraid of Grandpa. He had a square face with long, bushy white eyebrows that stuck out like stiff pine needles. She had never seen anyone with eyebrows that long.

She also had some trouble understanding him. Grandpa spoke Mandarin with a heavy accent from his native topolect. During dinner, when Mom explained to Grandpa that they needed to hire a caretaker for him, Grandpa kept on shaking his head emphatically and repeating, "Don't worry, eh!" Now Tongtong did understand *that* bit.

Back when Grandma had been ill, they had also hired a caretaker for her. The caretaker had been a lady from the countryside. She was short and small, but really strong. All by herself, she could lift Grandma—who had put on some weight—out of the bed, bathe her, put her on the toilet, and change her clothes. Tongtong had seen the caretaker lady accomplish these feats of strength with her own eyes. Later, after Grandma died, the lady didn't come anymore.

After dinner, Tongtong turned on the video wall to play some games. *The world in the game is so different from the world around me,* she thought. In the game, a person just died. They didn't get sick, and they didn't sit in a wheelchair. Behind her, Mom and Grandpa continued to argue about the caretaker.

Dad walked over and said, "Tongtong, shut that off now, please. You've been playing too much. It'll ruin your eyes."

Imitating Grandpa, Tongtong shook her head and said, "Don't worry, eh!"

Mom and Dad both burst out laughing, but Grandpa didn't laugh at all. He sat stone-faced, with not even a hint of smile.

A few days later, Dad came home with a stupid-looking robot. The robot had a round head, long arms, and two white hands. Instead of feet, it had a pair of wheels so that it could move forward and backward and spin around.

Dad pushed something in the back of the robot's head. The blank, smooth, egg-like orb blinked three times with a bluish light, and a young man's face appeared on the surface. The resolution was so good that it looked just like a real person.

"Wow," Tongtong said. "You're a robot?"

The face smiled. "Hello there! Ah Fu is my name."

"Can I touch you?"

"Sure!"

Tongtong put her hand against the smooth face, and then she felt the robot's arms and hands. Ah Fu's body was covered by a layer of soft silicone, which felt as warm as real skin.

Dad told Tongtong that Ah Fu was made by Guokr Technologies, Inc., and he was a prototype. His biggest advantage was that he was as smart as a person: he knew how to peel an apple, how to pour a cup of tea, even how to cook, wash the dishes, embroider, write, play the piano . . . Anyway, having Ah Fu around meant that Grandpa would be given good care.

Grandpa sat there, still stone-faced, still saying nothing.

After lunch, Grandpa sat on the balcony to read the newspaper. He dozed off after a while. Ah Fu came over noiselessly, picked up Grandpa with his strong arms, carried him into the bedroom, set him down gently in bed, covered him with a blanket, pulled the curtains shut, and came out and shut the door, still not making any noise.

Tongtong followed Ah Fu and watched everything.

Ah Fu gave Tongtong's head a light pat. "Why don't you take a nap, too?"

Tongtong tilted her head and asked, "Are you really a robot?"

Ah Fu smiled. "Oh, you don't think so?"

Tongtong gazed at Ah Fu carefully. Then she said very seriously, "I'm sure you are not."

"Why?"

"A robot wouldn't smile like that."

"You've never seen a smiling robot?"

"When a robot smiles, it looks scary. But your smile isn't scary. So you're definitely not a robot."

Ah Fu laughed. "Do you want to see what I really look like?"

Tongtong nodded. But her heart was pounding.

Ah Fu moved over by the video wall. From the top of his head, a beam of light shot out and projected a picture onto the wall. In the picture, Tongtong saw a man sitting in a messy room.

The man in the picture waved at Tongtong. Simultaneously, Ah Fu also waved in the exact same way. Tongtong examined the man in the picture. He wore a thin, long-sleeved gray bodysuit and a pair of gray gloves. The gloves were covered by many tiny lights. He also wore a set of huge goggles. The face behind the goggles was pale and thin and looked just like Ah Fu's face.

Tongtong was stunned. "Oh, so you're the real Ah Fu!"

The man in the picture awkwardly scratched his head and said, a little embarrassed, "Ah Fu is just the name we gave the robot. My real name is Wang. Why don't you call me Uncle Wang, since I'm a bit older?"

Uncle Wang told Tongtong that he was a fourth-year university student doing an internship at Guokr Technologies's R&D department. His group developed Ah Fu.

He explained that the aging population brought about serious social problems: many elders could not live independently, but their children had no time to devote to their care. Nursing homes made them feel lonely and cut off from society, and there was a lot of demand for trained, professional caretakers.

But if a home had an Ah Fu, things were a lot better. When not in use, Ah Fu could just sit there, out of the way. When it was needed, a request could be given, and an operator would come online to help the elder. This saved the time and cost of having caretakers commute to homes, and increased the efficiency and quality of care.

The Ah Fu they were looking at was a first-generation prototype. There were only three thousand of them in the whole country, being tested by three thousand families.

Uncle Wang told Tongtong that his own grandmother had also been ill and had to go to the hospital for an extended stay, so he had some experience with elder care. That was why he volunteered to come to her home to take care of Grandpa. As luck would have it, he was from the same region of the country as Grandpa and could understand his topolect. A regular robot probably wouldn't be able to.

Uncle Wang laced his explanation with many technical words, and Tongtong wasn't sure she understood everything. But she thought the idea of Ah Fu splendid, almost like a science fiction story.

"So does Grandpa know who you really are?"

"Your mom and dad know, but Grandpa doesn't know yet. Let's not tell him for now. We'll let him know in a few days, after he's more used to Ah Fu."

Tongtong solemnly promised. "Don't worry, eh!"

She and Uncle Wang laughed together.

Grandpa really couldn't just stay home and be idle. He insisted that Ah Fu take him out walking. But after just one walk, he complained that it was too hot outside and refused to go anymore.

Ah Fu told Tongtong in secret that it was because Grandpa felt self-conscious, having someone push him around in a wheelchair. He thought everyone in the street stared at him.

But Tongtong thought, *Maybe they were all staring at Ah Fu.*

Since Grandpa couldn't go out, being cooped up at home made his mood worse. His expression grew more depressed, and from time to time he burst out in temper tantrums. There were a few times when he screamed and yelled at Mom and Dad, but neither said anything. They just stood there and quietly bore his shouting.

But one time Tongtong went to the kitchen and caught Mom hiding behind the door, crying.

Grandpa was now nothing like the Grandpa she remembered. It would have been so much better if he hadn't slipped and got hurt. Tongtong hated staying at home. The tension made her feel like she was suffocating. Every morning, she ran out the door and would stay away until it was time for dinner.

Dad came up with a solution. He brought back another gadget made by Guokr Technologies: a pair of glasses. He handed the glasses to Tongtong and told her to put them on and walk around the house. Whatever she saw and heard was shown on the video wall.

"Tongtong, would you like to act as Grandpa's eyes?"

Tongtong agreed. She was curious about anything new.

※

Summer was Tongtong's favorite season. She could wear a skirt, eat watermelon and Popsicles, go swimming, find cicada shells in the grass, splash through rain puddles in sandals, chase rainbows after a thunderstorm, get a cold shower after running around and working up a sweat, drink iced sour plum soup, catch tadpoles in ponds, pick grapes and figs, sit out in the backyard in the evenings and gaze at stars, hunt for crickets after dark with a flashlight . . . In a word, everything was wonderful in summer.

Tongtong put on her new glasses and went to play outside. The glasses were heavy and kept on slipping off her nose. She was afraid of dropping them.

Since the beginning of summer vacation, she and more than a dozen friends, both boys and girls, had been playing together every day. At their age, play had infinite variety. Having exhausted old games, they would invent new ones. If they were tired or too hot, they would go by the river and jump in like a plate of dumplings going into the pot. The sun blazed overhead, but the water in the river was refreshing and cool. This was heaven!

Someone suggested that they climb trees. There was a lofty pagoda tree by the river shore, whose trunk was so tall and thick it resembled a dragon rising into the blue sky.

But Tongtong heard Grandpa's urgent voice by her ear: "Don't climb that tree! Too dangerous!"

Huh, so the glasses also act as a phone. Joyfully she shouted back, "Grandpa, don't worry, eh!" Tongtong excelled at climbing trees. Even her father said that in a previous life she must have been a monkey.

But Grandpa would not let her alone. He kept on buzzing in her ear, and she couldn't understand a thing he was saying. It was getting on her nerves, so she took off the glasses and dropped them in the grass at the foot of the tree. She took off her sandals and began to climb, rising into the sky like a cloud.

This tree was easy. The dense branches reached out to her like hands, pulling her up. She went higher and higher and soon left her companions behind. She was about to reach the very top. The breeze whistled through the leaves, and sunlight dappled through the canopy. The world was so quiet.

She paused to take a breath, but then she heard her father's voice coming from a distance. "Tongtong, get . . . down . . . here . . ."

She poked her head out to look down. A little ant-like figure appeared far below. It really was Dad.

On the way back home, Dad let her have it. "How could you have been so foolish?! You climbed all the way up there by yourself. Don't you understand the risk?"

She knew that Grandpa had told on her. Who else knew what she was doing?

Tongtong was livid. *He can't climb trees anymore, and now he won't let others climb trees, either? So stupid! And it was so embarrassing to have Dad show up and yell like that.*

The next morning, she left home super early again. But this time, she didn't wear the glasses.

※

"Grandpa was just worried about you," said Ah Fu. "If you fell and broke your leg, wouldn't you have to sit in a wheelchair just like him?"

Tongtong pouted and refused to speak.

Ah Fu told her that through the glasses left at the foot of the tree, Grandpa could see that Tongtong was really high up. He was so worried that he screamed himself hoarse and almost tumbled from his wheelchair.

But Tongtong remained angry with Grandpa. What was there to worry about? She had climbed plenty of trees taller than that one, and she had never once been hurt.

Since the glasses weren't being put to use, Dad packed them up and sent them back to Guokr. Grandpa was once again stuck at home with nothing to do. He somehow found an old Chinese Chess set and demanded Ah Fu play with him.

Tongtong didn't know how to play, so she pulled up a stool and sat next to the board just to check it out. She enjoyed watching Ah Fu pick up the old wooden pieces, their colors faded from age, with his slender, pale white fingers; she enjoyed watching him tap those fingers lightly on the table as he considered his moves. The robot's hand was so pretty, almost like it was carved out of ivory.

But after a few games, even she could tell that Ah Fu posed no challenge to Grandpa at all. A few moves later, Grandpa once again captured one of Ah Fu's pieces with a loud snap on the board.

"Oh, you suck at this," Grandpa muttered.

To be helpful, Tongtong also said, "You suck!"

"A real robot would have played better," Grandpa added. He had already found out the truth about Ah Fu and its operator.

Grandpa kept on winning, and after a few games, his mood improved. Not only did his face glow, but he was also moving his head about and humming folk tunes. Tongtong also felt happy, and her earlier anger at Grandpa dissipated.

Only Ah Fu wasn't so happy. "I think I need to find you a more challenging opponent," he said.

When Tongtong returned home, she almost jumped out of her skin. Grandpa had turned into a monster!

He was now dressed in a thin, long-sleeved gray bodysuit and a pair of gray gloves. Many tiny lights shone all over the gloves. He wore a set of huge goggles over his face, and he waved his hands about and gestured in the air.

On the video wall in front of him appeared another man, but not Uncle Wang. This man was as old as Grandpa, with a full head of silver-white hair. He wasn't wearing any goggles. In front of him was a Chinese Chess board.

"Tongtong, come say hi," said Grandpa. "This is Grandpa Zhao."

Grandpa Zhao was Grandpa's friend from back when they were in the army together. He had just had a heart stent put in. Like Grandpa, he was bored, and his family also got its own Ah Fu. He was also a Chinese Chess enthusiast and complained about the skill level of his Ah Fu all day.

Uncle Wang had the inspiration of mailing telepresence equipment to Grandpa and then teaching him how to use it. And within a few days, Grandpa was proficient enough to be able to remotely control Grandpa Zhao's Ah Fu to play chess with him.

Not only could they play chess, but the two old men also got to chat with each other in their own native topolect. Grandpa became so joyous and excited that he seemed to Tongtong like a little kid.

"Watch this," said Grandpa.

He waved his hands in the air gently, and through the video wall, Grandpa Zhao's Ah Fu picked up the wooden chessboard, steady as you please, dexterously spun it around in the air, and set it back down without disturbing a piece.

Tongtong watched Grandpa's hands without blinking. *Are these the same unsteady, jerky hands that always made it hard for Grandpa to do anything?* It was even more amazing than magic.

"Can I try?" she asked.

Grandpa took off the gloves and helped Tongtong put them on. The gloves were stretchy, and weren't too loose on Tongtong's small hands. Tongtong tried to wiggle her fingers, and the Ah Fu in the video wall wiggled its fingers, too. The gloves provided internal resistance that steadied and smoothed out Tongtong's movements, and thus also the movements of Ah Fu.

Grandpa said, "Come try shaking hands with Grandpa Zhao."

In the video, a smiling Grandpa Zhao extended his hand. Tongtong carefully reached out and shook hands. She could feel the subtle, immediate pressure changes within the glove, as if she were really shaking a person's hand—it even felt warm! *This is fantastic!*

Using the gloves, she directed Ah Fu to touch the chessboard, the pieces, and the steaming cup of tea next to them. Her fingertips felt the sudden heat from the cup. Startled, her fingers let go, and the cup fell to the ground and broke. The chessboard was flipped over, and chess pieces rolled all over the place.

"Aiya! Careful, Tongtong!"

"No worries! No worries!" Grandpa Zhao tried to get up to retrieve the broom and dustpan, but Grandpa told him to remain seated. "Careful about your hands!" Grandpa said. "I'll take care of it." He put on the gloves and directed Grandpa Zhao's Ah Fu to pick up the chess pieces one by one, and then swept the floor clean.

Grandpa wasn't mad at Tongtong and didn't threaten to tell Dad about the accident she caused.

"She's just a kid, a bit impatient," he said to Grandpa Zhao. The two old men laughed.

Tongtong felt both relieved and a bit misunderstood.

Once again, Mom and Dad were arguing with Grandpa.

The argument went a bit differently from before. Grandpa was once again repeating over and over, "Don't worry, eh!" But Mom's tone grew more and more severe.

The actual point of the argument grew more confusing to Tongtong the more she listened. All she could make out was that it had something to do with Grandpa Zhao's heart stent.

In the end, Mom said, "What do you mean, 'don't worry'? What if another accident happens? Would you please stop causing more trouble?"

Grandpa got so mad that he shut himself in his room and refused to come out even for dinner.

Mom and Dad called Uncle Wang on the videophone. Finally Tongtong figured out what had happened.

Grandpa Zhao was playing chess with Grandpa, but the game got him so excited that his heart gave out—apparently, the stent wasn't put in perfectly. There had been no one else home at the time. Grandpa was the one who operated Ah Fu to give CPR to Grandpa Zhao, and also called an ambulance.

The emergency response team arrived in time and saved Grandpa Zhao's life.

What no one could have predicted was that Grandpa suggested that he go to the hospital to care for Grandpa Zhao—no, he didn't mean he'd go personally, but that they send Ah Fu over, and he'd operate Ah Fu from home.

But Grandpa himself needed a caretaker, too. Who was supposed to care for the caretaker?

Furthermore, Grandpa came up with the idea that when Grandpa Zhao recovered, he'd teach Grandpa Zhao how to operate the tele-presence equipment. The two old men would be able to care for each other, and they would have no need of other caretakers.

Grandpa Zhao thought this was a great idea. But both families thought the plan absurd. Even Uncle Wang had to think about it for a while and then said, "Um . . . I have to report this situation to my supervisors."

Tongtong thought hard about this. Playing chess through Ah Fu was simple to understand. But caring for each other through Ah Fu? The more she thought about it, the more complicated it seemed. She was sympathetic to Uncle Wang's confusion.

Sigh, Grandpa is just like a little kid. He won't listen to Mom and Dad at all.

Grandpa now stayed in his room all the time. At first, Tongtong thought he was still mad at her parents. But then, she found that the situation had changed completely.

Grandpa got really busy. Once again, he started seeing patients. No, he didn't go to the clinic; instead, using his telepresence kit, he was operating Ah Fus throughout the country and showing up in other elders' homes. He would listen to their complaints, feel their pulse, examine them, and write out prescriptions. He also wanted to give acupuncture treatments through Ah Fus, and to practice this skill, he operated his own Ah Fu to stick needles in himself!

Uncle Wang told Tongtong that Grandpa's innovation could transform the entire medical system. In the future, maybe patients no longer needed to go to the hospital and waste hours in waiting rooms. Doctors could just come to your home through an Ah Fu installed in each neighborhood.

Uncle Wang said that Guokr's R&D department had formed a dedicated task force to develop a specialized, improved model of Ah Fu for such medical telepresence applications, and they invited Grandpa on board as a consultant. So Grandpa got even busier.

Since Grandpa's legs were not yet fully recovered, Uncle Wang was still caring for him. But they were working on developing a web-based system that would allow anyone with some idle time and interest in helping others to register to volunteer. Then the volunteers would be able to sign on to Ah Fus in homes across the country to take care of elders, children, patients, pets, and to help in other ways.

If the plan succeeded, it would be a step to bring about the kind of golden age envisioned by Confucius millennia ago: "And then men would care for all elders as if they were their own parents, love all children as if they were their own children. The aged would grow old and die in security; the youthful would have opportunities to contribute and prosper; and children would grow up under the guidance and protection of all. Widows, orphans, the disabled, the diseased—everyone would be cared for and loved."

Of course, such a plan had its risks: privacy and security, misuse of telepresence by criminals, malfunctions and accidents, just for starters. But since the technological change was already here, it was best to face the consequences and guide them to desirable ends.

There were also developments no one had anticipated.

Uncle Wang showed Tongtong lots of web videos: Ah Fus were shown doing all kinds of interesting things: cooking, taking care of children, fixing the plumbing and electric systems around the house, gardening, driving, playing tennis, even teaching children the arts of Go and calligraphy and seal carving and *erhu* playing . . .

All of these Ah Fus were operated by elders who needed caretakers themselves, too. Some of them could no longer move about easily, but still had sharp eyes and ears and minds; some could no longer remember things easily, but they could still replicate the skills they had perfected in their youth; and most of them really had few physical problems, but were depressed and lonely. But now, with Ah Fu, everyone was out and about, *doing* things.

No one had imagined that Ah Fu could be put to all these uses. No one had thought that men and women in their seventies and eighties could still be so creative and imaginative.

Tongtong was especially impressed by a traditional folk music orchestra made up of more than a dozen Ah Fus. They congregated around a pond in a park and played enthusiastically and loudly. According to Uncle Wang, this orchestra had become famous on the web. The operators behind the Ah Fus were men and women who had lost their eyesight, and so they called themselves "The Old Blinds."

"Tongtong," Uncle Wang said, "your grandfather has brought about a revolution."

Tongtong remembered Mom had often mentioned that Grandpa was an old revolutionary. "He's been working for the revolution all his life; it's time for him to take a break." But wasn't Grandpa a doctor? When did he participate in a "revolution"? And just what kind of work was "working for the revolution" anyway? And why did he have to do it all his life?

Tongtong couldn't figure it out, but she thought "revolution" was a splendid thing. Grandpa now once again seemed like the Grandpa she had known.

Every day Grandpa was full of energy and spirit. Whenever he had a few moments to himself, he preferred to sing a few lines of traditional folk opera:

> Outside the camp, they've fired off the thundering cannon thrice,
> And out of Tianbo House walks the woman who will protect her
>   homeland.
> The golden helmet sits securely over her silver-white hair,

The old iron-scaled war robe once again hangs on her shoulders.
Look at her battle banner, displaying proudly her name:
Mu Guiying, at fifty-three, you are going to war again!

Tongtong laughed. "But, Grandpa, you're eighty-three!"

Grandpa chuckled. He stood and posed as if he were an ancient general holding a sword as he sat on his warhorse. His face glowed red with joy.

In another few days, Grandpa would be eighty-four.

Tongtong played by herself at home.

There were dishes of cooked food in the fridge. In the evening, Tongtong took them out, heated them up, and ate by herself. The evening air was heavy and humid, and the cicadas cried without cease.

The weather report said there would be thunderstorms.

A blue light flashed three times in a corner of the room. A figure moved out of the corner noiselessly: Ah Fu.

"Mom and Dad took Grandpa to the hospital. They haven't returned yet."

Ah Fu nodded. "Your mother sent me to remind you: don't forget to close the windows before it rains."

Together, the robot and the girl closed all the windows in the house. When the thunderstorm arrived, the raindrops struck against the windowpanes like drumbeats. The dark clouds were torn into pieces by the white-and-purple flashes of lightning, and then a bone-rattling thunder rolled overhead, making Tongtong's ears ring.

"You're not afraid of thunder?" asked Ah Fu.

"No. You?"

"I was afraid when I was little, but not now."

An important question came to Tongtong's mind. "Ah Fu, do you think everyone has to grow up?"

"I think so."

"And then what?"

"And then you grow old."

"And then?"

Ah Fu didn't respond.

They turned on the video wall to watch cartoons. It was Tongtong's favorite show, *Rainbow Bear Village*. No matter how heavily it rained outside, the little bears of the village always lived together happily. Maybe everything else in the world was fake; maybe only the world of the little bears was real.

Gradually Tongtong's eyelids grew heavy. The sound of rain had a hypnotic effect. She leaned against Ah Fu. Ah Fu picked her up in his arms, carried her into the bedroom, set her down gently in bed, covered her with a blanket, and pulled the curtains shut. His hands were just like real hands, warm and soft.

Tongtong murmured, "Why isn't Grandpa back yet?"

"Sleep. When you wake up, Grandpa will be back."

Grandpa did not come back.

Mom and Dad returned. Both looked sad and tired.

But they got even busier. Every day, they had to leave the house and go somewhere. Tongtong stayed home by herself. She played games sometimes, and watched cartoons at other times. Ah Fu sometimes came over to cook for her.

A few days later, Mom called for Tongtong. "I have to talk to you."

Grandpa had a tumor in his head. The last time he fell was because the tumor pressed against a nerve. The doctor suggested surgery immediately.

Given Grandpa's age, surgery was very dangerous. But not operating would be even more dangerous. Mom and Dad and Grandpa had gone to several hospitals and gotten several other opinions, and after talking with one another over several nights, they decided they had to operate.

The operation took a full day. The tumor was the size of an egg.

Grandpa remained in a coma after the operation.

Mom hugged Tongtong and sobbed. Her body trembled like a fish. Tongtong hugged Mom back tightly. She looked and saw the white hairs mixed in with the black on Mom's head. Everything seemed so unreal.

Tongtong went to the hospital with Mom.

It was so hot, and the sun so bright. Tongtong and Mom shared a parasol. In Mom's other hand was a thermos of bright red fruit juice taken from the fridge.

There were few pedestrians on the road. The cicadas continued their endless singing. The summer was almost over.

Inside the hospital, the air conditioning was turned up high. They waited in the hallway for a bit before a nurse came to tell them that Grandpa was awake. Mom told Tongtong to go in first.

Grandpa looked like a stranger. His hair had been shaved off, and his face was swollen. One eye was covered by a gauze bandage, and the other eye was closed. Tongtong held Grandpa's hand, and she was scared. She remembered Grandma. Like before, there were tubes and beeping machines all around.

The nurse said Grandpa's name. "Your granddaughter is here to see you."

Grandpa opened his eye and gazed at Tongtong. Tongtong moved, and the eye moved to follow her. But he couldn't speak or move.

The nurse whispered, "You can talk to your grandfather. He can hear you."

Tongtong didn't know what to say. She squeezed Grandpa's hand, and she could feel Grandpa squeezing back.

Grandpa! she called out in her mind. *Can you recognize me?*

His eyes followed Tongtong.

She finally found her voice. "Grandpa!"

Tears fell on the white sheets. The nurse tried to comfort her. "Don't cry! Your grandfather would feel so sad to see you cry."

Tongtong was taken out of the room, and she cried—tears streaming down her face like she was a little kid, but she didn't care who saw—in the hallway for a long time.

Ah Fu was leaving. Dad packed him up to mail him back to Guokr Technologies.

Uncle Wang explained that he had wanted to come in person to say good-bye to Tongtong and her family. But the city he lived in was very far away. At least it was easy to communicate over long distances now, and they could chat by video or phone in the future.

Tongtong was in her room, drawing. Ah Fu came over noiselessly. Tongtong had drawn many little bears on the paper and colored them all different shades with crayons. Ah Fu looked at the pictures. One of the biggest bears was colored all the shades of the rainbow, and he wore a black eye patch so that only one eye showed.

"Who is this?" Ah Fu asked.

Tongtong didn't answer. She went on coloring, her heart set on giving every color in the world to the bear.

Ah Fu hugged Tongtong from behind. His body trembled. Tongtong knew Ah Fu was crying.

※

Uncle Wang sent a video message to Tongtong.

Tongtong, did you receive the package I sent you?

Inside the package was a fuzzy teddy bear. It was colored like the rainbow, with a black eye patch, leaving only one eye. It was just like the one Tongtong drew.

The bear is equipped with a telepresence kit and connected to the instruments at the hospital: your grandfather's heartbeat, breath, pulse, body temperature. If the bear's eye is closed, that means your grandfather is asleep. If your grandfather is awake, the bear will open its eye.

Everything the bear sees and hears is projected onto the ceiling of the room at the hospital. You can talk to it, tell it stories, sing to it, and your grandfather will see and hear.

He can definitely see and hear. Even though he can't move his body, he's awake inside. So you must talk to the bear, play with it, and let it hear your laughter. Then your grandfather won't be alone.

Tongtong put her ear to the bear's chest: *thump-thump*. The heartbeat was slow and faint. The bear's chest was warm, rising and falling slowly with each breath. It was sleeping deeply.

Tongtong wanted to sleep, too. She put the bear in bed with her and covered it with a blanket. *When Grandpa is awake tomorrow,* she thought, *I'll bring him out to get some sun, to climb trees, to go to the park and listen to those grandpas and grandmas sing folk opera. The summer isn't over yet. There are so many fun things to do.*

"Grandpa, don't worry, eh!" she whispered. *When you wake up, everything will be all right.*

AUTHOR'S NOTE

I'd like to dedicate this story to my grandfather. I composed this story in August, and it was also the anniversary of his passing. I will treasure the time I got to spend with him forever.

This story is also dedicated to all the grandmas and grandpas who, each morning, can be seen in parks practicing tai chi, twirling swords, singing opera, dancing, showing off their songbirds, painting, doing calligraphy, playing the accordion. You made me understand that living with an awareness of the closeness of death is nothing to be afraid of.

NIGHT JOURNEY OF THE DRAGON-HORSE

1.

The dragon-horse awakens in moonlight.

Drops of cold dew drip onto his forehead, where they meander down the curve of his steel nose.

Plink.

He struggles to open his eyes, rusted eyelids grinding against eyelashes. A pair of silvery specks reflects from those giant dark red pupils. At first he thinks it's the moon, but a careful examination reveals it to be a clump of white flowers blooming vibrantly in a crack in the cement, irrigated by the dew dripping from his nose.

He can't help but inhale deeply, as though trying to taste the fragrance of the flowers, but he smells nothing—after all, he is not made of flesh and blood and has never smelled anything. The air rushes into his nostrils, whistling loudly in the narrow gaps between mechanical components. He feels a slight buzzing all over his body, as if each one of his hundreds of scales is vibrating at a different frequency, and so he sneezes, two columns of white fog erupting from his nostrils. The white flowers tremble in the fog, drops of dew falling from the tips of the translucent petals.

Slowly the dragon-horse opens his eyes all the way and lifts his head to survey the world.

The world has been desolate for a long time and now looks very different from his memory of it. He remembers once having stood in the middle of a brightly lit hall, shaking his head and waving his tail at Chinese and foreign visitors, surrounded by cries of delight and surprised intakes of breath. He remembers nights when, after the lights in the museum had been extinguished, lingering visitors murmuring in strange tongues had disturbed his dreams.

The hall is now in ruins, the cracked walls askew with vines sprouting from fissures and seams, leaves susurrating in the wind. Vine-shrouded trees have punched holes large and small in the glass skylight overhead. Bathed by moonlight, dewdrops *plink-plonk* like pearls falling onto a jade platter.

The dragon-horse glances around the great hall of the museum— now a decayed courtyard—and sees that all the other inhabitants are gone, leaving only him dreaming for untold centuries amongst the rubble. He peers at the night sky through the holes in the skylight: the empyrean is a shade of midnight blue, and the stars twinkle like silver-white flowers. This is also a sight he can't remember having seen for a long, long time.

He recalls his birthplace, a small city named Nantes on the shores of the tranquil Loire, where the brilliant pinpricks of the stars reflected in the water resembled an oil painting. But in this metropolis, thousands of miles from Nantes, the sky always hung overhead like a thick, waxy gray membrane by day, varicolored neon lights turning it even more turbid at night.

Tonight the limpid moon and luminous stars arouse in him an intense nostalgia for his hometown, for the tiny workshop where he was born on an isle in the middle of the river, where the artisans drew the plans for his design using pens with nibs as fine as a single strand of hair, and then cast the components, polished, spray-painted, and assembled them until he was fully formed. His massive body weighed forty-seven tons, composed from tens of thousands of individual components.

With his reinforced steel frame and wooden scales, he stood erect, a terrifying sight. Then the gears, axles, motors, and cables inside him collaborated seamlessly in a mechanical symphony so that he could come alive: his four hoofed legs extending and flexing as though made of flesh, his neck curving and straightening like a startled wild goose, his spine gyrating like a playful dragon, his head lifting and dipping like a lazy tiger, his steps as light as an immortal dancing across water.

On top of his horse-like body is a dragon's neck and head, along with a long beard, deer antlers, and dark red glass eyes. Each of the golden scales covering his body is inscribed with a Chinese character: "dragon," "horse," "poem," "dream." These characters embody the romantic fantasies his clever artisan-creators harbored about another ancient civilization.

Long ago, he came here in a Year of the Horse. "Vigorous as dragon and horse" is an auspicious phrase the people of this land loved to say to one another, and it was this phrase that inspired his creators and endowed him with his present mythical form.

He remembers also parading across a square packed with crowds with his head held high and his legs stretched out. Children greeted him with curious eyes and delighted screams as the mist spewing from his nostrils drenched them. He remembers the lovely music that filled the air, a combination of Western symphonies and Chinese folk tunes—slowly and gracefully he strolled, swaying and stepping to the rhythm of the music. He remembers the streets and buildings spreading before him like a chessboard, stretching endlessly under the hazy gray sky. He remembers his performance partner, a mechanical spider who was almost as large as he was and whose eight legs sliced through the air menacingly. They performed together for three days and three nights, enacting a complete mythical tale.

Nüwa, the goddess of creation, sent the dragon-horse to survey the mortal world, where he encountered the spider, who had escaped from the heavenly court and was wreaking havoc everywhere. They fought an epic battle until—neither able to overcome the other—they forged a peace based on friendship. Then the four seas undulated in harmonious tranquility, and even the weather became mild and pleasant.

After the show, the spider returned to its birthplace, leaving the dragon-horse alone as guardian of this strange land.

Yet isn't this place another homeland for him? He was created to celebrate the lasting friendship between two nations, and from conception he was of mixed blood. The dreams and myths of this land were his original seed. After eons of being passed from one storyteller to another, the legends—transformed into the languages of strange lands, borne across oceans to new realms—were substantiated by the magic of steel and electricity, like those agile robots and spaceships. Finally, across thousands of miles, he came here to become a new legend to be passed down through the ages. Tradition and modernity, myth and technology, the East and the West—which is his old country, which the new?

The dragon-horse, unable to puzzle out the question, lowers his heavy head. He has been asleep for too long, and now the whole world has turned into a ruined garden. Are there still places in this garden for people to live? In the cold moonlight, the dragon-horse carefully lifts his legs and, step by step, begins to explore.

Every joint in his rusty body screeches. In a glass wall filled with spiderweb cracks, he sees a reflection of himself. His body has also been decaying. Time flows like a river, halting for no one. His scaled armor is now patchy, incomplete, like an aged veteran returning from the wars. Only his glass eyes continue to glow with that familiar dim light.

The wide avenue where cars had once streamed like a river of steel is now filled with lush trees dancing in the wind. As soon as there's a break in the rustling of leaves, birds and insects fill the silence with their chittering music, which only makes everything seem even more desolate. The dragon-horse looks around, uncertain where he should be headed.

Since it makes no difference, he picks a direction at random and strolls forward.

The clopping hoofbeats echo against the pavement. The moon stretches his lonely shadow a long way over the ground.

2.

The dragon-horse isn't sure how long he has been walking.

Silently the stars spin overhead, and the moon wanders across the firmament, but without clocks or watches, time's passage cannot be felt.

The avenue he's on was once this city's most famous street. Now it is a deep canyon whose craggy walls are formed from an amalgam of bricks, steel, concrete, and trees, the product of mixing the inorganic with the organic, decay with life, reality with dream, the steel-and-glass metropolis with ancient myths.

He remembers there was once a square nearby where bright lights remained lit throughout the night like a thousand-year dream. But in the end, the lights went out, and the dream ended. There's nothing in this world that can outlast time itself.

Coming into the valley that was once that square, he sees an impossible vision: thousands and thousands of steel wrecks heaped and stacked like the skeletal remains of beasts, the looming piles stretching as far as the eye can see. These were once automobiles of various makes and sizes, most of them so corroded by rust that only the frames remain. Twisted branches emerge from the dark, empty windows and stab into the sky as though clawing for some elusive prey. The dragon-horse experiences a nameless sorrow and terror. He lowers his eyes to gaze at his own rusty forelimbs. How is he different from these dead cars? Why should he not fall into a perpetual slumber alongside them?

No one can answer these questions.

A scale falls from his chest, rolling among the steel wrecks and echoing dully in the watery moonlight. The insects, near and far, fall silent for a moment before resuming their joyful chorus, as though what fell were nothing more than an insignificant pebble.

He becomes even more frightened, and picks up his pace as he continues his night journey.

※

Squeaks come from a certain spot in the ruins. The sound is thin and dreary, different from birdcall and insect chitter. The dragon-horse follows the sound to its source, searching among the thick grass with his nose. Suddenly, in the shadow of a shallow cave, he finds himself gazing at a pair of tiny, dark eyes.

"Who are you?" the dragon-horse asks. It has been so long since he has heard his own voice that the thrumming timbre sounds strange to him.

"Don't you recognize me?" a thin voice answers.

"I'm not sure."

"I'm a bat."

"A bat?"

"Half-beast, half-bird, I sleep during the day and emerge at night to swoop between dawn and dream."

The dragon-horse carefully examines his interlocutor: sharp snout, large ears, a soft body covered by fine gray fur and curled upon itself, and two thin, membranous wings shimmering in the moon.

"And who are you?" the bat squeaks.

"Who am I?" the dragon-horse repeats the question.

"You don't know who you are?"

"Maybe I do; maybe I don't," replies the dragon-horse. "I'm called Dragon-Horse, meaning I am both dragon and horse. I began as a myth in China, but I was born in France. I don't know if I'm a machine or a beast, alive or dead—or perhaps I've never possessed the animating spark. I also don't know if my walk through the night is real or only a dream."

"Like all poets who make dreams their horses."[2] The bat sighs.

"What did you say?"

"Oh, you reminded me of a line from a poem from long ago."

"A poem?" The word sounds familiar to the dragon-horse, but he's not certain what it means.

---

2 This and other lines recited by the bat are from Hai Zi's poem "With Dreams as Horses."

"Yes. I like poems," the bat says, and nods. "When the poets are gone, poems are even more precious."

"The poets are gone?" the dragon-horse asks carefully. "You are saying no one writes poems anymore?"

"Can't you tell? There are no longer any people in this world."

The dragon-horse doesn't bother looking around. He knows she's right.

"Then what should we do?" he asks, after being silent for a while.

"We can do whatever we want," says the bat. "Humans may be gone, but the world goes on. Look at how lovely the moon is tonight. If you want to sing, sing. If you don't want to sing, just lie still. When you sing, the world will listen; when you are quiet, you'll hear the song of all creation."

"But I can't hear it," admits the dragon-horse. "I can only hear the chitter of insects in the ruins. They frighten me."

"Poor baby—your ears aren't as good as mine," says the bat compassionately. "But you heard *me*. That's odd."

"Is it really that strange?"

"Usually only bats can hear other bats. But the world is so big, anything is possible." The bat shrugs. "Where are you going?"

"I don't know where I'm headed," the dragon-horse says. It's the truth.

"You don't even have a destination in mind?"

"I'm just walking about. Also, I don't know how to do anything except walk."

"I have a destination, but I got held up on the way." The bat's voice turns sorrowful. "I'd been flying for three days and three nights, and then an owl came after me. The owl almost tore my wings."

"You're hurt?" asks the dragon-horse solicitously.

"I said 'almost.' Do I look like I'm easy prey?" Her indignant speech is interrupted by a fit of coughing.

"Do you not feel well?"

"I'm thirsty. Flying parched my throat, and I want a drink. But the water here is full of the flavor of rust; I can't stand it."

"I have water," says the dragon-horse. "It's for my performance."

"Would you give me a drink? Just a sip."

The dragon-horse lowers his head, and a white mist sprays from his nostrils. The mist soaks the bat's tiny body, forming droplets on the fine fur. Satisfied, the bat spreads her wings and carefully licks up the droplets.

"You're nice," squeaks the bat. "I feel much better now."

"Are you leaving for where you want to go, then?"

"Yes. I have an important mission tonight. What about you?"

"I don't know. I guess I'll just keep on moving forward."

"Can you carry me for a while? I'm still tired and need rest, but I don't want to be late."

"But I walk very slowly," the dragon-horse says, embarrassed. "My body is designed so that I can only walk haltingly, step by step."

"I don't care." Briskly flapping her light wings, the bat lands next to the dragon-horse's right ear. The bat's claws lightly clutch a branch of his long antler, and then she's dangling upside down.

"See, now we get to talk as we walk. There's nothing better than a night journey with conversation."

The dragon-horse sighs and carefully shifts his limbs. The bat is so light that he almost can't feel the creature's presence. He can only hear that thin, reedy voice whispering poetry in his ear:

"Faced with the great river, I am consumed by shame. What has my exhaustion accomplished . . . ?"

3.

They pass through the graveyard of cars. The road is now more rugged and uneven, and the moon has hid itself behind wispy clouds so that the road is illuminated in patches.

The dragon-horse carefully picks his way through, fearful of falling and breaking a limb. With each step, his whole body creaks and groans, and gears and screws fall off him—*clink-clank*—and disappear in the gaps between rubble and weeds.

"Are you in pain?" asks the bat curiously.

"I've never known what pain is," confesses the dragon-horse.

"Wow, impressive. If it were me, I'd be dead from the pain by now."

"I don't know what death is, either." The dragon-horse falls silent. The nameless sorrow and terror have returned. If he is considered alive now, is that essence of life scattered among the tens of thousands of components making up his body, or is it concentrated in some special spot? If these components are all scattered along the path he has trodden, will he still be alive? How will he continue to sense all that is around him?

Time flows like a river, halting for no one. There's nothing in this world that can outlast time itself.

"Walking like this is boring," says the bat. "Why don't you tell me a story? You were born so long ago that you must know many stories I don't."

"Story? I don't know what a story is; I certainly can't tell you one."

"It's easy! Okay, repeat after me: 'Long, long ago.'"

"Long, long ago . . ."

"What comes to your mind now? Do you see something that doesn't exist?"

The dragon-horse does. The wheel of time seems to be reversing before his eyes. Trees shrink into the ground, and giant buildings shoot out of the earth, part to the sides like the sea, and leave a straight, wide avenue down the middle.

"Long, long ago, there was a bustling metropolis."

"Are there people in the city?" asks the bat.

"Many, many people."

"Can you see them clearly?"

The image before the dragon-horse's eyes clarifies like a long, painted scroll: everyone's expression is vivid and lifelike. He sees the people's joys and sorrows, partings and meetings, as though seeing the moon waxing and waning.

"Long, long ago, there was a bustling metropolis. In this city there lived a young woman . . ."

He starts to tell the stories of those people.

A young woman who'd never been in love fell for a stranger she met through the chat program on her phone, but then she discovered that her interlocutor was only a perfect bit of conversation software. Yet, the digital boy loved her back, and they happily spent a lifetime together. After the woman died, a record of her life—her frowns and laughter, her actions and reactions—was uploaded to the cloud, and she became the shared goddess of people and AIs.

A pious monk went to a factory to pray and bring blessings to the robot workers who were plagued by short-circuits and malfunctions. But the ghosts of the dead robot workers hounded him. Just as the investigation of the strange occurrences was about to end, the monk was found dead in a tiny hotel room, his nude body smeared with the blood of a woman. An autopsy revealed the truth: he was also a robot.

A famous actress was known for being able to portray a wide variety of roles. So skilled was she, the paparazzi suspected that she was only a software simulation. But by the time they managed to break into her well-secured mansion, all they saw was a cold corpse lying on a magnificent bed. Frighteningly, whether you were looking at her body with the naked eye or through a camera, everyone and every camera saw a different woman. And even years later, the actress continued to show up on the silver screen.

A blind child prodigy began to play go against the computer when he was five. As time passed, his skill improved, and his computer opponent also became smarter through competition with him. Many years later, as he lay dying, the blind Go player played one last match against his old opponent. But unbeknownst to him, as they played, others opened his skull and scanned each part of his brain layer by layer, digitizing the results into computer modules that his machine opponent could learn from, until this last Go match became so complicated that no one could follow it.

Delighted by the stories told by the dragon-horse, the bat dances upside down. In turn, she squeaks other stories into the dragon-horse's ear:

A bell that rang only once every hundred years was forgotten in the dark basement of an art museum in the heart of the city. But due to a marvelous resonance phenomenon, whenever the bell did ring, its sound would be echoed and magnified by the entire city until the ringing resounded like an ensemble of pipe organs, and everything stood still in awe.

An unmanned drone took to the skies every dawn. Each clockwise swoop over the city also served to recharge its solar-powered batteries. Whenever spring turned to summer, a flock of fledgling birds followed the drone to practice flying like a magnificent cloud.

Piles of paper books which no one ever read filled an ancient library where the temperature was always kept at sixty-two degrees Fahrenheit. The main computer of the library was capable of reciting every poem in every language. If you were lucky enough to find the way there, you would receive an unimaginably enthusiastic reception.

A musical fountain was capable of composing new music as soon as you deposited some coins. At dusk, feral cats and dogs often dropped coins they picked out of the ruins into the fountain; and so, as the birds and beasts took turns bathing in the fountain in an orderly manner, they also got to enjoy lovely music that never repeated itself.

"Is it really true?" they each ask the other, again and again. "And then? What happened then?"

Shadows dance in the moon. The longer they walk, the longer seems the road.

※

Gradually they hear gurgling water, like the babbling of a brook echoing through a deep canyon. Before the founding of the metropolis, creeks and brooks had crisscrossed this spot. Year by year, they were tamed as people multiplied, and turned into lakes, ditches, and dank underground sewers. But now the brooks have been freed, wantonly meandering their way over the rolling terrain, singing, nourishing the life on this patch of land.

The dragon-horse stops. The road he's on disappears into a wild lotus pond. The pond stretches as far as the horizon, covered by layer after layer of lotus leaves. A breeze passes, and the lotus leaves ruffle, causing undulating ripples through the dark-green-and-gray-white sea. Red and white lotus flowers peek out of the leaves as though they're pieces of frozen moonlight, with no trace of the merely terrestrial in their beauty.

"How lovely." The bat sighs lightly. "It's so beautiful that my heart aches."

The dragon-horse is startled because he feels the same, though he doesn't know if he has a heart.

"Shall we go on?" he asks.

"I need to fly over this lake," replies the bat. "But you can't go on any longer. You're made of metal; the water will probably cause you to short-circuit."

"Maybe." The dragon-horse hesitates. He has never been in the water.

"Then let us say farewell here." The bat's flapping wings tickle the dragon-horse's ear.

"You're leaving?"

"Yes, I don't want to be late."

"Bon voyage!"

"The same to you! Take care of yourself, and thank you for your stories."

"Thank you as well."

The dragon-horse stands at the shore and watches as the shadow of the bat diminishes until she has disappeared in the night.

He is alone again. The watery moon gently illuminates all creation.

4.

He looks at his reflection in the water. His body seems more skeletal than he remembers from before the start of this journey. The scales covering his body have mostly fallen off, and even one of his antlers is gone. Through the holes in his skin, messy bundles of wires and cables can be seen wrapped around his rusty steel skeleton.

Where shall I go? Should I go back? Back to where I started?

Or maybe I should head in the opposite direction. The Earth is round. No matter where I want to go, as long as I keep going, I'll get there.

Though he's pondering turning back, he has already, without realizing it, stepped forward.

His front hooves disappear underneath the ice-cold waves.

The lotus leaves scratch gently against his belly. Countless sparkling droplets roll across their surfaces: some return to the starting point after wandering about for a while; others coalesce like beads of mercury and then tumble off the edge of the leaf into the water.

The world is so lovely. I don't want to die.

The thought frightens him. *Why am I thinking about death? Am I about to die?*

But the endless lotus pond continues to tempt him. He moves forward, one step after another. He wants to reach the other shore, which he has never seen.

The water rises and covers his limbs, his belly, his torso, his spine, his neck.

His legs sink into the mud at the bottom of the pond, and he can't pull them out. His body sways, and he almost falls. The last scale falls from his body.

The golden scale splashes into the water like a lotus-shaped floating lantern. Slowly it drifts away, carried by the ripples.

The dragon-horse is exhausted, but he also feels as though all weight has been lifted from him. He closes his eyes.

He hears the sound of rushing water, as though he has returned to the place of his birth. Long-forgotten memories replay before his eyes. He seems to be on the ocean at this moment, riding in a giant ship headed for China. Perhaps all that he has seen and heard over the years are but a dream on this long voyage.

A breeze caresses his beard like a barely audible sigh.

The dragon-horse opens his eyes. The tiny figure of the bat is flattened against his nose.

"You're back!" Joy fills him. "Did you make it on time?"

"I got lost." The bat sighs. "The pond is too big. I can't seem to find the other shore."

"It's too bad that I'm stuck in the mud. I can't help carry you any farther."

"I wish we had fire."

"Fire?"

"Wherever there's fire, there's light. I want to lead the way for everyone!"

"For . . . who?"

"For the gods in darkness, for the lonely ghosts and lost souls, for anyone who doesn't know where to go—I will lead them all."

"You need fire?"

"Yes, but where would we find fire in all this water?"

"I have fire," says the dragon-horse. "I don't have much, but I hope it's enough for you."

"Where?"

"Give me a bit of space."

The bat flaps over to a lotus leaf nearby. The dragon-horse opens his jaw and sticks out his black tongue. Pure kerosene flows out of a seam under the tongue, and a dark blue electric spark comes to life at the tip of the tongue, lighting the kerosene spray. A golden-scarlet column of fire shoots into the sky.

"I had no idea you had such hidden talents!" the bat shouts in admiration. "More, more!"

The dragon-horse opens his mouth, and more flames shoot out. Kerosene burns easily, even after so many years of storage. He can't remember the last time he performed the fire-breathing trick—it's possible that he hasn't done it since the battle with the spider. Fire is so warm and beautiful, like a god whose shape is constantly shifting.

"Millions wish to extinguish the fire, but I alone will lift it high overhead." The bat's voice rings out clearly in the ear of the dragon-horse, resonating with each and every one of his components:

This fantastic fire, a storm of blossoms that blankets the sacred motherland.

Like all poets who make dreams their horses,
By this fire, I survive the long, dark night.

He feels like a burning match. But he doesn't feel any pain.

All around him, faint lights appear in the distance, gathering like fireflies.

Oh, what a collection of spirits and demons! They are of every shape and material, sporting every strange color and outline: hand-drawn door gods and buddhas; abstract graffiti on factory walls; tiny robots no bigger than a thumb made out of computer components; mechanical Guan Yu constructed from truck parts; dilapidated, ancient stone guardian lions; teddy bears as tall as a house and capable of telling stories; simple, clumsy robot dogs; strollers capable of singing a baby to sleep . . .

They are just like him, mixed-blood creations of tradition and modernity, myth and technology, dream and reality. They are made of Art, yet they are Natural.

"It's time!" the bat sings joyfully. "Come with us!"

"Where are we going?" asks the dragon-horse.

"Anywhere is fine. Tonight you will find eternal life and freedom in poetry and dream."

She sticks out a tiny claw and pulls him into the air, where he transforms into a fluttering butterfly with dark red eyes and golden wings full of Chinese characters. He looks down and sees the massive body of the dragon-horse still burning in the endless lotus pound, like a magnificent torch.

Along with all his companions, he flies higher into the sky. The rolling landscape of ruins diminishes in the distance. Next to his ear, the bat's voice continues to whisper.

A thousand years later, if I were to be born again on the river-
    bank of my motherland,
A thousand years later, I will again possess China's rice paddies
    and the snow-capped mountains of the King of Zhou, where
    sky-horses roam.

Farewell, and good-bye. He sighs.

The flame disappears in darkness.

They fly for a long time until they reach the end of the world.

Everywhere they look, gloom greets their eyes. Only a giant, sparkling river lies between heaven and earth.

The blue water gleams like fire, like mercury, like the stars, like diamonds—twinkling, shimmering, melding into the dark night. No one knows how wide it is, or how long.

The spirits flap and flutter their wings, heading for the opposite shore. Like mist, like a cloud, like a rainbow, like a bridge, they connect two worlds.

"Go on," says the bat. "Hurry."

"What about you?"

"I still have some tasks to finish. When the sun rises, I must return to my nest to sleep and wait for the next night."

"So we're to say farewell again?"

"Yes. But the world is so grand, I'm sure we'll meet somewhere else again."

They embrace, wrapping their tiny wings about each other. The dragon-horse spirit turns to leave, and the bat recites poetry to send him on his way.

> *Riding the five-thousand-year-old phoenix and a dragon whose name is "horse," I am doomed to fail.*
> *But Poetry itself, wielding the sun, will surely triumph.*

He heads for the opposite shore, and he isn't sure how long he has been flying. The starry river flows by.

Next to the shore is his birthplace, the tiny, tranquil isle of Nantes. The mechanical beasts have been slumbering for an unknown number of years: the twenty-five-meter-tall carousel horse of the ocean world; the fifty-ton giant elephant; the immense, frightening reptile; the heron with the eight-meter wingspan capable of carrying a man; the bizarre mechanical ants, cicadas, and carnivorous plants . . .

He sees his old partner, the spider, who lies tranquilly in the soft moonlight, his eight legs curled under him. Landing gently on the forehead of the spider, the dragon-horse spirit closes his wings like a dewdrop falling from the heavens.

> *When you sing, the world will listen; when you are quiet, you'll hear the song of all creation.*

The night breeze carries the sounds of collision, percussion, and metal creaking and grinding against metal. He smells the aroma of machine oil, rust, and electrical sparks. His friends have awakened, and to welcome his return, there will surely be a great feast.

But first, he falls into a deep slumber.

AUTHOR'S NOTE

For more about the dragon-horse, please see the following videos:
https://www.youtube.com/watch?v=QQxkVKBp6HY
https://www.youtube.com/watch?v=0nj0d_ZJQQw

MA BOYONG

Ma Boyong is a prolific and popular fiction writer, essayist, lecturer, Internet commentator, and blogger. His work crosses the boundaries of alternative history, historical fiction, wuxia (martial arts fantasy), fabulism, and more "core" elements of science fiction and fantasy.

Incisive, funny, and erudite, Ma's works are deeply allusive, featuring surprising and entertaining juxtapositions of traditional elements from Chinese culture and history against contemporary references. The ease with which Ma marshals his encyclopedic knowledge of Chinese history and traditions also makes it a challenge to translate his most interesting works. For example, he has written an imaginative history of coffee in China that applies the conventions of China's rich millennia-long tea culture to coffee, as well as a wuxia novella featuring Joan of Arc, in which the tropes and expectations of wuxia are mapped to medieval Europe. These stories are extremely entertaining for the reader with the right cultural context, and shed light on the genres and sources Ma plays with, but would be nigh impenetrable for a reader in translation without extensive footnotes.

"The City of Silence," the selection here, is different from the bulk of Ma's work. A dystopian tale of extreme censorship, the story won

China's Galaxy (Yinhe) Award in 2005. In its original published form, the story was set in "New York," and other changes were made to get past the censorship regime. For this translation, Ma and I worked together to restore the text to its original form, but also made additional changes to help the story work better for Anglophone readers.

Given the political background, it may be almost irresistible to read the story as purely a satire of China's government. I think it's better to resist that temptation.

THE CITY OF SILENCE

The year was 2046, the place the Capital of the State.

The State needed no name because other than it, there were no states. It was just as the Department of Propaganda kept emphasizing: there are no other states besides the State, It is who It is, and It always has been and always will be.

When the phone rang, Arvardan was sleeping with his face on the desk in front of the computer. The ringing was insistent, sharp. He rubbed his dry eyes and got up unwillingly. His brain felt heavy and slow.

The room was cramped, the air stagnant. The only window was shut tight. Even if the window were open, it would not have helped—the air outside was even murkier. The room was only about thirty square meters. An old army green cot stood in the corner, the serial number painted in white on one leg. Right next to the cot was a computer desk made from thin wooden boards, on top of which sat a pale white computer.

The phone continued, now on its seventh ring. Arvardan realized that he had no choice but to take the call.

"Your Web Access Serial, please." The voice on the other end was not in any hurry. Indeed, it contained no emotional content whatsoever because it was generated by a computer.

"ARVARDAN19842015BNKF."

Arvardan automatically recited the string of numerals and letters.

At the same time, he felt his chest grow even more congested. He did not like these empty electronic voices. Sometimes he thought, *Wouldn't it be nice if the voice on the phone belonged to a real woman, smooth and mellow?* Arvardan knew this was an unrealistic fantasy. But a fantasy like that still relaxed his body for a few seconds.

"Your application dated October fourth for an account to participate in the BBS discussion forums has been processed. The appropriate authorities have verified that the information you provided was in order. Please come to the processing center within three days with your Personal Identification Card, your Web Access Permit, your Web Access Serial Card, and other relevant documentation. You will receive your account username and password then."

"Understood. Thank you." Arvardan carefully chose his words, pausing between each.

It was time to get some work done. He sat down in front of the computer and moved the mouse. With a faint electronic pop, the screen came alive: "Please enter your Web Access Serial and name." Arvardan entered the requested information. Immediately the indicator LEDs on the front of the computer case began to blink rapidly, accompanied by the low hum of spinning fans.

Every Web user had a Web Access Serial, without which it was impossible to access the Web. This was the only representation of a user on the Web; it could not be changed or deleted. There was a homomorphism between the Web Access Serials and the names on the Personal Identification Cards that everyone carried. Thus, AR-VARDAN19842015BNKF *was* Arvardan, and Arvardan *was* AR-VARDAN19842015BNKF. Arvardan knew that some people with poor memories would print their Web Access Serials on the backs of their shirts.

The appropriate authorities explained that the Real ID Web Access System was designed to make administration of the Web more convenient and rational and eliminate the serious problems caused by anonymity on the Web. Arvardan was unsure what these "serious problems" were. He had never personally used the Web anonymously, and he knew no one who had—indeed, from a technical perspective, it was impossible for anyone to disguise themselves on the Web. The appropriate authorities had given this careful thought.

"The appropriate authorities" was a semantically vague phrase that nonetheless was full of authority and the power to intimidate. It was simultaneously general and specific, and included within its meaning a broad range of references. Sometimes it referred to the State Web Administration Committee, which had issued the Web Access Serial to Arvardan. Other times it referred to the server that e-mailed Arvardan the latest Web access announcements and regulations. Yet other times it referred to the Web Investigation Section of the Department of Public Security. Still other times it referred to the State News Agency. The "appropriate authorities" were everywhere and responsible for everything. They would always appear at the appropriate time to guide, supervise, or warn.

Now that the Web was almost equivalent to daily life, it was necessary to be ever vigilant and not allow the Web to become a tool for conspirators seeking to destabilize the State—so said the appropriate authorities.

The computer continued to hum. Arvardan knew this was going to take some time. The computer had been issued to him by the appropriate authorities, and he was uncertain about its technical specs and hardware configuration. The case was welded shut and could not be opened.

While waiting, Arvardan ferreted out a plastic cup from the mountain of trash at his feet and filled it with distilled water from the drinking spigot at his side. He swallowed a painkiller with the water. The distilled water went down his throat and settled into his stomach. Its empty taste nauseated him.

The speakers on the computer suddenly began to play the national anthem. Arvardan put down the cup and refocused his eyes on the computer screen. This meant that he had signed on to the Web. The screen first displayed a notice from the appropriate authorities: plain white background, black text, fourteen-point font. The notice described the meaning of using the Web and the latest regulations concerning such use.

The notice quickly disappeared. What followed was a desktop background emblazoned with the slogan "Let us build a healthy and stable Web!" Another window slowly floated up, containing several links: work, entertainment, e-mail, and BBS discussion forums. The BBS link was grayed out, indicating that choice was not yet available to him.

The operating system was simple and clear. The browser had no place to enter a URL. Only the bookmarks menu, which could not be edited, contained the addresses for a few Web sites. The reason for this was simple: all these Web sites were healthy and positive. If other Web sites had the same content as these, then, logically, having access to these Web sites alone was sufficient. On the other hand, if other sites had different content, then, logically, those other sites must be unhealthy and vulgar and should not be accessed.

Some said that outside the borders of the State there were other Web sites, but those were only urban legends.

Arvardan first clicked WORK. The screen displayed a menu of Web sites and software related to his work.

As a programmer, Arvardan's daily duty consisted of writing programs in accordance with instructions from his superiors. The work was boring, but it guaranteed a steady income. He did not know what the source code he wrote would be used for. His superiors never gave him such information.

He tried to continue the work left over from yesterday, but soon felt he couldn't concentrate. He tried to entertain himself, but the ENTERTAINMENT link only contained Solitaire and Minesweeper. According to the appropriate authorities, these two games were healthy: there was no violence and no sex, and they would not give players criminal desires.

A system alert popped up: "You have new mail." Arvardan had finally found a reason to pause in his work. He quickly moved the cursor onto the E-MAIL link and clicked, and soon a new window appeared on the screen.

To: ARVARDAN19842015BNKF
From: WANGHENG10045687XHDI
Subject: Module/Already/Complete, Start/Current/Project?

WANGHENG10045687XHDI was the Serial of a colleague. The body of the e-mail was written with a series of individual words and certain fixed expressions separated by slashes. This was a format suggested by the appropriate authorities. Although modern mainframe computers could now process natural-language digital texts easily, this style of writing was a gesture on the part of the citizen to indicate that he possessed the proper attitude.

Arvardan sighed. Every time he received a new e-mail, he hoped there would be some fresh stimulus to jolt his nervous system, which was growing duller by the day. On some level, he knew he would be disappointed each time, but he felt that keeping hope alive at least yielded a few seconds of excitement. It was like his wishing that the voice on the phone would be the smooth and mellow voice of a real woman. If he didn't keep for himself bits of remote, hopeless hope, Arvardan thought he would go mad sooner or later.

Arvardan clicked REPLY, and then opened a text file with the name "List of Healthy Words" in another window. This file contained the words and fixed expressions which the appropriate authorities required every Web user to use. When they wanted to compose e-mails or use the discussion forums, they must find the appropriate words from this list with which to express themselves. If the filtering software found any Web user using a word not on this list, then the word would be automatically shielded and replaced with the phrase "Please use healthy language."

Shielded was a technical term. A shielded word was forbidden in writing or in speech. Ironically, *shielded* itself was a shielded word.

The list was updated constantly. Every revision meant that a few more words disappeared from the list. This forced Arvardan to exercise his brain to come up with other words to substitute for the words that were shielded. For example, *movement* used to be allowed, but then the appropriate authorities decided that this was a sensitive word, so Arvardan had to use "change of position" to express the same idea.

He referred to the list and quickly composed a response similar in style to the e-mail he had received. The List of Healthy Words forced people to compress as much information as possible into the fewest words, and to eliminate all unnecessary flourishes and figures of speech. The resulting compositions were like that cup of distilled water: flavorless. Arvardan sometimes thought that one day he would become as bleached out as the e-mails and distilled water because he wrote such e-mails and drank such water.

Arvardan sent the e-mail but could not save a copy for himself. His computer had no hard drive, and no slots for floppy disks or CDs or even a USB port. Broadband technology had advanced to the point where software applications could be hosted on remote servers, and individual users would not suffer any speed issues related to remote access. Thus, there was no need for end users to have hard drives or local storage. Every document or program a user wrote, even every movement of the mouse or keystroke, would be automatically transmitted to the public server of the appropriate authorities. This made administration easier.

After completing the e-mail, Arvardan once again fell back into his anxious, listless mood, which he could not express because *tired, annoyed,* and other negative words were all dangerous words. If someone wrote an e-mail to others to complain about such feelings, the recipients would only get an e-mail full of "Please use healthy language."

This was Arvardan's life. Today was a little worse than yesterday, but should be a little better than tomorrow. But even this description was imprecise, because Arvardan himself was unclear what constituted "a little better" and what constituted "a little worse." *Better* and *worse* were variables, but his life was a constant, the value of which was *repression.*

Arvardan set aside the mouse, tilted his head back, and gave a long sigh. (At least *sigh* had not yet been shielded.) He wanted to hum a song, but he couldn't remember any songs. Instead, he whistled a few times, but it sounded like a dog with tuberculosis barking, and he had to stop. The appropriate authorities were like specters that filled the whole room, giving him no space. He was like a man stuck in a quagmire: as soon as he opened his mouth, mud flowed in, so he could not even scream for help.

He shook his head restlessly a few times, and his gaze happened to fall on the phone. Suddenly he remembered that he still had to go to the appropriate authorities to finish the application for the BBS permit. He was glad of an opportunity to be temporarily free of the Web. On the Web, he was nothing more than the sum of a series of dry numbers and "healthy words."

Arvardan put on his coat and covered his mouth with a filtering mask. He hesitated for a moment, and then picked up the Listener and put it over his ears. Then he left his room.

The Capital's streets had few pedestrians. Now that the Web was everywhere, most chores could be done there. Unlike in the primitive past, people no longer needed to go outside the home for the necessities of daily life. The appropriate authorities did not recommend too many outdoor activities, as they caused people to make physical contact with one another, and what happened after that was difficult to control.

The Listener, a portable language-filtering machine, was designed specifically to prevent that sort of thing. When the wearer said or heard some sensitive word, the Listener automatically gave a warning. Every citizen, before leaving home, must put on this device so that they could review and critique their own speech and conversation. When people realized that the Listener was present, they often chose silence. The appropriate authorities were attempting to gradually unify life on the Web and life in the physical world so that they would be equally healthy.

It was November, and the icy wind drove clouds across a leaden, oppressive sky. Along both sides of the street, utility poles stretched out in two rows like dead trees. Pedestrians were wrapped tightly in black or gray coats, shrinking into themselves so that they appeared as quick-moving black dots. A thin miasma covered the whole Capital. Breathing this air without a filtering mask would be a challenge.

Has it really been two months since I last left my room? Arvardan thought as he stood next to the sign for the bus stop.

A tall man in a blue uniform stood next to Arvardan. He looked suspiciously at Arvardan, wrapped in his black coat. Gradually the man shuffled closer and, with pretended casualness, said to Arvardan, "You, have, a, cigarette?"

The man enunciated each word and paused half a second between them. The Listener was not yet sufficiently advanced to adjust to the unique rhythm and intonation of each person. In response, the appropriate authorities required that all citizens speak in this manner, so that it would be more convenient to check if anyone used words outside the regulations.

Arvardan gave him a quick glance, licked his own dry lips, and replied, "No." The man was disappointed. Unwilling to give up, he opened his mouth again. "You, have, a, drink?"

"No."

It had been a long time since Arvardan had had any cigarettes or liquor. Perhaps it was due to the shortages, a common problem. But something was amiss: Arvardan's Listener had not issued a warning. In Arvardan's experience, whenever supplies of cigarettes, liquor, or other necessities suffered shortages, these words would temporarily become sensitive words that had to be shielded until the supply could be restored.

The man seemed exhausted. His puffy red eyes were a common sight these days, a result of long hours spent on the Web. His hair was a mess, and a few days' growth of stubble surrounded his mouth. A strong moldy smell wafted from the collar of the shirt under his uniform. It was obvious he had not been outside for days.

It was only now that Arvardan realized that the man's ears were unadorned. The space where the silver-gray Listener should have been was empty. Arvardan was stunned, and for a moment, he did not know whether to remind the man or to pretend that he hadn't

THE CITY OF SILENCE | 163

noticed. He thought, *Perhaps it would be better to report this to the appropriate authorities.*

Now the man inched even closer, and desire and yearning radiated from his eyes. Arvardan's heart squeezed tight, and unconsciously he took a step back. Was he going to be mugged? Or maybe this man was a sex maniac who had repressed his desires for too long? The man suddenly grabbed his sleeve. Arvardan struggled awkwardly but could not pull himself free.

The man did not make another move, but gave a loud yelp, and began to speak to Arvardan in a rapid manner that Arvardan was no longer accustomed to.

"I just want to talk to you, just a few sentences. I haven't spoken in so long. My name is Hiroshi Watanabe.[1] I'm thirty-two years old. Remember, thirty-two. I've always dreamed of having a house by a lake, with a small boat and a fishing pole. I hate the Web. Down with the Web Regulators! My wife has been poisoned by the Web. She only calls me by my Web Access Serial. This whole city is an asylum, and in it, the stronger inmates govern the weaker inmates and turn all the sane people into madmen like themselves. Fuck 'sensitive words.' I've fucking had it . . ."

The man's words poured out of him like soda from a bottle that had been shaken and the cap then popped. Arvardan's Listener beeped continuously. He stared in amazement but had no idea how to respond. Even more worrisome, he discovered in himself a sense of sympathy for the man, the sort of sympathy people who suffered from the same disease had for one another. The man had now gone from complaining to simply cursing, the most raw, direct kind of curses that had long been shielded. It had been five or six years since Arvardan himself had last cursed, and even the last time he had heard such language was four years ago.

But now this man was swearing at him in public, as though he wanted to say every single shielded sensitive word in a single breath.

1 Hiroshi Watanabe is also the name of a present-day Japanese animator.

Arvardan's eardrums began to throb with pain from the decibel level and the constant beeping from the Listener.

Just then, two police vehicles appeared at the end of the street and, lights flashing all the way, rushed toward the bus stop.

The man was still swearing when five or six officers in full riot gear rushed over and pushed him to the ground, beating him with their batons. The man kicked with his legs, and words poured out of his mouth even faster, and the curses grew even coarser. One of the officers pulled out a roll of tape and with a sharp *pa* tore off a piece, which he stuck over the man's mouth. Immediately before his mouth was taped, the man raised his voice and heartily yelled at the policeman, "Fuck you, you sonovabitch!" Arvardan watched as his expression turned from madness to a contented smile, as though he were intoxicated by the pleasure and release brought about by the swearing.

The police scrambled to push the man into one of the cars. One of the officers came to Arvardan. "Is, he, your, friend?"

"I, do, not, know, him." Arvardan responded in the same way.

The policeman stared at him. He took down Arvardan's Listener and checked its records. There was no record of Arvardan using any sensitive words. He put the Listener back on Arvardan's ear and warned Arvardan that everything the man had said was extremely reactionary, and he must immediately forget it. Then the officer turned around, and the police left with the arrested man.

Arvardan sighed with relief. Just now, for a second, he'd had an impulse to scream at the tops of his lungs on this empty street, "Fuck you, you sonovabitch!"

The street quickly returned to its customary quiescence. Ten minutes later, a bus slowly arrived at the station. The rusty doors opened with a *clang*, and an electronic female voice filled the empty space inside the bus: "Passengers, please pay attention and use civilized language. Adhere strictly to the List of Healthy Words as you speak."

Arvardan wrapped his coat even tighter around himself.

About an hour later, the bus arrived at his destination. The cold wind blew in through the broken windows of the bus, frosting

Arvardan's breath. The coal dust and sand in the wind stabbed at his face. He got up, shook the dust off himself like a wet dog shaking off water, and left the bus.

Arvardan needed to go to the appropriate authorities, the Department of Web Security in this case, responsible for processing BBS permit applications. Located across the street from the bus stop, this was a five-story building, cube shaped, completely covered in gray concrete. If it weren't for the few windows, the building would be indistinguishable from a solid block of concrete: hard and dead. Even mosquitoes and bats stayed away.

It was also very difficult to obtain a permit to use the BBS forums. An applicant had to go through close to twenty procedures and endure a long investigation process before being granted permission to browse the forums. Only after having had permission to browse the forums for three months could one be granted permission to post in designated forums. As for starting your own BBS, that was impossible.

Despite these obstacles, many used the BBS forums because this was the only place on the Web where one could have some limited conversation. Arvardan had decided to apply for a BBS permit simply out of a vague yet stubborn sense of nostalgia. He didn't know why he wanted to cause so much trouble for himself. Maybe it was just to bring a sense of excitement to his life. Maybe it was to emphasize the bits of connection between himself and the old times. Maybe it was both.

Arvardan vaguely remembered that when he was a kid, the Web was very different. Not that the technology was different, just the culture. He hoped to remember some of the things from that era through the BBS forums.

He walked into the building. Inside, it was just as cold as outside, and even darker. There were no lights in the hallways. The walls, painted a bluish white, were pasted over with Web-related regulations, policies, and slogans. Sucking the cold air into his lungs, Arvardan shuddered. Only the crack around the door at the end of the hall let in a sliver of light. On the door was a sign: "Department of Web Security, BBS Section."

Arvardan did not dwell on the irony that, in order to use some virtual functionality of the Web, one had to physically come here to apply.

Once he was behind the door, Arvardan immediately felt a blast of hot air. The heat in this room was turned way up, and Arvardan's hands, feet, and face, all frozen numb, now tingled and began to itch. He wanted to reach out and scratch himself.

An electronic female voice suddenly burst out of the speakers in the ceiling. "Citizen, please remain still as you wait in line."

Arvardan put down his hand as though he had been given an electric shock, and respectfully waited where he was. He observed the room he was in: a long and narrow lobby, divided in half by a marble counter that rose in the middle like the Great Wall. A fence made of silver-white poles connected the top of the counter to the ceiling.

"Please proceed to window number eight."

The counter was so tall that Arvardan could not even look over it to see what was on the other side. But he could hear the sound of someone approaching on the other side, then sitting down.

"Please place your application documents in the tray."

The speaker on top of the counter issued the order. Unexpectedly, the voice this time was different. Even though it was still dry and cold, Arvardan could tell that the voice did not belong to a computer— this was the voice of a real woman. He tried to lift his head even higher, but he could see nothing. The counter was just too tall.

"Please put the documents in the tray."

The voice repeated the order. There was some impatience in the tone.

Yes, this is the voice of a real woman . . ., Arvardan thought. The electronic female voice was always polite and never had any emotion in it. He put his Personal Identification Card, Web Access Permit, Web Access Serial Card, the record of sensitive word violations, and other similar documentation onto a small metallic tray, slid the tray into a slot in the side of the counter, and closed the flap over the slot. Immediately he heard a faint *whoosh*. He guessed that the person on the other side of the counter—perhaps a woman—had pulled the tray out on her side.

"What is the purpose for your application for BBS service?"

The woman's voice from the speaker was businesslike and professional.

"To, increase, Web-related, work, efficiency; to, create, a, healthy, and, stable, Web, environment; to, better, contribute, to, the, motherland."

Arvardan paused between each word, knowing this was only a formality. All he had to do was to give the standard answer.

The other side sank into silence. After about two minutes, the speaker came on again.

"The final procedure has been completed. You now have permission to use the BBS forums."

"Thank, you."

With a bang, the metallic tray bounced back out of the slot. In it, a few more pieces of paper had been added to the documents Arvardan had provided.

"The appropriate authorities have issued you a username and password for the BBS service, an index of available forums, a user guide, a copy of the applicable regulations, and the latest List of Healthy Words. Please also check your e-mail inbox."

Arvardan stepped forward, took out everything in the tray, and examined it. He was disappointed to see that his BBS username was identical to his Web Access Serial. He remembered that when he was little, it was possible to pick your own BBS forum username.

Memories of childhood were often mingled with fairy tales and fantasies, however, and might not match reality. The reality now was that you could only use the username and password issued by the appropriate authorities. The reason was simple: usernames and passwords also could contain sensitive words.

He shoved the papers into his coat pocket. The pieces of paper were actually meaningless, as the electronic copies had been sent to his e-mail already. But the appropriate authorities felt that formal documents on paper were helpful in inducing in users the proper feelings of fear and respect.

He hoped the speaker in the counter would speak a bit more. But he was disappointed by the sound of someone getting up and leaving. Based on the rhythm of the steps, Arvardan was even more certain that the person on the other side was a woman.

The empty electronic female voice again came from the ceiling: "You have completed the necessary procedures. Please leave the Department of Web Security and return to your work."

Arvardan wrinkled his nose in disgust, and turned to leave the warm lobby and return to the freezing cold hallway.

On the way home, Arvardan curled up in his seat on the bus without moving. The success of obtaining permission to use the BBS service gave him an illusory sense of excitement. His right hand fingered the documents in his pocket as he tried to remember the sound of that mysterious woman's voice. *It would be so nice to hear that voice again.* At the same time, he rubbed his thumb lightly over the piece of paper on top of the stack in his pocket, imagining that this document had been touched also by *her* slender, graceful, ivory-like fingers. He was so excited that he wanted to yell, "Fuck you, you sonovabitch!" The sound of that man cursing was stuck in his mind, and again and again the curse rose to the tip of his tongue.

Suddenly his finger felt something out of place on the back of the document. Arvardan looked around him, ascertained that there were no other passengers, and carefully took the document out and flipped it over. He examined it in the light from the bus window.

Arvardan realized that the top right corner of the document had been lightly creased by a fingernail. The crease was so light that if Arvardan hadn't been fingering it so closely he would never have noticed it. The crease was unusual: it was a straight line, but at the end of the line, not far from it, was another very short crease, as though the person had meant to make a dot. The whole thing looked like an exclamation point, or, if you looked at it from the opposite direction, the letter "i."

He looked through the other papers, and soon discovered that the other four documents also had similar creases. They were shaped differently, but all seemed to be symbols of some sort. Arvardan recalled the order in which the woman from the speaker had mentioned the documents, and began to write the symbols found on each document in order on the steamed-up bus window:

T-I-T-L-E
Title?

The bus stopped, and a few passengers got on. Arvardan moved his body to cover the writing on the window. Then, pretending to yawn, he lifted his sleeve and erased the letters.

After arriving home, Arvardan took off his coat and filtering mask, and threw down the Listener. Then he fell onto the cot and buried his head in the pillows. Every time he left home to go outside, he felt exhausted afterward, in part because his weakened physique was no longer used to being outside and in part due to the stress of being with the Listener.

When he woke up, he checked his e-mail. His inbox contained two work-related e-mails from colleagues and five e-mails containing the electronic copies of the BBS documents from the Department of Web Security.

Arvardan opened the index of BBS forums. All the forums were officially sanctioned. The forums had different subjects, but all basically revolved around how to better cooperate and respond to State directives and how to build a healthy Web. For example, on one of the computer technology forums, the main topic was how to improve the technology for shielding sensitive words.

Amazingly, one of the forums was about games. In it, the main topic of discussion was an online game about how to help others use healthy words. The player could control a little boy to patrol the streets and see if anyone was using sensitive words. If so, the little boy could choose to go up and criticize the offender or report the offender to the police. The more offenders the little boy caught, the higher the score and the better the rewards.

Arvardan opened a few other random forums. Everyone in them was polite and spoke very healthy language, just like people outside on the streets. No, it was even worse than on the streets. People on the streets at least had opportunities to perform a few private gestures, like the way Arvardan had written "title" on the bus window in secret. But on the BBS forums, even the last bits of privacy of the individual were stripped away. The appropriate authorities could examine every mouse movement, every keystroke, every bit that passed through your computer, and there was nowhere to hide.

Disappointment and a sense of loss overwhelmed Arvardan. He closed his eyes and lay back. He had been so naive to think that the BBS forums might be a little more open, but now it was clear that they were even more suffocating than real life. He was stuck in an electronic quagmire, and he couldn't breathe.

"Fuck you, you sonovabitch" once again rose to the tip of his tongue. The urge to shout was so strong that he struggled to contain himself.

Suddenly he thought of the mysterious "title." What did that really mean? Five documents, five e-mails. Maybe the e-mails had something hidden in them? Perhaps they had something to do with "title"?

Arvardan turned back to the screen and carefully examined the five e-mails from the Department of Web Security. He opened the e-mails and saw that each one had a title in larger font at the top. He arranged the titles in the order indicated by the letters in the word "title," taking each creased letter as indicating the position its corresponding e-mail's title should be in.

"Navigate/With/Care:/Your/Username/And/Password"

"To/Our/Users:/Newest/Index/Of/Available/Forums"

"User/Basics:/Guide/For/New/BBS/Users"

"Education/In/Health/And/Responsibility:/Applicable/BBS/Regulations"

"Forum/Etiquette:/List/Of/Healthy/Words/For/The/Web"

The first word from each title, when put together, formed a sentence: "Navigate To User Education Forum."

Arvardan remembered that he had indeed seen a forum with the name "User Education Forum." He clicked the link for that forum, hoping that this was not just some coincidence.

The User Education Forum was an administrative forum. All the posts in it were suggestions or complaints about BBS management. The forum moderator was someone named MICHEAL19387465LLKQ. There were few posts and responses, and the forum had little traffic. Arvardan opened the index of all posts in the forum and clicked open each one. The posts seemed completely random, and he could see no pattern.

Arvardan was disappointed. He seemed to have hit another dead end. But he had not been this excited for so long. He stubbornly kept on staring at the screen, trying to hold on to the sense of discovery and excitement, even if illusory, for just a little while longer.

Suddenly his eyes focused on the username of the forum administrator. *Micheal* was not the usual spelling for *Michael*.

He clicked through the posts in the forum again and noticed that some of the posts were also posted by usernames containing unusual spellings for common names.

Following the pattern from before, he took the initial words from the titles of posts by users with unusually spelled names and arranged them in the order of the number portion of the authors' usernames to form a new sentence:

"Every Sunday at the Simpson Tower, fifth floor, suite B."

There must be some meaning in this. The documents, the e-mails, and now the forum posts: three times in a row he had put clues together that led to more clues. This was no mere coincidence. Who had hidden these messages in the official documents from the appropriate authorities? What happened every Sunday at the Simpson Tower, fifth floor, suite B?

Arvardan had finally found the excitement long absent from his life. The novelty of the unknown stimulated his long-numbed nerves. More important, these word games, planted in the middle of official documents from the appropriate authorities, gave him the satisfaction of breathing freely, as though a solid iron mask had been punched through with a few air holes.

Let us build a healthy and stable Web!
Fuck you, you sonovabitch!

Arvardan stared at the desktop background, mouthed the curse silently, and lifted his middle finger to the computer screen.

For the next few days, Arvardan lived in a state of constant, barely subdued excitement. He was like a kid who was trying to hide a mouthful of candy with an innocent smile and who, after the adults had turned away, broke into a sly grin, enjoying the feeling of having a secret.

Day after day passed; the List of Healthy Words continued to shrink; the air outside the window grew even murkier. This was the way life was. Arvardan had begun to use the List of Healthy Words as a calendar. If three words had been deleted, that meant three days had passed. When seven words had been deleted, Arvardan knew it was Sunday.

Arvardan arrived at the Simpson Tower at noon. The clue that had brought him there did not mention a specific time. Arvardan thought it probably made sense to show up around noon. As he arrived wearing his dark green army coat, the filtering mask, and the Listener, his heart began to beat irregularly. He had imagined all kinds of possibilities for this moment, and now that the secret to the mystery was about to be revealed, he was nervous. *No matter what happens here, it can't be worse than my life now,* Arvardan thought.

He walked into the building and noticed that there were very few people here as well. The empty halls were filled only with his steps and their echo. An old elevator car had advertisements like "Let's build a beautiful home on the Web," and a poster with a man whose face shone with the light of truth and justice. The background of the poster was the Flag, and the man pointed at the viewer with his right index finger. Above him was the slogan, "Citizen, I need you to use healthy language." Arvardan turned away and saw that the other wall of the elevator car had the exact same poster. There was nowhere to hide.

Luckily, by then he had arrived at the fifth floor. The elevator doors opened, and opposite was the door to suite B. The door was green, the paint chipped, and splats of ink covered the doorframe.

Arvardan took a deep breath and pressed the doorbell.

He thought the rhythm of the steps within the door sounded familiar, as though he had heard it somewhere. The door cracked open halfway, and a young woman held on to the doorknob as she filled the doorway, leaning forward to stare at Arvardan. She said suspiciously, "Who, are, you, looking, for?"

It was the voice behind the counter at the Department of Web Security, BBS Section. She looked beautiful: hunter-green wool sweater, hair worn in a tight bun in the typical style, skin so fair it was pale, and lips glowing with the flush of health.

Looking into the woman's eyes, Arvardan hesitated, and then raised his right hand. "Title."

Arvardan stared at the woman tensely. If the woman reported his strange behavior to the police, then he would be arrested and interrogated as to why he had gone to a stranger's home. The crime of "willfully lolling about" was only slightly less serious than the crime of "using sensitive words."

The woman nodded, barely perceptibly, and carefully gestured with her right hand for him to come in. Arvardan was about to speak, but the woman glared at him, and he swallowed and obediently followed her into the apartment.

Once they were in, the woman shut the door immediately, and then pulled a lead-gray curtain over the doorway. Arvardan blinked anxiously, and looked about him. The apartment had two bedrooms and a living room. The living room had a couch and a coffee table, on top of which there were a few bunches of red and purple plastic flowers. Next to one of the walls was a desk with a computer. A common white calendar hung on the wall, but the owner had taken care to decorate its edges with pink paper, giving it a homier feel. Arvardan noticed that the shoe rack next to the door held four pairs of shoes, all of different sizes. This meant that he wasn't the only guest here today.

Arvardan was still uneasy. Suddenly the woman clapped him lightly on the back, indicating that he should continue inside. The two of them went across the living room, through a short hallway, and arrived at a bedroom. The bedroom door was veiled by the same kind of lead-gray curtain. The woman lifted the curtain and pushed open the bedroom door.

Arvardan saw three smiling individuals in a room decorated with real, fresh flowers. The room was also full of antiques that existed only in Arvardan's memory: an Impressionist painting, a wooden sculpture from Uganda, and a silver candelabra. But there was no computer.

As he hesitated, the woman entered the room. She carefully pulled the curtain closed and shut the door. She turned around. "Welcome to the Talking Club!"

The Talking Club?

Out of habit, Arvardan did not say the words aloud. He wasn't certain if the words were healthy, and so asked his question only with his eyes.

"You can speak as freely as you like. This damned device won't work in here." The woman pointed to his Listener. There was no warning beep. It didn't seem to hear the two sensitive words in her speech: *freely* and *damned*.

Arvardan remembered the man he had seen a week ago at the bus stop. If he took off his Listener, would what happened to that man also happen to him?

The woman saw that he was hesitant. She pointed to the lead-gray curtain at the door. "Don't worry. This can shield off the signal for the Listener. No one will know." Arvardan took off the Listener. He spoke in a low voice. It was still too difficult for him to shift out of the manner of speech demanded by the appropriate authorities. "Who, are, you? What, is, this, place?"

"This is the Talking Club. Here you may speak as you like," said another man as he got up. He was tall and thin, the glasses over his nose particularly thick.

Arvardan mumbled, but could not speak out loud. He was embarrassed by the stares of the four others, and his face flushed bright red.

The woman who had opened the door for him gave him a sympathetic look. "You poor thing. Don't be so tense. Everyone is like this when they first arrive. Over time you'll get used to it."

She put a hand on Arvardan's shoulder. "Actually, we've met. At least I've seen you, but you haven't seen me." As she spoke, she reached up and let down her hair. The black tresses fell to her shoulders, and in that moment Arvardan thought she was the most beautiful woman he had ever seen.

He finally spoke a whole sentence, though the words still did not flow smoothly. "I . . . remember you, remember your voice."

"Really?" The woman laughed. She sat him on a couch and handed him a glass of water. Arvardan noticed that this was an old-fashioned glass, etched with a flowery pattern. The water inside the glass gave off a faint fragrance. Arvardan tried a sip. The sweet taste was particularly stimulating for a tongue that had grown used to distilled water.

"This wasn't easy to obtain. Even we can't get it every week." The woman sat next to him, looking intently at him with her dark eyes. "How did you find out about us?"

Arvardan explained the process by which he had discovered the sequence of clues. The other four nodded in approval. "Smart man. Your brain hasn't become mush," said a thirty-something man with a few extra pounds. His voice was very loud.

The middle-aged man with glasses put his hands together in a gesture of agreement. "You are a natural for membership in the Talking Club."

"All right," the fat man said, "let's give a round of applause to formally welcome the new member."

The other four applauded, and the sound of their clapping filled the small bedroom. Arvardan lifted the glass to them, embarrassed. When the applause died down, he timidly lifted his head and asked, "Can I ask a question? What exactly is the Talking Club?"

The woman who had brought him in responded. "The Talking Club is a gathering where we can say anything we want. There are no sensitive words here, and no healthy Web. This is a space to release your soul and stretch out your body."

"Our principle is just this: talk," added the middle-aged man, and he adjusted his glasses.

"But what can I talk about?"

"Anything. You can talk about anything in your heart." The middle-aged man smiled.

This is an audacious gathering. It's clearly criminal, Arvardan thought. But he found himself attracted to the idea of being a criminal in this way.

"Of course, we need to make certain things clear," the woman said. "Talking is dangerous. Every member faces the danger of arrest by the appropriate authorities. State agents may break through the door at any moment and capture us under the charges of illegal assembly and using illegal language. You have the right to refuse to join us and leave immediately."

Arvardan listened to the woman's warning. He hesitated. But he thought if he left now, then he would go back to his life, suffocating in a quagmire. Arvardan had not known he had such a strong yearning to talk.

"I will not leave. I will join you, talking."

The woman was delighted. "Perfect! Oh, why don't we start with self-introductions?" She stood up. "Let's start with me. My name is Artemis. As for my Web Access Serial? To hell with it. Who cares? I have my own name."

Her words made everyone, including Arvardan, laugh. Then she continued. "Still, Artemis is just a pseudonym. She's a goddess from Greek mythology."

"Pseudonym?"

"Right. It's not the same as the name on my Personal Identification Card."

"But why?"

"Aren't you sick of the name they have for you in their files? I want to give myself a name that I like, even if there's just one place to use it. In the Talking Club we each have picked a name for ourselves. That's how we address one another."

Arvardan nodded thoughtfully. He understood Artemis's feeling.

When using the BBS forums, he had hoped to pick a name that he liked, and not be assigned a username.

Through Artemis's self-introduction, Arvardan learned that she was a staffer at the Department of Web Security, BBS Section. She was twenty-three, single, and hated cockroaches and spiders. Her hobbies included sewing and gardening, and the flowers in the bedroom were secretly cut and brought back by her from outside the Capital.

Next was the middle-aged man. His name was Lancelot. He was forty-one, an engineer at the Capital Electric Plant. The name "Lancelot" belonged to a faithful knight from the Arthurian legends. Lancelot was married and had two children: a boy (aged three) and a girl (aged four). They liked lemon-flavored candy the most. Lancelot hoped that he would be able to bring the kids to the next gathering of the Club. The children were still learning to talk, and he wanted them to learn real speech.

The thirty-something overweight man was a Web Regulator for the Department of Web Security named Wagner. This surprised Arvardan. He had had the impression that Web Regulators were all cold, expressionless men, but the man before Arvardan was corpuscular, oily, and his mustache curled up spiritedly at the ends. He loved cigars and the opera, and took advantage of the special privileges available to Web Regulators to obtain them.

"Wagner got us the curtains that can shield the signals from the Listener," Artemis added. Wagner tipped an imaginary hat and bowed to her.

The fourth member of the Talking Club was a woman in a black uniform. She had just turned thirty. Her name was Duras, and she worked as an editor at the *Capital Daily Times*. She was even thinner than Artemis, and her high cheeks contrasted with her sunken eyes. Her thin lips didn't part much from each other even when she spoke, and never revealed her teeth. She liked cats and dogs, even though she had no pets now.

"It's you next," Artemis said to Arvardan.

Arvardan took a minute to think, and then introduced himself to the group, stammering many times. When he tried to describe his hobbies, for a moment he couldn't come up with any. He had never had to think about hobbies before.

Artemis put her hand on his shoulder again and tried to help him. "Well, what's the one thing you really want to do?"

"I can really say anything?"

"Anything. There are no restrictions here."

Arvardan thought that he had finally found an opportunity. He cleared his throat, scratched his head, and broke into a loud, crisp shout. "Fuck you, you sonovabitch!"

All the others were stunned. Wagner was the first to recover. He held on to his cigar with his teeth and applauded vigorously. Then he took the cigar in his hand and loudly exclaimed, "Fantastic! This should be our formal membership oath."

Artemis and Duras both giggled. Arvardan thought that beyond the novelty of speaking with the Club, he really enjoyed the sense of contempt for the appropriate authorities in voicing the string of swearwords.

Artemis tilted her head and asked him, "What do you wish to name yourself?"

"Ummm . . . Wang Er," Arvardan said. This was a Chinese name. He had once had a Chinese friend who loved to tell stories. In all his stories, the main character was named Wang Er.[2]

The mood in the bedroom was now friendly and easy, and conversation became more natural. Everyone got into a comfortable position, and Artemis refilled everyone's cup from a kettle from time to time. Arvardan gradually let go of his tension, and felt that his brain had never been so relaxed.

Artemis filled his cup with sweet water again. "It's impossible to speak freely in our daily lives. We need this space. But we can't openly advertise for membership, and it's far too risky to try to find new members through physical contact. So Lancelot designed a system of

2 Wang Er is the name of the protagonist in stories by the Chinese writer Wang Xiaobo.

clues and hints, and Wagner and I used our system access privileges to leave the clues in places. Only those who discovered and solved the clues would find the Club."

"My system wasn't designed just for safety," Lancelot said. He took off his glasses and carefully polished them. "It's also a qualifying exam for potential new members. Members of the Talking Club must be in possession of intelligence and wisdom, passionate, and full of yearning for freedom."

Wagner held his cigar between two fingers, flicked the ash into an ashtray, then said loudly, "In my experience, most applicants for permission to use the BBS service are nostalgic for the past or desire something new and fresh in their lives. They think that the BBS forums will show them something different from daily life—of course, reality is otherwise, since the State's control over the BBS forums is even stricter than the regulation of e-mail—but their desire indicates they want to be free. Thus, we hide our clues in the BBS documents so that only applicants for BBS service can find them. And only those who are smart and observant can find all the hints and follow their trail to find this place."

"You are the second person to find the Talking Club. The first was Miss Duras," Artemis said to Arvardan. Arvardan gazed at Duras in admiration.

Duras lightly said, "It's no big deal. My job is all about playing with words."

Arvardan remembered the crazy man he had met at the bus stop a week ago. He told the others his story. When he was finished, Lancelot shook his head, and sighed.

"I've seen this sort of thing, too. It happened to a colleague of mine. This shows the necessity for something like the Talking Club as a pressure-release valve. Living constantly under the restrictions imposed by sensitive words will drive people crazy because they can neither think nor express themselves."

Wagner moved his heavy body to the side. "This is exactly what the appropriate authorities want to see. Then only the stupid will survive. A society full of stupid men is a stable one."

"You are also a member of the appropriate authorities, Mr. Wagner," Artemis said playfully as she refilled Wagner's cup.

"Miss Artemis, I'm an ordinary man just like any other, with the sole distinction that I'm allowed to use a few more sensitive words."

Everyone laughed. Arvardan had never heard so many people speak so much. He found, to his own surprise, that he quickly felt at home among these people. The distance and sense of unfamiliarity among them melted away quickly. Also, his dizziness and congested chest, problems that had become habits, disappeared.

Quickly the topic of conversation turned from the Talking Club itself to broader interests. Artemis sang a song; Lancelot told a few jokes; Duras told everyone about the customs of the southern provinces of the State; Wagner even sang an aria from an opera. Although Arvardan couldn't understand a word of this last contribution, he did not hold back his applause. In a shielded corner of the Capital, five individuals unwilling to sink into silence were enjoying a most precious luxury—talking.

"Wang Er, do you know *1984*?" Artemis asked. She sat down next to Arvardan.

Arvardan shook his head. "I only know that 1984 is part of my Web Access Serial."

"It's a book."

"Book?" This was an old word. Now that computer technology had advanced to the point that all information was contained by the Web, anyone could go to the online library to get the digital editions of published material. The appropriate authorities considered physical books to be an unnecessary waste, and so they had gradually disappeared.

Wagner said, "It is understandable that the appropriate authorities prefer electronic books. With electronic books, all you need is FIND and REPLACE to eliminate all unhealthy words in a book and decontaminate it. But to correct and edit physical books would take forever."

"*1984* is a great book. It's what an old philosopher predicted about our modern world," Artemis said earnestly. "Long ago, the book perceived the struggle between restraint and freedom over the flesh and over the soul. It's the foundation of the Talking Club."

"How can one read this book?" Arvardan asked, staring into Artemis's dark eyes.

"We can't find a paper copy, and of course the online library won't have it." Lancelot shook his head, and then broke into another smile. He gestured with his left hand at Duras. "Our Miss Duras should be proud of her memory. When she was young, she was fortunate enough to have read this book and can recall most of it."

"Wonderful! Then she wrote it out, right?"

"That would be far too dangerous. Right now, owning physical books is a great crime and would risk exposing the Talking Club. Instead, every time the Talking Club meets, we ask Miss Duras to recite some of it."

Everyone quieted. Duras stood up and walked to the middle of the room. Arvardan casually put his arm around Artemis's shoulders, and she leaned toward him, her hair drifting between them. A faint feminine fragrance found its way to his nose and caused his heart to skip a few beats.

Duras's voice was not loud, but clear and forceful. Her memory was indeed amazing: not only did she remember the plot, but also she could even recount many of the details and recite entire passages verbatim. Duras got to the part where Julia pretended to fall and secretly handed a note with the words "I love you" to Winston. Duras's retelling was so lively that she captivated everyone. Artemis was especially absorbed in the story and didn't notice Arvardan's eyes, which never left her.

Wagner gave his opinion as Duras paused for a drink. "The author of *1984* predicted the progress of totalitarianism, but could not predict the progress of technology." Arvardan thought that Wagner's appearance belied his quickness: he was a very perceptive technocrat.

"In Oceania, it was still possible to pass secret notes to others and express one's hidden thoughts. But now things are different. The appropriate authorities have forced all of us to live on the Web, where even if we wanted to pass secret notes to each other, the Web Regulators would see everything. There is no place to hide. And in real life? We still have to contend with the Listener." Wagner knocked his cigar against his thighs. "To put it simply: technology is neutral. But the progress of technology will cause a free world to become ever freer, and a totalitarian world to become ever more repressive."

"This seems like the pronouncement of some philosopher," Artemis said, winking at Arvardan. She retrieved some cookies from a drawer and handed them to everyone.

"Isn't this just like how the bits are just ones and zeros, but some will make them into useful tools while others will make them into malicious viruses?" Arvardan asked.

Wagner snapped his fingers happily. "Very good, Wang Er. That's exactly it. You are a credit to programmers."

Duras looked at the clock hanging on the wall, and reminded the other four that time was up. The Talking Club could not meet for too long each session. The longer their Listeners remained shielded and off the grid, the greater the risk of exposure.

"All right. Let's take the final half hour to complete today's activities."

Artemis cleaned away the empty cups on the table, and Lancelot and Wagner both got up to stretch out their shoulders and backs, a bit sore from sitting for so long. Only Duras remained seated without moving.

"Activities? What activities?" Arvardan asked. *What would the Talking Club do other than talk?*

"Oh, right. We do have other activities." Artemis moved her bangs out of the way and gave him a seductive smile. "We still have to have frank exchanges with each other."

"Frank exchanges?"

"Yes, fucking, to speak plainly."

Arvardan's face turned white, and his breathing quickened. His stomach felt as if it had just been injected with air chilled to thirty degrees below zero. He couldn't believe his ears.

Of course, the appropriate authorities *did* permit sexual activities, but only between married couples. And there was a complex set of algorithms that computed the legally permitted frequency and lengths of their couplings based on the couple's age, physical health, income level, professions, environment, climate, and record of rule-violations. As for unmarried individuals such as Arvardan, it was completely illegal to engage in any sexual activity whatsoever (including masturbation) or to read or view any material related to sex—all immoral words having been eliminated from the List of Healthy Words in any case.

"The Talking Club has freedom of speech as well as the freedom to go to bed with anyone," Artemis said without any embarrassment. "We talk to each other, and then choose whoever we like to make love with, just as we choose to speak the words that we like."

Lancelot saw the awkward expression on Arvardan's face. He walked over and lightly clapped Arvardan's shoulders. He said gently, "Of course we won't force anyone. This is all built on the foundation of consenting adults. I still have to leave early to pick up my kids. You have just the right number without me."

Arvardan flushed bright red. He felt hot, like the CPU in his computer during the summer. He couldn't even lift his eyes to look at Artemis. He had desired female company for so long, but this was the first time he had been so close to that goal.

Lancelot said his good-byes to everyone. Artemis left the bedroom to Wagner and Duras, took the hand of Arvardan, who was close to panicking, and led him to another bedroom. This one clearly belonged to Artemis herself. The room was appointed simply, very neat and clean.

Artemis took the initiative. Under her seductive ministrations, Arvardan gradually let himself go and allowed the primitive desires hidden deep within his heart to come out. He had yearned for any kind of release from his dry, boxed-in life by imagining the smooth, mellow voice of a real woman, and now his dreams were finally coming true. Arvardan did not know if there was a distinction between his desire for her and his desire to say, "Fuck you, you sonovabitch," but now was not the time for analysis.

When he woke up, he saw that Artemis was lying beside him, her naked body like a white jade statue. Even in sleep, her pose was beautiful. He lifted himself and yawned, and then Artemis opened her eyes.

"Feels good, doesn't it?" she asked.

"Yes . . ." Arvardan didn't know what else to say. He paused, then asked hesitantly, "Before, with Lancelot and Wagner, did you also . . . ummm, what I mean is, like we did just now?"

"Yes," Artemis said gently. She sat up, too, her hair hanging over her shoulder to cover her chest. Her forthrightness confused Arvardan. There was an uncomfortable hush in the room, and then Artemis broke the silence. "You remember the story today? The woman in the story handed the man a note that said, 'I love you.'"

"Yes," Arvardan said.

"The word *love* does not exist in the List of Healthy Words promulgated by the appropriate authorities." Artemis's eyes were filled with regret and loss.

"I love you," Arvardan said without thinking. He knew that it was possible to say anything he wanted in this room.

"Thank you." Artemis gave him a perfunctory smile. She put on her clothes and hurried Arvardan to do the same. Arvardan was a bit disappointed. She had not responded as enthusiastically as he had wished, but as though what he had just said was not all that important.

By now Duras and Wagner had already left. Artemis walked him to the door, handed him his Listener, and then reminded him, "Once outside, remember not to mention anything about the Talking Club or anyone here. Outside of the Talking Club, we are strangers."

"I understand," Arvardan said. He turned to leave.

"Wang Er."

Arvardan turned at her words. Before he knew what was happening, two soft lips covered his, and then a low voice sounded by his ear. "Thank you. I love you, too."

Arvardan felt his eyes grow wet. He put on the Listener, opened the door, and walked back into the suffocating world. But now he was in a very different mood from when he first showed up.

After this, Arvardan's mental condition clearly improved. He carefully treasured the joy of having a secret club. Every week or two weeks, the five members met. They talked, sang, or listened to Duras tell the story of *1984*. Arvardan enjoyed frank exchanges with Artemis a few more times, and occasionally did the same with Duras. Now he had two personas: one was Arvardan, who existed in real life and on the Web, and the other was Wang Er, member of the Talking Club.

At one meeting, Arvardan asked, "Are we the only ones who gather to talk in private in the whole State?"

"It is said that there are some places in the State, far from the Capital and deeply hidden in the mountains, where the truly radical not only gather to talk, but also to organize for violence. They shout as they rush at the State's agents, and even curse at the firing squads as they are executed," Wagner said.

"Can we join them?" Arvardan asked.

"Only if you are willing to give up your safe and still-comfortable life. The radicals live in places so desolate that except for free speech there is nothing else, not even enough clean water," Wagner said, a little coldly.

Arvardan flinched and did not pursue the topic further. He certainly desired talk, but not to the point where he was willing to give up all he had, little though it was. Distilled water was still better than no water. The Talking Club provided sufficient nourishment to sustain the dried husk of his spirit. Bottom line: he was easily satisfied.

At another meeting, the topic of conversation turned to sensitive words. Arvardan remembered that long ago—his memory was growing hazy—the appropriate authorities had actually issued a List of *Sensitive* Words. People who ran the various Web sites were told to refer to it secretly in administering the sites. He was not sure how that system had evolved into the present one. That day, Wagner brought a bottle of wine for the occasion and was in good spirits. He explained to them the history of the "shielding" system. As a Web Regulator, he had access to the historical records for this process.

Initially, the State only shielded certain sensitive words, but it quickly discovered that this was essentially useless. Many users simply mixed in special characters or numbers or misspelled words to get around the inspection system. The appropriate authorities had to respond by trying to shield these variant spellings. But as everyone knew, the combinations of different characters to approximate the appearance of different words were virtually limitless. Provided you had some imagination, it was always possible to come up with a novel combination and get your meaning across. For example, the word *politics* could be written as "polit/cs," " 政itics," "pol/itic$," and so on.

After the appropriate authorities finally caught on to the problem, they took a new tack. Since it was not possible to filter out all possible combinations of characters that might spell out a word, the solution was to forbid the use of anything except real dictionary words. This procedure was initially very successful. The number of rule-violators went down significantly. But very soon, people discovered it was possible to use puns, homonyms, or rhyming slang to continue to express the same dangerous ideas. Even if the appropriate authorities filtered out all sensitive words and all possible puns and homonyms with those words, it was useless. Imaginative citizens gave their creativity free rein and used metaphor, metonymy, analogy, etymology, rhyming slang, and other rhetorical tricks to substitute non-sensitive words for sensitive ones. The human mind was far more creative than the computer. The computer might shield off one path, but the people had many more paths to choose from.

This contest, under the surface, seemed to go the way of the people. But then a man who could think outside the box appeared. It was unclear who he really was: some said he was the chief administrator at the appropriate authorities; others said he was a dangerous man who had been arrested for using too many sensitive words. He was the cause of the turn in the tide of the battle between the State and the people.

He suggested to the appropriate authorities that the regulations should no longer explain what was forbidden. Instead, the regulations should set forth what *could* be said, and *how* to say it. The appropriate authorities immediately took this advice and issued new regulations. The List of Sensitive Words was eliminated, and in its place came the List of Healthy Words.

This time, the people were on the losing side. In the past, they had delighted in playing cat-and-mouse games with the appropriate authorities on the Web and in daily life. But now the appropriate authorities had them by the throat, since the entire framework and building blocks of language were now under their control.

Nonetheless, the people refused to give up. They began to select words from the List of Healthy Words and use them in novel combinations to express illegal meanings. For example, writing *stabilize* twice in a row meant "topple," *stabilize* plus *prosperity* meant "shield." The appropriate authorities had to keep an eye on this sort of trend and, day after day, eliminate more and more words from the List of Healthy Words to prevent their use in these new roles.

"So long as the world contained even two words or even two letters, then it would be possible to continue the free exchange of ideas—you know Morse code?"

Wagner paused, drained his cup, and gave a satisfied burp.

"But the price for this war is the loss of language. Our ability to express ourselves continues to get poorer, and more dry and banal. More and more people will choose silence. But this is a good thing as far as the appropriate authorities are concerned." Lancelot had a worried expression on his face, and rhythmically knocked against the desk. "If you think about it, isn't the people's desire for freedom the very thing that's pushing language to the edge of death? Ironic, isn't it? The appropriate authorities will have the last laugh."

"No, no. They will not understand the emotion behind laughter," Wagner said.

"Actually, I think the appropriate authorities have always operated in a state of fear. They are terrified that people will have the use of too many words and express too many thoughts, making their control difficult." Artemis put on the stiff, cold expression she wore for work and imitated the common speech pattern: "Let us build a healthy and stable Web!"

Duras, Lancelot, and Wagner all burst into laughter. The only one who didn't laugh was Arvardan. He was stuck on the last thing Lancelot had said: in the war between the people and the appropriate authorities, the final conclusion was the death of language. Then the Talking Club was nothing more than a chance to enjoy the final quiet moment that came from pulling shut the curtains on the windows of a train speeding toward the edge of a cliff.

Duras could not attend the frank exchange phase of the Talking Club that week because it was her time of the month, and she left early. Artemis washed the cups and smiled at the three men. "Should we try a three-on-one?"

Lancelot patted Arvardan on the shoulder. "I have some things I want to discuss with Wang Er. We'll stay here a bit." Artemis took Wagner to the other bedroom. Arvardan was confused, unsure of what Lancelot wanted.

Lancelot sat back on the couch. The engineer's expression became serious. "Wagner has told you about the radical organizations?" Arvardan nodded. "What do you think of them?"

"I admire them. But I'm not sure if it's necessary to go that far. Men cannot live on words alone." Although Arvardan had never been to the mountains, he had heard plenty about their desolation.

Lancelot laughed bitterly and drained the coffee cup in front of him. "I was once a member of the radicals. But now I'm a deserter."

Arvardan stared at him.

"In the beginning, I had lots of ideals. I went to the mountains and joined them. But when the rush of freedom had passed, what followed was only constant deprivation and suffering. I wavered and finally abandoned my friends, snuck back to the Capital, and now I hide in a girl's bedroom, chat, fuck, and drink coffee, and say I'm satisfied with my life."

"You regret leaving?"

"My regret is not what's important." Lancelot handed Arvardan a piece of paper. The paper was thin, light, and had a single address written on it.

"Memorize it and swallow the paper," Lancelot said. "This is how you get to the mountains and get in touch with them. If you change your mind about your life, you can go any time."

"Have you given this to the others, too?"

"No. The Talking Club is enough for the rest of us. But something is different about you. You remind me a lot of the younger me. Though you look quiet, inside you there is a dangerous spark. I have lost the ambition and the will to change the world, but I do not want to see everyone become like me."

"But I—"

"You don't need to promise me anything. This is only an option, that's all."

After returning home from the Talking Club, Arvardan lay on his cot with his hands under his head and sank into thought. He was infatuated with Artemis and could not help himself. Arvardan envied Winston from Duras's telling of *1984*. Winston and Julia had their own room, a world that only belonged only to the two of them.

(Arvardan also thought about what Lancelot had said to him about the radicals, but soon he put it out of his mind—the image of radicals hiding in the mountains was simply not as alluring as the body of Artemis.)

Once, when he was engaging in a "frank exchange" with Artemis, he had revealed his thoughts to her. She didn't answer him directly but only said the relationship between them could not go beyond what they had—the limit of what was possible. The appropriate authorities would not be napping forever. "We can only compress our emotional lives into the weekly meetings of the Talking Club. It's already a great luxury," she said, as she gently stroked his chest. "In the Talking Club, we are Artemis and Wang Er. But any other time, you are ARVARDAN19842015BNKF, and I am ALICE19387465BJHD."

Arvardan could only sigh in response. He really shouldn't have asked for more.

Along with his emotions, the Web also changed. Ever since he had joined the Talking Club, Arvardan had gradually begun noticing some of the hidden aspects of the Web. Just as Wagner had said, the war between the people and the appropriate authorities never ended. Always thought and speech leaked from the cracks.

Arvardan noticed that within the formulaic e-mails and BBS forum posts were hidden many details were worth paying attention to, just like his "title." There were all kinds of codes and hidden meanings. These puzzles came from different individuals, and the format and decoding technique differed for each. Arvardan didn't know what was hidden behind some of the codes, but one thing was certain: the Talking Club was not the only underground gathering. Wagner was right: individuals were always attempting to use "healthy" words to express "unhealthy" thoughts.

In the past, Arvardan had only vaguely felt that he was being constrained, but now he could see clearly the pulsing arteries and veins of this system—and the various tricks played on him by the appropriate authorities. The freedom he enjoyed at the Talking Club only made him even more aware of the lack of freedom in the rest of his life.

"Fuck you, you sonovabitch!"

At every meeting, the three male members would shout this curse out loud. They understood very well that this had no effect on the appropriate authorities, but they loved the feeling the curse brought them.

One week Arvardan was particularly busy. His colleague, for unknown reasons, had been shielded. This meant that the whole project fell on his shoulders. The project involved designing a piece of software for the appropriate authorities, which would be used to control the energy distribution for a new, high-powered, active Listener. (It was unusual for Arvardan to be told this much, but since his colleague was gone, his superiors had to give him the bigger picture.) The software was complex, and he had to spend more than twelve hours a day working in front of the computer, only pausing to eat, take a drink of distilled water, or nap briefly on his cot when his body could no longer take the abuse. His room was filled with the stench of sweaty socks and shirts.

Coincidentally, the heating system in his room failed. The gray radiators became ice cold and no longer circulated hot water. Arvardan checked them and realized the problem wasn't with the pipes. Since his neighbors were suffering the same fate, it meant the heating system was failing as a whole. The one positive effect of this failure was that it reduced the stench in his room. The negative effect, however, was that his room turned into an ice cellar. The low temperature covered everything in the already-uncomfortable room with an additional layer of frost. The only source of warmth in the room was the computer. Arvardan put on all his winter clothes, crawled into bed, and pointed the exhaust fans of the computer toward him.

The appropriate authorities decided that *heat* and *furnace* and other similar words were also temporarily sensitive words, so Arvardan had no way of drafting a complaint to the heating supply agencies. All he could do was to wait quietly. Other than his fingers moving over the keyboard, he tried to remain very still, so as to conserve body heat.

On the fourth day after the heating system had failed, the radiators finally began to clatter and rattle with the sound of hot water flowing through them. The room warmed up again, and *heat* and *furnace* and similar words returned to the List of Healthy Words. So e-mails and BBS forum posts were filled with sentiments like, "We congratulate the appropriate authorities for restoring heat so quickly to bring warmth to the people in need!" and "The people's government loves the people!" etc.

But this was too late for Arvardan. He fell sick with a cold, a terrible cold. His head hurt as though someone had shot a dumdum bullet into his skull. All he could do was lie on his bed and wait for the doctor.

The doctor arrived at his home, put him on an IV, gave him some nameless pills, and told him to rest. This sickness lasted several days, and he had to give up that week's Talking Club meeting. His body just wasn't up for it, and Arvardan thought he was going to die.

Arvardan lay on his bed, filled with regret. The Talking Club was his only joy in life, and now he couldn't even go. He covered his head with his blanket and thought, *Will Wagner bring something special to the meeting this time? Will Lancelot bring his two children? And Artemis . . .* If Arvardan weren't there, who would she have a "frank exchange" with? Wagner or Lancelot?

He also thought about Duras. At the last meeting, Duras had reached the point in the story where Winston told Julia in their secret meeting room, "We are the dead." Julia also said, "We are the dead." And a third voice then said, "You are the dead."

Duras had stopped when she got to this point. Arvardan had desperately wanted to know what happened next. Who was the third voice? Was it the Party? Would Winston and Julia be arrested? What was going to happen to them?

"Let it be a cliffhanger," Artemis said to him. "Then the whole of next week our lives will be spent in the joy of anticipation." And then the two went back to the joy of frankly exchanging.

Arvardan's sickness lasted ten days. The first thing he did after he felt well enough was get up and look at the calendar on the wall. Today was Sunday, a Talking Club meeting day. Arvardan had missed one meeting, and he felt like a man dying of starvation. Even in his sleep, he dreamed of talking at the Talking Club.

Arvardan washed his face and carefully shaved off his thick stubble with a rusty razor. He brushed his teeth and smoothed down his bed hair with a towel and some warm water. Due to his sickness, the appropriate authorities had issued him some extra supplies, including two croissants, two ginger beers, and a packet of fine sugar. He wrapped these carefully in a plastic bag, and put the package inside his coat pocket to bring to the Talking Club to share with everyone.

Arvardan got off the bus, felt for the package hidden inside his coat, and walked toward the Simpson Tower. Halfway there, he lifted his head, and an icy chill seized his heart, forcing him to stop in his tracks.

Something was very wrong.

He looked up to the fifth floor. Before, the window from Artemis's apartment that faced the street had been covered by pink curtains, but now the curtains were pulled to the sides, and the window was wide open. If there was a meeting of the Talking Club today, Artemis would never have left the shielding curtains open. And keeping the windows open was odd, period. The air in the Capital was terribly murky. No one would have opened the windows to let in "fresh air."

There was no Talking Club today. Something else was going on. Arvardan stared at the window, and his heart began to beat furiously. He took his hand out of his pocket, put a cigarette in his mouth, and leaned against a utility pole, forcing himself to be calm so as not to raise the suspicion of passing pedestrians. Suddenly he saw something that made him almost faint.

A single idea filled his mind. "There will be no meeting of the Talking Club this week. There will never be a meeting again," he mumbled to himself, his face the color of ashes.

He saw a contraption that looked like a radar dish, hidden in a corner on this side of the street. Arvardan knew exactly what this was. It was what he had been designing the software for: the new, high-powered, active Listener. The device was capable of sending out active electromagnetic waves to capture vibrations made by voices against walls and windows from a distance and examine such speech for sensitive words.

If such a device had been installed right near Artemis's home, then that meant the Talking Club was completely exposed to the view of the appropriate authorities. The active Listener's penetrating waves would easily pierce through the lead curtains and transmit the Club members' words verbatim to the ears of the appropriate authorities.

This invention defined a new era. The appropriate authorities no longer had to wait passively for warnings. Instead, they could at any time actively inspect any speech made by anyone. Arvardan could easily imagine what had happened next. Everything that Artemis and the others said had been recorded by the appropriate authorities. Then the police broke into her apartment and arrested all the members of the Talking Club who were present. After they conducted a search, all that was left was the empty room and the empty windows.

Arvardan felt a knife was being twisted inside his heart. He did not think that he was fortunate to have escaped capture. His stomach churned, and nausea rose from his stomach to his mouth. He wanted to vomit, but he couldn't—*vomit* was itself a sensitive word. His body, only just recovered, could not take the hit. He began to shake as though he was suffering chills.

He dared not continue forward. He turned around, boarded another bus, and shut his mouth even tighter. When Arvardan returned to his own building, he saw that another active Listener was being installed nearby. The dark antenna extended into the sky, and along with the other antennas around the Capital, it wove an invisible, giant Web in the sky that covered everything.

He dared not stop to look. Keeping his head low, he walked past the active Listener and returned home without stopping. Then he hid his face in the pillow, but dared not cry out loud. He couldn't even say, "Fuck you, you sonovabitch."

After that, Arvardan's life returned to normal—just as before, it was stagnant, restrained, passionless, healthy, and without any vulgar joys. Lancelot had said the result of the war was that the people's desire for freedom would push language to the edge of death. The death of the Talking Club led to the deletion of *talking, opera, frank,* and *exchange* from the List of Healthy Words.

Although it was still possible to use numbers, the number *1984* was shielded. One morning, without any warning, Arvardan was simply assigned a new Web Access Serial that no longer contained that string of numerals. This also meant that programmers like Arvardan had to constantly ensure that their programs did not compute illegal numbers. This added greatly to the workload, and Arvardan was even more exhausted.

What happened later in *1984* Arvardan would never know. Duras, the only one who did know, had disappeared completely. So what happened to Winston and Julia would forever be a mystery, like the fate of Lancelot, Wagner, Duras, and Artemis.

He worried the most about Artemis. Every time he thought of that name, Arvardan could not control how depressed he became. What happened to her? Was she completely shielded? If that was the case, then the only trace she left in this world would be a pseudonym in the memory of a programmer.

Three weeks after the disappearance of the Talking Club, everything remained calm. No one came after Arvardan. He thought maybe it was because the others had refused to give up any information about him. Or maybe it was because they didn't really know who he was—the person they knew was a programmer named Wang Er. In the Capital there were thousands of programmers, and Wang Er was just a pseudonym.

Life went on peacefully. No, to be precise, there was one bit of difference. That would be the List of Healthy Words: words disappeared from it at a faster and faster pace. Every hour, every minute, words vanished from it. As the pace of revision for the List quickened, e-mails and BBS forum posts became more and more vapid and banal. Since people had to use an extremely limited set of words to express an inexpressibly wide range of thoughts, everyone more and more preferred silence. Even the secret codes and hidden clues became fewer.

One day Arvardan lifted his head from the computer. He stared at the hazy gray sky outside the window, and his chest spasmed. He coughed in pain and drained the distilled water from his cup. He threw the disposable plastic cup into the trash can, also made of plastic. Listening to the dull sound of plastic hitting plastic, he thought his own brain was also filled with a pile of trash. He rapped his knuckles against his skull. Indeed, the same dull, empty sound came out.

He put on his coat and filtering mask and walked out the door. He did not wear a portable Listener because it was no longer necessary. The Capital was filled with active Listeners, ever vigilant for the presence of sensitive words. The entire Capital now was just like the Web, healthy and stable.

Arvardan had a legitimate excuse for going outside. He had decided to turn in his permit for BBS service. It was no longer necessary to use this service. E-mail, BBS forums, Web sites—everything was now the same.

The calendar said it was spring, but outside it was still very cold. Tall gray buildings stood like a forest of stone in absolute zero. Gusts of wind carrying yellow sand and polluting exhaust gas rushed between them and filled every available space, making it impossible for any-one to escape their suffocating presence. Arvardan put his hands in his pockets, shrank into his coat, and continued to the building for the Department of Web Security.

Suddenly he stopped, his feet froze in place, incapable of move-ment. He saw Artemis standing under the streetlight before him, wearing a black uniform. But what a change had come over her! Seen in profile, she seemed at least ten years older, her face full of wrin-kles. There was none of the vitality of youth left in her.

She heard his steps and turned to face him, and her dark eyes seemed especially empty. She stared past Arvardan into the distance, without focus.

Arvardan had never expected to meet her at this time and place. His heart, long dormant, now was lit by a few sparks. But his dull and exhausted nerves were incapable of feeling the simple emotion of excitement.

The two stared at each other for a while. He finally walked up to her and tentatively moved his lips as though he wanted to say some-thing. But when he took out the latest edition of the List of Healthy Words distributed earlier that day, he found it was empty—even the last word had been shielded by the appropriate authorities.

An address flashed in his mind—luckily, it was not yet possible to shield the mind with technology. Perhaps it was now time to take a trip to the mountains. He had nothing more to lose.

Someone has to do this.

And so, Arvardan maintained his silence. He passed by the expres-sionless Artemis and continued his forward progress. His silhouette eventually melted into the equally quiet gray crowd.

The whole city seemed especially silent.

HAO JINGFANG

Hao Jingfang is the author of several novels, a book of travel essays, and numerous short stories published in a variety of venues such as *Science Fiction World*, *Mengya*, *New Science Fiction*, and *ZUI Found*. Her fiction has been awarded the Galaxy (Yinhe) Award as well as the Nebula (Xingyun) Award. She majored in physics at Tsinghua University as an undergraduate, and afterward conducted graduate studies at the Center for Astrophysics at Tsinghua. Hao recently obtained her Ph.D. in Economics and Management from Tsinghua and currently works for a think tank.

Hao does not limit herself to "genre" writing. Her latest novel, *Born in 1984*, for instance, would be considered a literary novel. Imaginative and precise, her stories are carefully designed on multiple levels. Her wide range of interests and literary approaches are reflected in the two selections for this anthology, "Invisible Planets," a fabulist tale in the tradition of Italo Calvino, and "Folding Beijing," a near-future, economics-based dystopia. Both stories can be read in many ways. "Folding Beijing" was a finalist for the Hugo Award and the Sturgeon Award.

INVISIBLE PLANETS

"Tell me about the fascinating planets you've seen. But I don't want to hear anything cruel or disgusting," you say.

Good. I nod and smile. *Of course. No problem.*

CHICHI RAHA

Chichi Raha is a fascinating place, its flowers and lakes unforgettable to all visitors. There you cannot see a single inch of exposed soil because the land is covered by vegetation: the *anua* grass, as fine as silk thread; the *kuqin* tree, tall enough to scrape the clouds; and many varieties of unnameable, unimaginably strange fruits exuding seductive aromas.

The Chichi Rahans have never needed to worry about making a living. Their life expectancy is high, their metabolism is slow, and they have no natural enemies. They fill their bellies on a diet of various fruits and make their homes inside a type of tree with large, hollow trunks. The average diameter of these tubes is just wide enough to allow an adult Chichi Rahan to lie down comfortably. When the weather is good, the branches hang loosely, but when it rains, the branches rise so that the leaves form a canopy like an umbrella.

Those who visit Chichi Raha for the first time are always confused by how civilization could have developed on such a world. From the perspective of the visitors, in a place lacking crisis and competition, life should be able to survive very well without intelligence. But there is indeed civilization here, and indeed it is beautiful, vigorous, full of creativity.

Many visitors think they would like to retire here. Most of them think their greatest difficulty would be a matter of diet. So, anxiously and carefully, they taste every type of local fruit. But after they've stayed awhile, after they've attended enough local banquets, they discover—somewhat to their surprise—that while they enjoy the food, they cannot tolerate life here, especially those who are old.

It turns out all Chichi Rahans learn to lie from birth. Indeed, lying is their most important occupation. They spend the entire span of their existence fabricating stories concerning both events that have occurred and events that have not. They write them down, paint them, sing them, but never remember them. They do not care if there's a correspondence between their words and the facts, their only standard being whether the tale is interesting. If you ask them about the history of Chichi Raha, they will tell you a hundred versions. No one will contradict the version told by another, because each moment, they are already engaged in self-contradiction.

On this world, everyone is always saying, "Yes, I will," but nothing is ever done. No one takes such promises seriously, though promises do make life more interesting. Only in extremely rare circumstances do the inhabitants do as they promise. And such occasions are celebrated. For example, if two of them make an appointment and both happen to keep it, then they will most likely become a couple and live together. Of course, such occurrences are rare. Most live alone all their lives. The inhabitants do not feel any lack because of this. Indeed, they hear about the overpopulation problems of other planets and feel that their own world is the only one that understands the secret of good living.

So Chichi Raha developed brilliant literature, art, and history and became a famous center of civilization. Many visitors come with the hope that they might hear a local tell family stories in the grass beneath the crown of one of the house-trees.

At one time, some questioned whether a stable society could develop on a planet like this. They imagined Chichi Raha as a chaotic place with no government or commerce. But they were wrong. The planet has an advanced political culture, and the business of exporting fruits has gone on for several centuries without interruption. The habit of lying has never caused problems for these developments and may have even helped them. The only thing Chichi Raha lacks is science. Here every intelligent mind knows a bit of the universe's secret, but the bits never get the chance to be pieced together.

PIMACEH

This is another planet where you can't be sure about history. As you wander through its museums, restaurants, and hotels, you will hear many versions of its past. Eventually, you will be trapped in a miasma of confusion because every speaker's expression will be so sincere that you can't help but believe it, and yet there is no way to reconcile all the different stories.

The scenery of this world is legendary. Strictly speaking, the planet is not even spherical. The southern hemisphere is far lower in elevation than the northern, and an almost perpendicular cliff, going all the way around the equator, divides the planet into two completely different halves. Above the cliff: ice and snow; below: an endless ocean. The city of Pimaceh is built on this world-encircling cliff. From the sky to the sea, the lightly recessed houses and the perfect, straight, up-and-down avenues are like parts of a giant painting.

No one knows how this place was built. All you will hear is the various romances told by the current inhabitants. Every story is exciting: some are heroic legends; some are tragic and austere; some are full of doomed loves. The particular effect depends on the teller, but no one can give a version that convinces everyone. And so, as it passes from teller to teller, Pimaceh becomes more and more mysterious and charming.

Many visitors, entranced by the wondrous sights and stories, linger and do not wish to leave. This is an open and accommodating planet, and every visitor is welcomed with open arms. The visitors—now settlers—then build their own houses on the cliff and pass on the stories they hear to new visitors. Content, they gradually become locals.

This state of happiness will last until one day when they realize the truth about themselves. They'll suddenly understand that countless hints have already revealed Pimaceh's true history to them: Everyone on this world is a visitor. There are no natives at all.

Yes, Pimaceh did once have a glorious history, but for some reason it was abandoned. The original inhabitants left for unknown reasons, leaving behind only a lovely ghost town that astounded the interstellar travelers who later stumbled upon it. They also left behind fragments of a language no one could decipher, like metaphors that filled in the blank spaces between the buildings. These took root in the minds of those who came after and blossomed into the most lush and beautiful imaginary pasts for the planet.

No one knows who was the first to discover this uninhabited world. The history of the visitors has also faded, consciously or not, as it passed from generation to generation. All the visitors who have settled wish to think of themselves as the people of Pimaceh. They protect this planet and steadfastly play the role of hosts—until one day they themselves begin to believe this is their native land and the country where they will die.

Almost no one can discover Pimaceh's secret except a few true wanderers who have been to all corners of the universe. They can sense that the inhabitants here emphasize slightly too often that they are the *People of Pimaceh*. On planets where real natives have remained in charge, this is one of those things easily forgotten.

BINGWAUGH

Setting Pimaceh aside, in the sea of stars, you'll probably have to go all the way to Bingwaugh to see such a variety of different species from all over, each with its own culture and civilization, colliding, striking against one another, creating sparks.

Bingwaugh is not too big and not too small. Its seasons are indistinct and its climate mild. The surface of the planet is composed mostly of plains, with few mountains and little variation in elevation. The horizon is a smooth, gentle curve. Here there is everything an average planet should have, but nothing more: good soil, decent mineral deposits, various fauna and flora, and even the sort of circular fields surrounded by low bushes where tourists like to sing and dance. There's nothing remarkable at all.

The inhabitants of Bingwaugh are similarly average. They are mammals; not too big; a solid, good people; easily satisfied. Their social organization is loose, and everyone lives in harmony.

If one *had* to pick something unique about them, it would be their pleasant disposition. Rarely are they seen arguing, whether among themselves or with the multiplicity of interstellar visitors. They're great listeners. Adults and children alike would open their eyes wide and listen to you lecture, nodding frequently, their faces often breaking into expressions of being intoxicated by the wisdom you're imparting.

Having discovered this characteristic of Bingwaugh, all the ambitious adventurers in the universe rushed to take advantage of it. Who wouldn't want to rule over such a people and place? Plenty of resources, a comfortable living environment, and a great location at the intersection of so many trade routes.

So educators came, missionaries came, politicians came, revolutionaries and reporters all came. They described to the locals their visions of heaven, lectured them on their ideals, and again and again the inhabitants of Bingwaugh nodded and sighed with heartfelt admiration and accepted the new philosophies. Some remote planets even sent over "Supervisors" to rule over these new converts. The inhabitants never objected, not even a peep.

But after these triumphant developments, the interstellar guests would always be disappointed. Indeed, the longer they stayed on Bingwaugh, the more their disappointment grew.

As it turns out, the locals have never truly accepted any alien propaganda. Even when they agree with a new faith, they never actually do as they're told. As enthusiastically as they admire the new systems of laws being presented to them, they just as enthusiastically don't follow any of the alien laws at all.

Faced with this attitude from the locals, the ambitious colonizers can do nothing. This is because they realize this contrast between what the locals say and what they do is not at all the result of some deep conspiracy, but simply a matter of habit. If you ask them directly, they'll reply, very puzzled, "Yes, what you say sounds like Truth. But the world is full of Truths. So what if you have a Truth?"

Some planets, unable to tolerate this state of affairs, attempted to conquer Bingwaugh by force. But immediately some other planets would intervene. The balance of power is such that every possible conflict is always resolved outside the boundaries of the atmosphere of Bingwaugh.

So though it is a place where foreigners love to congregate, Bingwaugh is also one of the planets that has best preserved its native culture.

※

Do you like these stories?

"Yes . . . and no. Why is every planet filled with visitors from across the stars? I don't like this. It makes them sound like zoos."

You're right. I don't like it, either. The uniqueness of each planet disappears over time in this manner, like a fingerprint being rubbed away. All right, let's hear some stories about real natives.

AMIYACHI AND AIHUOWU

Let me tell you about two planets still ruled by their original inhabitants. On each, there are two different intelligent species. Yet each species believes itself to be the only master of its respective world.

Amiyachi orbits a double star: one a bright blue giant, the other a dim white dwarf. The two are similar in mass, but differ widely in volume and the type of emitted radiation. So Amiyachi's orbit is shaped like an irregular gourd. It dances a waltz along the hyperbolic paraboloid of the gravitational fields of the two stars.

Whenever Amiyachi is near the blue giant, it enters a long summer. But when it's near the white dwarf, it enters an equally long winter. The summer is when the planet's flora multiply and grow and stretch their vines like madness. In winter, most are dormant, and only a few hardy weeds quietly bloom over the empty earth.

Summer and winter—in each season Amiyachi is ruled by a different species: one dances through the lush forests of summer; the other marches alone over the barren plains of winter. The summer Amiyachians live in houses made of woven vines, and when the weather turns cold, the houses disappear as the vines wither and die. The winter Amiyachians live in caves dug into thick mountains, and when the weather turns hot, the mouths of the caves are hidden behind dense clumps of grass and fern, leaving no visible trace.

Whenever the summer Amiyachians are about to hibernate, they secrete a liquid covering to protect themselves and sink underground. The liquid stimulates a kind of insect known as the *wususu* to begin mating. The multiplying *wususu* then bring to life the cold-resistant shrub *aludon*. The flowering of this plant, unremarkable in appearance, begins the long and slow process of awakening the winter Amiyachians.

When the winter Amiyachians are near the end of their season's journey, they give birth. The new babies, protected by a hard membrane, develop in the soil. The ionic reactions of their growth change the pH level of the soil and cause other plants to germinate and grow, announcing the beginning of the planet's summer as well as the reign of the summer Amiyachians.

Thus, the two intelligent species of Amiyachi remain unaware of each other. Neither knows that its civilization's existence depends on the existence of the other—two sides of the same coin. Both races have composed works praising the divine wisdom of the gods, allowing them to be reborn as they awake from their slumber. But they

208 | HAO JINGFANG

have never realized that they're both the children called forth by the gods and the gods themselves.

As for Aihuowu, the situation is entirely different. On the surface of this world, the two intelligent species and their civilizations are very aware of each other's existence, yet neither is aware that the other is just like itself, possessing feelings, logic, and morality.

The reason is simple: the two species exist in different frames of time.

Aihuowu is a planet with a strange orbit. The angle between its axis of rotation and the plane of its orbit is very small, and the axis of rotation itself precesses slowly. Thus, the surface of the planet can be divided into four regions: the narrow strip near the equator has night and day in accordance with the rotation of the planet, while the polar regions have their own periods of brightness and darkness based on the precession of the axis of rotation. A day near the pole is hundreds of times longer than a day near the equator, and so the creatures born in each of these regions experience time at rates hundreds of times apart.

For the Aihuowuans near the equator, the mysterious poles seem to have very long nights and very long days. But for the polar Aihuowuans, the equator passes through darkness and light rapidly—in flashes. The equatorial Aihuowuans are dainty and agile, with hundreds of thousands of individuals living in dense colonies. The polar Aihuowuans, on the other hand, have slow metabolic rates matched to their long days and long nights, and their bodies are scaled large to fit their sense of time.

Sometimes the equatorial Aihuowuans come to the poles for adventure and exploration. They always get lost in the mazelike forests full of gigantic trees and mistake the occasional houses they encounter as unscalable cliffs. But when the polar Aihuowuans wander near the equator, they often miss the details and carelessly destroy the houses and fields of the equatorial Aihuowuans. They live on the same planet but belong to entirely separate worlds.

Sometimes the equatorial Aihuowuans venture to speculate that the giant creatures of the poles might also possess intelligence. But in their hearts, they believe that even if such slow-moving creatures, who in a hundred years might not shift more than a few feet, were intelligent, it would be a simple and rudimentary kind of intelligence. The polar Aihuowuans have similar suspicions of intelligence concerning the equatorial species. But then they sigh and shake their heads, realizing that such tiny creatures that are born and die in a single day would be incapable of experiencing real civilization.

And so the two intelligent species of Aihuowu experience the same process of learning, working, love, and war. Their histories play out on two time scales, each echoing the other. But they remain opaque to each other, unaware that when it comes to time, everyone is only measuring the universe using the ruler of their own lifespan.

"Wait a minute," you interrupt. "How can you know about all these civilizations? When did you go to Amiyachi? And what scale of time did you use to experience Aihuowu?"

I know. Of course I know. If you had been there, you would know as well. This is the difference between visitors and natives. This is the point of traveling.

"It is? This is why you travel?"

Yes and no. If you really want to know why I travel, then let me tell you about a planet devoted to travel.

LUNAJI

The people of Lunaji build the galaxy's most beautiful cars, boats, airships, and passenger catapults. The complexity and refinement of these vehicles far exceed the imaginations of visitors from other worlds, and also far exceed the technological levels of all other industries on this planet.

Those who are intuitive immediately jump to the conclusion that travel is especially meaningful for the Lunajians. But there's a deeper explanation which most cannot figure out. They can't imagine why so many intelligent beings would devote their entire lives to traveling and preparing for travel, rather than the accomplishment of some other, more rewarding task. Only those who know the life cycle of the Lunajians have some understanding of this seemingly irrational restlessness.

Lunaji has a large basin where the concentration of oxygen is higher than anywhere else. The soil is rich and moist; small waterfalls pour into a clear, pristine lake; flowers are in bloom every season of the year; and heavily laden, spherical fruit trees surround soft lawns strewn with mushrooms in all the colors of the rainbow. Every Lunajian spends their childhood here, none knowing how they arrived in this world. From the moment they open their eyes, this basin is all they know.

From time to time, some wish to discover the secret origin of their lives or seek the home of the gods. Then they start to grow up, tall enough to climb over the rocks blocking the gentle slope at the edge of the basin. They walk into the dense, labyrinthine forest, climbing up the slope toward the world outside the basin. They can't tell you their ages, because the age at which each one begins to mature is different.

After exiting the basin, they keep on walking, wandering, seeking—finding nothing. They meet others who left the basin before them, but they also are still searching, still traveling, still baffled by the mystery of their own lives. So a Lunajian's life is one long migration. They go from one place to another, never settling. They build boats, cars, airplanes with the purpose of accelerating their own pace so that they can cover every square inch of the planet until they reach the edge of the sky.

Sometimes, by coincidence, some follow an obscure path and arrive at a meadow in the wilderness. There a lovely silver flower blooms, giving off an intoxicating aroma. The fragrance makes every Lunajian nearby dizzy and causes unprecedented tender feelings to spring up among them. For the first time, they feel attraction for one another and embrace, clasp, give, and receive. Then they give birth by the edge of a brook, whose water bears the babies to the basin beneath the falls.

The parents? They die and sink into the muddy earth.

And so, such a simple cycle turns out to be the entirety of the meaning of the ceaseless travels of the Lunajians.

YANYANNI

Since we're on the topic of growing up, I want to tell you a few more stories. The first is about Yanyanni.

You can always tell a Yanyannian's age at a glance. Like trees, they never cease to grow. Every year, they become taller than they were the year before. An adult is several times the height of a child, and a young person is several feet shorter than an elder. The oldest person is always head and shoulders above the surrounding crowd, a lonely tower.

So in the world of the Yanyannians, there is no such thing as a friendship that crosses age gaps. Even talking to someone who is very different in age can be a chore. A long conversation would leave both interlocutors with sore necks and shoulders, as the younger looks up while the older looks down. Indeed, there's not much to talk about between people of very different ages. Their houses are of different heights, and the shelves from which they do their shopping are different. One can only see the belt of the other, and neither can see the other's expressions.

It's not true, however, that the Yanyannians can grow without limit. One day, they wake up and discover that their height hasn't increased. Then they know they are about to die. The knowledge does not make them sad, however. Growing taller is actually a very tiring process. Many have been exhausted by it and simply find an excuse to stop. Death for the Yanyannians takes a long time, but no one knows exactly how long. It's never been precisely measured. To simplify things, they list the age of death as the day when growth ceases.

In their eyes, the passage of time is a measure of change. When growth ceases, time stops.

The tallest house on Yanyanni was built more than a century ago. At the time, there was an old man who, year after year, grew and grew until his head touched the ceiling of the tallest building then in existence. So the people erected a tower for him designed to hold a single man. The base of the tower took up the space for a park. After the old man's death, no one else ever managed to reach his record of longevity, and so the tower was divided into two stories and turned into a museum.

Legend has it that the old man once left a diary next to each window of the tower, recording his life during the years when his height corresponded to that window. Afterward, others climbed ladders to retrieve these diaries for reading, but eventually the diaries became lost.

Now visitors wander past the empty windows and imagine how a man who could cross a river with a single step might brush his teeth and eat his food.

TISU ATI AND LUTIKAWULU

Tisu Ati and Lutikawulu are a pair of opposites. These two planets, a hundred thousand light-years apart, are like the two ends of a dipole: they negate each other and also define each other.

Tisu Atians are much smaller than the inhabitants of most planets. Their skin is especially soft, and their bodies can rapidly shift shapes. On this Lamarckian world, the development of gene expression reached its pinnacle—no, surpassed the pinnacle. All of evolution has been compressed into an individual's brief life.

The Tisu Atians can alter their bodies in accordance with their desires. Those who practice climbing mountains develop longer and longer arms until their arms are longer than their bodies. Those who operate machinery develop five or six arms until an individual can simultaneously control the opening and closing of numerous valves. On the street, no two Tisu Atians look alike. Everywhere one can see a mouth so large as to take up half a face, a waist thinner than a strand of noodle, or a round sphere covered by a layer of armor-like scales. These changes are unique to each individual, and it's impossible to detect anyone's parentage based on appearance. Even the parents themselves, if sufficient time has passed, have a hard time picking their children out of a crowd.

But "in accordance with their desires" is not quite accurate. It's not true that every Tisu Atian can attain the appearance they have in their minds. Most of the time, they're vague in their self-images. It's only when someone takes an extra-large step or bumps into something that person realizes their legs have grown another thirty percent or their back has grown a row of little spikes. Of course, in a few years that person has turned into a long-legged strider able to go up an entire flight of stairs in a single step, or a warrior whose body is covered by hard and sharp spikes.

So many Tisu Atians are even more cautious than the inhabitants of other planets. They speak carefully; they work carefully. They're terrified of the possibility that in a moment of carelessness, the silly face they made before going to bed will become permanent, will turn into a tumor impossible to remove.

On the busy streets of Lutikawulu, you can tell at a glance each person's career and daily life. This may be the only point on which Tisu Ati and Lutikawulu agree.

The Lutikawuluans also look very different from one another: runners, singers, sculptors, thinkers, etc. The difference between them can be clearly gleaned from differences in musculature, body shape, size, and facial features, just like on Tisu Ati.

But on Lutikawulu, the journey of life is the exact opposite of life on Tisu Ati. This is a Darwinian planet, where everyone is in agreement that any effort expended in directing the path of evolution is useless. The Lutikawuluans have stable genomes that evolve slowly in accordance with the principles of random variation and natural selection. But because the Lutikawuluans reproduce asexually, genetic changes in their somatic cells do continue to be expressed through inheritance. The cells, as they divide and change, pass on their adaptations without reservation to the next generation. And so children inherit the alterations in their parents.

As a result, a blacksmith's son is born stronger than other children, and a clocksmith's daughter is born with better vision and nimbler fingers. These differences, accumulated over thousands of years, slowly add up to the level of speciation. Every occupation has evolved into its own independent species. And even when some occupations have disappeared, the features associated with them continue to be expressed and continue to evolve.

All of these different species are united by their language. It's only through the common tongue and identical numbers of chromosomes that they can recognize themselves as possessing a common origin. Other than these, they have nothing in common. No one is jealous of another's work, just as a monkey would not be jealous of a dinosaur. As the proverb says, *the birds have the sky while the fish have the sea*. They pass by in the same town, but it's as if they see one another without seeing one another.

While the Tisu Atians have replayed evolution a hundred million times, they have always refused real evolution. No matter how they alter their own appearance, their children always begin in the same place, keeping the same original, primitive shape. The Lutikawuluans are just the opposite. No individual ever experiences any change, but when seen through the lens of eons, they are each points along numerous diverging curves.

"You lie," you say, pouting. "How can the same universe follow two opposite sets of rules?"

Why not? My dear, there's nothing that's impossible. Numerous steps, each meaningless by itself, when added together become a rule, a principle. Perhaps in this moment you laugh, or frown, and the future is divided into two paths, two sets of rules. But how can you, the you of this moment, know?

"Is that true?" you ask, tilting your head. And for a while you are quiet.

I look at you and laugh lightly. The swing you sit on sways back and forth, and the breeze causes the locks of hair next to your ears to flutter. The key to your question is the method of reproduction, of course, but this kind of answer is too dry. I have no wish to give it.

You know something? The real key isn't about whether what I say is true, but whether you believe it. From start to end, the direction of narrative is not guided by the tongue, but by the ear.

CHINCATO

The tongue and the ear have the most meaning on Chincato. For the people of this planet, speech is not a mere way to pass the time, but a necessity for existence.

There's nothing special about Chincato, save its thick atmosphere. It's so dense that no light can penetrate it, and the surface of the planet is covered by darkness. Chincato's life is born from warm, thick deep-sea currents full of organic material and warmed by bubbling lava, and gains its energy from the heat at the heart of the planet. For Chincatoans, the boiling crater of the underwater volcano is their sun, the home of the gods, the source of wisdom and strength. Outside the crater, they can find organic sugars, which are their food, the foundation of their life.

The Chincatoans do not have eyes or any organs that sense light. They rely on sound to locate one another. Their ears are both for listening and observing. Actually, to be precise, they don't have ears. They listen with their entire body. The upper halves of their bodies are covered by trapezoidal diaphragms, each of which is strung with thousands of hairs of different lengths, and each of which can resonate with the sound of a particular frequency. Using timing differences between when each trapezoidal diaphragm hears a sound and its position, the brain of a Chincatoan can deduce the location of the source of the sound, its distance, and even its precise shape.

So all day long, the Chincatoans talk and listen without pause. They emit sounds to feel the presence of others, and also to let others know of their own existence. They cannot be silent. Silence is dangerous and makes them panic. Only by continuously talking can they ascertain their own position, be sure that they're still alive. They compete with one another to speak louder, because only by doing so can they make themselves appear brighter, more noticeable to others.

Some children are born with defects in their voice organs. These children almost cannot survive. They're always in danger of being run over by others much bigger and faster. And then no one would even know such a child once existed.

※

"That is so sad. Your stories have become shorter and shorter, but why have they also become so much sadder?"

Sad? Is it that the story I'm telling is sad, or is it that the story you're hearing is sad?

"What's the difference?"

Very different. I've been to a planet where the people can make sounds at ten thousand different frequencies, but can only hear a small portion of the frequency range. The sensitivity of their ears is not matched to the versatility of their vocal cords, and so they never hear as much as they can speak. But the most interesting part is that the range of frequencies each of them can hear is different. While they all think they're hearing the same song, a thousand individuals would actually hear a thousand different songs, but none of them knows that.

"You're making things up again. How can such a place exist?" You bite your lips and widen your eyes. "Now I'm suspicious that you haven't been to these planets you've been telling me about. Have you made them all up to amuse me?"

My darling, starting with the Odyssey, *every knight errant has told romances of faraway places to court the ladies they love. Can you tell which stories are real and which are not? I travel through these planets like Marco Polo wandering through the cities of the Orient, like Kubla Khan riding through his endless realm: everything happens in the blink of an eye. You can say that I really have been to those places, or that I have never left. The planets I speak of are scattered at every corner of the universe, but sometimes collect themselves into the same place as though they have always been together.*

Hearing this, you giggle. "I understand now. They are gathered together by your stories, and now you tell these stories to me so they are gathered in my mind. Isn't that right?"

Looking at your happy face, I sigh. The sound is so quiet that you cannot see anything strange in my smile. How can I explain this to you? How do I make you understand? Stories cannot gather anything together, if they're fated to separate.

Yes, I say quietly. *We have been sitting here for an afternoon telling stories, and together, we possess a universe. But these stories are not something I tell you. This afternoon, you and I are both tellers and both listeners.*

JINJIALIN

Jinjialin is the last story I will tell you today. It's a short tale. I'll be finished soon.

The people of Jinjialin possess bodies unlike the bodies of the people of any other planet. They are like soft balloons, or maybe like jellyfish floating through the air, transparent and loose. The surface of the Jinjialinians is membranous, like a cell's outermost layer. When two membranes touch, they can merge into one.

When two Jinjialinians encounter each other, parts of their bodies briefly merge and mix the materials inside. When they separate, the materials are redistributed. Thus, the people do not care much about their physical bodies. Even they cannot tell how much of their current bodies comes from strangers they met along the road. They believe that they are still themselves, and it's no big deal to exchange some materials.

But they don't realize that this sense of "self" is an illusion. At the moment when two of them merge, the two original selves cease to exist. They become a combined person, and when separated, two new persons. The new persons do not know all that transpired before their encounter and each believes that the self is the self, never having changed at all.

※

Do you understand? When I am done telling you these stories, when you're done listening to these stories, I am no longer I, and you are no longer you. In this afternoon we briefly merged into one. After this, you will always carry a bit of me, and I will always carry a bit of you, even if we both forget this conversation.

"You're saying that Jinjialin is our own world?"

Our own world? Which one? Can any planet have belonged to us? Or can we have belonged to any planet?

Do not ask me about the coordinates of these planets. Those numbers are the oldest mystical proverbs of the universe. They are the air between your fingers. You reach out to grab them, but when you open your hands, there's nothing. You and I and they meet for a moment, and we are fated to again separate. We're only travelers, singing songs whose meanings are obscure, wandering through the dark sky. That is all. You know they are singing in the wind, singing in the wind of a distant homeland.

FOLDING BEIJING

1.

At ten of five in the morning, Lao Dao crossed the busy pedestrian lane on his way to find Peng Li.

After the end of his shift at the waste-processing station, Lao Dao had gone home first to shower and then to change. He was wearing a white shirt and a pair of brown pants—the only decent clothes he owned. The shirt's cuffs were frayed, so he rolled them up to his elbows. Lao Dao was forty-eight, single, and long past the age when he still took care of his appearance. As he had no one to pester him about domestic details, he had simply kept this outfit for years. Every time he wore it, he'd come home afterward, take off the shirt and pants, and fold them up neatly to put away. Working at the waste-processing station meant there were few occasions that called for the outfit save a wedding now and then for a friend's son or daughter.

Today, however, he was apprehensive about meeting strangers without looking at least somewhat respectable. After five hours at the station, he also had misgivings about how he smelled.

People who had just gotten off work filled the road. Men and women crowded every street vendor, picking through local produce and bargaining loudly. Customers packed the plastic tables at the food hawker stalls, which were immersed in the aroma of frying oil. They ate heartily with their faces buried in bowls of hot and sour rice noodles, their heads hidden by clouds of white steam. Other stands featured mountains of jujubes and walnuts, and hunks of cured meat swung overhead. This was the busiest hour of the day—work was over, and everyone was hungry and loud.

Lao Dao squeezed through the crowd slowly. A waiter carrying dishes shouted and pushed his way through the throng. Lao Dao followed close behind.

Peng Li lived some ways down the lane. Lao Dao climbed the stairs, but Peng wasn't home. A neighbor said that Peng usually didn't return until right before market closing time, but she didn't know exactly when.

Lao Dao became anxious. He glanced down at his watch: almost 5:00 A.M.

He went back downstairs to wait at the entrance of the apartment building. A group of hungry teenagers squatted around him, devouring their food. He recognized two of them because he remembered meeting them a couple of times at Peng Li's home. Each kid had a plate of chow mein or chow fun, and they shared two dishes family style. The dishes were a mess, and pairs of chopsticks continued to search for elusive, overlooked bits of meat amongst the chopped peppers. Lao Dao sniffed his forearms again to be sure the stench of garbage was off him. The noisy quotidian chaos around him assured him with its familiarity.

"Listen, do you know how much they charge for an order of twice-cooked pork over there?" a boy named Li asked.

"Fuck! I just bit into some sand," a heavyset kid named Ding said while covering his mouth with one hand, which had very dirty fingernails. "We need to get our money back from the vendor!"

Li ignored him. "Three hundred and forty yuan!" said Li. "You hear that? Three forty! For twice-cooked pork! And for boiled beef? Four hundred and twenty!"

"How could the prices be so expensive?" Ding mumbled as he clutched his cheek. "What do they put in there?"

The other two youths weren't interested in the conversation and concentrated on shoveling food from the plates into their mouths.

Li watched them, and his yearning gaze seemed to go through them and focus on something beyond.

Lao Dao's stomach growled. He quickly averted his eyes, but it was too late. His empty stomach felt like an abyss that made his body tremble. It had been a month since he last had a morning meal. He used to spend about a hundred each day on this meal, which translated to three thousand for the month. If he could stick to his plan for a whole year, he'd be able to save enough to afford two months of tuition for Tangtang's kindergarten.

He looked into the distance, where the trucks of the city cleaning crew were approaching slowly.

He began to steel himself. If Peng Li didn't return in time, Lao Dao would have to go on this journey without consulting him. Although it would make the trip far more difficult and dangerous, time was of the essence, and Lao Dao had to go.

The loud chants of the woman next to him hawking her jujubes interrupted his thoughts and gave him a headache. The peddlers at the other end of the road began to pack up their wares, and like fish in a pond disturbed by a stick, the crowd dispersed. No one was interested in fighting the city cleaning crew. As the vendors got out of the way, the cleaning trucks patiently advanced. Vehicles were normally not allowed in the pedestrian lane, but the cleaning trucks were an exception. Anybody who dillydallied would be packed up by force.

Finally Peng Li appeared, his shirt unbuttoned, a toothpick dangling between his lips, strolling leisurely and burping from time to time. Now in his sixties, Peng had become lazy and slovenly. His cheeks drooped like the jowls of a shar-pei, giving him the appearance of being perpetually grumpy. Looking at him now, one might get the impression that he was a loser whose only ambition in life was a full belly. However, even as a child, Lao Dao had heard his father recounting Peng Li's exploits from when he was a young man.

Lao Dao went up to meet Peng in the street. Before Peng Li could greet him, Lao Dao blurted out, "I don't have time to explain, but I need to get to First Space. Can you tell me how?"

Peng Li was stunned. It had been ten years since anyone had brought up First Space with him. He held the remnant of the toothpick in his fingers—it had broken between his teeth without his being aware of it. For some seconds, he said nothing, but then he saw the anxiety on Lao Dao's face and dragged him toward the apartment building. "Come into my place, and let's talk. You have to start from there anyway to get to where you want to go."

The city cleaning crew was almost upon them, and the crowd scattered like autumn leaves in a wind. "Go home! Go home! The Change is about to start," someone called from atop one of the trucks.

Peng Li took Lao Dao upstairs into his apartment. His ordinary single-occupancy public housing unit was sparsely furnished: six square meters in area with a washroom, a cooking corner, a table and a chair, and a cocoon-bed equipped with storage drawers underneath for clothes and miscellaneous items. The walls were covered with water stains and footprints, bare save for a few haphazardly installed hooks for jackets, pants, and linens. Once he entered, Peng took all the clothes and towels off the wall hooks and stuffed them into one of the drawers. During the Change, nothing was supposed to be unsecured.

Lao Dao had once lived in a single-occupancy unit just like this one. As soon as he entered, he felt the flavor of the past hanging in the air.

Peng Li glared at Lao Dao. "I'm not going to show you the way unless you tell me why."

It was already five thirty. Lao Dao had only half an hour left.

He gave Peng Li the bare outlines of the story: picking up the bottle with a message inside; hiding in the trash chute; being entrusted with the errand in Second Space; making his decision and coming here for guidance. He had so little time, he stressed, that he had to leave right away.

"You hid in the trash chutes last night to sneak into Second Space?" Peng Li frowned. "That means you had to wait twenty-four hours!"

"For two hundred thousand yuan?" Lao Dao said. "Even hiding for a week would be worth it."

"I didn't know you were so short on money."

Lao Dao was silent for a moment. "Tangtang is going to be old enough for kindergarten in a year. I've run out of time."

Lao Dao's research on kindergarten tuition had shocked him. For schools with decent reputations, the parents had to show up with their bedrolls to line up a couple of days before registration. The two parents had to take turns so that while one held their place in the line, the other could go to the bathroom or grab a bite to eat. Even after lining up for forty-plus hours, a place wasn't guaranteed. Those with enough money had already bought up most of the openings for their offspring, so the poorer parents had to endure the line, hoping to grab one of the few remaining spots. Mind you, this was just for decent schools. The really good schools? Forget about lining up—every opportunity was sold off to those with money.

Lao Dao didn't harbor unrealistic hopes, but Tangtang had loved music since she was an eighteen-month-old. Every time she heard music in the streets, her face lit up, and she twisted her little body and waved her arms about in a dance. She looked especially cute during those moments. Lao Dao was as dazzled as though she were surrounded by stage lights. No matter how much it cost, he vowed to send Tangtang to a kindergarten that offered music and dance lessons.

Peng Li took off his shirt and washed while he spoke with Lao Dao. The "washing" consisted only of splashing some drops of water over his face because the water was already shut off, and only a thin trickle came out of the faucet. Peng Li took down a dirty towel from the wall and wiped his face carelessly before stuffing the towel into a drawer as well. His moist hair gave off an oily glint.

"What are you working so hard for?" Peng Li asked. "It's not like she's your real daughter."

"I don't have time for this," Lao Dao said. "Just tell me the way."

Peng Li sighed. "Do you understand that if you're caught, it's not just a matter of paying a fine? You're going to be locked up for months."

"I thought you had gone there multiple times."

"Just four times. I got caught the fifth time."

"That's more than enough. If I could make it four times, it would be no big deal to get caught once."

Lao Dao's errand required him to deliver a message to First Space—success would earn him a hundred thousand yuan, and if he managed to bring back a reply, two hundred thousand. Sure, it was illegal, but no one would be harmed, and as long as he followed the right route and method, the probability of being caught wasn't great. And the cash—the cash was very real. He could think of no reason not to take the offer. He knew that when Peng Li was younger, he had snuck into First Space multiple times to smuggle contraband and made quite a fortune. There was a way.

It was a quarter to six. Lao Dao had to get going—now.

Peng Li sighed again. He could see it was useless to try to dissuade Lao Dao. He was old enough to feel lazy and tired of everything, but he remembered how he had felt as a younger man, and he would have made the same choice as Lao Dao. Back then, he didn't care about going to prison. What was the big deal? You lost a few months and got beaten up a few times, but the money made it worthwhile. As long as you refused to divulge the source of the money no matter how much you suffered, you could survive it. The Security Bureau's citation was nothing more than routine enforcement.

Peng Li took Lao Dao to his back window and pointed at the narrow path hidden in the shadows below.

"Start by climbing down the drainpipe from my unit. Under the felt cloth you'll find the hidden footholds I installed back in the day—if you stick close enough to the wall, the cameras won't see you. Once you're on the ground, stick to the shadows and head that way until you get to the edge. You'll feel as well as see the cleft. Follow the cleft and go north. Remember, go north."

Then Peng Li explained the technique for entering First Space as the ground turned during the Change. He had to wait until the ground began to cleave and rise. Then, from the elevated edge, he had to swing over and scramble about fifty meters over the cross section until he reached the other side of the turning earth, climb over, and head east. There he would find a bush that he could hold on to as the ground descended and closed up. He could then conceal himself in the bush.

Before Peng had even finished his explanation, Lao Dao was already halfway out the window, getting ready to climb down.

Peng Li held on to Lao Dao and made sure his foot was securely in the first foothold. Then he stopped. "I'm going to say something that you might not want to hear. I don't think you should go. Over there . . . is not so great. If you go, you'll end up feeling your own life is shit, pointless."

Lao Dao was reaching down with his other foot, testing for the next foothold. His body strained against the windowsill, and his words came out labored. "It doesn't matter. I already know my life is shit without having gone there."

"Take care of yourself," Peng Li said.

Lao Dao followed Peng Li's directions and groped his way down as quickly as he dared; the footholds felt very secure. He looked up and saw Peng Li light up a cigarette next to the window, taking deep drags. Peng Li put out the cigarette, leaned out, and seemed about to say something more, but ultimately he retreated back into his unit quietly. He closed his window, which glowed with a faint light.

Lao Dao imagined Peng Li crawling into his cocoon-bed at the last minute, right before the Change. Like millions of others across the city, the cocoon-bed would release a soporific gas that put him into a deep sleep. He would feel nothing as his body was transported by the flipping world, and he would not open his eyes again until tomorrow evening, forty hours later. Peng Li was no longer young; he was no longer different from the other fifty million who lived in Third Space.

Lao Dao climbed faster, barely touching the footholds. When he was close enough to the ground, he let go and landed on all fours. Luckily, Peng Li's unit was only on the fourth story, not too far up. He got up and ran through the shadow cast by the building next to the lake. He saw the crevice in the grass where the ground would open up.

But before he reached it, he heard the muffled rumbling from behind him, interrupted by a few crisp *clangs*. Lao Dao turned around and saw Peng Li's building break in half. The top half folded down and pressed toward him, slowly but inexorably.

Shocked, Lao Dao stared at the sight for a few moments before recovering. He raced to the fissure in the ground and lay prostrate next to it.

The Change began. This was a process repeated every twenty-four hours. The whole world started to turn. The sound of steel and masonry folding, grating, colliding filled the air, like an assembly line grinding to a halt. The towering buildings of the city gathered and merged into solid blocks; neon signs, shop awnings, balconies, and other protruding fixtures retracted into the buildings or flattened themselves into a thin layer against the walls, like skin. Every inch of space was utilized as the buildings compacted themselves into the smallest space.

The ground rose up. Lao Dao watched and waited until the fissure was wide enough. He crawled over the marble-lined edge onto the earthen wall, grabbing bits of metal protruding out of the soil. As the cleft widened and the walls elevated, he climbed, using his hands as well as his feet. At first, he was climbing down, testing for purchase with his feet. But soon, as the entire section of ground rotated, he was lifted into the air and flipped around.

Lao Dao was thinking about last night.

He had cautiously stuck his head out of the trash heap, alert for any sound from the other side of the gate. The fermenting, rotting garbage around him was pungent: greasy, fishy, even a bit sweet. He leaned against the iron gate. Outside, the world was waking up.

As soon as the yellow glow of the streetlights seeped into the seam under the lifting gate, he squatted and crawled out of the widening opening. The streets were empty; lights came on in the tall buildings, story by story; fixtures extruded from the sides of buildings, unfolding and extending segment by segment; porches emerged from the walls; the eaves rotated and gradually dropped down into position; stairs stretched out and descended to the street. On both sides of the road, one black cube after another broke apart and opened, revealing the racks and shelves inside. Signboards appeared from the tops of the cubes and connected together while plastic awnings extended from both sides of the lane to meet in the middle, forming a corridor of shops. The streets were empty, as though Lao Dao was dreaming.

The neon lights came on. Tiny flashing LEDs on top of the shops formed into characters advertising jujubes from Xinjiang, *lapi* noodles from Northeast China, bran dough from Shanghai, and cured meats from Hunan.

For the rest of the day, Lao Dao couldn't forget the scene. He had lived in this city for forty-eight years, but he had never seen such a sight. His days had always started with the cocoon and ended with the cocoon, and the time in between was spent at work or navigating dirty tables at hawker stalls and loudly bargaining crowds surrounding street vendors. This was the first time he had seen the world bare.

Every morning an observer at some distance from the city—say, a truck driver waiting on the highway into Beijing—could see the entire city fold and unfold.

At six in the morning, the truck drivers usually got out of their cabs and walked to the side of the highway, where they rubbed their eyes, still drowsy after an uncomfortable night in the truck. Yawning, they greeted one another and gazed at the distant city center. The break in the highway was just outside the Seventh Ring Road, while all the ground rotation occurred within the Sixth Ring Road. The distance was perfect for taking in the whole city, like gazing at an island in the sea.

In the early dawn, the city folded and collapsed. The skyscrapers bowed submissively like the humblest servants until their heads touched their feet; then they broke again, folded again, and twisted their necks and arms, stuffing them into the gaps. The compacted blocks that used to be the skyscrapers shuffled and assembled into dense, gigantic Rubik's Cubes that fell into a deep slumber.

The ground then began to turn. Square by square, pieces of the earth flipped 180 degrees around an axis, revealing the buildings on the other side. The buildings unfolded and stood up, awakening like a herd of beasts under the gray-blue sky. The island that was the city settled in the orange sunlight, spread open, and stood still as misty gray clouds roiled around it.

The truck drivers, tired and hungry, admired the endless cycle of urban renewal.

2.

The folding city was divided into three spaces. One side of the earth was First Space, population five million. Its allotted time lasted from six o'clock in the morning to six o'clock the next morning. Then the space went to sleep, and the earth flipped.

The other side was shared by Second Space and Third Space. Twenty-five million people lived in Second Space, and their allotted time lasted from six o'clock on that second day to ten o'clock at night. Fifty million people lived in Third Space, allotted the time from ten o'clock at night to six o'clock in the morning, at which point First Space returned. Time had been carefully divided and parceled out to separate the populations: five million enjoyed the use of twenty-four hours, and seventy-five million enjoyed the next twenty-four hours.

The structures on two sides of the ground were not even in weight. To remedy the imbalance, the earth was made thicker in First Space and extra ballast buried in the soil to make up for the missing people and buildings. The residents of First Space considered the extra soil a natural emblem of their possession of a richer, deeper heritage.

Lao Dao had lived in Third Space since birth. He understood very well the reality of his situation, even without Peng Li pointing it out. He was a waste worker; he had processed trash for twenty-eight years and would do so for the foreseeable future. He had not found the meaning of his existence or the ultimate refuge of cynicism; instead, he continued to hold on to the humble place assigned to him in life.

Lao Dao had been born in Beijing. His father was also a waste worker. His father told him that when Lao Dao was born, his father had just gotten his job, and the family had celebrated for three whole days. His father had been a construction worker, one of millions of other construction workers who had come to Beijing from all over China in search of work. His father and others like him had built this folding city. District by district, they had transformed the old city. Like termites swarming over a wooden house, they had chewed up the wreckage of the past, overturned the earth, and constructed a brand-new world. They had swung their hammers and wielded their adzes, keeping their heads down; brick by brick, they had walled themselves off until they could no longer see the sky. Dust had obscured their views, and they had not known the grandeur of their work. Finally, when the completed building stood up before them like a living person, they had scattered in terror as though they had given birth to a monster.

But after they calmed down, the workers realized what an honor it would be to live in such a city in the future, and so they had continued to toil diligently and docilely, to meekly seek out any opportunity to remain in the city. It was said that when the folding city was completed, more than eighty million construction workers had wanted to stay. Ultimately, no more than twenty million were allowed to settle.

It had not been easy to get a job at the waste-processing station. Although the work only involved sorting trash, so many hopefuls applied that stringent selection criteria had to be imposed: the desired candidates had to be strong, skillful, discerning, organized, diligent, and unafraid of the stench or difficult environment. Strong willed, Lao Dao's father had held fast to the thin reed of opportunity as the tide of humanity surged and then receded around him until at last he found himself a survivor on the dry beach.

His father had then kept his own head down and labored away in the acidic rotten fetor of garbage and crowding for twenty years. He had built this city; he was also a resident and a decomposer.

Construction of the folding city had been completed two years before Lao Dao's birth. He had never been anywhere else, and had never harbored the desire to go anywhere else. He finished elementary school, middle school, high school, and took the annual college entrance examination three times—failing each time. In the end, he became a waste worker, too. At the waste-processing station, he worked for five hours each shift, from eleven at night to four in the morning. Together with tens of thousands of coworkers, he mechanically and quickly sorted through the trash, picking out recyclable bits from the scraps of life from First Space and Second Space and tossing them into the processing furnace. Every day, he faced the trash on the conveyer belt flowing past him like a river, and he scraped off the leftover food from plastic bowls, picked out broken glass bottles, tore off the clean backing from blood-stained sanitary napkins and stuffed it into the recyclables can marked with green lines. This was their lot: to eke out a living by performing the repetitive drudgery as fast as possible, to toil hour after hour for rewards as thin as the wings of cicadas.

Twenty million waste workers lived in Third Space; they were the masters of the night. The other thirty million made a living by selling clothes, food, fuel, or insurance, but most people understood that the waste workers were the backbone of Third Space's prosperity. Each time he strolled through the neon-bedecked night streets, Lao Dao thought he was walking under rainbows made of food scraps. He couldn't talk about this feeling with others. The younger generation looked down on the profession of the waste worker. They tried to show off on the dance floors of nightclubs, hoping to find jobs as DJs or dancers. Even working at a clothing store seemed a better choice: their fingers would be touching thin fabric instead of scrabbling through rotting garbage for plastic or metal. The young were no longer so terrified about survival; they cared far more about appearances.

Lao Dao didn't despise his work. But when he had gone to Second Space, he had been terrified of being despised.

※

The previous morning, Lao Dao had snuck his way out of the trash chute with a slip of paper and tried to find the author of the slip using the address written on it.

Second Space wasn't far from Third Space. They were located on the same side of the ground, though they were divided in time. At the Change, the buildings of one space folded and retracted into the ground as the buildings of another space extended into the air, segment by segment, using the tops of the buildings of the other space as its foundation. The only difference between the spaces was the density of buildings. Lao Dao had to wait a full day and night inside the trash chute for the opportunity to emerge as Second Space unfolded. Although this was the first time he had been to Second Space, he wasn't anxious. He only worried about the rotting smell on him.

Luckily, Qin Tian was a generous soul. Perhaps he had been prepared for what sort of person would show up since the moment he put that slip of paper inside the bottle.

He knew at a glance why Lao Dao had come. He pulled Lao Dao inside his home, offered him a hot bath, and gave him one of his own bathrobes to wear. "I have to count on you," Qin Tian said.

Qin was a graduate student living in a university-owned apartment. He had three roommates, and besides the four bedrooms, the apartment had a kitchen and two bathrooms. Lao Dao had never taken a bath in such a spacious bathroom, and he really wanted to soak for a while and get rid of the smell on his body. But he was also afraid of getting the bathtub dirty and didn't dare to rub his skin too hard with the washcloth. The jets of bubbles coming out of the bathtub walls startled him, and being dried by hot jets of air made him uncomfortable.

After the bath, he picked up the bathrobe from Qin Tian and only put it on after hesitating for a while. He laundered his own clothes as well as a few other shirts casually left in a basin. Business was business, and he didn't want to owe anyone any favors.

Qin Tian wanted to send a gift to a woman he liked. They had gotten to know each other from work when Qin Tian had been given the opportunity to go to First Space for an internship with the UN Economic Office, where she was also working. The internship had lasted only a month. Qin told Lao Dao that the young woman was born and bred in First Space by very strict parents. Her father wouldn't allow her to date a boy from Second Space, and that was why he couldn't contact her through regular channels. Qin was optimistic about the future; he was going to apply to the UN's New Youth Project after graduation, and if he was to be chosen, he would be able to go to work in First Space. He still had another year of school left before he would get his degree, but he was going crazy pining for her. He had made a rose-shaped locket for her that glowed in the dark; this was the gift he would use to ask for her hand in marriage.

"I was attending a symposium, you know, the one that discussed the UN's debt situation? You must have heard of it. . . . Anyway, I saw her, and I was like, *Ah!* . . . I went over right away to talk to her. She was helping the VIPs to their seats, and I didn't know what to say, so I just followed her around. Finally I pretended that I had to find interpreters, and I asked her to help me. She was so gentle, and her voice was really soft. I had never really asked a girl out, you understand, so I was super nervous . . . Later, after we started dating, I brought up how we met . . . Why are you laughing? . . . Yes, we dated. . . . No, I don't think we quite got to that kind of relationship, but . . . well, we kissed." Qin Tian laughed as well, a bit embarrassed. "I'm telling the truth! Don't you believe me? Yes, I guess sometimes even I can't believe it. Do you think she really likes me?"

"I have no idea," Lao Dao said. "I've never met her."

One of Qin Tian's roommates came over and, smiling, said, "Uncle, why are you taking his question so seriously? That's not a real question. He just wants to hear you say, 'Of course she loves you! You're so handsome.'"

"She must be beautiful."

"I'm not afraid that you'll laugh at me." Qin Tian paced back and forth in front of Lao Dao. "When you see her, you'll understand the meaning of 'peerless elegance.'"

Qin Tian stopped, sinking into a reverie. He was thinking of Yi Yan's mouth. Her mouth was perhaps his favorite part of her: so tiny, so soft, with a full bottom lip that glowed with a natural, healthy pink, making him want to give it a loving bite. Her neck also aroused him. Sometimes it appeared so thin that the tendons showed, but the lines were straight and pretty. The skin was fair and smooth, extending down into the collar of her blouse so that his gaze lingered on her second button. The first time he tried to kiss her, she had moved her lips away shyly. He had persisted until she gave in, closing her eyes and returning the kiss. Her lips had felt so warm, and his hands had caressed the curve of her waist and backside again and again. From that day on, he had lived in the country of longing. She was his dream at night, and also the light he saw when he trembled in his own hand.

Qin Tian's roommate was called Zhang Xian, who seemed to relish the opportunity to converse with Lao Dao.

Zhang Xian asked Lao Dao about life in Third Space, and mentioned that he actually wanted to live in Third Space for a while. He had been given the advice that if he wanted to climb up the ladder of government administration, some managerial experience in Third Space would be very helpful. Several prominent officials had all started their careers as Third Space administrators before being promoted to First Space. If they had stayed in Second Space, they wouldn't have gone anywhere and would have spent the rest of their careers as low-level administrative cadres. Zhang Xian's ambition was to eventually enter government service, and he was certain he knew the right path. Still, he wanted to go work at a bank for a couple of years first and earn some quick money. Since Lao Dao seemed noncommittal about his plans, Zhang Xian thought Lao Dao disapproved of his careerism.

"The current government is too inefficient and ossified," he added quickly, "slow to respond to challenges, and I don't see much hope for systematic reform. When I get my opportunity, I'll push for rapid reforms: anyone who's incompetent will be fired." Since Lao Dao still didn't seem to show much reaction, he said, "I'll also work to expand the pool of candidates for government service and promotion, including opening up opportunities for candidates from Third Space."

Lao Dao said nothing. It wasn't because he disapproved; rather, he found it hard to believe Zhang Xian.

While he talked with Lao Dao, Zhang Xian was also putting on a tie and fixing his hair in front of the mirror. He had on a shirt with light blue stripes, and the tie was a bright blue. He closed his eyes and frowned as the mist of hairspray settled around his face, whistling all the while.

Zhang Xian left with his briefcase for his internship at the bank. Qin Tian said he had to get going as well since he had classes that would last until four in the afternoon. Before he left, he transferred fifty thousand yuan over the net to Lao Dao's account while Lao Dao watched, and explained that he would transfer the rest after Lao Dao succeeded in his mission.

"Have you been saving up for this for a while?" Lao Dao asked. "You're a student, so money is probably tight. I can accept less if necessary."

"Don't worry about it. I'm on a paid internship with a financial advisory firm. They pay me around a hundred thousand each month, so the total I'm promising you is about two months of my salary. I can afford it."

Lao Dao said nothing. He earned the standard salary of ten thousand each month.

"Please bring back her answer," Qin Tian said.

"I'll do my best."

"Help yourself to the fridge if you get hungry. Just stay put here and wait for the Change."

Lao Dao looked outside the window. He couldn't get used to the sunlight, which was a bright white, not the yellow he was used to. The street seemed twice as wide in the sun as what Lao Dao remembered from Third Space, and he wasn't sure if that was a visual illusion. The buildings here weren't nearly as tall as buildings in Third Space. The sidewalks were filled with people walking very fast, and from time to time some trotted and tried to shove their way through the crowd, causing those in front of them to begin running as well. Everyone seemed to run across intersections. The men dressed mostly in Western suits while the women wore blouses and short skirts with scarves around their necks and compact, rigid purses in their hands that lent them an air of competence and efficiency. The street teemed with cars, and as they waited at intersections for the light to change, the drivers stuck their heads out of the windows, gazing anxiously ahead. Lao Dao had never seen so many cars; he was used to the mass-transit maglev packed with passengers whooshing by him.

Around noon, he heard noises in the hallway outside the apartment. He peeked through the peephole in the door. The floor of the hallway had transformed into a moving conveyor belt, and bags of trash left at the door of each apartment were shoved onto the conveyor belt to be deposited into the chute at the end. Mist filled the hall, turning into soap bubbles that drifted through the air, and then water washed the floor, followed by hot steam.

A noise from behind Lao Dao startled him. He turned around and saw that another of Lao Dao's roommates had emerged from his bedroom. The young man ignored Lao Dao, his face impassive. He went to some machine next to the balcony and pushed some buttons, and the machine came to life, popping, whirring, grinding. Eventually, the noise stopped, and Lao Dao smelled something delicious. The young man took out a piping hot plate of food from the machine and returned to his room. Through the half-open bedroom door, Lao Dao could see that the young man was sitting on the floor in a pile of blankets and dirty socks and stared at his wall as he ate and laughed, pushing up his glasses from time to time. After he was done eating, he left the plate at his feet, stood up, and began to fight someone invisible as he faced the wall. He struggled, his breathing labored, as he wrestled the unseen enemy.

Lao Dao's last memory of Second Space was the refined air with which everyone conducted themselves before the Change. As he looked down from the window of the apartment, everything seemed so orderly that he felt a hint of envy. Starting at a quarter past nine, the stores along the street turned off their lights one after another; groups of friends, their faces red with drink, said good-bye in front of restaurants.

Young couples kissed next to taxicabs. And then everyone returned to their homes, and the world went to sleep.

It was ten at night. He returned to his world to go to work.

3.

There was no trash chute connecting First Space directly with Third Space. The trash from First Space had to pass through a set of metal gates to be transported into Third Space, and the gates shut as soon as the trash went through. Lao Dao didn't like the idea of having to go over the flipping ground, but he had no choice.

As the wind whipped around him, he crawled up the still-rotating earth toward First Space. He grabbed on to metal structural elements protruding from the soil, struggling to balance his body and calm his heart, until he finally managed to scrabble over the rim of this most distant world. He felt dizzy and nauseated from the intense climb, and, forcing down his churning stomach, he remained still on the ground for a while.

By the time he got up, the sun had risen.

Lao Dao had never seen such a sight. The sun rose gradually. The sky was a deep and pure azure, with an orange fringe at the horizon, decorated with thin, slanted wisps of cloud. The eaves of a nearby building blocked the sun, and the eaves appeared especially dark while the background was dazzlingly bright. As the sun continued to rise, the blue of the sky faded a little, but seemed even more tranquil and clear. Lao Dao stood up and ran at the sun; he wanted to catch a trace of that fading golden color. Silhouettes of waving tree branches broke up the sky. His heart leapt wildly. He had never imagined that a sunrise could be so moving.

After a while, he slowed down and calmed himself. He was standing in the middle of the street, which was lined on both sides with tall trees and wide lawns. He looked around, and he couldn't see any buildings at all. Confused, he wondered if he had really reached First Space. He pondered the two rows of sturdy ginkgoes.

He backed up a few steps and turned to look in the direction he had come from. There was a road sign next to the street. He took out his phone and looked at the map—although he wasn't authorized to download live maps from First Space, he had downloaded and stored some before leaving on this trip. He found where he was as well as where he needed to be: he was standing next to a large open park, and the seam he had emerged from was next to a lake in that park.

Lao Dao ran about a kilometer through the deserted streets until he reached the residential district containing his destination. Hiding behind some bushes, he observed the beautiful house from a distance.

❋

At eight thirty, Yi Yan came out of the house.

She was indeed as elegant as Qin Tian's description had suggested, though perhaps not as pretty. Lao Dao wasn't surprised, however. No woman could possibly be as beautiful as Qin Tian's verbal portrait. He also understood why Qin Tian had spoken so much of her mouth. Her eyes and nose were fairly ordinary. She had a good figure: tall, with delicate bones. She wore a milky white dress with a flowing skirt. Her belt was studded with pearls, and she had on black heels.

Lao Dao walked up to her. To avoid startling her, he approached from the front, and bowed deeply when he was still some distance away.

She stood still, looking at him in surprise.

Lao Dao came closer and explained his mission. He took out the envelope with the locket and Qin Tian's letter.

She looked alarmed. "Please leave," she whispered. "I can't talk to you right now."

"Uh . . . I don't really need to talk to you," Lao Dao said. "I just need to give you this letter."

She refused to take it from him, clasping her hands tightly. "I can't accept this now. Please leave. Really, I'm begging you. All right?" She took out a business card from her purse and handed it to him. "Come find me at this address at noon."

Lao Dao looked at the card. At the top was the name of a bank.

"At noon," she said. "Wait for me in the underground super-market."

Lao Dao could tell how anxious she was. He nodded, put the card away, and returned to hide behind the bushes. Soon a man emerged from the house and stopped next to her. The man looked to be about Lao Dao's age, or maybe a couple of years younger. Dressed in a well-fitted dark gray suit, he was tall and broad-shouldered. Not fat, just thickset. His face was nondescript: round, a pair of glasses, hair neatly combed to one side.

The man grabbed Yi Yan around the waist and kissed her on the lips. Yi Yan seemed to give in to the kiss reluctantly.

Understanding began to dawn on Lao Dao.

A single-rider cart arrived in front of the house. The black cart had two wheels and a canopy, and resembled an ancient carriage or rick-shaw one might see on TV, except there was no horse or person pull-ing the cart. The cart stopped and dipped forward. Yi Yan stepped in, sat down, and arranged the skirt of the dress neatly around her knees. The cart straightened and began to move at a slow, steady pace, as though pulled by some invisible horse. After Yi Yan left, a driverless car arrived, and the man got in.

Lao Dao paced in place. He felt something pushing at his throat, but he couldn't articulate it. Standing in the sun, he closed his eyes and inhaled. The clean, fresh air filled his lungs and provided some mea-sure of comfort.

A moment later, he was on his way. The address Yi Yan had given him was to the east, a little more than three kilometers away. There were very few people in the pedestrian lane, and only scattered cars sped by in a blur on the eight-lane avenue. Occasionally, well-dressed women passed Lao Dao in two-wheeled carts. The passengers adopted such graceful postures that it was as though they were in some fash-ion show. No one paid any attention to Lao Dao. The trees swayed in the breeze, and the air in their shade seemed suffused with the per-fume from the elegant women.

Yi Yan's office was in the Xidan commercial district. There were no skyscrapers at all, only a few low buildings scattered around a large park. The buildings seemed isolated from one another but were really parts of a single compound connected via underground passages.

Lao Dao found the supermarket. He was early. As soon as he came in, a small shopping cart began to follow him around. Every time he stopped by a shelf, the screen on the cart displayed the names of the goods on the shelf, their descriptions, customer reviews, and comparisons with other brands in the same category. All the merchandise in the supermarket seemed to be labeled in foreign languages. The packaging for all the food products was very refined, and small cakes and fruits were enticingly arranged on plates for customers.

There seemed to be no guards or clerks in the whole market, but Lao Dao didn't dare to touch anything, keeping his distance as though everything were a dangerous, exotic animal.

More customers appeared before noon. Some men in suits came into the market, grabbed sandwiches, and waved them at the scanner next to the door before hurrying out. Like on the street, no one paid any attention to Lao Dao as he waited in an obscure corner near the door.

Yi Yan appeared, and Lao Dao went up to her. Yi Yan glanced around and, without saying anything, led Lao Dao to a small restaurant next door. Two small robots dressed in plaid skirts greeted them, took Yi Yan's purse, brought them to a booth, and handed them menus. Yi Yan pressed a few spots on the menu to make her selection and handed the menu back to the robot. The robot turned and glided smoothly on its wheels to the back.

Yi Yan and Lao Dao sat mutely across from each other. Lao Dao pulled out the envelope.

Yi Yan still didn't take it from him. "Can you let me explain?"

Lao Dao pushed the envelope across the table. "Please take this first."

Yi Yan pushed it back. "Can you let me explain first?"

"You don't need to explain anything," Lao Dao said. "I didn't write this letter. I'm just the messenger."

"But you have to go back and give him an answer." Yi Yan looked down. The little robot returned with two plates, one for each of them. On each plate were two slices of some kind of red sashimi, arranged like flower petals. Yi Yan didn't pick up her chopsticks, and neither did Lao Dao. The envelope rested between the two plates, and neither touched it. "I didn't betray him," Yi Yan said. "When I met him last year, I was already engaged. I didn't lie to him or conceal the truth from him on purpose. . . . Well, maybe I did lie, but it was because he assumed and guessed. He saw Wu Wen come to pick me up once, and asked me if he was my father. I . . . I couldn't answer him, you know? It was just too embarrassing. I . . ."

Yi Yan couldn't speak anymore.

Lao Dao waited awhile before replying. "I'm not interested in what happened between you two. All I care about is that you take the letter."

Yi Yan kept her head down, and then she looked up. "After you go back, can you . . . help me by not telling him everything?"

"Why?"

"I don't want him to think that I was just playing with his feelings. I do like him, really. I feel very conflicted."

"None of this is my concern."

"Please, I'm begging you . . . I really do like him."

Lao Dao was silent for a minute. "But you got married in the end?"

"Wu Wen was very good to me. We'd been together several years. He knew my parents, and we'd been engaged for a long time. Also . . . I'm three years older than Qin Tian, and I was afraid he wouldn't like that. Qin Tian thought I was an intern, like him, and I admit that was my fault for not telling him the truth. I don't know why I said I was an intern at first, and then it became harder and harder to correct him. I never thought he would be serious."

Slowly Yi Yan told Lao Dao her story. She was actually an assistant to the bank's president and had already been working there for two years at the time she met Qin Tian. She had been sent to the UN for training and was helping out at the symposium. In fact, her husband earned so much money that she didn't really need to work, but she didn't like the idea of being at home all day. She worked only half days and took a half-time salary. The rest of the day was hers to do with as she pleased, and she liked learning new things and meeting new people. She really had enjoyed the months she spent training at the UN. She told Lao Dao that there were many wives like her who worked half time. As a matter of fact, after she got off work at noon, another wealthy wife worked as the president's assistant in the afternoon. She told Lao Dao that, though she had not told Qin Tian the truth, her heart was honest.

"And so"—she spooned a serving of the new hot dish onto Lao Dao's plate—"can you please not tell him, just temporarily? Please . . . give me a chance to explain to him myself."

Lao Dao didn't pick up his chopsticks. He was very hungry, but he felt that he could not eat this food. "Then I'd be lying, too," Lao Dao said.

Yi Yan opened her purse, took out her wallet, and retrieved five ten-thousand-yuan bills. She pushed them across the table toward Lao Dao. "Please accept this token of my appreciation."

Lao Dao was stunned. He had never seen bills with such large denominations or needed to use them. Almost subconsciously he stood up, angry. The way Yi Yan had taken out the money seemed to suggest that she had been anticipating an attempt from him to blackmail her, and he could not accept that. *This is what they think of Third Spacers.*

He felt that if he took her money, he would be selling Qin Tian out. It was true that he really wasn't Qin Tian's friend, but he still thought of it as a kind of betrayal. Lao Dao wanted to grab the bills, throw them on the ground, and walk away. But he couldn't. He looked at the money again: the five thin notes were spread on the table like a broken fan. He could sense the power they had over him. They were baby blue in color, distinct from the brown thousand-yuan note and the red hundred-yuan note. These bills looked deeper, most distant somehow, like a kind of seduction. Several times he wanted to stop looking at them and leave, but he couldn't.

Yi Yan continued to rummage through her purse, taking everything out until she finally found another fifty thousand yuan from an inner pocket and placed them together with the other bills. "This is all I have. Please take it and help me." She paused. "Look, the reason I don't want him to know is because I'm not sure what I'm going to do. It's possible that someday I'll have the courage to be with him."

Lao Dao looked at the ten notes spread out on the table, and then looked up at her. He sensed that she didn't believe what she was saying. Her voice was hesitant, belying her words. She was just delaying everything to the future so that she wouldn't be embarrassed now. She was unlikely to ever elope with Qin Tian, but she also didn't want him to despise her. Thus, she wanted to keep alive the *possibility* so she could feel better about herself.

Lao Dao could see that she was lying to herself, but he wanted to lie to himself, too. He told himself, *I have no duty to Qin Tian. All he asked was for me to deliver his message to her, and I've done that. The money on the table now represents a new commission, a commitment to keep a secret.* He waited, and then told himself, *Perhaps someday she really will get together with Qin Tian, and in that case I'll have done a good deed by keeping silent. Besides, I need to think about Tangtang. Why should I get myself all worked up about strangers instead of thinking about Tangtang's welfare?*

He felt calmer and realized that his fingers were already touching the money. "This is . . . too much." He wanted to make himself feel better. "I can't accept so much."

"It's no big deal." She stuffed the bills into his hand. "I earn this much in a week. Don't worry."

"What . . . what do you want me to tell him?"

"Tell him that I can't be with him right now, but I truly like him. I'll write you a note to bring him." Yi Yan found a notepad in her purse; it had a picture of a peacock on the cover, and the edges of the pages were golden. She ripped out a page and began to write. Her handwriting looked like a string of slanted gourds.

As Lao Dao left the restaurant, he glanced back. Yi Yan was still sitting in the booth, gazing up at a painting on the wall. She looked so elegant and refined, as though she were never going to leave.

He squeezed the bills in his pocket. He despised himself, but he wanted to hold on to the money.

4.

Lao Dao left Xidan and returned the way he had come. He felt exhausted. The pedestrian lane was lined with a row of weeping willows on one side and a row of Chinese parasol trees on the other side. It was late spring, and everything was a lush green. The afternoon sun warmed his stiff face and brightened his empty heart.

He was back at the park from this morning. There were many people in the park now, and the two rows of ginkgoes looked stately and luscious. Black cars entered the park from time to time, and most of the people in the park wore either well-fitted Western suits made of quality fabric or stylish, dark-colored Chinese suits, but everyone gave off a haughty air. There were also some foreigners. Some of the people conversed in small groups; others greeted one another at a distance, and then laughed as they got close enough to shake hands and walk together.

Lao Dao hesitated, trying to decide where to go. There weren't that many people in the street, and he would draw attention if he just stood here. But he would look out of place in any public area. He wanted to go back into the park, get close to the fissure, and hide in some corner to take a nap. He felt very sleepy, but he dared not sleep on the street.

He noticed the cars entering the park didn't seem to need to stop, and so he tried to walk into the park as well. Only when he was close to the gate did he realize that two robots were patrolling the area. While cars and other pedestrians passed their sentry line with no problems, the robots beeped as soon as Lao Dao approached and turned on their wheels to head for him. In the tranquil afternoon, the noise they made seemed especially loud. The eyes of everyone nearby turned to him.

Lao Dao panicked, uncertain if it was his shabby clothes that alerted the robots. He tried to whisper to the robots, claiming that his suit was left inside the park, but the robots ignored him while they continued to beep and flash the red lights over their heads. People strolling inside the park stopped and looked at him as though looking at a thief or eccentric person. Soon three men emerged from a nearby building and ran over. Lao Dao's heart was in his throat. He wanted to run, but it was too late.

"What's going on?" the man in the lead asked loudly.

Lao Dao couldn't think of anything to say, and he rubbed his pants compulsively.

The man in the front was in his thirties. He came up to Lao Dao and scanned him with a silver disk about the size of a button, moving his hand around Lao Dao's person. He looked at Lao Dao suspiciously, as though trying to pry open his shell with a can opener.

"There's no record of this man." The man gestured at the older man behind him. "Bring him in."

Lao Dao started to run away from the park.

The two robots silently dashed ahead of him and grabbed his legs. Their arms were cuffs and locked easily about his ankles. He tripped and almost fell, but the robots held him up. His arms swung through the air helplessly.

"Why are you trying to run?" The younger man stepped up and glared at him. His tone was now severe.

"I . . ." Lao Dao's head felt like a droning beehive. He couldn't think.

The two robots lifted Lao Dao by the legs and deposited his feet onto platforms next to their wheels. Then they drove toward the nearest building in parallel, carrying Lao Dao. Their movements were so steady, so smooth, so synchronized, that from a distance, it appeared as if Lao Dao was skating along on a pair of Rollerblades, like Nezha riding on his Wind Fire Wheels.

Lao Dao felt utterly powerless. He was angry with himself for being so careless. How could he think such a crowded place would be without security measures? He berated himself for being so drowsy that he could commit such a stupid mistake. *It's all over now,* he thought. *Not only am I not going to get my money, I'm also going to jail.*

The robots followed a narrow path and reached the back door of the building, where they stopped. The three men followed behind. The younger man seemed to be arguing with the older man over what to do with Lao Dao, but they spoke so softly that Lao Dao couldn't hear the details. After a while, the older man came up and unlocked the robots from Lao Dao's legs. Then he grabbed Lao Dao by the arm and took him upstairs.

Lao Dao sighed. He resigned himself to his fate.

The man brought him into a room. It looked like a hotel room, very spacious, bigger even than the living room in Qin Tian's apartment, and about twice the size of his own rental unit. The room was decorated in a dark shade of golden brown, with a king-sized bed in the middle. The wall at the head of the bed showed abstract patterns of shifting colors. Translucent white curtains covered the French window, and in front of the window sat a small circular table and two comfortable chairs. Lao Dao was anxious, unsure of who the older man was and what he wanted.

"Sit, sit!" The older man clapped him on the shoulder and smiled. "Everything's fine."

Lao Dao looked at him suspiciously.

"You're from Third Space, aren't you?" The older man pulled him over to the chairs and gestured for him to sit.

Lao Dao couldn't lie. "How do you know that?"

"From your pants." The older man pointed at the waist of Lao Dao's pants. "You never even cut off the label. This brand is only sold in Third Space; I remember my mother buying them for my father when I was little."

"Sir, you're . . . ?"

"You don't need to 'sir' me. I don't think I'm much older than you are. How old *are* you? I'm fifty-two."

"Forty-eight."

"See, just older by four years." The man paused, and then added, "My name is Ge Daping. Why don't you just call me Lao Ge?"

Lao Dao relaxed a little. Lao Ge took off his jacket and moved his arms about to stretch out the stiff muscles. Then he filled a glass with hot water from a spigot in the wall and handed it to Lao Dao. He had a long face, and the corners of his eyes, the ends of his eyebrows, and his cheeks all drooped. Even his glasses seemed about to fall off the end of his nose. His hair was naturally a bit curly and had been piled loosely on top of his head. As he spoke, his eyebrows bounced up and down comically. He made some tea for himself and asked Lao Dao if he wanted any. Lao Dao shook his head.

"I was originally from Third Space as well," said Lao Ge. "We're practically from the same hometown! So you don't need to be so careful with me. I still have a bit of authority, and I won't give you up."

Lao Dao let out a long sigh, congratulating himself silently for his good luck. He recounted for Lao Ge his experiencing of going to Second Space and then coming to First Space, but omitted the details of what Yi Yan had said. He simply told Lao Ge that he had successfully delivered the message and was just waiting for the Change before heading home.

Lao Ge also shared his own story with Lao Dao. He had grown up in Third Space, and his parents had worked as deliverymen. When he was fifteen, he entered a military school, and then joined the army. He served as a radar technician in the army, and because he worked hard, demonstrated good technical skills, and had some good opportunities, he was eventually promoted to an administrative position in the radar department with the rank of brigadier general. Since he didn't come from a prominent family, that was about as high as he could go in the army.

He then retired from the army and joined an agency in First Space responsible for logistical support for government enterprises, organizing meetings, arranging travel, and coordinating various social events. The job was blue collar in nature, but since his work involved government officials whose affairs he had to coordinate and manage, he was allowed to live in First Space. There were a considerable number of people in First Space like him—chefs, doctors, secretaries, housekeepers—skilled blue-collar workers needed to support the lifestyle of First Space. His agency had run many important social events and functions, and Lao Ge was its director.

Lao Ge might have been self-deprecating in describing himself as a "blue collar," but Lao Dao understood that anyone who could work and live in First Space had extraordinary skills. Even a chef here was likely a master of his art. Lao Ge must be very talented to have risen here from Third Space after a technical career in the army.

"You might as well take a nap," Lao Ge said. "I'll take you to get something to eat this evening."

Lao Dao still couldn't believe his good luck, and he felt a bit uneasy. However, he couldn't resist the call of the white sheets and stuffed pillows, and he fell asleep almost right away.

When he woke up, it was dark outside. Lao Ge was combing his hair in front of the mirror. He showed Lao Dao a suit lying on the sofa and told him to change. Then he pinned a tiny badge with a faint red glow to Lao Dao's lapel—a new identity.

The large lobby downstairs was crowded. Some kind of presentation seemed to have just finished, and attendees conversed in small groups. At one end of the lobby were the open doors leading to the banquet hall; the thick doors were lined with burgundy leather. The lobby was filled with small standing tables. Each table was covered by a white tablecloth tied around the bottom with a golden bow, and the vase in the middle of each table held a lily. Crackers and dried fruits were set out next to the vases for snacking, and a long table to the side offered wine and coffee. Guests mingled and conversed among the tables while small robots holding serving trays shuttled between their legs, collecting empty glasses.

Forcing himself to be calm, Lao Dao followed Lao Ge and walked through the convivial scene into the banquet hall. He saw a large hanging banner reading THE FOLDING CITY AT FIFTY.

"What is . . . this?" Lao Dao asked.

"A celebration!" Lao Ge was walking about and examining the

setup. "Xiao Zhao, come here a minute. I want you to check the table signs one more time. I don't trust robots for things like this. Sometimes they don't know how to be flexible."

Lao Dao saw that the banquet hall was filled with large, round tables with fresh flower centerpieces.

The scene seemed unreal to him. He stood in a corner and gazed up at the giant chandelier as though some dazzling reality was hanging over him, and he was but an insignificant presence at its periphery. There was a lectern set up on the dais at the front, and behind it, the background was an ever-shifting series of images of Beijing. The photographs were perhaps taken from an airplane and captured the entirety of the city: the soft light of dawn and dusk, the dark purple and deep blue sky, clouds racing across the sky, the moon rising from a corner, the sun setting behind a roof. The aerial shots revealed the magnificence of Beijing's ancient symmetry, the modern expanse of brick courtyards and large green parks that had extended to the Sixth Ring Road, Chinese-style theatres, Japanese-style museums, minimalist concert halls. And then there were shots of the city as a whole, shots that included both faces of the city during the Change: the earth flipping, revealing the other side studded with skyscrapers with sharp, straight contours; men and women energetically rushing to work; neon signs lighting up the night, blotting out the stars; towering apartment buildings, cinemas, nightclubs full of beautiful people.

But there were no shots of where Lao Dao worked.

He stared at the screen intently, uncertain if they might show pictures of the construction of the folding city. He hoped to get a glimpse of his father's era. When he was little, his father had often pointed to buildings outside the window and told him stories that started with, "Back then, we . . ." An old photograph had hung on the wall of their cramped home, and in the picture his father was laying bricks, a task his father had performed thousands, or perhaps hundreds of thousands of times. Lao Dao had seen that picture so many times he'd thought he was sick of it, and yet at this moment, he hoped to spot a scene of workers laying bricks, even if for just a few seconds.

He was lost in his thoughts. This was also the first time he had seen what the Change looked like from a distance. He didn't remember sitting down, and he didn't know when others had sat down next to him. A man began to speak at the lectern, but Lao Dao wasn't even listening for the first few minutes.

". . . advantageous for the development of the service sector. The service economy is dependent on population size and density. Currently the service industry of our city is responsible for more than eighty-five percent of our GDP, in line with the general characteristics of world-class metropolises. The other important sectors are the green economy and the recycling economy." Lao Dao was paying full attention now. "Green economy" and "recycling economy" were often mentioned at the waste-processing station, and the phrases were painted on the walls in characters taller than a man. He looked closer at the speaker on the dais: an old man with silvery hair, though he appeared hale and energetic. ". . . all trash is now sorted and processed, and we've achieved our goals for energy conservation and pollution reduction ahead of schedule. We've developed a systematic, large-scale recycling economy in which all the rare-earth and precious metals extracted from e-waste are reused in manufacturing, and even the plastics recycling rate exceeds eighty percent. The recycling stations are directly connected to the reprocessing plants . . ."

Lao Dao knew of a distant relative who worked at a reprocessing plant in the technopark far from the city. The technopark was just acres and acres of industrial buildings, and Lao Dao had heard that all the plants over there were very similar: the machines pretty much ran on their own, and there were very few workers. At night, when the workers got together, they felt like the last survivors of some dwindling tribe in a desolate wilderness.

He drifted off again. Only the wild applause at the end of the speech pulled him out of his chaotic thoughts and back to reality. He also applauded, though he didn't know what for. He watched the speaker descend the dais and return to his place of honor at the head table. Everyone's eyes were on him.

Lao Dao saw Wu Wen, Yi Yan's husband.

Wu Wen was at the table next to the head table. As the old man who had given the speech sat down, Wu Wen walked over to offer a toast, and then he seemed to say something that got the old man's attention. The old man got up and walked with Wu Wen out of the banquet hall.

Almost subconsciously, a curious Lao Dao also got up and followed them. He didn't know where Lao Ge had gone. Robots emerged to serve the dishes for the banquet.

Lao Dao emerged from the banquet hall and was back in the reception lobby. He eavesdropped on the other two from a distance and only caught snippets of conversation.

". . . there are many advantages to this proposal," said Wu Wen. "Yes, I've seen their equipment . . . automatic waste processing . . . they use a chemical solvent to dissolve and digest everything and then extract reusable materials in bulk . . . clean, and very economical . . . would you please give it some consideration?"

Wu Wen kept his voice low, but Lao Dao clearly heard "waste processing." He moved closer.

The old man with the silvery hair had a complex expression. Even after Wu Wen was finished, he waited awhile before speaking. "You're certain that the solvent is safe? No toxic pollution?"

Wu Wen hesitated. "The current version still generates a bit of pollution . . . but I'm sure they can reduce it to the minimum very quickly."

Lao Dao got even closer.

The old man shook his head, staring at Wu Wen. "Things aren't that simple. If I approve your project and it's implemented, there will be major consequences. Your process won't need workers, so what are you going to do with the tens of millions of people who will lose their jobs?"

The old man turned away and returned to the banquet hall. Wu Wen remained in place, stunned. A man who had been by the old man's side—a secretary, perhaps—came up to Wu Wen and said sympathetically, "You might as well go back and enjoy the meal. I'm sure you understand how this works. Employment is the number-one concern. Do you really think no one has suggested similar technology in the past?"

Lao Dao understood vaguely that what they were talking about had to do with him, but he wasn't sure whether it was good news or bad. Wu Wen's expression shifted through confusion, annoyance, and then resignation. Lao Dao suddenly felt some sympathy for him: he had his moments of weakness as well.

The secretary suddenly noticed Lao Dao. "Are you new here?" he asked.

Lao Dao was startled. "Ah? . . . Um . . ."

"What's your name? How come I wasn't informed about a new member of the staff?"

Lao Dao's heart beat wildly. He didn't know what to say. He pointed to the badge on his lapel, as though hoping the badge would speak or otherwise help him out. But the badge displayed nothing. His palms sweated. The secretary stared at him, his look growing more suspicious by the second. He grabbed another worker in the lobby, and the worker said he didn't know who Lao Dao was.

The secretary's face was now severe and dark. He grabbed Lao Dao with one hand and punched the keys on his communicator with the other hand.

Lao Dao's heart threatened to jump out of his throat, but just then, he saw Lao Ge.

Lao Ge rushed over and, with a smooth gesture, hung up the secretary's communicator. Smiling, he greeted the secretary and bowed deeply. He explained that he was shorthanded for the occasion and had to ask for a colleague from another department to help out tonight.

The secretary seemed to believe Lao Ge and returned to the banquet hall. Lao Ge brought Lao Dao back to his own room to avoid any further risks. If anyone really bothered to look into Lao Dao's identity, they'd discover the truth, and even Lao Ge wouldn't be able to protect him.

"I guess you're not fated to enjoy the banquet." Lao Ge laughed. "Just wait here. I'll get you some food later."

Lao Dao lay down on the bed and fell asleep again. He replayed the conversation between Wu Wen and the old man in his head.

Automatic waste processing. What would that look like? Would that be a good thing or bad?

The next time he woke up, he smelled something delicious. Lao Ge had set out a few dishes on the small circular table and was taking the last plate out of the warming oven on the wall. Lao Ge also brought over a half bottle of *baijiu* and filled two glasses.

"There was a table where they had only two people, and they left early, so most of the dishes weren't even touched. I brought some back. It's not much, but maybe you'll enjoy the taste. Hopefully you won't hold it against me that I'm offering you leftovers."

"Not at all," Lao Dao said. "I'm grateful that I get to eat at all. These look wonderful! They must be very expensive, right?"

"The food at the banquet is prepared by the kitchen here and not for sale, so I don't know how much it would cost in a restaurant." Lao Ge had already started to eat. "It's nothing special. If I had to guess, maybe ten thousand, twenty thousand? A couple might cost thirty, forty thousand. No more than that."

After a couple of bites, Lao Dao realized how hungry he was. He was used to skipping meals, and sometimes he could last a whole day without eating. His body would shake uncontrollably then, but he had learned to endure it. But now, the hunger was overwhelming. He wanted to chew quicker because his teeth couldn't seem to catch up to the demands of his empty stomach. He tried to wash the food down with *baijiu*, which was very fragrant and didn't sting his throat at all.

Lao Ge ate leisurely and smiled as he watched Lao Dao eat.

"Oh." Now that the pangs of hunger had finally been dulled a bit, Lao Dao remembered the earlier conversation. "Who was the man giving the speech? He seemed a bit familiar."

"He's always on TV," Lao Ge said. "That's my boss. He's a man with real power—in charge of everything having to do with city operations."

"They were talking about automatic waste processing earlier. Do you think they'll really do it?"

"Hard to say." Lao Ge sipped the *baijiu* and let out a burp. "I suspect not. You have to understand why they went with manual processing in the first place. Back then, the situation here was similar to Europe at the end of the twentieth century. The economy was growing, but so was unemployment. Printing money didn't solve the problem. The economy refused to obey the Phillips curve."

He saw that Lao Dao looked completely lost and laughed. "Never mind. You wouldn't understand these things anyway."

He clinked glasses with Lao Dao, and the two drained their *baijiu* and refilled the glasses.

"I'll just stick to unemployment. I'm sure you understand the concept," Lao Ge continued. "As the cost of labor goes up and the cost of machinery goes down, at some point, it'll be cheaper to use machines than people. With the increase in productivity, the GDP goes up, but so does unemployment. What do you do? Enact policies to protect the workers? Better welfare? The more you try to protect workers, the more you increase the cost of labor and make it less attractive for employers to hire people. If you go outside the city now to the industrial districts, there's almost no one working in those factories. It's the same thing with farming. Large commercial farms contain thousands and thousands of acres of land, and everything is automated, so there's no need for people. This kind of automation is absolutely necessary if you want to grow your economy—that was how we caught up to Europe and America, remember? Scaling! The problem is, now that you've gotten the people off the land and out of the factories, what are you going to do with them? In Europe they went with the path of forcefully reducing everyone's working hours and thus increasing employment opportunities. But this saps the vitality of the economy, you understand?

"The best way is to reduce the time a certain portion of the population spends living, and then find ways to keep them busy. Do you get it? Right, shove them into the night. There's another advantage to this approach: the effects of inflation almost can't be felt at the bottom of the social pyramid. Those who can get loans and afford the interest spend all the money you print. The GDP goes up, but the cost of basic necessities does not. And most people won't even be aware of it."

Lao Dao listened, only half grasping what was being said. But he could detect something cold and cruel in Lao Ge's speech. Lao Ge's manner was still jovial, but Lao Dao could tell Lao Ge's joking tone was just an attempt to dull the edge of his words and not hurt him. Not too much.

"Yes, it sounds a bit cold," Lao Ge admitted. "But it's the truth. I'm not trying to defend this place just because I live here. But after so many years, you grow a bit numb. There are many things in life we can't change, and all we can do is to accept and endure."

Lao Dao was finally beginning to understand Lao Ge, but he didn't know what to say.

Both men became a bit drunk. They began to reminisce about the past: the foods they ate as children, schoolyard fights. Lao Ge had loved hot and sour rice noodles and stinky tofu. These were not available in First Space, and he missed them dearly. Lao Ge talked about his parents, who still lived in Third Space. He couldn't visit them often because each trip required him to apply and obtain special approval, which was very burdensome. He mentioned that there were some officially sanctioned ways to go between Third Space and First Space, and a few select people did make the trip often. He hoped that Lao Dao could bring a few things back to his parents because he felt regret and sorrow over his inability to be by their side and care for them.

Lao Dao talked about his lonely childhood. In the dim lamplight, he recalled his childhood spent alone wandering at the edge of the landfill.

It was now late night. Lao Ge had to go check up on the event downstairs, and he took Lao Dao with him. The dance party downstairs was about to end, and tired-looking men and women emerged in twos and threes. Lao Ge said that entrepreneurs seemed to have the most energy and often danced until the morning. The deserted banquet hall after the party looked messy and grubby, like a woman who had taken off her makeup after a long, tiring day. Lao Ge watched the robots trying to clean up the mess and laughed. "This is the only moment when First Space shows its true face."

Lao Dao checked the time: three hours until the Change. He sorted his thoughts. *It's time to leave.*

5.

The silver-haired speaker returned to his office after the banquet to deal with some paperwork, and then got on a video call with Europe. At midnight, he felt tired. He took off his glasses and rubbed the bridge of his nose. It was finally time to go home. He worked till midnight on most days.

The phone rang. He picked up. It was his secretary.

The research group for the conference had reported something troubling. Someone had discovered an error with one of the figures used in the preprinted conference declaration, and the research group wanted to know if they should reprint the declaration. The old man immediately approved the request. This was very important, and they had to get it right. He asked who was responsible for this, and the secretary told him it was Director Wu Wen.

The old man sat down on his sofa and took a nap. Around four in the morning, the phone rang again. The printing was going a bit slower than expected, and they estimated it would take another hour.

He got up and looked outside the window. All was silent. He could see Orion's bright stars twinkling against the dark sky.

The stars of Orion were reflected in the mirrorlike surface of the lake. Lao Dao was sitting on the shore of the lake, waiting for the Change.

He gazed at the park at night, realizing this was perhaps the last time he would see a sight such as this. He wasn't sad or nostalgic. This was a beautiful, peaceful place, but it had nothing to do with him. He wasn't envious or resentful. He just wanted to remember the experience. There were few lights at night here, nothing like the flashing neon that turned the streets of Third Space bright as day. The buildings of the city seemed to be asleep, breathing evenly and calmly.

At five in the morning, the secretary called again to say that the declaration had been reprinted and bound, but the documents were still in the print shop, and they wanted to know if they should delay the scheduled Change.

The old man made the decision right away. Of course they had to delay it.

At forty minutes past the hour, the printed declarations were brought to the conference site, but they still had to be stuffed into about three thousand individual folders.

Lao Dao saw the faint light of dawn. At this time during the year, the sun wouldn't have risen by six, but it was possible to see the sky brightening near the horizon.

He was prepared. He looked at his phone: only a couple more minutes until six. But strangely, there were no signs of the Change. *Maybe in First Space, even the Change happens more smoothly and steadily.*

At ten after six, the last copy of the declaration was stuffed into its folder.

The old man let out a held breath. He gave the order to initiate the Change.

Lao Dao noticed that the earth was finally moving. He stood up and shook the numbness out of his limbs. Carefully he stepped up to the edge of the widening fissure. As the earth on both sides of the crack lifted up, he clambered over the edge, tested for purchase with his feet, and climbed down. The ground began to turn.

At twenty after six, the secretary called again with an emergency. Director Wu Wen had carelessly left a data key with important documents behind at the banquet hall. He was worried that the cleaning robots might remove it, and he had to go retrieve it right away.

The old man was annoyed, but he gave the order to stop the Change and reverse course.

Lao Dao was climbing slowly over the cross section of the earth when everything stopped with a jolt. After a moment, the earth started moving again, but now in reverse. The fissure was closing up. Terrified, he climbed up as fast as he dared. Scrabbling over the soil with hands and feet, he had to be careful with his movements.

The seam closed faster than he had expected. Just as he reached the top, the two sides of the crack came together. One of his lower legs was caught. Although the soil gave enough to not crush his leg or break his bones, it held him fast, and he couldn't extricate himself despite several attempts. Sweat beaded on his forehead from terror and pain. *Have I been discovered?*

Lao Dao lay prostrate on the ground, listening. He seemed to hear steps hurrying toward him. He imagined that soon the police would arrive and catch him. They might cut off his leg and toss him in jail with the stump. He couldn't tell when his identity had been revealed.

As he lay on the grass, he felt the chill of morning dew. The damp air seeped through collar and cuffs, keeping him alert and making him shiver. He silently counted the seconds, hoping against hope that this was but a technical malfunction. He tried to plan for what to say if he was caught. Maybe he should mention how honestly and diligently he had toiled for twenty-eight years and try to buy a bit of sympathy. He didn't know if he would be prosecuted in court. Fate loomed before his eyes.

Fate now pressed into his chest. Of everything he had experienced during the last forty-eight hours, the episode that had made the deepest impression was the conversation with Lao Ge at dinner. Lao Dao felt he had approached some aspect of truth, and perhaps that was why he could catch a glimpse of the outline of fate. But the outline was too distant, too cold, too out of reach. He didn't know what was the point of knowing the truth. If he could see some things clearly but was still powerless to change them, what good did that do? In his case, he couldn't even see clearly.

Fate was like a cloud that momentarily took on some recognizable shape, and by the time he tried to get a closer look, the shape was gone. He knew that he was nothing more than a figure. He was but an ordinary person, one out of 51,280,000 others just like him. And if they didn't need that much precision and spoke of only fifty million, he was but a rounding error, the same as if he had never existed. He wasn't even as significant as dust. He grabbed on to the grass.

At six thirty, Wu Wen retrieved his data key. At six forty, Wu Wen was back in his home.

At six forty-five, the white-haired old man finally lay down on the small bed in his office, exhausted. The order had been issued, and the wheels of the world began to turn slowly. Transparent covers extended over the coffee table and the desk, securing everything in place. The bed released a cloud of soporific gas and extended rails on all sides; then it rose into the air. As the ground and everything on the ground turned, the bed would remain level, like a floating cradle.

The Change had started again.

After thirty minutes spent in despair, Lao Dao saw a trace of hope again. The ground was moving. He pulled his leg out as soon as the fissure opened, and then returned to the arduous climb over the cross section as soon as the opening was wide enough. He moved with even more care than before. As circulation returned to his numb leg, his calf itched and ached as though he was being bitten by thousands of ants. Several times, he almost fell. The pain was intolerable, and he had to bite his fist to stop from screaming. He fell; he got up; he fell again; he got up again. He struggled with all his strength and skill to maintain his footing over the rotating earth.

He couldn't even remember how he had climbed up the stairs. He only remembered fainting as soon as Qin Tian opened the door to his apartment.

Lao Dao slept for ten hours in Second Space. Qin Tian found a classmate in medical school to help dress his wound. He suffered massive damage to his muscles and soft tissue, but luckily, no bones were broken. However, he was going to have some difficulty walking for a while.

After waking up, Lao Dao handed Yi Yan's letter to Qin Tian. He watched as Qin Tian read the letter, his face filling up with happiness as well as loss. He said nothing. He knew that Qin Tian would be immersed in this remote hope for a long time.

Returning to Third Space, Lao Dao felt as though he had been traveling for a month. The city was waking up slowly. Most of the residents had slept soundly, and now they picked up their lives from where they had left off the previous cycle. No one would notice that Lao Dao had been away.

As soon as the vendors along the pedestrian lane opened shop, he sat down at a plastic table and ordered a bowl of chow mein. For the first time in his life, Lao Dao asked for shredded pork to be added to the noodles. *Just one time*, he thought. *A reward*.

Then he went to Lao Ge's home and delivered the two boxes of medicine Lao Ge had bought for his parents. The two elders were no longer mobile, and a young woman with a dull demeanor lived with them as a caretaker.

Limping, Lao Dao slowly returned to his own rental unit. The hallway was noisy and chaotic, filled with the commotion of a typical morning: brushing teeth, flushing toilets, arguing families. All around him were disheveled hair and half-dressed bodies.

He had to wait awhile for the elevator. As soon as he got off at his floor, he heard loud arguing noises. It was the two girls who lived next door, Lan Lan and Ah Bei, arguing with the old lady who collected rent. All the units in the building were public housing, but the residential district had an agent who collected rent, and each building, even each floor, had a subagent. The old lady was a long-term resident. She was thin, shriveled, and lived by herself—her son had left, and nobody knew where he was. She always kept her door shut and didn't interact much with the other residents. Lan Lan and Ah Bei had moved in recently, and they worked at a clothing store. Ah Bei was shouting while Lan Lan was trying to hold her back. Ah Bei turned and shouted at Lan Lan; Lan Lan began to cry.

"We all have to follow the lease, don't we?" The old lady pointed at the scrolling text on the screen mounted on the wall. "Don't you dare accuse me of lying! Do you understand what a lease is? It's right here in black and white: in autumn and winter, there's a ten-percent surcharge for heat."

"Ha!" Ah Bei lifted her chin at the old lady while combing her hair forcefully. "Do you think we are going to be fooled by such a basic trick? When we're at work, you turn off the heat. Then you charge us for the electricity we haven't been using so you can keep the extra for yourself. Do you think we were born yesterday? Every day when we get home after work, the place is cold as an ice cellar. Just because we're new, you think you can take advantage of us?"

Ah Bei's voice was sharp and brittle, and it cut through the air like a knife. Lao Dao looked at Ah Bei, at her young, determined, angry face, and thought she was very beautiful. Ah Bei and Lan Lan often helped him by taking care of Tangtang when he wasn't home, and sometimes even made porridge for him. He wanted Ah Bei to stop shouting, to forget these trivial things and stop arguing. He wanted to tell her that a girl should sit elegantly and quietly, cover her knees with her skirt, and smile so that her pretty teeth showed. That was how you got others to love you. But he knew that that was not what Ah Bei and Lan Lan needed.

He took out a ten-thousand-yuan bill from his inner pocket and handed it to the old lady. His hand trembled from weakness. The old lady was stunned, and so were Ah Bei and Lan Lan. He didn't want to explain. He waved at them and returned to his home.

Tangtang was just waking up in her crib, and she rubbed her sleepy eyes. Lao Dao gazed into her face, and his exhausted heart softened. He remembered how he had found Tangtang and her dirty, tear-stained face in front of the waste-processing station. He had never regretted picking her up that day.

Now she laughed and smacked her lips. Lao Dao thought he was fortunate. Although he was injured, he hadn't been caught and had managed to bring back money. He didn't know how long it would take Tangtang to learn to dance and sing and become an elegant young lady.

He checked the time. It was time to go to work.

TANG FEI

Tang Fei is a speculative fiction writer whose work has been featured (under various pen names) in magazines in China such as *Science Fiction World, Jiuzhou Fantasy,* and *Fantasy Old and New.* She has written fantasy, science fiction, fairy tales, and wuxia (martial arts fantasy), but prefers to write in a way that straddles or stretches genre boundaries. She is also a genre critic, and her critical essays have been published in *The Economic Observer.*

When not writing, Tang Fei is a documentary photographer and dancer. Her portraits of the lives of China's LGBT communities have received much attention. She is currently working on a multiyear project documenting WorldCons held across the globe.

In translation, her fiction has appeared in *Clarkesworld* and *Apex.* "Call Girl" was selected for inclusion in Rich Horton's *Year's Best Science Fiction & Fantasy, 2014 Edition.*

Many of Tang Fei's stories defy easy genre classifications. She employs surreal images and playful language to great effect, and she does not hesitate to mislead the reader when it serves the tale's purpose.

Although she lives in Beijing, she tries to escape it as often as she can and considers herself a foodie with a particular appreciation for dark chocolate, blue cheese, and good wine.

CALL GIRL

1.

Morning climbs in through the window as shadow recedes from Tang Xiaoyi's body like a green tide imbued with the fragrance of trees. Where the tidewater used to be, now there is just Xiaoyi's slender body, naked under the thin sunlight.

She opens her eyes, gets up, dresses, brushes her teeth, wipes away the foam at the corner of her mouth with a towel. Staring at the mirror, all serious, her face eventually breaks into a fifteen-year-old's smile. Above her, a section of the rose-colored wallpaper applied to the ceiling droops down. This is the fourth place where this has happened.

My house is full of blooming flowers, Xiaoyi thinks.

"There must be another leak in the pipes," her mother says. "There's a large water stain growing on the wall."

They sit down together to have a lavish breakfast: soy milk, eggs, pan-fried *baozi*, porridge. Xiaoyi eats without speaking.

When she's ready to leave the apartment, she takes out a stack of money from her backpack and leaves it on the table. Her mother pretends not to see as she turns to do the dishes. She has turned up the faucet so that the sound of the gushing water is louder than Xiaoyi's footsteps.

Xiaoyi walks past her mother and the money on the table and

closes the door. She can no longer hear the water. It's so quiet she doesn't hear anything at all.

Her knees shake.

She reaches up for the silver pendant hanging from her neck, a dog whistle.

2.

The school is on the other side of the city, and Xiaoyi has to transfer buses three times to get there.

Li Bingbing once asked Xiaoyi whether she wanted to get a ride with her in Bingbing's father's car. *Being chauffeured around in a BMW is very comfortable.*

But Xiaoyi had said no because she didn't think it was a big deal to ride the bus. School was so boring anyway; it was like riding another bus. Since she had to ride the bus, as it were, what did it matter where she got on? Of course Xiaoyi didn't say *that* to Bingbing. As a general rule, she doesn't like talking, unless it's to *them*.

They would never appear at the school, which makes school even more boring. Xiaoyi sits in the last row, next to the window. All day long, she sits and broods. Whether it's during class or recess, no one bothers her.

She has no friends. No one talks to her. No one sees her. The girls like to form cliques: those with bigger boobs in one clique, those with smaller boobs in another. Once in a while a busty girl might be friends with a flat-chested girl, but that never lasts.

Xiaoyi is different from all of them. She doesn't wear a bra. Never. Many found this odd. Then the girls found out about *them*. So wherever Xiaoyi goes, there's a sudden circle of silence. But as soon as she leaves the area—but not so far that she can't hear them—the buzz of conversation starts again: "Look, that's Tang Xiaoyi!"

Yes, that's Tang Xiaoyi. No one knows what to do with her. If it weren't for Bingbing, who sometimes gets obsessive, Xiaoyi would have a completely peaceful life.

"Hey, you know that Li Jian and Ding Meng are together now?" says Bingbing.

It's the end of geography, the last morning class. Bingbing sits down next to Xiaoyi and starts babbling. Once in a while, she pauses in her monologue and takes a drag from her cigarette. When she's finally done with the cigarette, she can't hold back any longer.

"Xiaoyi, you know that lots of people are talking about you behind your back. Is it true? Are they all really old and really rich? Are they richer than my dad? How much do they pay you each time?"

Xiaoyi rests her chin on a palm and stares out the window. The lunch queue outside the cafeteria grows longer and longer, all the way to the *wutong* tree at the school gate.

Just then a nondescript little car stops at the gate. The car door opens, but no one gets out. He's waiting, waiting for Xiaoyi.

Xiaoyi stands up slowly and strides out of the classroom, her steps lightly echoing against the ground, her hair waving over her shoulder as though a breeze were blowing in her face.

There's no sound around her. Sunlight slices across her shoulders like a knife blade.

3.

"I did as you said and switched to a different car. Can you tell me why? It's . . . unusual."

The middle-aged man turns to gaze at Xiaoyi. This is the first time they've met. The two are squeezed tightly into the backseat of the little Daihatsu Charade: the schoolgirl in her short dark blue skirt, the man in his elegant *hanfu*. Once in a while, in a moment of careless-ness, their knees bump into each other and separate immediately.

In the driver's seat is the chauffeur, his uniform neatly pressed, sil-ver epaulettes on his shoulders, brand-new white gloves on his hands.

"You brought a chauffeur." Xiaoyi frowns.

"I haven't driven in a long time."

Xiaoyi turns her eyes to the flow of traffic outside the window—which is not flowing at all. It's Friday, and the traffic jam started at noon. It doesn't really matter. They're not in any hurry. The man takes out a handkerchief to wipe the sweat from his brow. The Charade's air conditioning isn't working—unpleasant for those used to Cadillacs.

"Where to?" he asks.

"Nowhere."

"Okay. Just so long as you're happy."

They are always so good-tempered, treating her like a pet, adoration mixed with contempt. Before they really start, they're all the same.

Xiaoyi turns to give the middle-aged man a careful look. His eyes are dark, strange but friendly. They seize her and don't let go.

"What do you want me to do?" she asks.

"What you do with the others."

"So you haven't thought through what you want yourself."

The man laughs. "I just can't be sure that you can satisfy me."

"You're greedy." Xiaoyi winks. Her eyelashes are long and dark, fanning seductively.

The man's Adam's apple moves up and down. The way Xiaoyi's shirt clings to her body tells him that she's not wearing a bra.

"Let's start now," Xiaoyi says.

"In the car?"

Xiaoyi reaches out and closes the man's eyelids. Her hands are ice cold.

4.

The man opens his eyes and looks around. Nothing has changed. The Charade is still the Charade. The road is still as congested as a constipated colon.

But the chauffeur is gone.

He's an experienced man. He knows when he must remain calm. "They're right about you. I guess I finally found the right one."

"You can straighten out your legs. There's lots of legroom."

The man does as she suggests. He sees his own legs slowly passing through the front seat as easily as passing through a shadow. He relaxes and leans back. Much more comfortable. He has paid the fee, and he should enjoy it; this is part of the transaction.

For a long time now, private clubs, custom services, and other forms of high-class entertainment haven't been able to satisfy him. He's been looking for special experiences like this girl. The website described her this way: *I sell stories. Special. Expensive. No substitutes. You must come in a beat-up car. You must bring enough money. No matter what happens, you may never come see me again.*

His right index finger trembles. Everything is set. He sits, expectant. He begins to believe that she can offer him what she claims.

"I'm ready," he says.

Xiaoyi nods. Without him noticing it, she's now sitting across from him, in an armchair located where the driver's seat ought to be.

"I'm going to ask you again. What do you want?"

"I have everything."

Xiaoyi says nothing as she stares at the man. Suddenly she takes off her shoes and tucks her feet under her on the armchair. She curls her whole body into a ball and sinks into the soft white leather. "When you've thought it through, tell me. I'm on the clock, by the way."

This is a difficult client, she thinks. *He's going to wear me out.* She decides to close her eyes and conserve her strength.

"Why don't you tell me something special, something I don't have or haven't experienced?"

"A story," Xiaoyi says.

"That's right."

Xiaoyi opens her eyes but keeps her body in the same position.

"They tell me that you're really good, unique. But you're expensive. All those who had used your services, they say that you . . ." The man seems not to notice that his voice is too excited.

The noise of other cars honking interrupts his speech. The sounds seem to come from far away. He begins to feel that something is wrong. The air feels thin; the sunlight seems harsh; a susurration fills his ears. He has trouble telling the density of things. This is another world.

The man stands and walks around the confines of the shadowy outline of the little Charade. But the walk takes him ten minutes to complete. He's never even dared to think that the passage of time could change.

When the man sits down again, Xiaoyi says, "I'll tell you a gentle story."

"I've heard such stories. They're liquid. Sticky, wet, filled with the smell of tears and mucus. I don't like them."

"Stories are not liquid." Xiaoyi glares at him.

Before the man can argue with her, something tumbles from above and falls into his lap. It's warm, furry, and squirms around—a pure white puppy! Round, dark eyes. Wet nose. Oh, it's sticking out its pink tongue and licking the man's finger.

"Stories are like dogs," Xiaoyi explains. "When called, they appear."

"How did you do this?" the man asks, carefully cradling the puppy and watching it suck on his finger.

"With this." She shakes the pendant hanging from her neck.

"A dog whistle?"

"Only I can work it. When stories hear my call, they come, and then people take them away." Xiaoyi sits up. "So do you want this one?"

The man looks at the puppy. "I'd like to see some others."

5.

"How about this one? Do you like it?" Xiaoyi asks.

The man shakes his head.

Xiaoyi glances around the car. It's filled with the dogs she's called here. They sit quietly, their faces expectant. More than twenty pairs of eyes stare at her innocently.

The rottweiler she just summoned pushes against her hand with its wet nose. Xiaoyi absentmindedly strokes its ears. She's tired and cold. The feeling is close to her skin, like a soaked-through shirt.

"Do you need to take a break?" the man asks. But his eyes say, *Keep going! Faster! Faster! I want my story!*

Xiaoyi stands up and grabs the man's hand.

Wind against their faces. An unfamiliar smell.

The sky spins. An ancient, somber prayer song echoes around them.

The herdsmen have lit a bonfire of cypress leaves. Goshawks gather from all around and land with puffs of dust around them.

The old priest-shaman sings with a trembling voice. He sharpens his knife and hook until they glisten. The living bow their backs as the dead lie with their naked chests exposed. The goshawks flap their wings and take off, circle in the air, cry out.

In the far distance, at the limit of vision, bright flags flap in the wind.

They're standing under a big sky on a limitless prairie, bathed in bright, harsh sunlight.

The man blanches. "What the . . . ?"

"To simplify somewhat, this story is too big. Moving us is simpler than having him move." Xiaoyi moves to the side.

The man now sees the hound. Though strictly speaking, it's not a "hound" at all.

It's gigantic. Its mouth is wide and its nose broad. Its teeth are as sharp as knives. It crouches, not moving, only its thick fur waving in the wind. Blood thousands of years old courses through its veins. It is the embodiment of the cruel and strict law of nature. It is a sacred beast.

"Do you like him? He's very expensive."

"You're saying that I can bring him with me?"

"Yes, if you're willing to spend that much."

"A very high price to pay, and not just in money?"

Xiaoyi's throat tightens. She nods.

The man looks at the massive hound, which still isn't moving but seems to arrogantly take in everything before it. In the end, the man shakes his head. "Any others?"

"You are sure you want to keep looking?"

The man doesn't say anything. He doesn't need to.

Saaaaa-saaaa. The sound of the wind comes from Xiaoyi's chest: thin, dry, lingering, like sand passing through an hourglass.

6.

Everywhere they look, it's the same. The world is one substance. Bright light sparkles from the deep blue.

They're at the bottom of the sea. The water pushes and pulls noiselessly.

Xiaoyi's hair and skirt drift alongside the kelp.

The man opens his mouth. No bubbles. There is no need to breathe at the bottom of the sea.

"This is my last story."

The man's eyes quickly grow used to the ocean. He looks around but cannot see any dogs. "Where is it?"

"The dog is only a shape to make them easier to call and to be accepted. But here, you see them in their native state. No, that's not exactly right, either. Fundamental nature consists of zeros and ones, part of the ultimate database. This sea is an illusion, a projection of that fundamental nature. The sea of data is too big to be compressed into the shape of a dog. Of course, you may still call it a dog. From the perspective of the story, nothing is impossible."

Xiaoyi pauses and takes a drink of seawater. It's salty, and makes her even thirstier. "This place has existed for a long time, and it's too strong. My computing power is insufficient to alter it, to call it. I can only . . . be called *by* it."

"You've brought others here before?"

"Most people are easier to satisfy."

"What happened to those you did bring here?"

Xiaoyi smiles without answering.

The man can feel the transparent currents—11001101111—pass by him. They'll flow to the countless trenches and caves at the bottom of the sea and leave this place behind. Someday this ancient source will dry up, too. But not now. As far as the man is concerned, it is eternity.

He takes a step forward. The sea trembles; the sky trembles; everything in the sky and in the sea trembles. If someday a bird dives toward the surface of the sea, then he will feel the excitement and joy of that dive through the seawater as well.

"You like this?"

"Yes."

"It's even more expensive than you think."

"I know."

"What I mean is that I don't have any way for you to bring it with you."

The man is silent. Far to the north, a part of the sea roils with dark, surging currents. He can no longer think it over. "Then I won't leave."

Xiaoyi bites her lips. After a long silence, she opens her mouth and lets out a word soundlessly.

A school of orange lyretails swims between them, obscuring their faces from each other.

When they can see each other again, both are smiling.

7.

Six P.M. Rush hour. A tidal wave of humanity emerges from the subway stations, fills the shops, the roads, the overpasses.

Xiaoyi gets out of the Charade. This is the world of the present. Dusk burns brightly and gently. Pedestrians part around her.

Behind her is her shadow, stretched very long. Together they walk slowly, with great effort.

Xiaoyi lifts her hand to find the dog whistle hanging around her neck, touches it.

They exist. They've always existed.

She's not alone at all.

She does not cry.

CHENG JINGBO

Cheng Jingbo's fiction has won many accolades, among them the Galaxy (Yinhe) Award and Nebula (Xingyun) Award as well as being selected for various Year's Best anthologies in Chinese. Unusual among genre writers, she has been published in *People's Literature,* perhaps the most prestigious mainstream literary market in China. She lives in Chengdu, China, and works as a children's book editor.

Cheng's stories are difficult to classify. They feature multilayered, dreamlike images connected by the logic of metaphor, dense syntax, and evocative, allusive expressions. Leaping from thought to thought, they invite the reader to navigate like a water strider stepping across ripples in a pond. The stories pose a challenge to the reader and the translator alike, but the effort is worth it.

GRAVE OF THE
FIREFLIES

February 16: Through the Door Into Summer

The Snow-No-More birds appeared in the sky, adding to the chaos that enveloped the world.

The fluttering wings that were supposed to signal clear weather scraped across the orange sky like the return of snow-laden billows. Ash white feathers filled the air, drifting down until they fell into the black orbs of my eyes, turning them into snowy globes.

On the sixteenth of February, I was born on the road to light, a refugee. My ebony eyes were luminous and vivid, but no one came to kiss my forehead. All around, people sighed heavily. I lifted my head and saw the ash white flock heading southward, their cries as dense as their light-stealing wings.

To the south was the Door Into Summer, built from floating asteroids like a road to heaven.

The giant star that lit the way for the refugees gradually dimmed, the shadow crawling up everyone's face. After the briefest experience of daylight, I saw the first twilight of my life: my mother's image bloomed in the dim glow like a secret flower.

Mankind streamed across the river of time, aiming straight for the Door Into Summer. In that moment, our tiny planet was falling like a single drop of dew in a boundless universe, tumbling toward that plane made up of the broken remains of a planet.

New cries arose from the Snow-No-More birds. Gliding through the gravity-torn clouds, the soft, gentle creatures were suddenly seized by some unknown force. Alarmed, the flock wound through the sky like a giant electric eel, each individual bird a scale. They hovered near one another, their wingtips brushing from time to time with delicate snaps. The snaps quickly grew louder and denser—the birds drew closer together to resist the unknown force that threatened to divert them, and electric sparks generated by the friction of the wings hopped from wingtip to wingtip. A great, invisible hand wrapped its fingers around the throat of the flock, and the ash white electric eel in the sky began to tremble, its entire body enshrouded by a blue flame.

And in a moment, the invisible force that had been pulling them higher into the sky dissipated. The eel writhed in its death throes among the clouds, the feathers shed by struggling birds falling like volcanic ash. Soon the feathery snow descended over us. It slid in through gaps around the oxhide flaps, fell mothlike against the greasy glass of the gas lamps, floated in clumps over the dirty water in copper basins, caught in my eyebrows and the corners of my eyes.

The oxcart rolled forward slowly. My mother began to sing in the midst of this snowstorm of ash and sorrow. Gradually, I fell asleep, listening to her lovely voice. But her eyes were filled with the sights from outside the cart: in the suffocating, fiery air, tens of thousands of oxcarts headed in the same direction. The remnants of humanity flooded across the hills and plains. The farther she looked, the more oxcarts she saw—each like the one we were in.

An old man rushed before our cart and knelt down. "The star is about to go out."

Even before he had spoken, my mother already knew about the star. Even before he had opened his lips, her eyes had already sunk into gloom. Since the oxen's eyes were covered by black cloth, the animals showed no signs of panic. But as the darkness fell, they felt the strange chill.

Rising clouds of dust drowned out the old man's words, just like the endless night drowned out my mother's beautiful, bottomless eyes.

He had failed to notice the spiked wheels of the oxcart. Blood soaked into earth, a dark stain melting into the night. In my sleep, I felt the oxcart lurch momentarily, as though something had caught against its wheels. And then it rolled on as though nothing had happened.

My mother continued to sing. In her song, the white-bearded High Priest died on the way to see the Queen—because the news he was bringing was ill.

After that day, I never saw a Snow-No-More bird again.

Legend has it that on the day I was born, my small planet passed through the Door Into Summer. All the Snow-No-More birds died outside the door. Though they were birds of spring, when they died, it snowed: every flake was an ash white feather; every flake was limned in pale blue fire.

On the day the Snow-No-More birds disappeared in the southern sky, we penetrated a wall made of 1,301 asteroids and exited the Garden of Death through the Door Into Summer.

February 19: Curtain Call for the Crimson Universe

People called me Rosamund because they said I'm the rose of the world.

I thought the world was a fading rose. The cooling universe was filled with ancient stars like our sun—they collapsed, lost heat, aged, contracted into infinitesimal versions of themselves and stopped giving us light. Now, with shrunken bodies and failing sight, they could only offer us a useless prayer as they watched us flee at the edge of night.

A thousand years ago, nine priests secretly debated among themselves around a circular table and probed the will of the gods for the answer to one question: why had the stars suddenly decided to grow old and die?

In the end, because the priests could not answer the question satisfactorily, the king punished them by taking their heads.

But one of them, the most powerful priest of them all, managed to survive. He lived because he had two faces, the second one hidden by his long, thick hair, and no one ever knew of its existence. If one gathered enough courage to pull aside the curtain of snakelike hair, one would see tightly pursed lips and wide-open eyes. When the king demanded that the priests yield up their heads, this priest split apart his own head with a double-edged sword and gave up the front half. Thereafter he became a wanderer far from home, and lived only with the secret half of his head.

It was rumored that the descendants of this man created Weightless City, the first planet we arrived at after passing through the Door Into Summer. The star collapsed behind us while the army of refugees dove like moths toward the last lit lamp in the universe.

No one could explain why the stars were dying. A thousand years ago, following an ancient prophecy, our ancestors altered the structure of our planet and adjusted its gravity to turn it into an Ark to flee toward those stars that seemed young still.

When we arrived at Weightless City, everyone was going to leave our own planet and move there. After its thousand-year flight, the Ark could no longer go on. And after we left our home, this planet that had once birthed and nurtured all of humanity would fall into the heat of a strange star and dissolve into a million droplets of dew.

That year, I turned six. The nineteenth of February was a special day. My mother, the Queen, set me on the back of a white bull, and I saw thousands, tens of thousands of oxen, all of them pitch-black, pulling my subjects over the earth like a flood.

A lonely golden tower rose from the distant horizon. By dusk, the refugees arrived at its foot. The tower, too, appeared as if it had been on a long journey. Behind it was a deep trench like a surgical incision; the rich, fleshy loam brought up from the depths gave off a burned scent.

This was the Dock. The inhabitants of Weightless City, the dark green planet revolving overhead, had dropped it down. On this special day, the gravity between the two planets achieved perfect balance, enabling us to ascend this tower to our new home.

If anyone could have witnessed the coupling between these two tiny planets from a distance, they would have seen this: a golden rod emerged from one of the planets like a raised matchstick. As the two planets spun, the matchstick struck the surface of the other planet, scratching out a groove on its surface, and then stopped.

But for those on the ground, the sight seemed like a manifestation of divinity. Occasionally, through an opening in the clouds, we could see our future home—darkgreen, serene Weightless City. The mammoth golden tower in front of us had extended from that heaven like a dream and then fixed itself inexorably into the earth. Everyone cried out in joy. They busied themselves with reshoeing the oxen with strong, magnetic shoes, gilding the wheel spikes with silvery powder, patching the leaky oxhide tents . . .

Afterward, the oxcarts began to climb the tower in order of precedence. Far away from the tower, barefoot, I ran. A few flowers hid in the grass, twinkling here and there. Wind seemed to come from somewhere deep within the ground, and I thought I heard a voice cry out between sky and earth: *Rosamund, Rosamund.* I placed my ear against the tips of the blades of grass: I wanted to know if it was my planet calling my name.

When I turned to look back, I saw the sky turn slowly, the horizon already tilted. The tower leaned away from the zenith until finally anyone could walk on it barefoot like me.

Night fell, and the whole human race trod along this road to heaven. A woman carelessly knocked over a kitchen pail, and it fell down the tower, clanging, banging all the way, until it plunged into a moist black cloud, leaving nothing but ripples on the surface. It was so quiet that everyone heard the woman muttering her complaint. But then she pulled the rope attached to the pail—almost everything in the oxcarts had been tied down by rope to prevent it from moving about during the journey—and so her pail returned, filled with clear water.

We marched in the dark, silent night. In front of us was a new city shining like a piece of jade. All we could see around the massive and long bridge formed by the golden tower was the star-studded night.

The universe was like a gigantic stage curtain that gradually fell. Fewer and fewer stars remained. We walked faster.

February 22: The Magician of Weightless City

My mother was the only one who did not cry after she saw Weightless City.

After we descended the tower, the sky rotated back into its original location. The horizon was no longer tilted. Everyone got a clear view of heaven: just another ruin.

This was the first thing my mother said to the first stranger she met: "Take me to your king, archon, headman, or . . . whatever you call him."

"There's no one like that here," the man answered. "We just have a magician."

And so we came upon a machine-man made of steel. It sat in the middle of an open space like a heap of twisted metal. Walking from its left foot to its right foot took five minutes. But to climb from its right foot to its waist took a whole afternoon.

"Listen," my mother said. She squatted down to look into my eyes. "Rosamund, my precious, I have to go in there to talk to the magician. Wait for me here. My darling, my baby, do not leave before I come out."

I nodded. She smiled and lightly kissed my forehead. No one saw this farewell, and that was why, in the stories people told afterward, the Queen died from mistakenly eating a poisonous mushroom in Weightless City. But I saw with my own eyes my mother climb onto the shoulder of that gigantic robot, enter through an ear, and then disappear.

In the six years after I became an orphan, after my planet and my mother had abandoned and forgotten me, I grew into a twelve-year-old, a willful young woman. Everyone now called me Wild Rose.

In the new world of Weightless City, I discovered a plant that had also existed on my planet. The vines extended hundreds of miles and had fragile stalks that ended in thin, delicate tips. I liked to run among them barefoot. As my feet crushed the stalks, bright yellow liquid oozed out, and the wind brought indistinct cries: *Rosamund, Rosamund*. I put my ear against the black soil: I wanted to know if it was my planet calling me now through this new earth. My loneliness grew without cease during those six years until it took root deep in my blood and bones.

One time, when I heard the calls and put my ear against the muddy earth, I closed my eyes and saw my mother's face. "Rosamund, my precious . . ." She smiled and kissed my forehead as though I really were the world's rose. Then I opened my eyes. Nothing.

Another time, when I opened my eyes, what I saw shocked and frightened me: a young man (barely more than a boy) was puffing out his cheeks. He was buried in the earth up to his neck, but his face was practically touching my forehead. He blinked his eyes, blue as water, and a breeze caressed my face. I stood up. "Who are you?"

"A free person of Weightless City," he said, joy in his voice. As he answered, he climbed out from his hole nimbly, as though the earth provided no resistance at all. "But who are you?"

I looked at him, stunned. He brushed off the mud from his clothes. There were flowers blooming now in the place where he had been buried.

"Let me guess," he said. "I bet I can guess your name."

And so he found a comfortable place to sit down and set himself to the serious task of guessing my name.

It was an unforgettable sight: the silhouette of a young man sitting alone in the light of dawn. I couldn't see his face, but I could imagine his expression. Slender grass shot up wildly around him, extending farther and farther away.

"All right," he said finally. "I give up. Why don't you try to guess my name?"

But then he glanced up at the sky and slapped his head. "Ah, I forgot what I came for. Rosamund, my sweet girl, where are you?"

As he said this, he was already running away like the wind. And so I had no choice but to cup my hands around my mouth and shout at his back, "Do you know Rosamund?"

"No." He was already some distance away. "I have to find her first. And then I'll know her."

"Why are you looking for Rosamund?"

He was almost at the horizon. "Because she's my guest."

I sighed. He was already invisible. "*I* am Rosamund."

A whirlwind swept from the horizon. The young man was standing in front of me again. He combed his hair with his hands, smoothed out the wrinkles on his shirt, and then bowed toward me very chivalrously. "Pleased to make your acquaintance, my . . . guest."

"But who are you?"

"Neither of us could guess the other's name. If you're truly Rosamund, then permit me to present you with my true name: the Magician of Weightless City."

February 25: The Knight of the Rose

Six years after meeting me, the Magician of Weightless City no longer looked so young. His castle was the secret to his eternal youth.

But I still enjoyed running barefoot on the wild heath. To see me, he often had to leave his castle. And in this way we grew up together.

Now that I was eighteen, he was like a knight, with a steel will and iron-hard shoulders. But when I was twelve, I had entered his castle for the first time.

The castle was the silent robot sitting on the ground. Since the robot had no need of a bladder, that was the location of the castle gate. After we entered, the Magician (still boyish back then) held my hand with his right hand, and, with a *puff,* a torch appeared in his left hand. The interior of the castle was completely dark.

We passed by many murals, set foot on countless carpets, and after the seventh turn in the staircase, we knocked over three silver bottles and a crystal ball. The Magician's eyes and hair glinted brightly in the light from the torch. Both of us talked only of the journey we had taken and what we had encountered along the way, as though we hadn't been paying attention to each other at all.

Finally I saw my mother, sitting on a chair covered by a tiger skin. She looked serene; her face hadn't changed at all from how I remembered her.

"Let me take a look at you, young lady," she said. Then she recognized me with a start. "What in the world happened to you?"

The Magician clapped his hands, and the torch disappeared from his left hand. Innumerable points of light suddenly appeared in the dark ceiling of the great hall, like stars, like fireflies.

The man who brought forth light said to my mother, "Your Majesty, while you have only been here a little while, she has been living outside on her own for six years."

"What kind of witchcraft is this?!" My mother hugged me and then pushed me back, holding on to my arms tightly so she could examine me in detail. I was too embarrassed to look back at her.

The Magician said, "A thousand years ago, one of my ancestors came through the Door Into Summer. Using magic and witchcraft, he built this castle of eternal youth. Whether something is living or dead, as soon as it comes inside, it ceases to be eroded by the river of time. The short periods that I have lived outside the castle caused me to grow into this boyish form you see."

My mother spoke in the darkness. The starry light that bathed her forehead could not illuminate her eyes. The Queen confirmed the claim of this fugitive's descendant to his domain and made him Weightless City's first knight.

The answer to this grant of peerless honor came six years later. My knight found the dust-covered silver armor in the depths of the castle, put it on, and bowed slightly to the Queen on her tiger-skin throne. "Please allow me to be Rosamund's knight. She's come of age and is ready to have a knight of her own."

I hid in a dark corner, watching him with my wide-open eyes like a fawn.

"Why?" my mother asked.

"Because she needs a knight. Not just any knight, but me. And I need to become the knight for a pure lady. Not just any lady, but her."

"Then," my mother said, "what can a knight do for a princess? Perhaps he doesn't even know what she truly needs, and neither does she."

The Magician of Weightless City, once a proud youth, and now a knight standing tall, full of courage, trembled as he heard this. His cold, rigid shadow stretched long and narrow, and as he trembled, it seemed about to take off from the ground.

Finally the corners of his mouth lifted, and he answered the woman sitting high on her throne. "The loneliness in her heart is as dark as her eyes. But I will give her eternal light."

And with that, my knight departed his gloomy castle without looking back.

Behind him, the Queen, driven mad by the terror of eternity, screamed, "The stars are going out! You cannot bring back lasting light!"

The stars are going out. You cannot bring back lasting light. But the barefoot princess remained hidden in the darkness, expectant.

February 28: A Skeleton or Two

I was sick.

I'd lost count of the passing years. Six years? Sixty? Or even six hundred? February twenty-eighth was the last day of that suspended period, the end coming like a cliff cleaving space into two halves.

The Queen of mankind had gone mad in the castle. She could not tolerate the erosion of the river of time, and could tolerate even less the passing days that now skipped over her like migrating birds over a forgotten tree. And so she constantly paced the halls of the castle, too frightened to abandon this heaven of eternal life, and yet unable to derive joy from the absolute stillness.

In her face, I could no longer detect the bloom of that secret flower. The permanent starry night of the great hall's ceiling cast two gloomy shadows under her eyes against her pale mask of a face. My mother's once-luminous black eyes had, after many, many, *many* years of unchanging life, finally dimmed and merged into the darkness.

I thought of the man who had once built this castle, that great priest with only half a head. Where had he gone?

When the world outside was drenched in heavy rain, I made torches out of bundles of straw and played hide-and-go-seek in the castle. I passed through room after room full of dust, perusing books whose pages shattered at my touch—perhaps time had touched them now and then, after all? Among them was a diary kept by another princess who had lived here long ago. She had poured out her heart through her quill.

Sometimes I carried an oil lamp, and as its shifting light cast shadows on the walls, they coalesced into unfamiliar faces; sometimes I lit a candle inside a rose-colored paper lantern, and the light flickered, almost going out.

I walked through the Cimmerian castle, got lost, searched, and occasionally, at the end of a long hallway, I'd see a figure, hear a low murmur, and then everything would once again disappear into darkness and silence—it was my mother, walking, losing her way, seeking, like me.

Finally our paths brought each of us to the same room, a room I had never been in before. Everything inside seemed as new as the long-ago day when the castle had been first erected. I found my mother sitting on the bed, inside the calla lily–colored netting, sobbing like a ghost. That luxurious room had floor-length curtains, bright red, fresh, as though drops of blood were about to ooze out.

I went up and pulled the bed nets aside. But only a pair of empty sockets greeted me. It was a corpse. He had died long ago.

My game was over. The riddle revealed its answer. This dry husk of a body had once been famous—he was that priest who had escaped, the creator of Weightless City, the powerful wizard who once possessed two faces. I saw a ring on a string around his neck, and when I recognized it, I gasped.

From the day I was born, I also wore such a ring around my neck.

The inside of the ring was etched with a secret: the name of the lover my mother had lost a thousand years ago. He was once the most respected priest in the whole kingdom, but he had fallen in love with the princess, and they made love in her bedroom. The king, furious, ordered his guards to seize all nine high priests and cut off their heads. As for the princess who had lost her virginity, he sealed her inside a bronze mirror—she had been intended for the prince of another kingdom and was supposed to become a queen beloved by her subjects and husband alike.

I had read this story in an old book, but I did not know that the legendary princess who had been sealed away was, in fact, my mother. The priest with two faces did not have a chance to say good-bye to his beloved. He cut off half his head, handed it to the king's guards, and then became a fugitive through the Door Into Summer. A thousand years later, the princess awoke from the bronze mirror and became the wife of a king, and then the queen regnant of a people. By the time I was born, my father—who had never gotten my mother's heart—had already disappeared. My mother ruled over her realm as the disaster of the collapsing star unfolded, and then she led her people on the route her lover had taken a thousand years earlier.

Though the priest had built this timeless castle to wait for her, she had still come too late.

In his diary, she read of the suffering he had endured for a thousand years. His quill had turned into her lips, and she spoke to him every day. The diary I found had in fact been composed by the priest as he sank into these hallucinated conversations with my mother.

Finally one day, seized by the ecstasy and rage of waiting, he cut his own heart open. Loneliness poured out of it, bright, fresh, and so he died in this murky castle.

He spent a thousand years to extinguish each and every star; she spent a thousand years to escape to the last star that remained lit.

He knew she would come; she knew he would wait—even though when he had cut off half his head with his sword, he had no chance to tell her anything.

My mother had known the truth for a long time. She had seen in the corpse's empty sockets the cruelest ending possible. From then on, she became an insubstantial ghost wandering through this empty, massive, ancient castle. The fleeting glimpses and murmurs I had caught of her had been nothing but figments of my imagination.

I finally understood why my mother would rather turn her rotting passion into ghosts that danced at the edge of light than set foot outside this eternal hell. When she saw the stars wink out, one after another, she was the happiest woman in the world. When darkness covered her eyes like a flood, she and the man she loved disappeared together on the shore of life and time.

Now that I understood this most impossible love in the world, I found myself an orphan. Truly this time, my mother and my planet had abandoned me.

I lay on the cold floor of the castle, inches and seconds from death.

I seemed to be back on my little planet spinning in space, blue like water. Slender grass shot up wildly around me, extending farther and farther away. I put my ear to the tips of the grass, a few flowers twinkling here and there. I knew I was going to die. Everyone who was about to die saw visions of the most beautiful scenes in her life.

I saw all the flowers blooming, the rain falling, a bright red lantern shining in the forest. I saw legends that flared up and dimmed, the face of a youth, fragile but stubborn grass. I saw the Magician of Weightless City: his silver armor had been burnished by the ice and snow at the peak of the world's tallest mountain, had been washed by the water in the deepest ocean, had protected him through desert, swamp, the ruins of mankind's cities, and the Eden of fierce beasts, had been borne up a tower that reached into the sky and, following the planet that had abandoned me, reached an undying star—finally, the armor was dented, broken, full of holes. I saw the Magician's long, narrow shadow sweep across the cold floor before my eyes. I saw the return of the Knight of the Rose.

I could recognize only his eyes, the rest of him hidden behind his long-suffering armor. I couldn't tell if his chestnut hair had turned white. I could only smell wind and earth from the wounds in that silver shell.

My knight came before me, opened his left hand: a black pearl.

He found a slender thread and began to pull on it. The black pearl spun in his hand—ah, it was a tiny ball of thread. He pulled and pulled. In this castle of eternal night, the thread seemed to also have no end.

Finally he picked me up from the floor. Until that moment, his silence had caused me in my weakened state to suspect I had also turned into an insubstantial shade like my mother, a second living ghost wandering through the castle.

He pressed his left hand into my palm and squeezed my fingers into a fist. Then he pulled the rest of the thread out from between my fingers with his right hand. In that moment, I understood that I was still alive.

Thousands, millions of rays of searing light shot out of my clenched fist. He gave me the most dazzling light in the universe, a fistful of fireflies.

The Magician of Weightless City really did bring back a fragment of the star for me. My eyes had never seen such splendor. I saw my birth and death, feathers drifting down like volcanic ash, the clear, distant cries of Snow-No-More birds—that snowstorm had been kept on the other side of the Door Into Summer, and now the flakes fell into my eyes, dark as night.

My knight bent to kiss my forehead. The luminous heat dissolved his armor. He and I were pierced by a thousand, a million rays.

The light melted our hair and eyes, skin and organs, until he had no more lips and I no more forehead. Our bodies were fixed in place: two skeletons with our arms entwined about each other.

Many years later, more explorers would come here. They would smash through the gate in the robot where the bladder ought to be. They'd walk into the castle and discover in this perpetual radiance a strange skeleton.

"Maybe this was the priest who had escaped tens of thousands of years ago," one of them would say.

The others, after long debate, would reach consensus and publicize the cause for the extinguishing stars: "Due to the irresistible gravity of their mass, the red giants tragically collapsed to death after exhausting the fuel in their cores."

They would not be able to search through the entire castle—that fragment of an eternal star would blind many of the explorers. They would not be able to examine that strange skeleton closely because no one dared to look at it directly for even a thousandth of a second.

The priest extinguished all the lanterns in the universe just so he could recognize the woman he loved at a glance in a flood of refugees. My knight brought back that star fragment so the inextinguishable flame could warm the loneliness in my dark eyes. The night completed my mother; the day completed me.

Here in our luminous crypt, the fire can never be blown out.

LIU CIXIN

Liu Cixin is widely recognized as the leading voice in Chinese science fiction. He won China's Galaxy (Yinhe) Award for eight consecutive years, from 1999 to 2006, and again in 2010. He received the Nebula (Xingyun) Award in both 2010 and 2011.

An engineer by profession—until 2014, he worked for the China Power Investment Corporation at a power plant in Niangziguan, Shanxi Province—Liu began writing science fiction short stories as a hobby. However, his popularity soared with the publication of the Three-Body series of novels (the first volume, *The Three-Body Problem,* was serialized in *Science Fiction World* in 2006 and then published as a stand-alone book in 2008). An epic story of alien invasion and humanity's journey to the stars, the series begins with a secret Mao-era military effort at establishing communications with extraterrestrial intelligence and ends (literally) with the end of the universe. Tor Books began publishing the English translation of the Three-Body series in November 2014, and the first volume, *The Three-Body Problem,* which I translated, received the Hugo Award in 2015, thus becoming the first novel in translation ever to win that award. Tor Books has also published English translations of the book's two sequels: *The Dark Forest* (2015, trans. Joel Martinsen), and *Death's End* (2016, trans. Ken Liu).

Liu's work generally fits the definition of "hard SF" and is in the tradition of writers like Arthur C. Clarke. Some have called him a "classical" writer for that reason, as his stories prioritize the romance and grandeur of science and humankind's effort to discover nature's secrets.

Two of Liu's short works are featured here. "The Circle" is an adaptation of a chapter from *The Three-Body Problem*. It gives a hint of Liu's imagination. "Taking Care of God" shows another side of Liu, which is deeply concerned with the humanistic values of Chinese culture in a universe guided by grander laws.

THE CIRCLE

Jing Ke slowly unrolled the silk scroll of a map across the low, long table.

On the other side of the table, King Zheng of Qin sighed satisfactorily as he watched the mountains and rivers of his enemy being slowly revealed. Jing Ke was here to present the surrender of the King of Yan. It was easy to feel in control looking at the fields, roads, cities, and military bases drawn on a map. The real land, so vast, sometimes made him feel powerless.

When Jing Ke reached the end of the scroll, there was a metallic glint, and a sharp dagger came into view. The air in the Great Hall of the Palace seemed to solidify in an instant.

All the king's ministers stood at least thirty feet away, and in any event, had no weapons. The armed guards were even farther away, below the steps leading into the Great Hall. These measures were intended to improve the king's security, but now they only made the assassin's task easier.

1 This story is set during the Warring States Period, when China was divided into several independent states: Qin, Qi, Chu, Wei, Zhao, Yan, and Han. King Zheng of Qin would eventually conquer the other six states and unify China under the Qin Dynasty. He is known more familiarly as Qin Shihuang, the First Emperor of China.

But King Zheng remained calm. After giving the dagger a brief glance, he focused his sharp and somber eyes on Jing Ke. The king was a careful man, and he had noticed that the dagger was positioned such that the handle pointed at *him* while the tip pointed back toward the assassin.

Jing Ke picked up the dagger, and all those present in the Great Hall gasped. But King Zheng sighed in relief. He saw that Jing Ke held the dagger only by the tip of the blade, with the dull handle pointing at the king.

"Your Majesty, please kill me with this weapon." Jing Ke raised the dagger over his head and bowed. "Crown Prince Dan of Yan ordered me to make this attempt on your life, and I cannot disobey an order from my master. But my great admiration for you makes it impossible for me to carry through."

King Zheng made no move.

"Sire, all you have to do is to stab lightly. The dagger has been soaked in poison. A slight prick is enough to end my life."

King Zheng sat still and raised his hands to signal the guards rushing into the Great Hall to stop. Without changing his expression he said, "I do not have to kill you to feel safe. Your words have convinced me that you do not have the heart of an assassin."

In a single, smooth motion, Jing Ke wrapped the fingers of his right hand around the handle of the dagger. The tip of the dagger was aimed at his own chest as though he was about to commit suicide.

"You're a learned man." King Zheng's voice was cold. "Dying now would be a waste. I'd like to have your skills and knowledge assisting my army. If you insist on dying, do so only after you've accomplished some things for me first." He waved at Jing Ke, dismissing him.

The assassin from Yan gently put the dagger down on the table and, still bowing, backed out of the Great Hall.

King Zheng stood up and walked out of the Great Hall. The sky was perfectly clear, and he saw the pale white moon in the blue sky like a delicate dream left behind by the night.

"Jing Ke," he called after the assassin still descending the steps. "Does the moon appear during the day often?"

The assassin's white robe reflected the sunlight like a bright flame. "It's not unusual to have the sun and the moon appear in the sky simultaneously. On the lunar calendar, between the fourth and twelfth days of each month, it's possible to see the moon at different times during the day as long as the weather is good."

King Zheng nodded. "Oh, not an uncommon sight," he muttered to himself.

Two years later, King Zheng summoned Jing Ke to an audience.

When Jing Ke arrived outside the palace in Xianyang, he saw three officials being marched out of the Great Hall by armed guards. Having been stripped of the insignia of their rank, their heads were bare. Two of them walked between the guards with faces drained of blood while the third was so frightened he could no longer walk and had to be carried by two soldiers. This last man continued to mumble, begging King Zheng to spare his life. Jing Ke heard him muttering the word "medicine" a few times. He guessed that the three men had been sentenced to death.

King Zheng's mood was jovial when he saw Jing Ke, as though nothing had happened. He pointed to the three departing officials and said by way of explanation, "Xu Fu's fleet has never returned from the East Sea. Someone has to be held responsible."

Jing Ke knew that Xu Fu was an occultist who claimed he could go to three magical mountains on islands out in the East Sea to find the elixir of eternal life. King Zheng gave him a large fleet of ships loaded with three thousand youths and maidens and heaped with treasure, gifts for the immortals who held the secret of eternal life. But the fleet had set sail three years ago, and not a peep had been heard from him since.

King Zheng waved the sore topic away. "I hear that you've invented many wonders in the last couple years. The new bow you designed can shoot twice as far as the old models; the war chariots you devised are equipped with clever springs to ride smoothly over rough ground without having to slow down; the bridges whose construction you supervised use only half as much material but are even stronger—I'm very pleased. How did you come up with these ideas?"

"When I follow the order of the Heavens, all things are possible."

"Xu Fu said the same thing."

"Sire, please permit me to be blunt. Xu Fu is nothing more than a fraud. Casting lots and empty meditation are not appropriate ways to understand the order of the universe. Men like him cannot understand the way the Heavens speak at all."

"What is the language of the Heavens, then?"

"Mathematics. Numbers and shapes are the means by which the Heavens write to the world."

King Zheng nodded thoughtfully. "Interesting. So what are you working on now?"

"I'm always striving to understand more of the Heavens' messages for Your Majesty."

"Any progress?"

"Yes, some. At times, I even feel I'm standing right in front of the door to the treasury filled with the secrets of the universe."

"How do the Heavens tell you these mysteries? Just now, you explained that the language of the Heavens consists of numbers and shapes."

"The circle."

Seeing that King Zheng was utterly confused, Jing Ke asked for and received permission to pick up a brush. He drew a circle on the silk cloth spread out on the low table. Though he didn't use a compass or other tools to assist him, the circle appeared to be perfect.

"Sire, other than objects made by men, have you ever seen a perfect circle in nature?"

King Zheng pondered this for a moment. "Very rarely. Once, a falcon and I stared at each other, and I noticed that its eyes were very round."

"Yes, that's true. I can also suggest as examples eggs laid by certain aquatic creatures, the intersecting plane between a dewdrop and a leaf, and so on. But I've carefully measured all of these, and none of them are perfect circles. It's the same with the circle I drew here: It may look round, but it contains errors and imperfections undetectable by the naked eye. In fact, it's an oval, not a perfect circle. I've been searching for the perfect circle for a long time, and I finally realized it does not exist in the world below, but only in the Heavens above."

"Oh?"

"Sire, please accompany me outside the palace."

Jing Ke and King Zheng strode outside the palace. It was another beautiful day with the moon and the sun both visible in the clear sky.

"The sun and the full moon are both perfect circles," said Jing Ke as he pointed at the sky. "The Heavens placed the perfect circle— impossible to find on earth—in the sky. Not just one, but two examples, and they're the most notable features of the firmament. The meaning couldn't be clearer: the secret of the Heavens resides inside the circle."

"But the circle is the simplest of shapes. Other than a straight line, it's the least complicated figure." King Zheng turned around and returned inside the palace.

"That apparent simplicity disguises a profound mystery," Jing Ke said as he followed the king back inside. When they returned to the low table, he drew a rectangle on the silk with the brush. "Observe this rectangle if you would. The longer dimension measures four inches, and the shorter dimension two. The Heavens speak also through this figure."

"What does it say?"

"The Heavens tell me that the ratio between the longer side and the shorter side is two."

"Are you mocking me?"

"I wouldn't dare. This is just an example of a simple message. Please observe this other figure." Jing Ke drew another rectangle. "This time, the long side is nine inches and the shorter seven. The ideas expressed by the Heavens in this figure are far richer."

"From what I can see, it's still extremely simple."

"Not so. Sire, the ratio between the longer side and the shorter side in this rectangle is 1.285714285714285714 . . . The sequence '285714' repeats forever. Thus, you can calculate the ratio to be as precise as you like, but it will never be exact. Though the message is still simple, much more meaning can be extracted from it."

"Interesting," said King Zheng.

"Next, let me show you the most mysterious shape the Heavens gifted us: the circle." Jing Ke drew a straight line through the center of the circle he had drawn earlier. "Observe that the ratio between the circumference and the diameter of a circle is an endless string of numbers beginning with 3.1415926. But it keeps on going after that, never repeating itself."

"Never?"

"Yes. Imagine a silk cloth as large as all-under-heaven. The string of numbers in the circle's ratio could be written in tiny script, each numeral no bigger than the head of a fly, all the way from here to the edge of the sky, and then coming back here start on a new line. Continued this way, the entire cloth could be filled, and there would still be no end to the numbers, and the sequence still wouldn't repeat. Your Majesty, this endless string of numbers contains the mysteries of the universe."

King Zheng's expression didn't change, but Jing Ke saw that his eyes had brightened. "Even if you obtained this number, how would you read from it the message the Heavens want to express?"

"There are many ways. For example, by treating the numbers as coordinates, it's possible to turn the numbers into new shapes and pictures."

"What will the pictures show?"

"I don't know. Maybe it will be an illustration of the enigma of the universe. Or maybe it will be an essay, or perhaps even a whole book. But the key is that we must obtain enough digits of the circular ratio first. I estimate that we must compute tens of thousands, perhaps even hundreds of thousands, of digits before the meaning can be discerned. Right now, I've only computed about a hundred digits, inadequate to detect any hidden meaning."

"A hundred? That's all?"

"Sire, even so few digits have taken me more than ten years of effort. To compute the circular ratio, one must approach it by inscribing and circumscribing a circle with polygons. The mores sides in the polygons, the more precise the calculations and the more digits that can be obtained. But the complexity of the calculations increases rapidly, and progress is slow."

King Zheng continued to stare at the circle crossed by a straight line. "Do you think you'll find the secret of eternal life in it?"

"Yes, of course." Jing Ke grew excited. "Life and death are the basic rules given to the world by the Heavens. Thus, the mystery of life and death must be contained in this message as well, including the secret of eternal life."

"Then you must compute the circular ratio. I will give you two years to compute ten thousand digits. In five more years, I need you to get to a hundred thousand digits."

"That's . . . that's impossible!"

King Zheng whipped his long sleeves across the table, scattering the silk cloth and ink and brush onto the floor. "You have but to name whatever resources you need." He stared at Jing Ke coldly. "But you must complete the calculations in time."

Five days later, King Zheng called for Jing Ke again. This time, Jing Ke didn't come to the palace in Xianyang; instead, he met the royal entourage on the road as the king was touring around his domain. Right away, King Zheng asked Jing Ke for updates on the progress of the calculations.

Jing Ke bowed and spoke. "Sire, I gathered all the mathematicians who are capable of such calculations in the entire realm: they number only eight. Based on the amount of calculations necessary, even if all nine of us devote the rest of our lives to this task, we will only be able to obtain about three thousand digits of the circular ratio. In two years, the best that we can do is three hundred digits."

King Zheng nodded and indicated that Jing Ke should walk with him. They came to a granite monument about twenty feet high.

A hole was drilled through the top of the monument, and a thick rope made of twisted oxhide passed through the hole to suspend the monument from a wooden platform like the weight of a giant pendulum. The smooth bottom of the monument hovered about a man's height above the ground. There were no inscriptions on the monument.

King Zheng pointed to the hanging monument and said, "Look, if you can finish the calculations in time, this will become a monument of your triumph. We will erect it on the ground and fill it with inscriptions of your many accomplishments. But if you can't finish the calculations, this will become a memento of your shame. In that case, it will also be erected on the ground, but before the rope is cut to drop it, you will have to sit below it so that it can be your tombstone."

Jing Ke lifted his eyes to gaze at the gigantic suspended stone that filled his field of vision. Against the moving clouds in the sky, the dark mass appeared oppressive.

Jing Ke turned to the king and said, "Your Majesty has spared my life once, and even if I could finish the calculations in time, it wouldn't be enough to erase the crime of my attempt on your life. I'm not afraid to die. Please give me five more days to think about this. If I still can't come up with a plan, I'll sit under the monument willingly."

Four days later, Jing Ke requested an audience with the king, which was immediately granted. Calculating the circular ratio was the most important task on the king's mind.

"From your expression, I gather that you have indeed come up with a plan." The king smiled.

Jing Ke did not answer directly. "Your Majesty, you once said that you would give me all the resources that I require. Is that still the case?"

"Of course."

"I need three million men from your army."

The number did not astonish the king. His eyebrows only lifted briefly. "What kind of soldiers?"

"The common soldiers under your command now are sufficient."

"I think you should be aware that most of the soldiers in my army are illiterate. In two years, you cannot possibly teach them complex mathematics, let alone finish the calculations."

"Sire, the skills they would need can be taught to the least intelligent soldier in an hour. Please give me three soldiers so that I can demonstrate."

"Three? Only three? I can easily give you three thousand."

"I only need three."

King Zheng waved his hand and summoned three soldiers. They were all very young. Like other Qin soldiers, they moved like order-obeying machines.

"I don't know your names," Jing Ke said, tapping the shoulders of two of the soldiers. "The two of you will be responsible for number input, so I'll call you 'Input One' and 'Input Two.'" He pointed to the last soldier. "You will be responsible for number output, so I'll call you 'Output.'" He shoved the soldiers to where he wanted them to stand. "Like this. Form a triangle. Output is the apex. Input One and Input Two form the base."

"You could have just told them to stand in the Wedge Attack Formation," King Zheng said, glancing at Jing Ke with a smile.

Jing Ke took out six small flags—three white, three black—and handed them out to the three soldiers so that each held a black flag and a white flag. "White represents zero; black represents one. Good. Now listen to me. Output, you turn around and look at Input One and Input Two. If they both raise black flags, you raise the black flag as well. Under all other circumstances, you raise the white flag."

Jing Ke repeated the instructions one more time to be sure the three soldiers understood. Then he began to shout orders. "Let's begin! Input One and Input Two, you can raise whichever flag you want. Good. Raise! Good. Raise again! Raise!"

Input One and Input Two raised their flags three times. The first time they were black-black, the second time white-black, and the third time black-white. Output reacted correctly each time, raising the black flag once and the white one twice.

"Very good. Sire, your soldiers are very smart."

"Even an idiot would be capable of that. Tell me, what are they really doing?" King Zheng looked baffled.

"The three soldiers form a component for a calculation system, which I call an AND gate. If both numbers input into the gate are one, the result output is also one; otherwise, if one of the numbers input is zero, such as zero-one, one-zero, or zero-zero, the result output is zero." Jing Ke paused to let King Zheng digest the information.

The king said impassively, "All right. Continue."

Jing Ke turned to the three soldiers again. "Let's form another component. You, Output, if you see either Input One or Input Two raise a black flag, you raise the black flag. There are three situations where that will be true: black-black, white-black, black-white. When it's white-white, you raise the white flag. Understand? Good lad, you're really clever. You're the key to the correct functioning of the gate. Work hard, and you will be rewarded. Let's begin operation. Raise! Good, raise again! Raise again! Perfect. Your Majesty, this component is called an OR gate. Whenever one of the two inputs is one, the output is also one."

Then Jing Ke used the three soldiers to form what he called a NAND gate, a NOR gate, an XOR-gate, an XNOR-gate, and a tri-state gate. Finally, using only two soldiers, he made the simplest gate, a NOT gate: Output always raised the flag that was opposite in color from the one raised by Input.

Jing Ke bowed to the Emperor. "All calculating components have been demonstrated. This is the scope of the skills that the three million soldiers must learn."

"How can you perform complex calculations using such simple, childish tricks?" King Zheng's face was full of distrust.

"Great King, the complexity in everything in the universe is built up from the simplest components. Similarly, an immense number of simple components, when structured together appropriately, can generate extremely complex capabilities. Three million soldiers can form a million of these gates I've just demonstrated, and these gates can be put together into a whole formation capable of any complex calculation. I call my invention a calculating formation."

"I still don't understand how the calculations will be carried out."

"The precise process is complicated. If Your Majesty continues to be interested, I can explain in detail later. For now, it's enough to know that the operation of the calculating formation is based on a novel method of thinking about and writing down numbers. In this method, only two numerals, zero and one, corresponding to the white and black flags, are needed. But this new method can use zero and one to represent any number, and this allows the calculating formation to use a large number of simple components to collectively carry out high-speed calculations."

"Three million is almost the entirety of my arm, but I will give them to you." King Zheng sighed meaningfully. "Hurry. I'm feeling old."

A year passed.

It was another beautiful day with the sun and the moon both out. King Zheng and Jing Ke stood together on a high stone dais, with the king's numerous ministers in rows behind them. Below them, a magnificent phalanx of three million Qin soldiers stood arrayed on the ground, the entire formation a square three miles[2] on each side. Lit by the freshly risen sun, the phalanx remained still like a giant carpet made of three million terra-cotta warriors. But when a flock of birds wandered above the phalanx, the birds immediately felt the potential for death from below and scattered anxiously.

Jing Ke said, "Your Majesty, your army is truly matchless. In an extremely short time, we have completed such complex training."

King Zheng held on to the hilt of his long sword. "Even though the whole is complex, what each soldier must do is very simple. Compared to the military training they went through, this is nothing."

2 For the benefit of English readers, Chinese measurement units (such as *li, zhang, chi,* and *cun*) throughout the text have been translated and converted into approximate English equivalents.

"Then, Your Majesty, please give the great order!" Jing Ke's voice trembled with excitement.

King Zheng nodded. A guard ran over, grabbed the hilt of the king's sword, and stepped backward. The bronze sword was so long that it was impossible for the king to pull it out of the scabbard without help. The guard knelt and presented the sword to the king, who lifted the sword to the sky and shouted, "Calculating formation!"

Battle drums began to beat, and four giant bronze cauldrons at the corners of the stone dais came to life simultaneously with roaring flames. A group of soldiers standing at the edge of the dais facing the phalanx chanted in unison, "Calculating formation!"

On the ground below, colors in the phalanx began to shift and move. Complicated and detailed circuit patterns appeared and gradually filled the entire formation. Ten minutes later, the army had rearranged itself into a nine-mile-square calculating formation.

Jing Ke pointed to the formation and began to explain. "Your Majesty, we have named this formation Qin One. Look, there in the center is the central processing subformation, the core calculating component, made up of the best divisions of your army. By referencing this diagram, you can locate the adding subformations, quick storage subformations, and stack memory subformation. The part around it that looks highly regular is the memory subformation. When we built that part, we found that we didn't have enough soldiers. But luckily, the work done by the elements in this component is the simplest, so we trained each soldier to hold more colored flags. Each man can now complete the work that initially required twenty men. This allowed us to increase the memory capacity to meet the minimum requirements for running the calculating procedure for the circular ratio. Observe also the open passage that runs through the entire formation, and the light cavalry waiting for orders in the passage: that's the system's main communication line, responsible for transmitting information between the components of the whole system."

Two soldiers brought over a large scroll, tall as a man, and spread it open before King Zheng. When they reached the scroll's end, everyone present remembered the scene in the palace a few years ago, and they all held their breath. But the imaginary dagger did not appear. Before them was only a large sheet of thin silk filled with symbols, each the size of a fly's head. Packed so densely, the symbols were as dazzling to behold as the calculating formation on the ground below.

"Your Majesty, these are the orders in the procedure I developed for calculating the circular ratio. Please look here"—Jing Ke pointed to the calculating formation below—"where the soldiers standing ready for what I call the 'hardware.' What's on this cloth is what I call the 'software,' the soul of the calculating formation. The relationship between hardware and software is like that between the *guqin* zither and sheet music."

King Zheng nodded. "Good. Begin."

Jing Ke lifted both hands above his head and solemnly chanted, "As ordered by the Great King, initiate the calculating formation! System self-test!"

A row of soldiers standing halfway down the face of the stone dais repeated the order using flag signals. In a moment, the phalanx of three million men seemed to turn into a lake filled with sparkling lights as millions of tiny flags waved.

"Self-test complete! Begin initialization sequence! Load calculation procedure!"

Below, the light cavalry on the main communication line that passed through the entire calculating formation began to ride back and forth swiftly. The main passage soon turned into a turbulent river. Along the way, the river fed into numerous thin tributaries, infiltrating all the modular subformations. Soon the ripples of black and white flags coalesced into surging waves that filled the entire phalanx. The central processing subformation area was the most tumultuous, like tinder set on fire.

Suddenly, as though the fuel had been exhausted, the movements in the central processing subformation slackened and eventually stopped. Starting with the central processing subformation in the center, the stillness spread in every direction like a lake being frozen over. Finally the entire calculating formation came to a stop, with only a few scattered components flashing lifelessly in infinite loops.

"System lockup!" a signal officer called out. Shortly after, the reason for the malfunction was determined: there was an error with the operation of one of the gates in the central processing subformation's status storage unit.

"Restart system!" Jing Ke ordered confidently.

"Not yet," King Zheng said as he grasped his sword. "Replace the malfunctioning gate and behead all the soldiers who made up that gate. In the future, any other malfunctions will be dealt with the same way."

A few riders dashed into the phalanx with their swords drawn. They killed the three unfortunate soldiers and replaced them with new men. From the vantage point of the dais, three eye-catching pools of blood appeared in the middle of the central processing subformation.

Jing Ke gave the order to restart the system. This time, it went very smoothly. Ten minutes later, the soldiers were carrying out the circular-ratio-calculating procedure. As the phalanx rippled with flag signals, the calculating formation settled into the long computation.

"This is really interesting," King Zheng said, pointing to the spectacular sight. "Each individual's behavior is so simple, yet together, they can produce such complex intelligence."

"Great King, this is just the mechanical operation of a machine, not intelligence. Each of these lowly individuals is just a zero. Only when someone like you is added to the front as a one is the whole endowed with meaning." Jing Ke's smile was ingratiating.

"How long would it take to calculate ten thousand digits of the circular ratio?" King Zheng asked.

"About ten months. Maybe even sooner if things go right."

General Wang Jian[3] stepped forward. "Your Majesty, I must urge caution. Even in regular military operations, it's extremely dangerous to concentrate so much of our force in an open area like this. More-

---

3 One of the four great generals of King Zheng's campaigns against the other six states. The historical Wang Jian was responsible for the destruction of the states of Yan (where Jing Ke was from), Zhao, and Chu.

over, the three million soldiers in this phalanx are unarmed, carrying only signal flags. The calculating formation is not intended for battle and will be extremely vulnerable if attacked. Even under normal conditions, to effectuate an orderly retreat of this many men packed so tightly would take most of a day. If they were attacked, retreat would be impossible. Sire, this calculating formation will appear in the eyes of our enemies as meat placed on a cutting board."

King Zheng did not reply, but turned his gaze to Jing Ke. The latter bowed and said, "General Wang is absolutely right. You must be cautious when deciding whether to pursue this calculation."

Then Jing Ke did something bold and unprecedented: he lifted his eyes and locked gazes with King Zheng. The king immediately understood the meaning in that gaze: *All your accomplishments so far are like zeros; only with the addition of eternal life for yourself, a one, can all of those become meaningful.*

"General Wang, you're overly concerned." King Zheng whipped his sleeves contemptuously. "The states of Han, Wei, Zhao, and Chu have all been conquered. The only two remaining states, Yan and Qi, are led by foolish kings who have exhausted their people. They're on the verge of total collapse and pose no threat. Given the way things are going, by the time the circular ratio calculation is complete, those two states may already have fallen apart on their own and surrendered to the Great State of Qin. Of course, I appreciate the general's caution. I suggest that we form a line of scouts at some distance from the calculating formation and step up our surveillance of the movements of the Yan and Qi armies. This way, we will be secure." He lifted his long sword toward the sky and solemnly declared, "The calculations must be finished. I have decided that it must be so."

The calculating formation ran smoothly for a month, and the results were even better than expected. Already, more than two thousand digits of the circular ratio had been computed, and as the soldiers in the formation grew used to the work and Jing Ke further refined the calculating procedure, speed in the future would be even faster. The estimate was that only three more years would be needed to reach the target of a hundred thousand digits.

※

The morning of the forty-fifth day after the start of the calculations was foggy. It was impossible to see the calculating formation, enveloped in mist, from the dais. Soldiers in the formation could see no farther than about five men.

But the calculating formation's operation was designed to be unaffected by the fog and continued. Shouted orders and the hoofbeats of the light cavalry on the main communication line echoed in the haze.

However, those soldiers in the north of the calculating formation heard something else. At first, the noise came intermittently and seemed illusory, but soon the noise grew louder and formed a continuous boom, like thunder coming from the depths of the fog.

The noise came from the hooves of thousands of horses. A powerful division of cavalry approached the calculating formation from the north, and the banner of the state of Yan flew at their head. The riders moved slowly, forcing their horses to maintain ranks. They knew they had plenty of time.

Only when the riders were about a third of a mile from the edge of the calculating formation did they begin the charge. By the time the vanguard of the cavalry had torn into the calculating formation, the Qin soldiers didn't even get a proper look at their enemies. In this initial charge, tens of thousands of Qin soldiers died just from being trampled under the hooves of the attacking riders.

What followed was not a battle at all, but a massacre. Before the battle, the Yan commanders already knew that they would not meet with meaningful resistance. In order to increase the efficiency of the slaughter, the riders abandoned the traditional cavalry weapons, long-handled lances and halberds, and instead equipped themselves with swords and morning stars. The several hundred thousand Yan heavy cavalry became a death-dealing cloud, and wherever they rode, the bodies of Qin soldiers carpeted the land.

In order to avoid giving warning to the core of the calculating formation, the Yan riders killed in silence, as though they were machines, not men. But the screams of the dying Qin soldiers, whether cut down or trampled, spread far and wide in the thick fog.

However, all the Qin soldiers in the calculating formation had been trained under threat of death to ignore outside interference and to devote themselves single-mindedly to the simple task of acting as calculating components. Combined with the disguise provided by the thick fog, the result was that most of the calculating formation did not realize the northern edge of the formation was already under attack. As the death-dealing region slowly and orderly ate through the formation, turning it into piles of corpses strewn over blood-soaked, muddy ground, the rest of the formation continued to calculate as before, even though more and more errors began to plague the system.

Behind the first wave of cavalry, more than a hundred thousand Yan archers loosened volleys from their long bows, aimed at the heart of the calculating formation. In a few moments, millions of arrows fell like a thunderstorm, and almost every arrow found a target.

Only then did the calculating formation start to fall apart. At the same time, information of the enemy attack began to spread, increasing the chaos. The light cavalry on the main communication line carried reports of the sudden attack, but as the situation deteriorated, the main passage became blocked, and the panicked riders began to trample through the densely packed phalanx. Countless Qin soldiers thus died under the hooves of friendly forces.

On the eastern, southern, and western edges of the calculating formation, which weren't under attack, Qin soldiers began to retreat without any semblance of order. Amidst the utter lack of information and broken chain of command, the retreat was slow and confused. The calculating formation, now purposeless, became like a thick, concentrated bubble of ink that refused to dissolve in water, with only wispy tendrils leaving at the edges.

Those Qin soldiers running toward the east were soon stopped by the disciplined ranks of the Qi army. Instead of charging, the Qi commanders ordered the infantry and cavalry to form impregnable defensive lines to wait for the escaping Qin soldiers to enter the trap before surrounding them and beginning the slaughter.

The only direction left for the remainder of the hopeless Qin army, now without any will to fight, was toward the southwest. Hundreds of thousands of unarmed men poured over the plains like a dirty flood. But they soon encountered a third enemy force: unlike the disciplined armies from Yan and Qi, this third force consisted of the ferocious riders of the Huns. They tore into the Qin army like wolves into a flock of sheep and quickly overwhelmed them.

The slaughter continued until noon, when the strong breeze from the west lifted the fog, and the wide expanse of the battlefield was exposed to the glare of the midday sun.

The Yan, Qi, and Hun armies had combined in multiple places, surrounding what remained of the Qin army in small pockets. The cavalry of the three armies continued to charge the Qin soldiers, leaving the wounded and the few escapees to be mopped up by the infantry. Oxen formations, urged on by fire, and catapults were also put into operation to kill the remaining Qin men even more efficiently.

By evening, the sorrowful notes of battle horns echoed over a field covered with bodies and crisscrossed by rivulets of blood. The final survivors of the Qin army were now surrounded in three shrinking pockets.

The night that followed had a full moon. The pure, cold moon floated impassively over the slaughter below, bathing the mountains of corpses and seas of blood in its calm, liquid light. The killing continued throughout the night and wasn't over until the next morning.

The army of the Qin Empire was entirely eliminated.

One month later, the allied forces of Qi and Yan entered Xianyang and captured King Zheng. The Qin Empire was over.

The day selected for the execution of King Zheng was another day when the sun and the moon appeared together. The moon floated in the azure sky like a snowflake.

The monument that had been intended for Jing Ke still hung in the air. King Zheng sat below it, waiting for the Yan executioner to cut the oxhide rope.

Jing Ke walked out of the crowd observing the execution, still dressed all in white. He came before King Zheng and bowed. "Your Majesty."

"In your heart, you've always remained a Yan assassin," the king said. He did not look up at Jing Ke.

"Yes. But I didn't want to just kill you. I also needed to eliminate your army. If I had succeeded a few years ago in killing you, Qin would have remained powerful. Advised by brilliant strategists and led by veteran commanders, the million-strong Qin army would still have posed an unstoppable threat to Yan."

King Zheng asked the last question of his life. "How could you have sent so many men so close to my army without my notice?"

"During the year when the calculating formation was being trained and operating, Yan and Qi focused on digging tunnels. Each tunnel was many miles long and wide enough to allow cavalry to pass through. It was my idea to use these tunnels to allow the allies to bypass your sentries and appear suddenly near the defenseless calculating formation."

King Zheng nodded and said nothing more. He closed his eyes to wait to die. The supervising official gave the order, and an executioner began to climb up the platform, a knife held between his teeth.

King Zheng heard movements next to him. He opened his eyes and saw that Jing Ke was sitting next to him.

"Your Majesty, we'll die together. When the heavy stone falls, it will become a monument to both of us. Our blood and flesh will mix together. Perhaps this will give you some comfort."

"What is the point of this?" King Zheng asked coldly.

"It's not that I want to die. The King of Yan has ordered my execution."

A smile quickly appeared on King Zheng's face and disappeared just as quickly, like a passing breeze. "You have accomplished so much for Yan that your name is praised more than the king's. He fears your ambition. This result is expected."

"That is indeed one reason, but not the main one. I also advised the King of Yan to build Yan's own calculating formation. This gave him the excuse he needed to kill me."

King Zheng turned to gaze at Jing Ke. The surprise in the king's eyes was genuine.

"I don't care if you believe me. My advice was given with the hope of strengthening Yan. It's true that the calculating formation was a stratagem I came up with to destroy Qin by taking advantage of your obsession with eternal life. But it's also a genuinely great invention. Through its calculating power, we can understand the language of mathematics and divine the mysteries of the universe. It could have opened a new era."

The executioner had reached the top of the platform and stood in front of the rope holding up the stone monument, waiting for the final order as he held the knife in his hand.

In the distance, under a bright baldachin, the King of Yan waved his hand in assent. The supervising official shouted the order to carry out the sentence.

Jing Ke suddenly opened his eyes wide as though awakening from a dream. "I've got it! The calculating formation doesn't have to rely on the army, not even people. All those gates—AND, NOT, NAND, NOR, and so on—can be made from mechanical components. These components can be made very small, and when they're put together they will be a mechanical calculating formation! No, it shouldn't be called a calculating formation at all, but a calculating machine! Listen to me, King; wait!" Jing Ke shouted at the King of Yan in the distance. "The calculating machine! The calculating machine!"

The executioner cut the rope.

"The calculating machine!" Jing Ke shouted the three words with the last of his breath.

As the giant stone fell, in that moment when its massive shadow blotted out everything in the world, King Zheng felt the end of his life. But in the eyes of Jing Ke, a faint ray of light heralding the beginning of a new era was extinguished.

TAKING CARE OF GOD

1.

Once again, God had upset Qiusheng's family.

This had begun as a very good morning. A thin layer of white fog floated at the height of a man over the fields around Xicen village like a sheet of rice paper that had just become blank: the quiet countryside being the painting that had fallen out of the paper. The first rays of morning fell on the scene, and the year's earliest dewdrops entered the most glorious period of their brief life . . . but God had ruined this beautiful morning.

God had gotten up extra early and gone into the kitchen to warm some milk for himself. Ever since the start of the Era of Support, the milk market had prospered. Qiusheng's family had bought a milk cow for a bit more than ten thousand yuan, and then, imitating others, mixed the milk with water to sell. The unadulterated milk had also become one of the staples for the family.

After the milk was warm, God took the bowl into the living room to watch TV without turning off the liquefied petroleum gas stove.

When Qiusheng's wife, Yulian, returned from cleaning the cowshed and the pigsty, she could smell gas all over the house. Covering her nose with a towel, she rushed into the kitchen to turn off the stove, opened the window, and turned on the fan.

"You old fool! You're going to get the whole family killed!" Yulian shouted into the living room. The family had switched to using lique-fied petroleum gas for cooking only after they began supporting God. Qiusheng's father had always been opposed to it, saying that gas was not as good as honeycomb coal briquettes. Now he had even more ammunition for his argument.

As was his wont, God stood with his head lowered contritely, his broom-like white beard hanging past his knees, smiling like a kid who knew he had done something wrong. "I . . . I took down the pot for heating the milk. Why didn't it turn off by itself?"

"You think you're still on your spaceship?" Qiusheng said, com-ing down the stairs. "Everything here is dumb. We aren't like you, being waited on hand and foot by smart machines. We have to work hard with dumb tools. That's how we put rice in our bowls!"

"We also worked hard. Otherwise how did you come to be?" God said carefully.

"Enough with the 'how did you come to be?' Enough! I'm sick of hearing it. If you're so powerful, go and make other obedient children to support you!" Yulian threw her towel on the ground.

"Forget it. Just forget it," Qiusheng said. He was always the one who made peace. "Let's eat."

Bingbing got up. As he came down the stairs, he yawned. "Ma, Pa, God was coughing all night. I couldn't sleep."

"You don't know how good you have it," Yulian said. "Your dad and I were in the room next to his. You don't hear us complaining, do you?"

As though triggered, God began to cough again. He coughed like he was playing his favorite sport with great concentration.

Yulian stared at God for a few seconds before sighing. "I must have the worst luck in eight generations." Still angry, she left for the kitchen to cook breakfast.

God sat silently through breakfast with the rest of the family. He ate one bowl of porridge with pickled vegetables and half a *mantou* bun. During the entire time he had to endure Yulian's disdainful looks—maybe she was still mad about the liquefied petroleum gas, or maybe she thought he ate too much.

After breakfast, as usual, God got up quickly to clean the table and wash the dishes in the kitchen. Standing just outside the kitchen, Yulian shouted, "Don't use detergent if there's no grease on the bowl! Everything costs money. The pittance they pay for your support? Ha!"

God grunted nonstop to show that he understood.

Qiusheng and Yulian left for the fields. Bingbing left for school. Only now did Qiusheng's father get up. Still not fully awake, he came downstairs, ate two bowls of porridge, and filled his pipe with tobacco. At last he remembered God's existence.

"Hey, old geezer, stop the washing. Come out and play a game with me!" he shouted into the kitchen.

God came out of the kitchen, wiping his hands on his apron. He nodded ingratiatingly at Qiusheng's father. Playing Chinese Chess with the old man was a tough chore for God; winning and losing both had unpleasant consequences. If God won, Qiusheng's father would get mad: *You fucking old idiot! You trying to show me up? Shit! You're God! Beating me is no great accomplishment at all. Why can't you learn some manners? You've lived under this roof long enough!* But if God lost, Qiusheng's father would still get mad: *You fucking old idiot! I'm the best chess player for fifty kilometers. Beating you is easier than squishing a bedbug. You think I need you to let me win? You . . . to put it politely, you are* insulting *me!*

In any case, the final result was the same: the old man flipped the board, and the pieces flew everywhere. Qiusheng's father was infamous for his bad temper, and now he'd finally found a punching bag in God.

But the old man didn't hold a grudge. Every time after God picked up the board and put the pieces back quietly, he sat down and played with God again—and the whole process was repeated. After a few cycles of this, both of them were tired, and it was almost noon.

God then got up to wash the vegetables. Yulian didn't allow him to cook because she said God was a terrible cook. But he still had to wash the vegetables. Later, when Qiusheng and Yulian returned from the fields, if the vegetables hadn't been washed, she would be on him again with another round of bitter, sarcastic scolding.

While God washed the vegetables, Qiusheng's father left to visit the neighbors. This was the most peaceful part of God's day. The noon sun filled every crack in the brick-lined yard and illuminated the deep crevasses in his memory. During such periods God often forgot his work and stood quietly, lost in thought. Only when the noise of the villagers returning from the fields filled the air would he be startled awake and hurry to finish his washing.

He sighed. *How could life have turned out like this?*

This wasn't only God's sigh. It was also the sigh of Qiusheng, Yulian, and Qiusheng's father. It was the sigh of more than five billion people and two billion Gods on Earth.

2.

It all began with an autumn evening three years ago.

"Come quickly! There are toys in the sky!" Bingbing shouted in the yard. Qiusheng and Yulian raced out of the house, looked up, and saw that the sky really was filled with toys, or at least objects whose shapes could only belong to toys.

The objects spread out evenly across the dome of the sky. In the dusk, each reflected the light of the setting sun—already below the horizon—and each shone as bright as the full moon. The light turned Earth's surface as bright as it is at noon. But the light came from every direction and left no shadow, as though the whole world was illuminated by a giant surgical lamp.

At first, everyone thought the objects were within our atmosphere because they were so clear. But eventually, humans learned that these objects were just enormous. They were hovering about thirty thousand kilometers away in geostationary orbits.

There were a total of 21,530 spaceships. Spread out evenly across the sky, they formed a thin shell around Earth. This was the result of a complex set of maneuvers that brought all the ships to their final locations simultaneously. In this manner, the alien ships avoided causing life-threatening tides in the oceans due to their imbalanced mass.

The gesture assured humans somewhat, as it was at least some evidence that the aliens did not bear ill will toward Earth.

During the next few days, all attempts at communicating with the aliens failed. The aliens maintained absolute silence in the face of repeated queries. At the same time, Earth became a nightless planet. Tens of thousands of spaceships reflected so much sunlight onto the night side of Earth that it was as bright as day, while on the day side, the ships cast giant shadows onto the ground. The horrible sight pushed the psychological endurance of the human race to the limit, so that most ignored yet another strange occurrence on the surface of the planet and did not connect it with the fleet of spaceships in the sky.

Across the great cities of the world, wandering old people had begun to appear. All of them had the same features: extreme old age, long white hair and beards, long white robes. At first, before the white robe, white beard, and white hair got dirty, they looked like a bunch of snowmen. The wanderers did not appear to belong to any particular race, as though all ethnicities were mixed in them. They had no documents to prove their citizenship or identity and could not explain their own history.

All they could do was to gently repeat, in heavily accented versions of various local languages, the same words to all passersby:

"We are God. Please, considering that we created this world, would you give us a bit of food?"

If only one or two old wanderers had said this, then they would have been sent to a shelter or nursing home, like the homeless with dementia. But millions of old men and women all saying the same thing—that was an entirely different thing.

Within half a month, the number of old wanderers had increased to more than thirty million. All over the streets of New York, Beijing, London, Moscow . . . these old people could be seen everywhere, shuffling around in traffic-stopping crowds. Sometimes it seemed as if there were more of *them* than the original inhabitants of the cities.

The most horrible part of their presence was that they all repeated the same thing: "We are God. Please, considering that we created this world, would you give us a bit of food?"

Only now did humans turn their attention from the spaceships to the uninvited guests. Recently, large-scale meteor showers had been occurring over every continent. After every impressive display of streaking meteors, the number of old wanderers in the corresponding region greatly increased. After careful observation, the following incredible fact was discovered: the old wanderers came out of the sky, from those alien spaceships.

One by one, they leaped into the atmosphere as though diving into a swimming pool, each wearing a suit made from a special film. As the friction from the atmosphere burned away the surface of the suits, the film kept the heat away from the wearer and slowed their descent. Careful design ensured that the deceleration never exceeded 4G, well within the physical tolerance of the bodies of the old wanderers. Finally, at the moment of their arrival at the surface, their velocity was close to zero, as though they had just jumped down from a bench. Even so, many of them still managed to sprain their ankles. Simultaneously, the film around them had been completely burned away, leaving no trace.

The meteor showers continued without stopping. More wanderers fell to Earth. Their number rose to almost one hundred million.

The government of every country attempted to find one or more representatives among the wanderers. But the wanderers claimed that the "Gods" were absolutely equal, and any one of them could represent all of them. Thus, at the emergency session of the United Nations General Assembly, one random old wanderer, who was found in Times Square and who now spoke passable English, entered the General Assembly Hall.

He was clearly among the earliest to land: his robe was dirty and full of holes, and his white beard was covered with dirt, like a mop. There was no halo over his head, but a few loyal flies did hover there. With the help of a ratty bamboo walking stick, he shuffled his way to the round meeting table and lowered himself under the gaze of the leaders. He looked up at the Secretary-General, and his face displayed the childlike smile particular to all the old wanderers.

"I . . . ha— . . . I haven't had breakfast yet."

So breakfast was brought. All across the world, people stared as he ate like a starved man, choking a few times. Toast, sausages, and a salad were quickly gone, followed by a large glass of milk. Then he showed his innocent smile to the Secretary-General again.

"Haha . . . uh . . . is there any wine? Just a tiny cup will do."

So a glass of wine was brought. He sipped at it, nodding with satisfaction. "Last night, a bunch of new arrivals took over my favorite subway grille, one that blew out warm air. I had to find a new place to sleep in the Square. But now with a bit of wine, my joints are coming back to life. . . . You, can you massage my back a little? Just a little."

The Secretary-General began to massage his back. The old wanderer shook his head, sighed, and said, "Sorry to be so much trouble to you."

"Where are you from?" asked the President of the United States.

The old wanderer shook his head. "A civilization only has a fixed location in her infancy. Planets and stars are unstable and change. The civilization must then move. By the time she becomes a young woman, she has already moved multiple times. Then they will make this discovery: no planetary environment is as stable as a sealed space-ship. So they'll make spaceships their home, and planets will just be places where they sojourn. Thus, any civilization that has reached adulthood will be a starfaring civilization, permanently wandering through the cosmos. The spaceship is her home. Where are we from? We come from the ships." He pointed up with a finger caked in dirt.

"How many of you are there?"

"Two billion."

"Who are you really?" The Secretary-General had cause to ask this. The old wanderers looked just like humans.

"We've told you many times." The old wanderer impatiently waved his hand. "We are God."

"Could you explain?"

"Our civilization—let's just call her the God Civilization—had existed long before Earth was born. When the God Civilization entered her senescence, we seeded the newly formed Earth with the beginnings of life. Then the God Civilization skipped across time by traveling close to the speed of light. When life on Earth had evolved to the appropriate stage, we came back, introduced a new species based on our ancestral genes, eliminated its enemies, and carefully guided its evolution until Earth was home to a new civilized species just like us."

"How do you expect us to believe you?"

"That's easy."

Thus began the half-year-long effort to verify these claims. Humans watched in astonishment as spaceships sent the original plans for life on Earth and images of the primitive Earth. Following the old wanderer's direction, humans dug up incredible machines from deep below Earth's crust, equipment that had through the long eons monitored and manipulated the biosphere on this planet.

Humans finally had to believe. At least with respect to life on Earth, the Gods really were God.

3.

At the third emergency session of the United Nations General Assembly, the Secretary-General, on behalf of the human race, finally asked God the key question: why did they come to Earth?

"Before I answer this question, you must have a correct understanding of the concept of civilization." God stroked his long beard. This was the same God who had been at the first emergency session half a year ago. "How do you think civilizations evolve over time?"

"Civilization on Earth is currently in a stage of rapid development. If we're not hit by natural disasters beyond our ability to resist, I think we will continue our development indefinitely," said the Secretary-General.

"Wrong. Think about it. Every person experiences childhood, youth, middle age, and old age, finally arriving at death. The stars are the same way. Indeed, everything in the universe goes through the same process. Even the universe itself will have to terminate one day.

Why would civilization be an exception? No, a civilization will also grow old and die."

"How exactly does that happen?"

"Different civilizations grow old and die in different ways, just like different people die of different diseases or just plain old age. For the God Civilization, the first sign of her senescence was the extreme lengthening of each individual member's life span. By then, each individual in the God Civilization could expect a life as long as four thousand Earth years. By age two thousand, their thoughts had completely ossified, losing all creativity. Because individuals like these held the reins of power, new life had a hard time emerging and growing. That was when our civilization became old."

"And then?"

"The second sign of the civilization's senescence was the Age of the Machine Cradle."

"What?"

"By then our machines no longer relied on their creators. They operated independently, maintained themselves, and developed on their own. The smart machines gave us everything we needed: not just material needs, but also psychological ones. We didn't need to put any effort into survival. Taken care of by machines, we lived as though we were lying in comfortable cradles.

"Think about it; if the jungles of primitive Earth had been filled with inexhaustible supplies of fruits and tame creatures that desired to become food, how could apes evolve into humans? The Machine Cradle was just such a comfort-filled jungle. Gradually we forgot about our technology and science. Our civilization became lazy and empty, devoid of creativity and ambition, and that only sped up the aging process. What you see now is the God Civilization in her final dying gasps."

"Then . . . can you now tell us the goal for the God Civilization in coming to Earth?"

"We have no home now."

"But . . ." The Secretary-General pointed upward.

"The spaceships are old. It's true that the artificial environment on the ships is more stable than any natural environment, including Earth's. But the ships are so old, old beyond your imagination. Old components have broken down. Accumulated quantum effects over the eons have led to more and more software errors. The system's self-repair and self-maintenance functions have encountered more and more insurmountable obstacles. The living environment on the ships is deteriorating. The amount of life necessities that can be distributed to individuals is decreasing by the day. We can just about survive. In the twenty thousand cities on the various ships, the air is filled with pollution and despair."

"Are there no solutions? Perhaps new components for the ships? A software upgrade?"

God shook his head. "The God Civilization is in her final years. We are two billion dying men and women each more than three thousand years old. But before us, hundreds of generations had already lived in the comfort of the Machine Cradle. Long ago, we forgot all our technology. Now we have no way to repair these ships that have been operating for tens of millions of years on their own. Indeed, in terms of the ability to study and understand technology, we are even worse than you. We can't even connect a circuit for a lightbulb or solve a quadratic equation . . .

"One day, the ships told us that they were close to complete breakdown. The propulsion systems could no longer push the ships near the speed of light. The God Civilization could only drift along at a speed not even one-tenth the speed of light, and the ecological support systems were nearing collapse. The machines could no longer keep two billion of us alive. We had to find another way out."

"Did you ever think that this would happen?"

"Of course. Two thousand years ago, the ships already warned us. That was when we began the process of seeding life on Earth so that in our old age we would have support."

"Two thousand years ago?"

"Yes. Of course I'm talking about time on the ships. From your frame of reference, that was three-point-five billion years ago, when Earth first cooled down."

"We have a question: you say that you've lost your technology. But doesn't seeding life require technology?"

"Oh. To start the process of evolving life on a planet is a minor operation. Just scatter some seeds, and life will multiply and evolve on its own. We had this kind of software even before the Age of the Machine Cradle. Just start the program, and the machines can finish everything. To create a planet full of life, capable of developing civilization, the most basic requirement is time, a few billion years of time.

"By traveling close to the speed of light, we possess almost limitless time. But now, the God Civilization's ships can no longer approach the speed of light. Otherwise we'd still have the chance to create new civilizations and more life, and we would have more choices. We're trapped by slowness. Those dreams cannot be realized."

"So you want to spend your golden years on Earth."

"Yes, yes. We hope that you will feel a sense of filial duty toward your creators and take us in." God leaned on his walking stick and trembled as he tried to bow to the leaders of all the nations, and he almost fell on his face.

"But how do you plan to live here?"

"If we just gathered in one place by ourselves, then we might as well stay in space and die there. We'd like to be absorbed into your societies, your families. When the God Civilization was still in her childhood, we also had families. You know that childhood is the most precious time. Since your civilization is still in her childhood, if we can return to this era and spend the rest of our lives in the warmth of families, then that would be our greatest happiness."

"There are two billion of you. That means every family on Earth would have to take in one or two of you." After the Secretary-General spoke, the meeting hall sank into silence.

"Yes, yes, sorry to give you so much trouble . . ." God continued to bow while stealing glances at the Secretary-General and the leaders of all the nations. "Of course, we're willing to compensate you."

He waved his cane, and two more white-bearded Gods walked into the meeting hall, struggling under the weight of a silvery, metallic trunk they carried between them. "Look, these are high-density information storage devices. They systematically store the knowledge the God Civilization had acquired in every field of science and technology. With this, your civilization will advance by leaps and bounds. I think you will like this."

The Secretary-General, like the leaders of all the nations, looked at the metal trunk and tried to hide his elation. "Taking care of God is the responsibility of humankind. Of course this will require some consultation between the various nations, but I think in principle . . ."

"Sorry to be so much trouble. Sorry to be so much trouble . . ." God's eyes filled with tears, and he continued to bow.

After the Secretary-General and the leaders of all the nations left the meeting hall, they saw that tens of thousands of Gods had gathered outside the United Nations building. A white sea of bobbing heads filled the air with murmuring words. The Secretary-General listened carefully and realized that they were all speaking, in the various tongues of Earth, the same sentence:

"Sorry to be so much trouble. Sorry to be so much trouble . . ."

4.

Two billion Gods arrived on Earth. Enclosed in suits made of their special film, they fell through the atmosphere. During that time, one could see the bright, colorful streaks in the sky even during the day. After the Gods landed, they spread out into 1.5 billion families.

Having received the Gods' knowledge about science and technology, everyone was filled with hopes and dreams for the future, as though humankind was about to step into paradise overnight. Under the influence of such joy, every family welcomed the coming of God.

That morning, Qiusheng and his family and all the other villagers stood at the village entrance to receive the Gods allocated to Xicen.

"What a beautiful day," Yulian said.

Her comment wasn't motivated solely by her feelings. The spaceships had disappeared overnight, restoring the sky's wide open and limitless appearance. Humans had never been allowed to step onto any of the ships. The Gods did not really object to that particular request from the humans, but the ships themselves refused to grant permission. They did not acknowledge the various primitive probes which Earth sent and sealed their doors tightly. After the final group of Gods leaped into the atmosphere, all the spaceships, numbering more than twenty thousand, departed their orbit simultaneously. But they didn't go far, only drifting in the asteroid belt.

Although these ships were ancient, the old routines continued to function. Their only mission was to serve the Gods. Thus, they would not move too far. When the Gods needed them again, they would come.

Two buses arrived from the county seat, bringing the one hundred and six Gods allocated to Xicen. Qiusheng and Yulian met the God assigned to their family. The couple stood on each side of God, affectionately supported him by the arms, and walked home in the bright afternoon sun. Bingbing and Qiusheng's father followed behind, smiling.

"Gramps, um, Gramps God." Yulian leaned her face against God's shoulder, her smile as bright as the sun. "I hear that the technology you gave us will soon allow us to experience true Communism! When that happens, we'll all have things according to our needs. Things won't cost any money. You just go to the store and pick them up."

God smiled and nodded at her, his white hair bobbing. He spoke in heavily accented Chinese. "Yes. Actually, 'to each according to need' fulfills only the most basic needs of a civilization. The technology we gave you will bring you a life of prosperity and comfort surpassing your imagination."

Yulian's laughed so much her face opened up like a flower. "No, no! 'To each according to need' is more than enough for me!"

"Uh-huh," Qiusheng's father agreed emphatically.

"Can we live forever without aging like you?" Qiusheng asked.

"We can't live forever without aging. It's just that we can live longer than you. Look at how old I am! In my view, if a man lives longer than three thousand years, he might as well be dead. For a civilization, extreme longevity for the individual can be fatal."

"Oh, I don't need three thousand years. Just three hundred." Qiusheng's father was now laughing as much as Yulian. "In that case, I'd still be considered a young man right now. Maybe I can . . . hahahaha."

※

The village treated the day like it was Chinese New Year. Every family held a big banquet to welcome its God, and Qiusheng's family was no exception.

Qiusheng's father quickly became a little drunk with cups of vintage *huangjiu*. He gave God a thumbs-up. "You're really something! To be able to create so many living things—you're truly supernatural."

God drank a lot, too, but his head was still clear. He waved his hand. "No, not supernatural. It was just science. When biology has developed to a certain level, creating life is akin to building machines."

"You say that. But in our eyes, you're no different from immortals who have deigned to live among us."

God shook his head. "Supernatural beings would never make mistakes. But for us, we made mistake after mistake during your creation."

"You made mistakes when you created us?" Yulian's eyes were wide open. In her imagination, creating all those lives was a process similar to her giving birth to Bingbing eight years ago. No mistake was possible.

"There were many. I'll give a relatively recent example. The world-creation software made errors in the analysis of the environment on Earth, which resulted in the appearance of creatures like dinosaurs: huge bodies and low adaptability. Eventually, in order to facilitate your evolution, they had to be eliminated.

"Speaking of events that are even more recent, after the disappearance of the ancient Aegean civilizations, the world-creation software believed that civilization on Earth was successfully established. It ceased to perform further monitoring and microadjustments, like leaving a wound-up clock to run on its own. This resulted in further errors. For example, it should have allowed the civilization of ancient Greece to develop on her own and stopped the Macedonian conquest and the subsequent Roman conquest. Although both of these ended up as the inheritors of Greek civilization, the direction of Greek development was altered . . ."

No one in Qiusheng's family could understand this lecture, but all respectfully listened.

"And then two great powers appeared on Earth: Han China and the Roman Empire. In contrast to the earlier situation with ancient Greece, the two shouldn't have been kept apart and left to develop in isolation. They ought to have been allowed to come into full contact . . ."

"This 'Han China' you're talking about? Is that the Han Dynasty of Liu Bang and Xiang Yu?" Finally Qiusheng's father heard something he knew. "And what is this 'Roman Empire'?"

"I think that was a foreigners' country at the time," Qiusheng said, trying to explain. "It was pretty big."

Qiusheng's father was confused. "Why? When the foreigners finally showed up during the Qing Dynasty, look how badly they beat us up. You want them to show up even earlier? During the Han Dynasty?"

God laughed at this. "No, no. Back then, Han China was just as powerful as the Roman Empire."

"That's still bad. If those two great powers had met, it would have been a great war. Blood would have flowed like a river."

God nodded. He reached out with his chopsticks for a piece of beef braised in soy sauce. "Could have been. But if those two great civilizations, the Occident and the Orient, had met, the encounter would have generated glorious sparks and greatly advanced human progress.... Eh, if those errors could have been avoided, Earth would now probably be colonizing Mars, and your interstellar probes would have flown past Sirius."

Qiusheng's father raised his bowl of *huangjiu* and spoke admiringly. "Everyone says that the Gods have forgotten science in their cradle, but you are still so learned."

"To be comfortable in the cradle, it's important to know a bit about philosophy, art, history, etc—just some common facts, not real learning. Many scholars on Earth right now have much deeper thoughts than our own."

※

For the Gods, the first few months after they entered human society were a golden age, when they lived very harmoniously with human families. It was as though they had returned to the childhood of the God Civilization, fully immersed in the long-forgotten warmth of family life. This seemed the best way to spend the final years of their extremely long lives.

Qiusheng's family's God enjoyed the peaceful life in this beautiful southern Chinese village. Every day he went to the pond surrounded by bamboo groves to fish, chat with other old folks from the village, play chess, and generally enjoy himself. But his greatest hobby was attending folk operas. Whenever a theatre troupe came to the village or the town, he made sure to go to every performance.

His favorite opera was *The Butterfly Lovers*. One performance was not enough. He followed one troupe around for more than fifty kilometers and attended several shows in a row. Finally Qiusheng went to town and bought him a VCD of the opera. God played it over and over until he could hum a few lines of *Huangmei* opera and sounded pretty good.

One day Yulian discovered a secret. She whispered to Qiusheng and her father-in-law, "Did you know that every time Gramps God finishes his opera, he always takes a little card out from his pocket? And while looking at the card, he hums lines from the opera. Just now I stole a glance. The card is a photo. There's a really pretty young woman on it."

That evening, God played *The Butterfly Lovers* again. He took out the photograph of the pretty young woman and started to hum. Qiusheng's father quietly moved in. "Gramps God, is that your . . . girlfriend from a long time ago?"

God was startled. He hid the photograph quickly and smiled like a kid at Qiusheng's father. "Haha. Yeah, yeah. I loved her two thousand years ago."

Yulian, who was eavesdropping, grimaced. *Two thousand years ago!* Considering his advanced age, this was a bit gag inducing.

Qiusheng's father wanted to look at the photograph. But God was so protective of it that it would have been embarrassing to ask. So Qiusheng's father settled for listening to God reminisce.

"Back then we were all so young. She was one of the very few who wasn't completely absorbed by life in the Machine Cradle. She initiated a great voyage of exploration to sail to the end of the universe. Oh, you don't need to think too hard about that. It's very difficult to understand. Anyway, she hoped to use this voyage as an opportunity to awaken the God Civilization, sleeping so soundly in the Machine Cradle. Of course, that was nothing more than a beautiful dream. She wanted me to go with her, but I didn't have the courage. The endless desert of the universe frightened me. It would have been a journey of more than twenty billion light-years. So she went by herself. But in the two thousand years after that, I never stopped longing for her."

"Twenty billion light-years? So like you explained to me before, that's the distance that light would travel in twenty billion years? Oh my! That's way too far. That's basically good-bye for life. Gramps God, you have to forget about her. You'll never see her again."

God nodded and sighed.

"Well, isn't she now about your age, too?"

God was startled out of his reverie. He shook his head. "Oh, no. For such a long voyage, her explorer ship would have to fly at close to the speed of light. That means she would still be very young. The only one that has grown old is me. You don't understand how large the universe is. What you think of as 'eternity' is nothing but a grain of sand in space-time.

"Well, the fact that you can't understand and feel this is sometimes a blessing."

5.

The honeymoon between the Gods and humans quickly ended.

People were initially ecstatic over the scientific material received from the Gods, thinking that it would allow mankind to realize its dreams overnight. Thanks to the interface equipment provided by the Gods, an enormous quantity of information was retrieved successfully from the storage devices. The information was translated into English, and in order to avoid disputes, a copy was distributed to every nation in the world.

But people soon discovered that realizing these God-given technologies was impossible, at least within the present century. Consider the situation of the ancient Egyptians if a time traveler had provided information on modern technology to them, and you will have some understanding of the awkward situation these humans faced.

As the exhaustion of petroleum supplies loomed over the human race, energy technology was at the top of everyone's minds. But scientists and engineers discovered that the God Civilization's energy technology was useless for humans at this time. The Gods' energy source was built upon the basis of matter-antimatter annihilation. Even if people could understand all the materials and finally create an annihilation engine and generator (a basically impossible task within this generation), it would still have been for naught. This was because the fuel for these engines, antimatter, had to be mined from deep space. According to the material provided by the Gods, the closest antimatter ore source was between the Milky Way and the Andromeda galaxy, about 550,000 light-years away.

The technology for interstellar travel at near the speed of light also involved every field of scientific knowledge, and the greater part of the theories and techniques revealed by the Gods were beyond human comprehension. Just to get a basic understanding of the foundations would require human scholars to work for perhaps half a century. Scientists, initially full of hope, had tried to search the material from the Gods for technical information concerning controlled nuclear fission, but there was nothing. This was easy to understand: our current literature on energy science contained no information on how to make fire from sticks, either.

In other scientific fields, such as information science and life sciences (including the secret of human longevity), it was the same. Even the most advanced scholars could make no sense of the Gods' knowledge. Between the Gods' science and human science, there was still a great abyss of understanding that could not be bridged.

The Gods who arrived on Earth could not help the scientists in any way. Like the God at the United Nations had said, among the Gods now there were few who could even solve quadratic equations. The spaceships adrift among the asteroids also ignored all hails from the humans. The human race was like a group of new elementary school students who were suddenly required to master the material of Ph.D. candidates, and were given no instructor.

On the other hand, Earth's population suddenly grew by two billion. These were all extremely aged individuals who could no longer be productive. Most of them were plagued by various diseases and put unprecedented pressure on human society. As a result, every government had to pay each family living with a God a considerable support stipend. Health care and other public infrastructures were strained beyond the breaking point. The world economy was pushed near the edge of collapse.

The harmonious relationship between God and Qiusheng's family was gone. Gradually the family began to see him as a burden that fell from the sky. They began to despise him, but each had a different reason.

Yulian's reason was the most practical and closest to the underlying problem: God made her family poor. Among all the members of the family God also worried the most about her; she had a tongue as sharp as a knife, and she scared him more than black holes and supernovas. After the death of her dream of true Communism, she unceasingly nagged God: *Before you came, our family had lived so prosperously and comfortably. Back then everything was good. Now everything is bad. All because of you. Being saddled with an old fool like you was such a great misfortune.* Every day, whenever she had the chance, she would prattle on like this in front of God.

God also suffered from chronic bronchitis. This was not a very expensive disease to treat, but it did require ongoing care and a constant outlay of money. Finally one day Yulian forbade Qiusheng from taking God to the town hospital to see doctors and stopped buying medicine for him. When the Secretary of the village branch of the Communist Party found out, he came to Qiusheng's house.

"You have to pay for the care of your family God," the Secretary said to Yulian. "The doctor at the town hospital already told me that if left untreated, the chronic bronchitis might develop into pulmonary emphysema."

"If you want him treated, then the village or the government can pay for it," Yulian shouted at the Secretary. "We're not made of money!"

"Yulian, according to the God Support Law, the family has to bear these kinds of minor medical expenses. The government's support fee already includes this component."

"That little bit of support fee is useless!"

"You can't talk like that. After you began getting the support fee, you bought a milk cow, switched to liquefied petroleum gas, and bought a big, new color TV! You're telling me now that you don't have money for God to see a doctor? Everyone knows that in your family, your word is law. I'm going to make it clear to you: right now I'm helping you save face, but don't push your luck. Next time, it won't be me standing here trying to persuade you. It will be the County God Support Committee. You'll be in real trouble then."

Yulian had no choice but to resume paying for God's medical care. But after that she became even meaner to him.

One time, God said to Yulian, "Don't be so anxious. Humans are very smart and learn fast. In only another century or so, the easiest aspects of the Gods' knowledge will become applicable to human society. Then your life will become better."

"Damn. *A whole century.* And you say 'only.' Are you even listening to yourself?" Yulian was washing the dishes and didn't even bother looking back at God.

"That's a very short period of time."

"For you! You think we can live as long as you? In another century, you won't even find my bones! But I want to ask you a question: how much longer do you think *you'll* be living?"

"Oh, I'm like a candle in the wind. If I can live another three or four hundred years, I'll be very satisfied."

Yulian dropped a whole stack of bowls on the ground. "This is not how 'support' is supposed to work! Ah, so you think not only I should spend my entire life taking care of you, but you have to have my son, my grandson, for ten generations and more!? Why won't you die?"

⚹

As for Qiusheng's father, he thought God was a fraud, and in fact, this view was pretty common. Since scientists couldn't understand the Gods' scientific papers, there was no way to prove their authenticity. Maybe the Gods were playing a giant trick on the human race. For Qiusheng's father, there was ample support for this view.

"You old swindler, you're way too outrageous," he said to God one day. "I'm too lazy to expose you. Your tricks are not worth my trouble. Heck, they're not even worth my grandson's trouble."

God asked him what he had discovered.

"I'll start with the simplest thing: our scientists know that humans evolved from monkeys, right?"

God nodded. "More accurately, you evolved from primitive apes."

"Then how can you say that you created us? If you were interested in creating humans, why not directly make us in our current form? Why bother first creating primitive apes and then go through the trouble of evolving? It makes no sense."

"A human begins as a baby, and then grows into an adult. A civilization also has to grow from a primitive state. The long path of experience cannot be avoided. Actually, humans began with the introduction of a much more primitive species. Even apes were already very evolved."

"I don't believe these made-up reasons. All right, here's something more obvious. This was actually first noticed by my grandson. Our scientists say that there was life on Earth even three billion years ago. Do you admit this?"

God nodded. "That estimate is basically right."

"So you're three billion years old?"

"In terms of your frame of reference, yes. But according to the frame of reference of our ships, I'm only thirty-five hundred years old. The ships flew close to the speed of light, and time passed much more slowly for us than for you. Of course, once in a while a few ships dropped out of their cruise and decelerated to come to Earth so that further adjustments to the evolution of life on Earth could be made. But this didn't require much time. Those ships would then return to cruise at close to the speed of light and continue skipping over the passage of time here."

"Bullshit," Qiusheng's father said contemptuously.

"Dad, this is the Theory of Relativity," Qiusheng interrupted. "Our scientists already proved it."

"Relativity, my ass! You're bullshitting me, too. That's impossible! How can time be like sesame oil, flowing at different speeds? I'm not so old that I've lost my mind. But you—reading all those books has made you stupid!"

"I can prove to you that time does indeed flow at different rates," God said, his face full of mystery. He took out that photograph of his beloved from two thousand years ago and handed it to Qiusheng. "Look at her carefully and memorize every detail."

The second Qiusheng looked at the photograph, he knew that he would be able to remember every detail. It would be impossible to forget. Like the other Gods, the woman in the picture had a blend of the features of all ethnicities. Her skin was like warm ivory, her two eyes were so alive that they seemed to sing, and she immediately captivated Qiusheng's soul. She was a woman among Gods, the God of women. The beauty of the Gods was like a second sun. Humans had never seen it and could not bear it.

"Look at you! You're practically drooling!" Yulian grabbed the photograph from the frozen Qiusheng. But before she could look at it, her father-in-law took it away from her.

"Let me see," Qiusheng's father said. He brought the photograph to his ancient eyes, as close as possible. For a long time he did not move, as though the photograph provided sustenance.

"Why are you looking so close?" Yulian said, her tone contemptuous.

"Shut it. I don't have my glasses," Qiusheng's father said, his face still practically on the photograph.

Yulian looked at her father-in-law disdainfully for a few seconds, curled her lips, and left for the kitchen.

God took the photograph out of the hands of Qiusheng's father, whose hands lingered on the photo for a long while, unwilling to let go. God said, "Remember all the details. I'll let you look at it again this time tomorrow."

The next day, father and son said little to each other. Both thought about the young woman, so there was nothing to say. Yulian's temper was far worse than usual.

Finally the time came. God had seemingly forgotten about it and had to be reminded by Qiusheng's father. He took out the photograph that the two men had been thinking about all day and handed it first to Qiusheng. "Look carefully. Do you see any change in her?"

"Nothing really," Qiusheng said, looking intently. After a while, he finally noticed something. "Aha! The opening between her lips seems slightly narrower. Not much, just a little bit. Look at the corner of the mouth here . . ."

"Have you no shame? To look at some other woman that closely?"

Yulian grabbed the photo again, and again, her father-in-law took it away from her.

"Let me see—" Qiusheng's father put on his glasses and carefully examined the picture. "Yes, indeed the opening is narrower. But there's a much more obvious change that you didn't notice. Look at this wisp of hair. Compared to yesterday, it has drifted farther to the right."

God took the picture from Qiusheng's father. "This is not a photograph, but a television receiver."

"A . . . TV?"

"Yes. Right now it's receiving a live feed from that explorer spaceship heading for the end of the universe."

"Live? Like live broadcasts of football matches?"

"Yes."

"So . . . the woman in the picture, she's alive!" Qiusheng was so shocked that his mouth hung open. Even Yulian's eyes were now as big as walnuts.

"Yes, she's alive. But unlike a live broadcast on Earth, this feed is subject to a delay. The explorer spaceship is now about eighty million light-years away, so the delay is about eighty million years. What we see now is how she was eighty million years ago."

"This tiny thing can receive a signal from that far away?"

"This kind of super long-distance communication across space requires the use of neutrinos or gravitational waves. Our spaceships can receive the signal, magnify it, and then rebroadcast to this TV."

"Treasure, a real treasure!" Qiusheng's father praised sincerely. But it was unclear whether he was talking about the tiny TV or the young woman on the TV. Anyway, after hearing that she was still "alive," Qiusheng and his father both felt a deeper attachment to her. Qiusheng tried to take the tiny TV again, but God refused.

"Why does she move so slowly in the picture?"

"That's the result of time flowing at different speeds. From our frame of reference, time flows extremely slowly on a spaceship flying close to the speed of light."

"Then . . . can she still talk to you?" Yulian asked.

God nodded. He flipped a switch behind the TV. Immediately a sound came out of it. It was a woman's voice, but the sound didn't change, like a singer holding a note steady at the end of a song. God stared at the screen, his eyes full of love.

"She's talking right now. She's finishing three words: 'I love you.' Each word took more than a year. It's now been three and a half years, and right now she's just finishing 'you.' To completely finish the sentence will take another three months." God lifted his eyes from the TV to the domed sky above the yard. "She still has more to say. I'll spend the rest of my life listening to her."

Bingbing actually managed to maintain a pretty good relationship with God for a while. The Gods all had some childishness to them, and they enjoyed talking and playing with children. But one day, Bingbing wanted God to give him the large watch he wore, and God steadfastly refused. He explained that the watch was a tool for communicating with the God Civilization. Without it, he would no longer be able to connect with his own people.

"Hmm, look at this. You're still thinking about your own civilization and race. You've never thought of us as your real family!" Yulian said angrily.

After that, Bingbing was no longer nice to God. Instead, he often played practical tricks on him.

The only one in the family who still had respect and feelings of filial piety toward God was Qiusheng. Qiusheng had graduated from high school and liked to read. Other than a few people who passed the college-entrance examination and went away for college, he was the most learned individual in the village. But at home, Qiusheng had no power. On practically everything he listened to the direction of his wife and followed the commands of his father. If somehow his wife and father had conflicting instructions, then all he could do was to sit in a corner and cry. Given that he was such a softy, he had no way to protect God at home.

6.

The relationship between the Gods and humans had finally deteriorated beyond repair.

The complete breakdown between God and Qiusheng's family occurred after the incident involving instant noodles. One day, before lunch, Yulian came out of the kitchen with a paper box and asked why half the box of instant noodles she had bought yesterday had already disappeared.

"I took them," God said in a small voice. "I gave them to those living by the river. They've almost run out of things to eat."

He was talking about the place where the Gods who had left their families were gathering. Recently there had been frequent incidents of abuse of the Gods in the village. One particularly savage couple had been beating and cursing out their God, and even withheld food from him. Eventually that God tried to commit suicide in the river that ran in front of the village, but luckily others were able to stop him.

This incident caused a great deal of publicity. It went beyond the county, and the city's police eventually came, along with a bunch of reporters from CCTV and the provincial TV station, and took the couple away in handcuffs. According to the God Support Law, they had committed God abuse and would be sentenced to at least ten years in jail. This was the only law that was universal among all the nations of the world, with uniform prison terms.

After that, the families in the village became more careful and stopped treating the Gods too poorly in front of other people. But at the same time, the incident worsened the relationship between the Gods and the villagers. Eventually, some of the Gods left their families, and other Gods followed. By now almost one-third of the Gods in Xicen had already left their assigned families. These wandering Gods set up camp in the field across the river and lived a primitive, difficult life.

In other parts of the country and across the world, the situation was the same. Once again, the streets of big cities were filled with crowds of wandering, homeless Gods. The number quickly increased like a repeat of the nightmare three years ago. The world, full of Gods and people, faced a gigantic crisis.

"Ha, you're very generous, you old fool! How dare you eat our food while giving it away?" Yulian began to curse loudly.

Qiusheng's father slammed the table and got up. "You idiot! Get out of here! You miss those Gods by the river? Why don't you go and join them?"

God sat silently for a while, thinking. Then he stood up, went to his tiny room, and packed up his few belongings. Leaning on his bamboo cane, he slowly made his way out the door, heading in the direction of the river.

Qiusheng didn't eat with the rest of his family. He squatted in a corner with his head lowered and not speaking.

"Hey, dummy! Come here and eat. We have to go into town to buy feed this afternoon," Yulian shouted at him. Since he refused to budge, she went over to yank his ear.

"Let go," Qiusheng said. His voice was not loud, but Yulian let him go as though she had been shocked. She had never seen her husband with such a gloomy expression on his face.

"Forget about him," Qiusheng's father said carelessly. "If he doesn't want to eat, then he's a fool."

"Ha, you miss your God? Why don't you go join him and his friends in that field by the river, too?" Yulian poked a finger at Qiusheng's head.

Qiusheng stood up and went upstairs to his bedroom. Like God, he packed a few things into a bundle and put it in a duffel bag he had once used when he had gone to the city to work. With the bag on his back, he headed outside.

"Where are you going?" Yulian yelled. But Qiusheng ignored her.

She yelled again, but now there was fear in her voice. "How long are you going to be out?"

"I'm not coming back," Qiusheng said without looking back.

"What? Come back here! Is your head filled with shit?" Qiusheng's father followed him out of the house. "What's the matter with you? Even if you don't want your wife and kid, how dare you leave your father?"

Qiusheng stopped but still did not turn around. "Why should I care about you?"

"How can you talk like that? I'm your father! I raised you! Your mother died early. You think it was easy to raise you and your sister? Have you lost your mind?"

Qiusheng finally turned back to look at his father. "If you can kick the people who created our ancestors' ancestors' ancestors out of our house, then I don't think it's much of a sin for me not to support you in your old age."

He left, and Yulian and his father stood there, dumbfounded.

※

Qiusheng went over the ancient arched stone bridge and walked toward the tents of the Gods. He saw a few of the Gods had set up a pot to cook something in the grassy clearing strewn with golden leaves. Their white beards and the white steam coming out of the pot reflected the noon sunlight like a scene out of an ancient myth.

Qiusheng found his God and said stubbornly, "Gramps God, let's go."

"I'm not going back to that house."

"I'm not, either. Let's go together into town and stay with my sister for a while. Then I'll go into the city and find a job, and we'll rent a place together. I'll support you for the rest of my life."

"You're a good kid," God said, patting his shoulder lightly. "But it's time for us to go." He pointed to the watch on his wrist. Qiusheng now noticed that all the watches of all the Gods were blinking with a red light.

"Go? Where to?"

"Back to the ships," God said, pointing at the sky. Qiusheng lifted his head and saw that two spaceships were already hovering in the sky, standing out starkly against the blue. One of them was closer, and its shape and outline loomed huge. Behind it, another was much farther away and appeared smaller. But the most surprising sight was that the first spaceship had lowered a thread as thin as spider silk, extending from space down to Earth. As the spider silk slowly drifted, the bright sun glinted on different sections like lightning in the bright blue sky.

"A space elevator," God explained. "Already more than a hundred of these have been set up on every continent. We'll ride them back to the ships." Later Qiusheng would learn that when a spaceship dropped down a space elevator from a geostationary orbit, it needed a large mass on its other side, deep in space, to act as a counterweight. That was the purpose of the other ship he saw.

When Qiusheng's eyes adjusted to the brightness of the sky, he saw that there were many more silvery stars deep in the distance. Those stars were spread out very evenly, forming a huge matrix. Qiusheng understood that the twenty thousand ships of the God Civilization were coming back to Earth from the asteroid belt.

7.

Twenty thousand spaceships once again filled the sky above Earth. In the two months that followed, space capsules ascended and descended the various space elevators, taking away the two billion Gods who had briefly lived on Earth. The space capsules were silver spheres. From a distance, they looked like dewdrops hanging on spider threads.

The day that Xicen's Gods left, all the villagers showed up for the farewell. Everyone was affectionate toward the Gods, and it reminded everyone of the day a year ago when the Gods first came to Xicen. It was as though all the abuse and disdain the Gods had received had nothing to do with the villagers.

Two big buses were parked at the entrance to the village, the same two buses that had brought the Gods here a year ago. More than a hundred Gods would now be taken to the nearest space elevator and ride up in space capsules. The silver thread that could be seen in the distance was in reality hundreds of kilometers away.

Qiusheng's whole family went to send off their God. No one said anything along the way. As they neared the village entrance, God stopped, leaned against his cane, and bowed to the family. "Please stop here. Thank you for taking care of me this year. Really, thank you. No matter where I will be in this universe, I will always remember your family." Then he took off the large watch from his wrist and handed it to Bingbing. "A gift."

"But . . . how will you communicate with the other Gods in the future?" Bingbing asked.

"We'll all be on the spaceships. I have no more need for this," God said, laughing.

"Gramps God," Qiusheng's father said, his face sorrowful, "your ships are all ancient. They won't last much longer. Where can you go then?"

God stroked his beard and said calmly, "It doesn't matter. Space is limitless. Dying anywhere is the same."

Yulian suddenly began to cry. "Gramps God, I . . . I'm not a very nice person. I shouldn't have made you the target of all my complaints, which I'd saved up my whole life. It's just as Qiusheng said: I've behaved as if I don't have a conscience . . ." She pushed a bamboo basket into God's hands. "I boiled some eggs this morning. Please take them for your trip."

God picked up the basket. "Thank you." Then he took out an egg, peeled it, and began to eat, savoring the taste. Yellow flakes of egg yolk soon flaked his white beard. He continued to talk as he ate. "Actually, we came to Earth not only because we wanted to survive. Having already lived for two, three thousand years, what did we have to fear from death? We just wanted to be with you. We like and cherish your passion for life, your creativity, your imagination. These things have long disappeared from the God Civilization. We saw in you the childhood of our civilization. But we didn't realize we'd bring you so much trouble. We're really sorry."

"Please stay, Gramps," Bingbing said, crying. "I'll be better in the future."

God shook his head slowly. "We're leaving not because of how you treated us. The fact that you took us in and allowed us to stay was enough. But one thing made us unable to stay any longer: in your eyes, the Gods are pathetic. You pity us. Oh, you *pity* us."

God threw away the pieces of eggshell. He lifted his face, trailing a full head of white hair, and stared at the sky, as though through the blue he could see the bright sea of stars. "How can the God Civilization be pitied by man? You have no idea what a great civilization she was. You do not know what majestic epics she created, or how many imposing deeds she accomplished.

"It was 1857, during the Milky Way Era, when astronomers discovered a large number of stars was accelerating toward the center of the Milky Way. Once this flood of stars was consumed by the supermassive black hole found there, the resulting radiation would kill all life found in the galaxy.

"In response, our great ancestors built a nebula shield around the center of the galaxy with a diameter of ten thousand light-years so that life and civilization in the galaxy would continue. What a magnificent engineering project that was! It took us more than fourteen hundred years to complete . . .

"Immediately afterward, the Andromeda galaxy and the Large Magellanic Cloud united in an invasion of our galaxy. The interstellar fleet of the God Civilization leaped across hundreds of thousands of light-years and intercepted the invaders at the gravitational balance point between Andromeda and the Milky Way. When the battle entered into its climax, large numbers of ships from both sides mixed together, forming a spiraling nebula the size of the Solar System.

"During the final stages of the battle, the God Civilization made the bold decision to send all remaining warships and even the civilian fleet into the spiraling nebula. The great increase in mass caused gravity to exceed the centrifugal force, and this nebula, made of ships and people, collapsed under gravity and formed a star! Because the proportion of heavy elements in this star was so high, immediately after its birth, the star went supernova and illuminated the deep darkness between Andromeda and the Milky Way! Our ancestors thus destroyed the invaders with their courage and self-sacrifice, and left the Milky Way as a place where life could develop peacefully . . .

"Yes, now our civilization is old. But it is not our fault. No matter how hard one strives, a civilization must grow old one day. Everyone grows old, even you.

"We really do not need your pity."

"Compared to you," Qiusheng said, full of awe, "the human race is really nothing."

"Don't talk like that," God said. "Earth's civilization is still an infant. We hope you will grow up fast. We hope you will inherit and continue the glory of your creators." God threw down his cane. He put his hands on the shoulders of Bingbing and Qiusheng. "I have some final words for you."

"We may not understand everything you have to say," Qiusheng said, "but please speak. We will listen."

"First, you must get off this rock!" God spread out his arms toward space. His white robe danced in the autumn wind like a sail.

"Where will we go?" Qiusheng's father asked in confusion.

"Begin by flying to the other planets in the solar system, then to other stars. Don't ask why, but use all your energy toward the goal of flying away, the farther the better. In that process, you will spend a lot of money, and many people will die, but you must get away from here. Any civilization that stays on her birth world is committing suicide! You must go into the universe and find new worlds, new homes, and spread your descendants across the galaxy like drops of spring rain."

"We'll remember," Qiusheng said and nodded, even though neither he nor his wife nor father nor son really understood God's words.

"Good," God sighed, satisfied. "Next I will tell you a secret, a great secret." He stared at everyone in the family with his blue eyes. His stare was like a cold wind and caused everyone's heart to shudder. "You have brothers."

Qiusheng's family looked at God, utterly confused. But Qiusheng finally figured out what God meant. "You're saying that you created other Earths?"

God nodded slowly. "Yes, other Earths, other human civilizations. Other than you, there were three others. All are close to you, within two hundred light-years. You are Earth Number Four, the youngest."

"Have you been to the other Earths?" Bingbing asked.

God nodded again. "Before we came to you, we went first to the other three Earths and asked them to take us in. Earth Number One was the best among the bunch. After they obtained our scientific materials, they simply chased us away.

"Earth Number Two, on the other hand, kept one million of us as hostages and forced us to give them spaceships as ransom. After we gave them one thousand ships, they realized that they could not operate the ships. They then forced the hostages to teach them how, but the hostages didn't know how, either, since the ships were autonomous. So they killed all the hostages.

"Earth Number Three took three million of us as hostages and demanded that we ram Earth Number One and Earth Number Two with several spaceships each because they were in a prolonged state of war with the other two Earths. Of course, even a single hit from one of our antimatter-powered ships would destroy all life on a planet. We refused, and so they killed all the hostages."

"Unfilial children!" Qiusheng's father shouted in anger. "You should punish them!"

God shook his head. "We will never attack civilizations we created. You are the best of the four brothers. That's why I'm telling you all this. Your three brothers are drawn to invasion. They do not know what love is or what morality is. Their capacity for cruelty and bloodlust are impossible for you to imagine.

"Indeed, in the beginning we created six Earths. The other two were in the same solar systems as Earth Number One and Earth Number Three, respectively. Both were destroyed by their brothers. The fact that the other three Earths haven't yet destroyed one another is only due to the great distances separating their solar systems. By now, all three know of the existence of Earth Number Four and possess your precise coordinates. Thus, you must go and destroy them first before they destroy you."

"This is too frightening!" Yulian said.

"For now, it's not yet too frightening. Your three brothers are indeed more advanced than you, but they still cannot travel faster than one-tenth the speed of light, and cannot cruise more than thirty light-years from home. This is a race of life and death to see which one among you can achieve near-light-speed space travel first. It is the only way to break through the prison of time and space. Whoever can achieve this technology first will survive. Anyone slower will die a sure death. This is the struggle for survival in the universe. Children, you don't have much time. Work hard!"

"Do the most learned and most powerful people in our world know these things?" Qiusheng's father asked, trembling.

"Yes. But don't rely on them. A civilization's survival depends on the effort of every individual. Even the common people like you have a role to play."

"You hear that, Bingbing?" Qiusheng said to his son. "You must study hard."

"When you fly into the universe at close to the speed of light to resolve the threat of your brothers, you must perform another urgent task: find a few planets suitable for life and seed them with some simple, primitive life from here, like bacteria and algae. Let them evolve on their own."

Qiusheng wanted to ask more questions, but God picked up his cane and began to walk. The family accompanied him toward the bus. The other Gods were already aboard.

"Oh, Qiusheng." God stopped, remembering. "I took a few of your books with me. I hope you don't mind." He opened his bundle to show Qiusheng. "These are your high school textbooks on math, physics, chemistry."

"No problem. Take them. But why do you want these?"

God tied up the bundle again. "To study. I'll start with quadratic equations. In the long years ahead, I'll need some way to occupy myself. Who knows? Maybe one day, I'll try to repair our ships' antimatter engines and allow us to fly close to the speed of light again!"

"Right," Qiusheng said, excited. "That way, you'll be able to skip across time again. You can find another planet, create another civilization to support you in your old age!"

God shook his head. "No, no, no. We're no longer interested in being supported in our old age. If it's time for us to die, we die. I want to study because I have a final wish." He took out the small TV from his pocket. On the screen, his beloved from two thousand years ago was still slowly speaking the final word of that three-word sentence. "I want to see her again."

"It's a good wish, but it's only a fantasy," Qiusheng's father said. "Think about it. She left two thousand years ago at the speed of light. Who knows where she is now? Even if you repair your ship, how will you ever catch her? You told us that nothing can go faster than light."

God pointed at the sky with his cane. "In this universe, as long as you're patient, you can make any wish come true. Even though the possibility is minuscule, it is not nonexistent. I told you once that the universe was born out of a great explosion. Now gravity has gradually slowed down its expansion. Eventually the expansion will stop and turn into contraction. If our spaceship can really fly again at close to the speed of light, then we will endlessly accelerate and endlessly approach the speed of light. This way, we will skip over endless time until we near the final moments of the universe.

"By then, the universe will have shrunk to a very small size, smaller even than Bingbing's toy ball, as small as a point. Then everything in the entire universe will come together, and she and I will also be together."

A tear fell from God's eye and rolled onto his beard, glistening brightly in the morning sun. "The universe will then be the tomb at the end of *The Butterfly Lovers*. She and I will be the two butterflies emerging from the tomb . . ."

8.

A week later, the last spaceship left Earth. God left.

Xicen village resumed its quiet life.

On this evening, Qiusheng's family sat in the yard, looking at a sky full of stars. It was deep autumn, and insects had stopped making noises in the fields. A light breeze stirred the fallen leaves at their feet. The air was slightly chilly.

"They're flying so high. The wind must be so severe, so cold—" Yulian murmured to herself.

"There isn't any wind up there," Qiusheng said. "They're in space, where there isn't even air. But it is really cold. So cold that in the books they call it *absolute zero*. It's so dark out there, with no end in sight. It's a place that you can't even dream of in your nightmares."

Yulian began to cry again. But she tried to hide it with words. "Remember those last two things God told us? I understand the part about our three brothers. But then he told us that we had to spread bacteria onto other planets and so on. I still can't make sense of that."

"I figured it out," Qiusheng's father said. Under the brilliant, starry sky, his head, full of a lifetime of foolishness, finally opened up to insight. He looked up at the stars. He had lived with them above his head all his life, but only today did he discover what they really looked like. A feeling he had never had before suffused his blood, making him feel as if he had been touched by something greater. Even though it did not become a part of him, the feeling shook him to his core. He sighed at the sea of stars, and said,

"The human race needs to start thinking about who is going to support us in our old age."

ESSAYS

THE WORST OF ALL POSSIBLE UNIVERSES AND THE BEST OF ALL POSSIBLE EARTHS: *THREE-BODY* AND CHINESE SCIENCE FICTION

by Liu Cixin

A few years ago, a science fiction novel appeared in China under the strange title *Three-Body*.

There were, in total, three volumes, and the title for the entire work is *Remembrance of Earth's Past*. After volume one, *Three-Body* (note: the official English title for volume one is *The Three-Body Problem*), the next two volumes are *The Dark Forest* and *Death's End*. However, Chinese readers habitually refer to the entire work as *Three-Body*.

Science fiction is not a genre that has much respect in China. Critics have long been discouraged from paying attention to the category, dismissed as a branch of juvenile literature. The subject of *Three-Body*—an alien invasion of Earth—is not unheard of, but rarely discussed.

Thus it surprised everyone when the book gained widespread interest in China and stimulated much debate. The amount of ink and pixels that have been spilled on account of *Three-Body* is unprecedented for a science fiction novel.

Let me give a few examples. The main consumers of science fiction books in China are high school and college students. But *Three-Body* somehow gained the attention of information technology entrepreneurs; on Internet forums and elsewhere, they debated and discussed the book's various details (such as the "Dark Forest Theory" of the cosmos—an answer to the Fermi Paradox—and the dimension-reduction attack on the solar system launched by aliens) as metaphors for the cutthroat competition among China's web companies. Next, *Three-Body* came to the attention of China's mainstream literary world, which had always been dominated by realist fiction. *Three-Body* was like some monster that suddenly erupted onto the scene, and literary critics were baffled by it while feeling they couldn't ignore it.

The book even had an effect on scientists and engineers. Li Miao, a cosmologist and string theorist, wrote a book titled *The Physics of* Three-Body. Many aerospace engineers became fans, and China's aerospace agency even asked me to consult with them (despite the fact that in my novel, China's aerospace establishment was described as so conservative and hidebound that an extremist officer had to engage in mass assassinations to allow new ideas to flourish). These sorts of reactions are probably familiar to American readers (e.g., *The Physics of* Star Trek, and NASA scientists regularly teaming up with science fiction writers), but they're unheard of in China, and they contrast sharply with the official policy of suppressing science fiction during the 1980s.

On the web, one can find many fan-composed songs for *Three-Body* and readers yearning for a movie adaptation—some have even gone to the trouble of creating fake trailers out of clips from other movies. Sina Weibo—a Chinese microblogging service analogous to Twitter—has numerous user accounts based on characters in *Three-*

Body, and these users stay in character and comment on current events, expanding the story told in the novel. Based on these virtual identities, some have speculated that the ETO, the fictional organization of human defectors who form a fifth column for the alien invaders, is already in place. When CCTV, China's largest state television broadcaster, tried to hold an interview series on the topic of science fiction, a hundred-plus studio audience members erupted into chants of, "Eliminate human tyranny! The world belongs to Trisolaris!"—a quote from the novel. The two TV hosts were utterly flummoxed and didn't know what to do.

Of course, these events are only the latest entries in the century-long history of science fiction in China.

Chinese science fiction was born at the turn of the twentieth century, when the Qing dynasty was teetering on the edge of ruin. At the time, Chinese intellectuals were entranced by and curious about Western science and technology, and thought of such knowledge as the only hope for saving the nation from poverty, weakness, and general backwardness. Many works popularizing and speculating about science were published, including works of science fiction. One of the leaders of the failed Hundred Days' Reform (June 11–September 21, 1898), the renowned scholar Liang Qichao, wrote a science fiction story called "A Chronicle of the Future of New China." In it, he imagined a Shanghai World's Fair—a vision that would not become true until 2010.

Like most genres of literary expression, science fiction in China was subject to instrumentalist impulses and had to serve practical goals. At its birth, it became a tool of propaganda for the Chinese who dreamed of a strong China free of colonial depredations. Thus, science fiction works from the end of the Qing dynasty and the early Republican years almost always presented a future in which China was strong, prosperous, and advanced, a nation which the world respected rather than subjugated.

After the founding of the People's Republic in 1949, science fiction became a tool for popularizing scientific knowledge, and its main intended readers were children. Most of these stories put technology at the core and contained little humanism, featuring simplistic characters and basic, even naïve literary techniques. Few of the novels ventured outside the orbit of Mars, and most stuck to the near future. In these works, science and technology were always presented as positive forces, and the technological future was always bright.

An interesting observation can be made when one surveys the science fiction published during this period. In the early years after the Communist Revolution, politics and revolutionary fervor infused every aspect of daily life, and the very air one breathed seemed filled with propaganda for Communist ideals. Given this context, one might have expected that science fiction would also be filled with descriptions of Communist utopias of the future. But as a matter of fact, not a single work of this type can be found. There were practically no science fiction stories that featured Communism as the subject, not even simplistic sketches to promote the concept.

By the 1980s, as Deng Xiaoping's reforms took effect, the influence of Western science fiction on Chinese science fiction became more apparent. Chinese science fiction writers and critics began to debate whether science fiction was more about "science" or "fiction," and ultimately the literary camp won out. The debate had tremendous influence on the direction of the future development of Chinese science fiction, and in some ways can be seen as a delayed Chinese response to the New Wave movement in the West. Science fiction was finally able to escape the fate of being a mere tool to serve the goal of popularizing science, and could develop in new directions.

During the period between the mid-1990s and now, Chinese science fiction experienced a renaissance. New writers and their fresh ideas had little connection to the last century, and as Chinese science fiction became more diverse, it also began to lose its distinctness as particularly "Chinese." Contemporary Chinese science fiction is becoming more similar to world science fiction, and styles and subjects that have been explored by American writers, for instance, can find easy analogs in Chinese science fiction.

It's interesting to note that the optimism toward science that underlay much of last century's Chinese science fiction has almost completely vanished. Contemporary science fiction reflects much suspicion and anxiety about technological progress, and the futures portrayed in these works are dark and uncertain. Even if a bright future appears occasionally, it comes only after much suffering and a tortuous path.

At the time of *Three-Body*'s publication, China's science fiction market was anxious and depressed. The long marginalization of science fiction as a genre led to a small and insular readership. Fans saw themselves as a tribe on an island and felt misunderstood by outsiders. Writers struggled to attract readers outside the tribe and felt they had to give up their Campbellian "science fiction fundamentalism" and raise the genre's literary qualities and realism.

The first two volumes of *Three-Body* show some efforts made in this direction. Much of the first volume was set during the Cultural Revolution, and in the second volume, the China of the future still existed under sociopolitical institutions similar to the present. These were attempts to increase the sense of realism for readers, to give the speculative elements some foundation in the present. As a result, both my publisher and I had little faith in the third volume prior to its publication. As the story continued to develop, it was impossible to root the third volume in present realities, and I had to describe distant futures and distant corners of the cosmos—and by consensus, Chinese readers were not interested in such things.

My publisher and I reached the conclusion that since it was impossible for the third volume to succeed in the market, maybe it was best to give up trying to attract readers who were not already science fiction fans. Instead, I would write a "pure" science fiction novel, which I found comforting, as I considered myself a hard-core fan. And so I wrote the third volume for myself and filled it with multidimensional and two-dimensional universes, artificial black holes and mini-universes, and I extended the time line to the heat death of the universe.

And to our utter surprise, it was this third volume, written only for science fiction fans, which led to the popularity of the series as a whole.

The experience of *Three-Body* caused science fiction writers and critics to reevaluate Chinese science fiction and China. They realized they had been ignoring changes in the thinking patterns of Chinese readers. As modernization accelerated its pace, the new generation of readers no longer confined their thoughts to the narrow present as their parents did, but were interested in the future and the wide-open cosmos. The China of the present is a bit like America during science fiction's Golden Age, when science and technology filled the future with wonder, presenting both great crises and grand opportunities. This is rich soil for the growth and flourishing of science fiction.

Science fiction is a literature of possibilities. The universe we live in is also one of countless possibilities. For humanity, some universes are better than others, and *Three-Body* shows the worst of all possible universes, a universe in which existence is as dark and harsh as one can imagine.

Not long ago, Canadian writer Robert Sawyer came to China, and when he discussed *Three-Body,* he attributed my choice of the worst of all possible universes to the historical experience of China and the Chinese people. As a Canadian, he argued that he had an optimistic view of the future relationship between humans and extraterrestrials.

I don't agree with this analysis. In the Chinese science fiction of the last century, the universe was a kind place, and most extraterrestrials appeared as friends or mentors, who, endowed with Godlike patience and forbearance, pointed out the correct path for us, a lost flock of sheep. In Jin Tao's *Moonlight Island,* for example, the extraterrestrials soothed the spiritual trauma of the Chinese who experienced the Cultural Revolution. In Tong Enzheng's *Distant Love,* the human-alien romance was portrayed as poignant and magnificent. In Zheng Wenguang's *Reflections of Earth,* humanity was seen as so morally corrupt that gentle, morally refined aliens were terrified and had to run away, despite their possession of far superior technology.

But if one were to evaluate the place of Earth civilization in this universe, humanity seems far closer to the indigenous peoples of the Canadian territories before the arrival of European colonists than the Canada of the present. More than five hundred years ago, hundreds of distinct peoples speaking languages representing more than ten language families populated the land from Newfoundland to Vancouver Island. Their experience with contact with an alien civilization seems far closer to the portrayal in *Three-Body*. The description of this history in the essay "Canadian History: An Aboriginal Perspective," by Georges Erasmus and Joe Saunders, is unforgettable.

I wrote about the worst of all possible universes in *Three-Body* in the hope that we can strive for the best of all possible Earths.

THE TORN GENERATION: CHINESE SCIENCE FICTION IN A CULTURE IN TRANSITION

by Chen Qiufan

This past March, I attended the *Huadi* Literary Awards in Guangzhou, where my debut novel, *The Waste Tide,* was honored with the top distinction for genre (SF) fiction. Published in the capital of China's most developed province, *Huadi* is the magazine supplement for the *Yangcheng Evening News,* one of the largest newspapers in the world by circulation (in excess of one million). This was also the second literary award my novel has received (after a Chinese Nebula). As a former Googler, I want to invoke the button that rarely gets pressed: "I'm feeling lucky!"

The *Huadi* Awards was a joint effort by the local government and media, and as one might expect, it was suffused with the trappings of officialdom. Even the ceremony itself was held in a government auditorium. The winners were led on a night tour of the Pearl River, and our hosts excitedly pointed out the splendor of the postmodern architecture on both shores. However, one of the winners, Chen Danqing, a noted liberal opinion leader and artist, reminisced about his childhood visit to Guangzhou in the midst of the Cultural Revolution.

"From here to there," he said, sweeping his arm across the night, "bodies dangled from every tree." We looked at where he was pointing, and all we could see were lit-up commercial skyscrapers indistinguishable from those you'd find in Manhattan. "The young are always at the vanguard."

As the youngest winner among the group—I was the only one born after 1980—I played the role of the eager student seizing an opportunity to learn from respected elders. "Do you have any advice for us, the younger generation?"

Chen Danqing puffed on his cigarette thoughtfully for a while, and then said, "I'll give you eight words: 'Stay on the sidelines; hope for the best.' "

I gazed at the reflections of the profusion of neon lights and pondered these eight words. The short voyage was soon over, and the river's surface disappeared in darkness. I thought there was much wisdom in his words, though the somewhat cynical values they advocated were at odds with the spirit of the "Chinese Dream" promoted by the government.

In the eyes of Han Song, a Chinese science fiction writer born in the 1960s, the Chinese born after 1978 belong to a "Torn Generation." Han Song's perspective is interesting. While he is a member of China's most powerful state-run news agency, Xinhua, he is also the author of extraordinary novels such as *Subway* and *Bullet Train*. In these surrealist novels, the order of nature on speeding trains is subverted by events such as accelerated evolution, incest, cannibalism, and so on. Critics have suggested that "the world on the subway reflects a society's explosive transformation and is a metaphor for the reality of China's hyper-accelerated development."

In a widely distributed recent essay, Han Song wrote, "The younger generation is torn to a far greater degree than our own. The China of our youth was one of averages, but in this era, when a new breed of humanity is coming into being, China is being ripped apart at an accelerated pace. The elite and the lowly alike must face this fact. Everything, from spiritual dreams to the reality of life, is torn."

As a journalist with Xinhua, Han Song has a broader perspective than most. He points out that the young people who have been grouped into one generation by the accident of their dates of birth have wildly divergent values and lifestyles, like fragments seen in a kaleidoscope.

My generation includes the workers at Foxconn, who, day after day, repeat the same motions on the assembly line, indistinguishable from robots; but it also includes the sons and daughters of the wealthy and of important Communist officials, princelings who treat luxury as their birthright and have enjoyed every advantage in life. It includes entrepreneurs who are willing to leave behind millions in guaranteed salary to pursue a dream as well as hundreds of recent college graduates who compete ruthlessly for a single clerical position. It includes the "foreigners' lackeys" who worship the American lifestyle so much that their only goal in life is to emigrate to the United States as well as the "fifty-cent party" who are xenophobic, denigrate democracy, and place all their hopes in a more powerful, rising China.

It's absurd to put all these people under the same label.

Take myself as an example. I was born in a tiny city in Southern China (population: a million-plus). In the year of my birth, the city was designated one of the four "special economic zones" under Deng Xiaoping, and began to benefit from all the special government policies promoting development. My childhood was thus spent in relative material comfort and an environment with improved education approaches and a growing openness of information. I got to see *Star Wars* and *Star Trek* and read many science fiction classics. I became a fan of Arthur C. Clarke, H. G. Wells, and Jules Verne. Inspired by them, I published my first story when I was sixteen.

Not even seventy kilometers from where I lived, though, was another small town—administratively, it was under the jurisdiction of the same city government—where a completely different way of life held sway. In this town of fewer than two hundred thousand people, more than 3,200 businesses, many of them nothing more than family workshops, formed a center for e-waste recycling. Highly toxic electronic junk from around the world, mostly the developed world, was shipped here—often illegally—and workers without any training or protection processed them manually to extract recyclable metals. Since the late 1980s, this industry has managed to create multiple millionaires but also turned the town into one of the most polluted areas in all of Guangdong Province.

It was this experience in contrasts and social rips that led me to write *The Waste Tide*. The novel imagines a near future in the third decade of this century. On Silicon Isle, an island in Southern China built on the foundation of e-waste recycling, pollution has made the place almost uninhabitable. A fierce struggle follows in which powerful native clans, migrant workers from other parts of China, and the elites representing international capitalism vie for dominance. Mimi, a young migrant worker and "waste girl," turns into a posthuman after much suffering and leads the oppressed migrant workers in rebellion.

Han Song described my novel this way: "*The Waste Tide* shows the fissures ripping China apart, the cleavages dividing China from the rest of the world, and the tears separating different regions, different age cohorts, different tribal affiliations. This is a future that will make a young person feel the death of idealism."

In fact, I am not filled with despair and gloom for the future of China. I wrote about the suffering of a China in transformation because I yearn to see it change gradually for the better. Science fiction is a vehicle of aesthetics to express my values and myself.

In my view, "what if" is at the heart of science fiction. Starting with reality itself, the writer applies plausible and logically consistent conditions to play out a thought experiment, pushing the characters and plot toward an imagined hyperreality that evokes a sense of wonder and estrangement. Faced with the absurd reality of contemporary China, the writer cannot fully explore or express the possibilities of extreme beauty and extreme ugliness without resorting to science fiction.

Since the 1990s, the ruling class of China has endeavored to produce an ideological fantasy through the machinery of propaganda: development (increase in GDP) is sufficient to solve all problems. But the effort has failed and so created even more problems. In the process of this ideological hypnosis of the entire population, a definition of "success" in which material wealth is valued above all has choked off the younger generation's ability to imagine the possibilities of life and the future. This is a dire consequence of the policy decisions of those born in the 1950s and 1960s, a consequence which they neither understand nor accept responsibility for.

These days, I work as a mid-level manager in one of China's largest web companies. I'm in charge of a group of young people born after 1985, some even after 1990. In our daily contact, what I sense in them above all is a feeling of exhaustion about life and anxiety for success. They worry about skyrocketing real estate prices, pollution, education for their young children, medical care for their aging parents, growth and career opportunities—they are concerned that as the productivity gains brought about by China's vast population have all but been consumed by the generation born during the 1950s–1970s, they are left with a China plagued by a falling birthrate and an aging population, in which the burdens on their shoulders grow heavier year after year and their dreams and hopes are fading.

Meanwhile, the state-dominated media are saturated with phrases like "the Chinese Dream," "revival of the Chinese people," "the rise of a great nation," "scientific development" . . . Between the feeling of individual failure and the conspicuous display of national prosperity lies an unbridgeable chasm. The result is a division of the population into two extremes: one side rebels against the government reflexively (sometimes without knowing what its "cause" is) and trusts nothing it says; the other side retreats into nationalism to give itself the sense of mastering its own fate. The two sides constantly erupt into flame wars on the Internet, as though this country can hold only One True Faith for the future: things are either black or white; either you're with us, or you're against us.

If we pull back far enough to view human history from a more elevated perspective, we can see that society builds up, invents, creates utopias—sketches of perfect, imagined futures—and then, inevitably, the utopias collapse, betray their ideals, and turn into dystopias. The process plays out in cycle after cycle, like Nietzsche's eternal recurrence.

"Science" is itself one of the greatest utopian illusions ever created by humankind. I am by no means suggesting that we should take the path of antiscience—the utopia offered by science is complicated by the fact that science disguises itself as a value-neutral, objective endeavor. However, we now know that behind the practice of science lie ideological struggles, fights over power and authority, and the profit motive. The history of science is written and rewritten by the allocation and flow of capital, favors given to some projects but not others, and the needs of war.

While micro fantasies burst and are born afresh like sea spray, the macro fantasy remains sturdy. Science fiction is the byproduct of the process of gradual disenchantment with science. The words create a certain vision of science for the reader. The vision can be positive or full of suspicion and criticism—it depends on the age we live in. Contemporary China is a society in the transition stage when old illusions have collapsed but new illusions have not yet taken their place; this is the fundamental cause of the rips and divisions, the confusion and the chaos.

In 1903, another revolutionary time in Chinese history when the new was replacing the old, Lu Xun, the father of modern Chinese literature, said, "The progress of the Chinese people begins with scientific fiction." He saw science fiction as a tool to inspire the nation with the spirit of science and to chase away the remnants of feudal obscurantism. More than a hundred years later, the problems facing us are far more complicated and likely not amenable to scientific solutions, but I still believe that science fiction is capable of wedging open small possibilities: to mend the torn generation, to allow different visions and imagined future Chinas to coexist in peace, to listen to one another, to reach consensus, and to proceed together.

Even if it's only an insignificant, slow, hesitant step.

WHAT MAKES CHINESE SCIENCE FICTION CHINESE?

by Xia Jia

In the summer of 2012, I was on a panel on Chinese science fiction at Chicon 7. One of the attendees asked me and the other Chinese authors: "What makes Chinese science fiction Chinese?"

This is not at all an easy question to answer, and everyone will have a different response. It is true, however, that for the last century or so, "Chinese science fiction" has occupied a rather unique place in the culture and literature of modern China.

Science fiction's creative inspirations—massive machinery, new modes of transportation, global travel, space exploration—are the fruits of industrialization, urbanization, and globalization, processes with roots in modern capitalism. But when the genre was first introduced via translation to China at the beginning of the twentieth century, it was mostly treated as fantasies and dreams of modernity, material that could be woven into the construction of a "Chinese Dream."

"Chinese Dream" here refers to the revival of the Chinese nation in the modern era, a prerequisite for realizing which was reconstructing the Chinese people's dream. In other words, the Chinese had to wake up from their five-thousand-year-old dream of being an ancient civilization and start to dream of becoming a democratic, independent, prosperous modern nation-state. As a result, the first works of science fiction in Chinese were, in the word of the famous writer Lu Xun, seen as literary tools for "improving thinking and assisting culture." On the one hand, these early works, as myths of science, enlightenment, and development based on imitating "the West"/"the world"/"modernity," attempted to bridge the gap between *reality* and *dream*. On the other hand, the limitations of their historical context endowed them with deeply Chinese characteristics that only emphasized the depth of the chasm between *dream* and *reality*.

One such early work was Lu Shi'e's "New China" (published in 1910). The protagonist wakes up in the Shanghai of 1950 after a long slumber. He sees around him a progressive, prosperous China, and is told that all this is due to the efforts of a certain Dr. Su Hanmin, who had studied abroad and invented two technologies: "the spiritual medicine" and "the awakening technique." With these technologies, a population mired in spiritual confusion and the daze of opium awakened in an instant and began an explosive bout of political reform and economic development. The Chinese nation has not only been revived, but is even able to overcome abuses which the West could not overcome on its own. In the author's view, "European entrepreneurs were purely selfish and cared not one whit for the suffering of others. That was why they had stimulated the growth of the Communist parties." However, with the invention of Dr. Su's spiritual medicine, every Chinese has become altruistic, and "everyone views everyone else's welfare as their responsibility; it is practically socialism already, and so of course we're not plagued by Communists."

After the founding of the People's Republic, Chinese science fiction, as a branch of socialist literature, was handed the responsibility for popularizing scientific knowledge as well as describing a beautiful plan for the future and motivating society to achieve it. For instance, the writer Zheng Wenguang once said, "The realism of science fiction is different from the realism of other genres; it is a realism infused with revolutionary idealism because its intended reader is the youth." This "revolutionary idealism," at its root, is a continuation of the Chinese faith and enthusiasm for the grand narrative of modernization. It represents optimism for continuing development and progress, and unreserved passion for building a nation-state.

A classic example of revolutionary idealism is Zheng Wenguang's "Capriccio for Communism" (published in 1958). The story describes the celebration at Tiananmen Square in 1979 at the thirtieth anniversary of the founding of the People's Republic. The "builders of Communism" parade across the square, presenting their scientific achievements to the motherland: the spaceship *Mars I,* the gigantic levee that connects Hainan Island with the mainland, factories that synthesize all sorts of industrial products from ocean water, even artificial suns that melt the glaciers of the Tianshan Mountains to transform deserts into rich farmland . . . Faced with such wonders, the protagonist exclaims, "Oh, such fantastic scenes made possible by science and technology!"

After the lull imposed by the Cultural Revolution, the passion for building a modern nation-state reignited in 1978. Ye Yonglie's *Little Smart Roaming the Future* (published August 1978), a thin volume filled with enticing visions of a future city seen through the eyes of a child, heralded a new wave of science fiction in China with its initial print run of 1.5 million copies. Paradoxically, as China actually modernized with the reforms of the Deng Xiaoping era, these enthusiastic dreams of the future gradually disappeared from Chinese science fiction. Readers and writers seemed to fall out of romantic, idealistic utopias and back into reality.

In 1987, Ye Yonglie published a short story called "Cold Dream at Dawn." On a cold winter night in Shanghai, the protagonist has trouble falling asleep in his unheated home. A series of grand science fictional dreams fills his mind: geothermal heating, artificial suns, "reversing the South and North Poles," even "covering Shanghai with a hothouse glass dome." However, reality intrudes in the form of concerns about whether the proposed projects would be approved, how to acquire the necessary materials and energy, potential international conflicts, and so forth—every vision ends up being rejected as unfeasible. "A thousand miles separate the lovers named Reality and Fantasy!" The distance and the gap, one surmises, demonstrate the anxiety and discomfort of the Chinese waking up from the fantasy of Communism.

Starting at the end of the 1970s, large numbers of European and American science fiction works were translated and published in China, and Chinese science fiction, long under the influence of Soviet scientific literature for children, suddenly realized its own lag and marginal status. Motivated by binary oppositions such as *China-the West, underdeveloped-developed,* and *tradition-modernity* as well as the desire to reintegrate into the international order, Chinese science fiction writers attempted to break away from the science-popularization mode that had long held sway. They hoped to rapidly grow (or perhaps evolve) Chinese science fiction from an underdeveloped, suppressed, juvenile state to a mature, modern mode of literary expression. Simultaneously, controversy erupted as writers and critics debated how to approach international standards in content and literary form while exploring unique "national characteristics" of Chinese science fiction so that "China" could be relocated in global capitalism. Chinese writers had to imitate and reference the subjects and forms of Western science fiction while constructing a position for Chinese culture in a globalizing world, and from this position participate in the imagination of humanity's shared future.

The end of the Cold War and the accelerating integration of China into global capitalism in the 1990s led to a process of social change whose ultimate demand was the application of market principles to all aspects of social life, especially manifested in the shock and destruction visited upon traditions by economic rationality. Here, "traditions" include both the old ways of life in rural China as well as the country's past equality-oriented socialist ideology. Thus, as

China experienced its great transformation, science fiction moved away from future dreams about modernization to approach a far more complex social reality.

The science fiction of Europe and America derives its creative energy and source material from the West's historical experience of political and economic modernization and, through highly allegorical forms, refines the fears and hopes of humanity for its own fate into dreams and nightmares. After taking in a variety of settings, images, cultural codes, and narrative tropes through Western science fiction, Chinese science fiction writers have gradually constructed a cultural field and symbolic space possessing a certain degree of closure and self-discipline vis-à-vis mainstream literature and other popular literary genres. In this space, gradually maturing forms have absorbed various social experiences that cannot yet be fully captured by the symbolic order, and after a series of transformations, integrations, and reorganizations, resulted in new vocabularies and grammars. It is in this sense that the Chinese science fiction of the era dating from the 1990s to the present can be read as a national allegory in the age of globalization.

Overall, Chinese science fiction writers are faced with a particular historic condition. On the one hand, the failure of Communism as an alternative for overcoming the crises of capitalism means that the crises of capitalist culture, accompanied by the process of globalization, are manifesting in the daily lives of the Chinese people. On the other hand, China, after a series of traumas from the economic reforms and paying a heavy price for development, has managed to take off economically and resurge globally. The simultaneous presence of crisis and prosperity guarantees a range of attitudes toward humanity's future among the writers: some are pessimistic, believing that we're powerless against irresistible trends; some are hopeful that human ingenuity will ultimately triumph; still others resort to ironic observation of the absurdities of life. The Chinese people once believed that science, technology, and the courage to dream would propel them to catch up with the developed nations of the West. However, now that Western science fiction and cultural products are filled with imaginative visions of humanity's gloomy destiny, Chinese science fiction writers and readers can no longer treat "where are we going?" as an answered question.

Contemporary Chinese science fiction writers form a community full of internal differences. These differences manifest themselves in age, region of origin, professional background, social class, ideology, cultural identity, aesthetics, and other areas. However, by carefully reading and parsing their work, I can still find aspects of commonality among them (myself included). Our stories are written primarily for a Chinese audience. The problems we care about and ponder are the problems facing all of us sharing this plot of land. These problems, in turn, are connected in a thousand complicated ways with the collective fate of all of humanity.

In reading Western science fiction, Chinese readers discover the fears and hopes of Man, the modern Prometheus, for his destiny, which is also his own creation. Perhaps Western readers can also read Chinese science fiction and experience an alternative Chinese modernity and be inspired to imagine an alternative future.

Chinese science fiction consists of stories that are not just about China. For instance, Ma Boyong's "The City of Silence" is an homage to Orwell's *1984* as well as a portrayal of the invisible walls left after the Cold War; Liu Cixin's "Taking Care of God" explores the common tropes of civilization expansion and resource depletion in the form of a moral drama set in a rural Chinese village; Chen Qiufan's "The Flower of Shazui" spreads the dark atmosphere of cyberpunk to the coastal fishing villages near Shenzhen, where the fictional village named "Shazui" is a microcosm of the globalized world as well as a symptom. My own "A Hundred Ghosts Parade Tonight" includes fleeting images of other works by masters: Neil Gaiman's *The Graveyard Book,* Tsui Hark's *A Chinese Ghost Story,* and Hayao Miyazaki's films. In my view, these disparate stories seem to speak of something in common, and the tension between Chinese ghost tales and science fiction provides yet another way to express the same idea.

Science fiction—to borrow the words of Gilles Deleuze—is a literature always in the state of *becoming,* a literature that is born on the frontier—the frontier between the known and unknown, magic and science, dream and reality, self and other, present and future, East and West—and renews itself as the frontier shifts and migrates. The development of civilization is driven by the curiosity that compels us to cross this frontier, to subvert prejudices and stereotypes, and in the process, complete our self-knowledge and growth.

At this critical historic moment, I am even firmer in my faith that reforming reality requires not only science and technology, but also the belief by all of us that life should be better—and *can* be made better—if we possess imagination, courage, initiative, unity, love, and hope as well as a bit of understanding and empathy for strangers. Each of us is born with these precious qualities, and it is perhaps also the best gift that science fiction can bring us.